T0312465

Amanda Jennings lives in Oxfordshire with her husband, three daughters, and a menagerie of animals. She studied History of Art at Cambridge and before writing her first book, was a researcher at the BBC. With a deep fascination for the far-reaching effects of trauma, her books focus on the different ways people find to cope with loss, as well as the moral struggles her protagonists face. When she isn't writing she can usually be found walking the dog. Her favourite place to be is up a mountain or beside the sea.

Also by Amanda Jennings

The Haven
The Storm
The Cliff House
In Her Wake
The Judas Tree
Sworn Secret

AMANDA JENNINGS

ONE PLACE. MANY STORIES

HQ
An imprint of HarperCollins*Publishers* Ltd
1 London Bridge Street
London SE1 9GF

www.harpercollins.co.uk

HarperCollins*Publishers*
Macken House, 39/40 Mayor Street Upper,
Dublin 1, D01 C9W8, Ireland
This edition 2024

1
First published in Great Britain by
HQ, an imprint of HarperCollins*Publishers* Ltd 2024

Copyright © Amanda Jennings 2024

Amanda Jennings asserts the moral right to be
identified as the author of this work.
A catalogue record for this book is
available from the British Library.

ISBN: 9780008410377

MIX
Paper | Supporting
responsible forestry
FSC
www.fsc.org
FSC™ C007454

This book contains FSC™ certified paper and other controlled sources to ensure responsible forest management.

For more information visit: www.harpercollins.co.uk/green

Set in Sabon LT Std by HarperCollins*Publishers* India

Printed and bound in the UK using 100% Renewable Electricity at CPI Group (UK) Ltd

To my sister, with love

PROLOGUE

She reaches out to touch him with the tip of her shoe. Her leg trembles. There is no movement from him, no sound. Blood seeps from his crooked body, creeping along the grooves between salt-weathered paving stones. His eyes are open, glassy like polished marbles, the moonlight reflected in them strangely beautiful. She glances upwards to follow his gaze. The sky is almost black and dotted with a million pinpricks of light, the music and laughter from the wedding an unsettling backdrop. The air around them is warm and still, holding its breath, waiting for someone to speak.

She is surprised she feels no guilt. Not even a pinch of it. There is regret, not for what she's done, but for what she left unspoken. Words she'd kept tucked away inside her where they festered and grew like bacteria, infecting every part of her life. She'd allowed him to live inside her head for so many years. Allowed him to lurk in the shadows, strolling into her thoughts without warning, flashes of memory that left her short of breath. How many nights had she woken drenched in sweat, heart pounding, his face leering through the darkness?

Too many to count.

She crouches down and locks eyes on his lifeless body. Is she rid of him?

Is she free?

In the marquee on the lawn behind her, the wedding guests revel, drunk on privilege and expensive champagne, blissfully unaware of the horror sprawled on the terrace. She pictures them hearing the news. Gasps of disbelief. Screaming. Sobbing. Clinging to each other with ashen-faced shock.

As she stares at this man lying dead on the terrace of Lowencliffe Hall, his belly full of flash-fried venison, Courvoisier, and unchecked entitlement, her thoughts crystallise like the surface of a frozen lake and a feeling of cold satisfaction settles over her.

She is right to feel no guilt.

The world is better off without him.

'You deserved this,' she whispers. 'Good riddance, you bastard.'

CHAPTER ONE

June 2024

'She loves it,' Celeste said. 'Which is great news.'

A wave of relief swept through me. The thought of having to deal with a dissatisfied version of Ingrid wasn't appealing. Twenty-seven years old and one of the hottest young stars of the British film industry, Ingrid Olsson was top of casting wish-lists on both sides of the Atlantic. She was also a woman who got what she wanted. Celeste was the on-call twenty-four-seven personal assistant who headed up Ingrid's team. She was fearsomely efficient, with one of those brusque, clipped voices that gave the impression she was far too busy to talk.

'Ingrid will give the painting to her husband at the reception dinner. She'd like you there. She feels it gives the painting more gravitas if the artist is present.' Celeste sounded like she was reading from a script, as if she'd had this conversation a hundred times before.

'She's inviting me to the wedding?'

'As the artist of her gift. Yes. The florist and dress designer are both coming. As are the couple who are hand-gilding the after-dinner chocolates and the calligrapher of the menus. Ingrid likes to surround herself with talented people from other creative industries.'

'My diary is actually—'

'You'll be flown over first class and met by a chauffeur.'

When Anne-Marie told me that winning the Visage d'Or prize

for emerging artists marked a moment of change, I didn't believe her. I'd lived hand-to-mouth for so long – working in Fabian's café, doing the odd commission here and there – the idea of a single portrait paying a year's rent was surreal enough, let alone putting me on the radar of bona fide film stars.

Ingrid Olsson had contacted me through Anne-Marie's gallery with her proposition. Anne-Marie insisted I'd be a fool to say no.

'Non!' she'd said, shocked at my suggestion I turn the commission down. 'Victoria – putain – are you fucking crazy?'

So reluctantly I'd agreed to a sitting with Ingrid at the Hotel du Cap-Eden-Roc. A silent driver with a bushy grey moustache chauffeured me to Antibes in a limousine with blacked-out windows. There I was met in the hotel lobby by a herd of people, led by Celeste, who escorted me through the marble opulence to Ingrid's expansive suite, all brocade and gold, with double-height windows that framed the glittering azure of the Mediterranean sea.

As I set up my easel, Ingrid reclined on a chaise and scrolled her phone. A hairdresser arranged her hair so it tumbled artfully over her shoulders, reverentially placing a garland of white daisies on her head, while Celeste stood guard with set mouth and folded arms.

'Obviously don't put the phone in,' Ingrid trilled. 'And I want to look regal. Elegant. Like Nefertiti or the Princess of Wales. Pensive, too, as if I'm distracted by faraway but important thoughts, you know? The look I'm going for,' she went on, her voice heavy with sincerity, 'is Pre-Raphaelite queen.' Then she lowered her phone and stared at me, head slightly cocked to one side, eyes quizzical. 'You know the Pre-Raphaelites, right?'

I managed to smile. 'I do.'

Halfway through the sitting, Ingrid hurled her phone down and exploded in sudden rage, leaping off the chaise and storming into the bathroom screeching, 'That jealous cow!' over and over. It took Celeste twenty minutes to calm her down before Ingrid reappeared with a flick of her white-blonde hair to reassume her pose. She closed her eyes while she was retouched, a make-up girl dabbing her face with translucent powder, the hairdresser rearranging her waves, a stylist organising the folds of her dress so they revealed just the right amount of alabaster thigh.

'*Bitch*,' Ingrid muttered, shaking her head and breathing in through her nose and out through her mouth. 'I can't stand her. *Jesus*.' She looked at Celeste with a flash of vulnerability. 'Why would she say that?'

'Like you always say, the world is full of so many arseholes, you can't always avoid the stench.'

Ingrid closed her eyes and took a moment. I watched as her body relaxed, her fists uncurling, mouth loosening. She opened her eyes and smiled at me. 'I'm sorry about that.'

'I think,' I said, glancing at Celeste, who eyed me suspiciously, worrying that whatever I was thinking hadn't been OK'd by her first, 'that now I've captured your essence, I can finish the rest of the painting in Marseille using photographs.'

'Really? God, that would be *amazing*. Honestly, lying here is a nightmare. I'm one of those people who always needs to be *doing* something, you know?'

I loathed working from photographs, but the thought of finishing the portrait in the quiet of my studio was infinitely more appealing than spending any more time in this hotel room with Ingrid and her simpering groupies. 'Absolutely.'

'You're a total *legend*!' Ingrid jumped off the chaise and skipped over to me, planting a kiss on my cheek. I tried to stop myself recoiling. 'Thank you, *thank* you, darling,' she sang.

The portrait had taken three weeks to complete. I was relieved to get it finished. I had no love for it whatsoever. It was too whimsical, too superficial, the colours too joyful. I'd have preferred to paint the version of Ingrid Olsson I'd seen having a tantrum. Edgier and more vulnerable. Darker. But despite my reservations, I was pleased when Celeste said Ingrid loved it. Still, there was no way I could contemplate returning to England.

'It's kind of her to invite me, but I'm afraid I can't make the wedding.'

Celeste wasn't taking *I can't* for an answer. 'You must come.'

'My diary is full,' I said, taken aback by her insistence. 'I've a couple of events in July I can't change.'

'Ingrid won't be happy.'

'I'm sorry about—'

The phone went dead.

I went to the fridge and grabbed the half-bottle of white wine, pulled out the cork and took a coffee mug from the draining board. My apartment was filled with noise and scents from the market in the square below. Freshly baked patisserie, warm ripe fruit, cut flowers and cured meats. Simple people going about their everyday lives, buying and selling produce, sharing jokes, counting out pennies. Ingrid Olsson inhabited a different world, a world where people rented four-thousand-euro-a-night rooms to pose for a painting and thought nothing of flying the artist to a different country, first class, because it seemed like a cute idea.

The idea was anything but cute.

I hadn't been back to England since I'd left twenty-five years earlier, shell-shocked and bewildered, in a haze of guilt, self-loathing and agonising grief. I couldn't recall much from those first days in France. I'd arrived with no plan beyond Paris, but being in the city without Nick was too hard, so I made my way south, hitch-hiking from one town to the next in a semi-conscious state until I found myself in Marseille. I hadn't expected to stay. I might have spent the rest of my life wandering the continent like a nomadic zombie, but I got drunk and had sex with a man I met in a bar near the station. He was older than me, mid thirties, husky-voiced, and called me *belle anglaise* as he filled my glass with pastis and lavished me with Gallic charm. The one-night stand I'd hoped would take my mind off my shattered heart turned into a second night, then a third, then seamlessly into a relationship I didn't have the energy to get out of. Beneath his attractive facade, Jean was numbingly bland, only interested in football, underwhelming in bed, and the language barrier made conversation stilted. Everything about him reminded me of what I'd lost. What chance did he have when I'd tasted Nick? But I stayed because it was easy. Six years I gave him. Every day a fraction greyer than the last. It wasn't until Nicole died that I made the break.

Nicole was another caricaturist on the strip. She had the spot next to me and she was as close to a friend as I had. We chatted, shared cigarettes, joked about the punters behind their backs. She died from an overdose, her ravaged body found next to the bins behind a restaurant on the Plage des Catalans. Her death was enough to jolt me out of my stupor. I didn't want to go back to my easel on the strip. I didn't want to spend one more night with Jean. As I walked the streets, trying to get my thoughts in order, going over the words I would use to end things with him, I spotted a job advertised in the window of Fabian's café. There was something fateful about it, that small yellow index card with scrawled handwriting offering me some sort of route out.

I took a breath and walked in.

Fabian gave me the job there and then.

'*Demain à huit heures?*' he said, pulling the card off the window.

Jean sobbed like a baby when I told him we were finished, but I felt nothing more than a vague sense of relief. He moved out of our apartment, and I stayed. It was on the outskirts of Marseille, about twenty minutes from the centre by bus, neither city nor suburb, and was the nearest thing to a home I had. I had a yearning to paint again. The landlord was happy for me to turn the bedroom into a studio. I moved the bed into the living room and repainted the walls and woodwork a light, airy white. Though it was small and up four flights of stairs, I'd made it my own, and I never had any desire to look for another place.

My phone interrupted my thoughts. It was Celeste again. I hesitated before accepting the call.

'I have Ingrid for you,' came the clipped voice.

I didn't have time to reply before Ingrid was on the line. '*Darling*. Victoria. I love love *love* it. Now I won't take no for an answer. You *have* to come to the wedding. It will mean so much more to have you there. Please. I can't imagine giving it to him in front of all those people without being able to toast the artist.'

The thought made me queasy. 'Ingrid, I really—'

'No, no, *no*. Don't speak. It's going to be *such* a fun day. You'll love it. Please say you'll be there.' I pictured her pouting.

I shook my head and looked at the ceiling. 'I'm already busy that weekend.'

Ingrid tittered with laughter as if I'd made a joke, and I wondered if anybody had ever told her they were too busy to do something she asked.

'Will you at least talk to whoever you're seeing and explain the situation? I'm *certain* they'll understand.'

'I mean, I could have a chat with the organiser and see—'

'Oh my God. Yes. *Amazing*. Thank you, darling!'

'But I don't think I can—'

'We appreciate you changing your plans,' came Celeste's staccato voice.

'I said I'd talk—'

'I'll send you the details. Please remember, their privacy is of the utmost importance. Anybody involved in set-up, as well as all guests and staff on the day, will be required to sign an NDA. The press are vultures, and Ingrid has no intention of giving away any scraps.'

'I honestly don't—'

She was gone.

Ten minutes later, an email landed in my inbox.

To: victoria.fisher@aol.com
From: Celeste@IngridOlssonWorld.com
Subject: Follow-up

As you know, Ingrid is keen for you to be at her wedding. She wants me to tell you how much of a fan she is and how valuable this event will be in terms of your career. We appreciate you are having to change your plans. As discussed, we will provide return flights, first class, from Marseille to Heathrow, and a chauffeur to meet you at the airport. You will be welcomed as a guest, though Ingrid has suggested you oversee the hanging of the painting, for which we will pay you a fee of £500. This fee is negotiable. You are welcome to expense your overnight accommodation as well. All you need to do is forward the receipt and I will reimburse you. By accepting these terms you are agreeing to our non-disclosure policy. As you can imagine, with such a high-profile couple, discretion is of the utmost importance. Any breach of trust will result in us pursuing legal action.

If you could get back to us soonest, we would be most grateful.

I shook my head in disbelief. Who were these people? Legal action? This was a different world.

'So who are you marrying?' I whispered under my breath as I opened Google and typed *Ingrid Olsson fiancé*. I drank some wine and pressed enter. The search results flashed onto my screen. It took a few seconds for what I was seeing to make sense.

When it did, it was a punch in the gut.

What?

Surely not …

Ingrid Olsson to marry Julian Draper.

Hot bile rose in my throat.

Julian Draper?

My body started to tremble as his name sank hooks into me. My head reeled. It couldn't be him. It would be too much of a coincidence. How many Julian Drapers could there be in the world? Hundreds? Thousands? Surely Ingrid was marrying someone young and beautiful, a film star or model, someone as glamorous as she was. Wouldn't the Julian Draper I was thinking of be too old for her?

It *had* to be a different man.

But then snippets of her chatter in Antibes came back to me. The way she'd joked with Celeste about her fiancé's receding hairline. Her mentioning he'd been born in 1979 with as much incredulity as if he'd been born on the moon.

'The seventies? My God. *Insane!*'

My eye fell on the thumbnail images.

I clicked on one with trepidation and his face filled my screen.

Nausea swept through me.

I slammed my laptop closed and pushed back from the table, my chair scraping against the floorboards as I inhaled sharply. I let the breath out slowly in an attempt to stay focused, and walked back to the kitchenette.

'No,' I whispered, topping up my wine. 'Delete the email. Block their phone numbers. Walk away.'

But I couldn't stop myself.

My heart thrashed against my ribcage as I opened my laptop again. I clicked on the first link and there he was. Straight out of my nightmares. He was older now, with less hair and deep wrinkles. There was an unhealthy pallor to his skin and he'd developed a jowl and puffy bags beneath his eyes. I sat back, pressing both palms against my face as memories hit me. Then I went in again. Leaning forward. Clicking a link. It was an article from *Marie-Claire*.

Top Ten Power Couples to Watch in 2024
Number 2: Julian Draper and Ingrid Olsson

New entry this year! It might not be the pairing we would have put money on, but there's no doubt Julian Draper and Ingrid Olsson are catapulting themselves straight to the top of the power chart with their engagement in September last year. Draper, the wealthy businessman who rubs shoulders with political hard-hitters from around the world, has caused quite a stir by hooking up with the brightest star of the British film industry, Ingrid Olsson. The pair met at the fortieth birthday of mutual friend Fraser Jenner at the film agent's multimillion-pound villa on the shores of Lake Como. Jenner will be best man at the wedding of his oldest university friend, a wedding rumoured to have an array of chart-topping performers and DJs to entertain the guests at an undisclosed location. Counting both Hollywood and British royalty amongst their circle of friends, this is one heck of an influential pairing. So what's in store for them this year? We predict an Oscar for her, a nod from the Prime Minister in the New Year honours list for him and, who knows, maybe news of a baby Olsson-Draper?! Watch this space ...

The article was accompanied by a photograph of the couple on a boat in Venice. The caption said the photo was taken the day they announced their engagement. Ingrid and Julian held champagne flutes. His arm was draped around her shoulder, her ivory silk dress fluttered in the breeze, they wore matching sunglasses and smiles. The cherry-sized diamond I'd painted weighed down her delicate ring finger. A sharp pain dug me in the ribs. They looked so happy, basking in the glow of their polished golden world.

My head spun.

Everything screamed at me to stop torturing myself. I should have closed the laptop. I should have shoved him back into the darkest recesses of my mind. But I couldn't – I wasn't strong enough – so instead I sat there and allowed a ghoulish obsession to take hold.

The internet spewed out scores of articles and I read every single one. His Wikipedia page was a mile long. Raised in Gloucestershire. Educated at Eton. Failed his A levels. Retook them at a college in Oxford. Then to the Queen's School of Architecture (QSA), where he scraped a third-class degree. He went on to pursue a career in property renovation using money inherited from his grandfather. He made a fortune in 2008 buying up vacant buildings and turning them into cheap student housing. Then came a series of high-profile office builds and a number of government contracts. He emerged unscathed from multiple controversies surrounding high-ranking politicians and grubby backhanders between 2016 and 2022. There were photographs of him rubbing shoulders with an array of powerful men from around the world, smoking cigars with a US president, clinking pint glasses with Brexit bigwigs, a paparazzi snap of him dancing in a nightclub with a disgraced member of the aristocracy. Then a messy divorce following a number of infidelities, one of which resulted in his engagement to Ingrid, an actress eighteen years his junior, famous for playing wide-eyed ingénues with porcelain skin and bovine lashes in lavish period dramas. Her thick white-blonde hair, one article informed me, was inherited from her infamous Swedish rally-driver father who had drunk and screwed his way through the eighties and nineties.

I returned to the photograph of them in Venice again. I felt sick to my core. Julian Draper was happy and I hated him for that. I hated myself too. Hated myself for hating he was happy. Hated myself for allowing him to turn me into such a bitter, lonely husk.

'You bastard,' I whispered.

I poured myself more wine and continued to click through the pictures. In one, Julian was with another man I recognised. Fraser. It had been taken in an airport. I leant forward to study the photograph, my nose close to the screen. Fraser hadn't changed at all, still youthful, with thick dark hair and smooth, unwrinkled skin. The headline told me he was a film agent in LA, which didn't surprise me at all. It was then I noticed another face in the background. Blurry and concealed by shadow. I peered more closely and my heart stopped.

'Oh my God,' I whispered.

Nick?

My breathing grew shallow. I touched his face with the tip of my finger. Electric pulses fizzed along my arm. I recalled the last time we were together. Me lying in his arms, sadness coursing my veins as dawn grew closer, bringing with it the bitter pill of our devastating goodbye. Flashes of memory came at me. His touch as he brushed a tear from my cheek. The sound of the hotel door closing. The ache in the pit of my stomach as I collapsed on the floor and sobbed.

I sat back and stared at the photograph. Those three faces. Fraser, Julian and Nick. Still friends. Friendly enough to go to Italy together.

Friendly enough for Nick to be on Julian's wedding guest list?

The wine bottle was nearly empty, so I went to the fridge for another. Though I'd had too much already, and knew it wouldn't help, I didn't care. I filled the mug then walked over to my bed, my vision wavering. Nick filled my head. Thoughts of the last time we were together. Eleven years ago in Paris. The evening sunlight streaming through the window, warming my skin, illuminating him and giving the illusion of a halo. The solidity of his chest beneath my cheek as we lay together. Digging my nails into my hand, fighting to stay awake, not wanting to lose one moment of that precious time to sleeping.

The alcohol had eroded my willpower. Though I knew it was wrong, I couldn't stop myself reaching for my phone and opening a new text. I typed his name. Then a message.

Are you going to Julian's wedding?

I pressed send, then swore under my breath. What was I doing? I'd worked so hard to put what had happened – all the pain and humiliation – behind me. I turned my phone off and angrily threw it on the floor.

I managed to drag myself to the bathroom and as I brushed my teeth, I stared at myself in the mirror. 'You're an idiot,' I said. My slurred voice was deafening in the silence.

I was woken in the morning by the street cat who had appeared on the balcony a few years earlier and never left. He purred like a train, his paw tapping my cheek, demanding his breakfast.

'Let me sleep, you pest.' But he was having none it, his large brown eyes begging, rubbing his face against mine. 'Fine,' I said. 'You win.'

He jumped off the bed and trotted over to the kitchenette with his tail held up like a knight's standard.

I sat up gingerly. My head throbbed with a deathly hangover and I squinted against the sun that streamed in through the open window. The cat wound himself around my ankles in an impatient figure-of-eight as I drank thirstily from the tap. The sight of the empty wine bottle and the second, near-empty, beside it made me queasy. I grabbed both and dropped them into the bin, then flicked the kettle on.

With the cat fed and my mug filled with strong black coffee,

I retrieved my phone from the floor and stepped out onto the balcony, breathing healing slugs of scented air. The balcony was my tiny patch of heaven, with window boxes holding bright flowers and herbs, and just enough room for a chair. Here I was hidden from sight, but still able to enjoy the anonymous bustle from the street below. I closed my eyes and listened to the shouts of greeting, traffic buzzing, impatient horns, and laughter.

As I drank my coffee, I absently turned on my phone. My heart missed a beat when I saw a message from Nick. It was only then I remembered the text I'd sent him. A flash of horror struck me.

'Shit,' I muttered. 'Shit, shit. *Shit.*'

I trembled as I opened his message, trepidation adding to the nausea I was already battling.

Hello! Long time no speak! Hope you're OK? Yes I am going. Are you? If so it will be lovely to see you. There will be a few old (haha) faces from QSA. Tilly, Fraser, Giles and a couple of others. Did you know Noah and Rob? Think we got friendly with them after you left. Will be a great party! BW Nick

The names he'd listed came at me like sniper shots. Those people were ghosts from a part of my life I'd tried to erase. Apart from Nick, there was nobody I wanted to see from my brief time at university. I'd never understood why people agreed to school or college reunions. Friends drifted apart or escaped each other for good reason. Why did people think it was a good idea to reconnect with 'old faces' you'd moved on from? Nostalgia? Morbid curiosity? A desperation to find out who'd put the most weight on, who'd lost their hair, who had the best job, the best marriage, the biggest house and cleverest children? The thought was hideous, and even more reason to keep as far away from Ingrid's wedding as possible.

But then there was Nick …

I'd resigned myself to never seeing him again. He'd made that clear in Paris. Though it devastated me, I'd always respected his decision to stay with his family. That was the type of man he was. Responsible, loyal, and duty-bound to do the right thing, however difficult the 'right thing' was. Yet now he was saying it would be lovely to see me?

I reread his text over and over. It was chatty, at ease, warm. A shiver of pleasure passed through me as I pictured his fingers typing words meant only for me. I chewed lightly on the inside of my lip, my finger poised to reply. But then I hesitated. Would it be easier to talk?

The thought of his voice made me giddy.

I read his text again. Then I dialled.

He didn't pick up straight away, and sudden panic grabbed me as I thought of him staring at my name on his phone and ignoring me. As I was about to hang up, he answered. 'Vix?'

I hadn't used that name in over two decades, and hearing it floored me.

'Vix? Is that you?'

'Yes,' I managed. 'Sorry, nobody's called me that since I left England. I'm Victoria now.'

He laughed. 'You'll always be Vix to me. And if I remember rightly, you never liked the name Victoria.' He laughed again, a soft, honey-sweet sound. 'It's good to hear from you. Are you well? It's been ages.'

'It has,' I said. 'I'm fine … I … I wasn't sure if I should phone.' My throat was drier than sandpaper. 'You said not to, but … well, I mean, it was so long ago. And you replied to my text. No. I shouldn't have called. Sorry.' I was rambling like a madwoman. I swore silently. 'It's … well … I was a bit drunk when I sent …' Sweat was creeping over my skin like mould. 'I was going to text you back but then wondered if it was better to speak …' My voice trailed off.

'No, no, it's nice to hear from you.'

There was movement. Footsteps. A door closing. He'd shut his family out. We were alone.

'I can't talk for long. We're about to have breakfast.'

'Sure. No problem. That's OK. I need to be somewhere in a bit as well.' My heart thumped against my chest as if desperate to get to him.

'That's great. You sound …' He faltered, hesitating. 'You sound good?'

'I am.'

There was another pause, and I wondered if he was expecting me to say more about how I was.

'So,' he said, when I stayed quiet, 'you've been invited to the wedding?'

'Yes. Well, no. Not properly. It was through Ingrid. Julian doesn't even know I know her. It's to do with work.'

'Work?'

'I'm not supposed to tell anybody – you know, the NDA? – but I did a portrait of Ingrid. It's her present to him – a surprise – and she's got it into her head that I need to be there when she gives it to him.'

'You're an artist?'

Disappointment jabbed at me. Had I hoped he'd know about me? That he might have kept an eye on my life from afar? 'I sell a few paintings.'

'And Ingrid commissioned something?'

'Mm-hmm.'

'Small world,' he said. 'How did she find you?'

'You sound suspicious.'

'Do I? No. Not suspicious. Interested.'

'I won an award over here. One of her friends lives in Paris and told her about me. Something like that anyway.'

'That's impressive.'

'It wasn't the Turner.'

'Still impressive, and great that she's invited you to the wedding. You should definitely come.'

'I can't. I'm the last person Julian would want there. Especially without warning.' My skin crawled at the thought.

'I'll have a chat with him. Tell him you and I have been in touch and that you'll be in England that weekend? I'm sure he'll suggest you come.'

'God, no, please don't!' I was unable to keep the horror from my voice. 'We've not had any contact since I left, and seriously, it's not worth risking Ingrid's surprise. She'd never forgive me – or you – if he found out about the painting before the big reveal.'

'I wouldn't tell him. Honestly, I imagine he'd be delighted to invite you, especially as the rest of the gang are going.'

I gave a quiet laugh. 'Not sure I was ever part of the *gang*.'

'Of course you were.'

'Either way, believe me, I'm the last person Julian Draper wants to see. It would be far too awkward. I'm busy anyway. I've already told Ingrid I can't make it.'

There was a pause. He took a breath, hesitating. 'He asked after you last time I saw him.'

A chill ran through me. I gripped the balcony railing to steady myself.

'How come?' I tried to keep my voice as level as possible.

'I can't remember exactly. I guess we were talking about our time in London, the QSA crowd, and you came up in conversation.'

Raging anxiety grabbed hold of me. I didn't want to come up in their conversations. A flood of conflicting emotions made me weak. Regret, shame, guilt, of course, but then confusingly the comfort of talking to him. It was as if we'd never been apart, like finding a lost sweater, slipping it on and remembering how much I loved it.

'From what Julian told me, this is going to be a proper spectacle. You should come just to experience it. It'll be once in a lifetime. Apparently he gave Ingrid free rein and an unlimited budget and she's gone for it.' Nick laughed.

His casual mention of Julian's name skewered me. 'I don't want to see him.'

'Really? I mean, I get it. You and he were never best friends and what he did was awful, but it was an insensitive student stunt. He thought it was funny. And, well, it's been twenty-five years.' He hesitated. 'Maybe it's time to forgive him?'

Forgive him?

If Nick knew the truth, he would never tell me to forgive him. There was no forgiving Julian Draper for what he'd done to me.

'I don't want to see him.'

Nick was quiet for a beat. 'Well, if you change your mind, it will be nice to see you.'

'I won't change my mind,' I said. 'But I hope you and Cami have a lovely time.' Bitterness crept into my mouth as her name left my lips.

'Cami isn't coming.'

My heart quickened. 'Oh? Why not?'

'I don't know, some clash she can't get out of. Something at school. I've no idea why someone else can't do it. We had a fight about it—' He stopped himself. 'Sorry,' he said. 'You don't need to know any of that.'

I smiled. I'd always found Nick's tendency to overshare endearing. A wave of longing swept through me. I'd tried so hard to forget him, thrown myself into my painting, made a life for myself in France, endured disappointing sex with men who weren't him in the vain hope I might find somebody else to love. To some extent, I'd managed it. Not quite forgetting him, but certainly easing the pain of him. Speaking to him again had reopened the wounds and doused them with acid.

I heard the faint sound of a woman's voice calling to him from somewhere beyond the door.

'Coming,' he called back. He sounded weary. It wasn't fair. Nick didn't deserve to be bound to a woman he didn't love. He deserved to be happy.

'I should go,' he said. 'But seriously, if you can make the wedding, you should come. It would be great to catch up.'

He rang off, and I stood on the balcony for a while, both hands on the railing, my head spinning. Nick was the closest friend I'd ever had. Our attraction to each other had complicated things. Though I mourned our love – our intimacy, his body, the way his lips felt on mine – speaking to him made me realise how much I missed his friendship. I had a few friends in Marseille, but I kept them at arm's length, even Fabian and Anne-Marie. It felt safer that way. If I didn't let people in, then I couldn't be hurt. Talking to him again had rocked me to the core. That and thoughts of Julian. It was impossible to know which one of them had destabilised me more. The combination was dizzying.

I walked into my studio and took three deep breaths. The smell of oil paint, linseed and turps usually acted like Valium, but not this time. It wasn't even taking the edge off.

I focused my attention on the painting of Madame Girroux. The portrait had been commissioned by her granddaughter to mark Madame's ninetieth birthday. She was a delightful woman, a seamstress, soft and gentle, her eyes lit by the joy of a simple, fulfilling life. Though I'd been enjoying the painting, as I pressed greys and greens and shades of terracotta into the canvas, I now found myself fighting an unbearable urge to turn the palette knife vertically and hack dear Madame Girroux to shreds.

When I heard my phone buzzing on the table in the other room, I threw down the knife and ran to grab it. I was desperate for it to be Nick, but it was Ingrid's name on the screen. I stared at the phone, the vibrations causing it to shudder and dance on the table, waiting until it fell silent. A voicemail alert pinged moments later. I played the message on loudspeaker, arms crossed, glaring at the phone as if it were Ingrid herself.

'Oh my *God*, Victoria! I've just had Nick on the phone! Isn't he an absolute *darling*? By far the nicest of Julian's friends. What an amazing coincidence! I can't believe you know Julian! I will totally forgive you for telling Nick about the painting, but *only* if you come to the wedding. You *have* to. It's a *must*. Don't worry, I'll put you on a table with Nick and the others. Seriously though, isn't it *crazy* how things *always* work out?'

CHAPTER TWO

I hadn't managed a wink of sleep since speaking to Nick. I was exhausted. At the café, I absorbed myself in menial, repetitive tasks, folding napkins, cleaning the coffee machine, stacking boxes of UHT milk, anything that might still my mind.

Fabian appeared at the store-cupboard door. He wiped his hands on a cloth then reached into his breast pocket for cigarettes. 'Ça va?' he asked gruffly, his heavy brow knotted.

Fabian was a man of few words. He loved two things in life, patisserie and hunting. I enjoyed watching him meticulously arrange his *tartes aux framboises* and *pommes*, and would smile to myself as he impatiently checked the clock every Friday morning, grumbling as he waited for it to hit midday, when he'd rip off his apron and dash out of the café to meet his brother for their weekend trip to shoot boar and drink red wine in the Calanques.

Though I knew he cared for me, his raspy *ça va* was as close as Fabian got to spoken sympathy and was enough to make me cry. I pressed my sleeve against my eyes and forced a nod. He was quiet for a moment or two, then silently held out the cigarettes, gesturing with his head in the direction of the back door.

I took them from him and went out to the small concrete yard scattered with cigarette butts and fallen leaves from the oleander tree that grew on the other side of the wall.

He appeared a few minutes later and handed me a double espresso.
'Sorry,' I said, taking the coffee. 'Difficult news from home.'

He didn't ask what the news was.

As I drank the coffee and smoked, I texted Anne-Marie to see if she had time for lunch.

'*Quel est le problème, chérie?*' she said, as soon as she saw me an hour or so later.

'Ah. Same as usual. My head, you know?'

Anne-Marie locked the gallery and together we walked down to our favourite brasserie, our silence punctuated every now and then by her irritated huffing at meandering tourists in front of her. Anne-Marie was good company and I valued her no-nonsense opinions. She had a sharp sense of humour and called a spade a spade. It was Anne-Marie who had submitted my painting of Monsieur Lafiche – the white-bearded stationmaster at Gare de Sainte-Marthe – into the Visage d'Or. '*Chérie*,' she'd said, when I'd questioned why she'd do such a thing. '*Mon dieu*. For the money! If you win, *tout le monde* will want your paintings and buy them from me, *oui?*'

We sat at a table on the pavement in the sunshine, and ordered the bouillabaisse for me, *tarte à l'oignon* for Anne-Marie, and half a carafe of white wine to share.

She waited until the waiter had poured the wine, then looked at me. 'So?'

She opened her cigarette case, took out a white Gitanes and lit it with her silver lighter. Anne-Marie was unfeasibly stylish, her dark hair cut into a blunt bob, oversized designer sunglasses, a pristine white T-shirt beneath a Burberry blazer, her tiny frame holding her clothes as if on a coat hanger. She wore red Chanel on her lips, from which poured an almost continuous torrent of swear words in both French and fluent English.

'And don't bullshit me.'

She listened without reacting as I gave her a sanitised precis of the mess I'd left behind in England. I included sufficient information to give context, the bones but not the sinew, enough for her to understand the implications of the wedding invitation. However, all she seemed to focus on was the Hollywood glamour.

'Ingrid *Olsson*? Shit! *Putain!* Of course you must go!'

I shook my head and pushed a crouton in circles around the orange soup with my spoon.

'*Es-tu sérieuse?* Ingrid Olsson invited you to her wedding and you think two times?'

'But her husband won't want me there. It's complicated.'

'*Pfft!*' She gave a dismissive flick of her perfectly manicured hand. 'Forget him.'

'Did you listen to anything I said?' I smiled and reached for my wine glass.

'Sure.' She shrugged. 'But *fuck* them. This wedding will be, like, the bees fucking feet. Plus this man, your ex-lover, he calls the fucking bride and arranges for you to go? And he knows his wife isn't there? You think he does this for friendship?' She drew on her cigarette and shook her head. '*Non.* For sure he wants sex with you, *oui?*'

'Wife there or not, he's still married.'

Anne-Marie considered this. 'Is she a friend?'

I bristled. 'God, no. She's dreadful.'

She grinned triumphantly. 'Then we don't worry about her. *Alors.* Decision done. Go to the wedding. Have sex with the man you love. And who knows? Maybe he is leaving this dreadful wife.'

'You think so?'

'You will not know this if you stay in Marseille.' Anne-Marie suddenly laughed. 'And – *merde* – even if there's no sex, you are at a fucking Hollywood *mariage*.'

I smiled. 'I asked you to lunch so you could tell me not to go. You were supposed to say, Victoria, you do not need this fucking stress in your life. Forget these *connards*.'

Anne-Marie flicked her hand with another *pfft*. 'No, *chérie*, you need sex. You haven't had it in fucking ages.'

'Not true.'

She raised her eyebrows over the reach of her sunglasses. 'Oh no? When, then?'

'Sex?' I glanced over my shoulder self-consciously. 'I've no idea.'

She growled and made a face. 'Don't bullshit me. Everybody knows this.'

I rolled my eyes. 'Maybe a year?' This was a lie. It was nearly three, with a Norwegian who smelt of Polytar shampoo. The sex was quick and disappointing, and the man – whose name I couldn't remember – fell asleep as soon as he came, collapsed on top of me, so heavy I thought I might suffocate.

'Oh my *God*!' She snatched her glasses off and leant forward in horror. 'A *year*? You have to go to this wedding.'

'But what about the other man? Ingrid's husband. He's an arsehole, and we have …' I hesitated, 'bad history.'

Bad history.

Understatement of the decade.

Anne-Marie pressed her finger to a pastry crumb on the edge of her plate and popped it into her mouth. 'It's no problem. You go to Ingrid Olsson's wedding. Have sex with the man you like and tell the other one to fuck off. Get up in his ugly face. *Va te faire foutre*, you will say. You will feel *so* fucking good. Or …' she sat back in her chair with a chuckle, 'you can kill him.'

I laughed. 'I can't kill him on his wedding day.'

She shrugged. 'The day after, then.'

My smile slipped from my face as I reached for the carafe and topped up our glasses. Anne-Marie didn't know what kind of man Julian was. As tempting as it sounded, there was no way I'd have the courage to be in the same room as him, let alone tell him what I thought of him. The brave Vix Fisher, the girl who might have stood up for herself twenty-five years ago, had faded like an old photograph on a windowsill.

'Seriously, *chérie*. Don't look sad. Why let this *connard* make you feel like a piece of shit? He is nothing. Not worth your thought. But the sex? Yeah, sure. Why not? And this wedding, well, the champagne will be the best, right? And you are tired in your eyes. Maybe a *petites vacances* would do you some good? A holiday, some great sex—' She stopped herself and leant forward, lowering her sunglasses. 'The sex *is* great, yes?'

I glanced over my shoulder again, blushing, then gave a small nod, my skin tingling with recalled pleasure. 'But what if he doesn't want to?'

'It's a wedding. Anybody can get sex at a wedding. If not him, then another. Maybe Timothée Chalamet?' Anne-Marie laughed. 'So there you have it! Great sex, great *champagne* and tell the *connard* he's a donkey's arse.'

Despite myself, I smiled at the image of me calling Julian a donkey's arse.

'These *connards* should not get away with this shit. Good for him to hear *la vérité*, you know?'

'But the café? Fabian needs me.'

Anne-Marie leant forward and rested her hand on mine. 'This is not your problem. The café will survive without you.' She smiled. 'Come on, *chérie*. You deserve some fun. This wedding will be *formidable*! You must go. *Amuse-toi bien*. Dance with sexy men, drink good wine and live like a queen. Why fucking not, *hein*?'

She'd made it sound so easy, and after all the rekindled emotion, she'd brought a welcome shot of positivity. I'd loved Nick for twenty-five years, and for all of those years I'd had to accept we would never be together. Was all that about to change? But of course this fantasy was short-lived. As I sat on the bus, watching the suburbs of Marseille pass by in a blur, I heard Nick's whispered voice in my head, each word like the sting of a scorpion.

'I can't leave my family.'

'But you don't love her.' I'd struggled to get the words out through my sobbing. 'If you loved her, you wouldn't have come to me.'

For months after he left me in that hotel room, hollowed out by devastation, I'd been consumed with darkness and self-loathing. At points it got so bad I'd thought about taking my own life. Why on earth was I opening myself up to that again? I banged my head softly against the bus window as if hoping to knock the pain away.

Back at my apartment, I headed into my studio to continue with the portrait of Madame Girroux, but was once again interrupted by a buzz from my phone.

It was an email from Celeste.

Sense told me to delete it and walk away from this sorry tangled mess. But I couldn't do it.

The email contained a link, and when I clicked on it, an animated invitation slid out of a gold envelope in a flurry of butterflies, hearts and doves.

Ms Ingrid Olsson and Mr Julian Draper
are delighted to invite you to attend their wedding on

27 July 2024 at 2 p.m.
Full details will only be supplied
when you accept this invitation

Accept   Decline

By pressing Accept, you agree to privacy terms as
laid out in the accompanying document.

'Don't,' I whispered.

I hovered the cursor over the *Accept* button.

'It's ridiculous.' My voice echoed around the apartment. 'Why the hell would I go?'

Then I clicked the mouse.

Accept.

An automated response landed in my inbox instantly.

Ingrid and Julian are delighted you're able to join them in celebrating their wedding! The reception will be held from 2 p.m. at Lowencliffe Hall in Cornwall following an intimate registry office service for close friends and family.

Ingrid and Julian have taken the hotel for the weekend and I will be contacting separately those who have been allocated a room. For those not allocated a room at the venue, I can provide a list of local hotels should you require it. If you are arriving by helicopter, please let me know so I can arrange logistics with the hotel. The wedding reception will go on until late. Dress code is coastal glam. The couple have requested that if you're bringing a gift, you make it unusual!

By clicking Accept, you have agreed to a confidentiality clause. Any breaking of this will constitute a breach of the law and you will be open to legal action. The couple are intent on keeping their wedding private, for friends and family only, and that newspapers and photographers aren't given location information. Ingrid and Julian have signed an exclusive photographic rights deal and any photographs shared without consent of the couple are not permitted. Hence, we will be politely requesting that phones are handed over on arrival.

Please reply to this email with dietary requirements. If you have any other questions, don't hesitate to contact me.

Julian and Ingrid are so looking forward to celebrating their deep love and commitment to each other with you!

At the bottom was the photo of Julian and Ingrid on the boat in Venice. I stared at it. The smiles. The glamour. His undeserved happiness.

'You have no idea what kind of monster he really is,' I whispered to Ingrid.

CHAPTER THREE

Late September 1999

Mum changed beyond recognition after Dad went to prison. She used to be bright and bubbly, immaculately dressed, always in full make-up, with a vibrant social life that centred around her tennis and bridge clubs. After he left, she drew into herself like a tortoise. She didn't like leaving the house. She'd sit for hours and stare at the wall. She stopped colouring her hair. I'd had no idea she wasn't a natural blonde until I noticed the muddy grey inching out of her skull in the weeks following his trial. It was as if the shame had sucked the colour from her.

'I thought you wanted me to go to university?'

'I do.' Though she didn't sound convinced. 'Oh Victoria ... I just don't understand why you have to go so far.'

'It's not that far.'

'They do architecture at Manchester, don't they? That's a train ride away. You could live at home if you went to Manchester.'

Live at home? God. No. Getting away was pretty much the only reason I was going to university. 'The course isn't great.' The lie came easily. 'And QSA is one of the best. Most parents would be desperate for their child to go there.'

'But I'll miss you.' Her voice was a feeble whisper as her eyes welled with tears.

'I'll miss you too.' I tried to sound as convincing as possible.

The truth was, I couldn't wait to escape. When I left the exam hall after my final A level, I didn't stop to dissect the paper or celebrate with the others, I just kept walking. Along the corridor, out of the front entrance, onto the street. I didn't look back. I was ready to close the door on the lot of it, school, home, everything about the life I was living. I was desperate for a fresh start, to get to university, to reinvent myself. I didn't want to be the girl with a father in prison and a broken mother and a brother who swung between violent rage and morose silence any longer. I wanted to shed my skin like a snake and wriggle into a whole different me. It was time to leave the old Victoria Fisher behind.

My dad swore blind the north of England was the 'jewel in the country's crown', but I couldn't wait to get to London. I'd looked at architecture courses in other places – Cambridge, Bath, St Andrews, in fact everywhere but Manchester – but I kept coming back to London. Was it the promise of golden pavements? The city conjured a world of opportunity. If there was anywhere that could offer me a new life it was London.

'Oh, me? Yeah. I study in *London*,' I'd whisper to my reflection in the mirror, whilst rehearsing a nonchalant shrug. 'That's right. London. What do I do? I'm studying architecture. In *London*.'

The more I played around with the idea of the city, the more convinced I became that London was my spiritual home. Like millions before me, I was joining the throng of people seeking fortunes and new beginnings in the capital. My blood fizzed at the thought.

Mum wanted to come with me to drop me off. 'You've hardly been on a train. And there are changes. What if you can't find the platforms?'

'I'll ask a guard.' There was no way I wanted her coming with me. 'If you come, I'll find it too hard to say goodbye, and it means you'll have to be out of the house for a whole day.'

She dropped her head, her hands rubbing the length of her

thighs repeatedly. 'I'm not sure how I'll cope without you.' Her words were so quiet I pretended I hadn't heard them.

She waved me off from her bedroom window, tears streaming down her cheeks, watching me walk in the direction of Knutsford station with my bags, a tin-foil parcel of cheese and pickle sandwiches and a Thermos flask of sugary tea. She'd packed the remaining tea bags into my suitcase along with two pink toilet rolls and a freezer bag of washing powder.

'You'll want your sheets to smell like home,' she'd said as she tucked the Daz into the corner of the case and wiped away a tear that had rolled down her cheek.

I was used to her crying – she cried all the time – but it was usually because of Dad or Mikey, not me. The guilt was overwhelming.

I'd read the Queen's School of Architecture prospectus so many times I knew the text by heart. I'd pored over the photographs, floor plans and maps until I had every detail memorised. The school occupied a row of grandiose grey-brick buildings on Bedford Square. What were once residential houses had been converted into a number of studios, two lecture rooms, a library and a workshop. There was a large space in a semi-glazed extension on the ground floor that housed a canteen and a student-run bar and opened onto a small courtyard. My accommodation was a twenty-minute walk away in a narrow three-storey private house owned by a lady called Mrs Drummond, who rented rooms out to students. I hadn't realised I'd have to apply for accommodation, and when I'd called the office a week before I was due to arrive without the faintest clue where I was supposed to be heading, the woman informed me the halls of residence were all full.

'Don't worry, I've a number of alternatives,' she went on, her voice reassuring as she picked up on my panic. 'In fact, we've just this morning had a space free up in a house on Frederick

Street. The landlady, Louise Drummond, is a friend of mine and it's a *very* nice house. Walking distance from Bedford Square, which is pretty good for London accommodation.' She paused momentarily. 'She takes people from any London university, but looking at the list, there's another QSA student there, which is a bit of luck, isn't it?'

I nearly missed my first connection in Chester, then found myself sharing the train from Crewe with a group of rowdy men who drank and sang the entire way to London. It was all so new and I was jittery with nerves, filled with anticipation and the thrill – and fear – of the unknown. It was my first time away from home on my own, and as the train sped towards London, I was overwhelmed by a heady sense of freedom, as if I'd been tied up in a windowless room and was breathing fresh air for the first time.

When I stepped off the train at Euston, it was bedlam. People came at me from all directions, lights and smells too, an assault of unfamiliar noises so different to the laid-back murmur of my home town. Traffic horns, police sirens, whistles and yelling, a woman crouched in a doorway banging the side of her head and shouting at the sky. The mayhem was bewildering. It was a world away from Knutsford, with its cobbled streets, colourful hanging baskets and recognisable faces. Of course I'd known London would be different – I'd been desperate to come for that very reason – but having landed, I felt small and lost and incredibly alone. I stared blindly at the Tube map, trying to work out if it was easier to take a train to Frederick Street rather than walk with my bag and suitcase, and was struck with the sickening fear I'd made a terrible mistake.

In the end I chose to walk, but as I dragged my suitcase, trying to avoid the crowds of people, who as far as I could tell were unable to see me, it didn't take long for me to doubt my decision. Lost and confused, I plucked up the courage to ask a man at a bus stop if he knew where Frederick Street was. He scowled and waved me away without a word.

More by luck than design, I somehow made it to Mrs Drummond's. She opened the door and looked me up and down, but not unkindly, more as if assessing me, working out whether I was an acceptable lodger. Thankfully, I apparently was, and she stepped to one side and opened an arm to welcome me in.

'You've had a long journey. Would you like a rest before I show you around?'

'I'm fine,' I said. 'It wasn't too bad.'

Mrs Drummond was a no-nonsense woman. Tall and angular, with the bookish air of a librarian or headmistress, short grey hair, a pink cardigan over a matching sweater, black trousers and camel-coloured slippers lined with sheepskin. She rubbed one hand absently with the other and I noticed her knuckles were enlarged, the skin around them tight and pale. On each wrist she wore a copper bangle.

As I followed her along the hall towards the staircase, she indicated a closed door to her right. 'My rooms are through there. They're out of bounds. There's a payphone under the stairs.'

We walked up one flight of stairs and she gestured through to a bathroom with a salmon-pink bath and basin, beige carpet patched with orange stains, smelling strongly of the blue block of bleach I'd later discover melting slowly in the bowl of the discoloured toilet. Next to it was a small kitchen with a fridge, a two-ring hob blackened by years of use, a toaster and a grubby white kettle.

'You each have a shelf.' She opened a cupboard and tapped the empty shelf. The other two were brimming over with delicious-looking things like hot chocolate powder, biscuits, jars of colourful pasta sauces and jam. I thought of the squashed box of tea bags in my case.

Nerves began to build as I realised that behind the food on those shelves were actual people I was going to have to interact with. I hadn't made a new friend since primary school. I wasn't even sure I remembered how to.

We passed two closed doors on the next floor. Mrs Drummond didn't say anything, but continued up the next flight. 'This is you,' she said, opening the door at the top.

The room was tucked into the eaves, with a sloping ceiling, a single bed, a desk, a chest of drawers and a flimsy wardrobe. A small window overlooked the back garden, which was more of a yard, with a clothes line strung across its width. The window ledge was buried by a thick layer of bird poo, on top of which stood two slate-grey pigeons, one with a mangled leg, feathers puffed up, cooing loudly.

'Right then. I'll leave you be. If you need anything, knock on my door. London can be a daunting city.'

The door closed and I was alone.

When I left home, I'd been intent on throwing myself headlong into university life and was dismayed to discover how petrifying this was in reality. London was supposed to be my new beginning. I'd imagined wild and unusual friends. I'd fantasised about falling in love and doing things I'd never done before. The friends I'd had in primary school had fallen away when my father was arrested. Invites to after-school tea dried up. There was nobody to walk home from school with. Nobody to partner up with in PE. Even my best friend, Sadie, abandoned me, and I'd known her since we were four.

'Mum says we're not to talk any more. She says you're not our type of people now.' Sadie looked sad, but only for a moment. 'Sorry about that,' she said, as she shrugged and skipped off to eat lunch with Becky Davidson, who'd hated me for ever.

When it was time to apply for secondary school, I'd asked Mum if we could look out of catchment.

'But you can walk to Valley Park.'

'*Please?*' I'd begged, tears welling. 'I want to go where nobody knows me.'

She'd nodded heavily, then said she had a headache and went up to bed. I ended up at school in Northwich, but of course it wasn't far enough to escape my story. From day one, I was the girl from Knutsford whose dad was in prison for defrauding two local charities. Much of the money he'd stolen had been donated by members of the wider community, including a couple of teachers at the school. Our family were forced to carry his mantle of shame everywhere we went. It wasn't only Sadie's mum; lots of our peers were told by their parents not to associate with us. 'Those Fishers are rotten apples,' I imagined them saying. I wanted to scream that it was nothing to do with me, that I hated my father as much as they did, but it was easier to keep my mouth shut and my head down. I set my sights on escaping to university and threw myself into my work. I spent all my spare time in the library or the art room, and this way school was lonely but bearable. There were times I'd overhear the others – joking about, arranging parties, gossiping – and feel envious. From the art room window I'd watch some of them, the rebellious ones, slipping out of school to play truant in their modified uniform, cigarettes in their mouths, desperate to be with them.

I'd vowed to keep Dad a secret when I got to QSA, and nobody needed to know about my mum's depression or my brother's moods either. I went over what I would say if asked about my family. My dad was easy. When he was let out of prison, he'd disappeared off the face of the planet. He could be in Timbuktu for all I knew. I'd tell them he'd left when I was a baby. That I didn't know him. I'd say I wasn't that close to my mum and brother. I'd be vague. Offhand. I convinced myself I didn't need to feel guilty about it. It was a survival tactic. Over the summer, while I was washing up in the pub and saving for my university fund, I mused about who

I would be with Victoria gone. I decided I'd call myself Vicky, but I'd spell it Vikki. Vikki was confident and brave and funny. Vikki was popular. Vikki was life and soul of the party. I had it all planned out.

The day after I arrived in London, I managed to get myself to the school for registration. It was surreal walking into the building, having stared at it for so long in the prospectus. It felt both familiar and alien simultaneously. I hovered in the corner of the reception area and observed the others, searching for someone as alone and nervous as me. But everybody else seemed fine, gathered in groups, chattering and laughing as if they'd known each other for years. The noise of them was overwhelming. I had to get out of there. I told the woman on the desk my name, and she ticked me off and handed me an information pack.

'Everything you need to know about freshers' week and the course is in there,' she said brightly. 'Don't look so worried. Everybody feels nervous.'

I mumbled something unintelligible and left, running back to Frederick Street, the buildings towering over me, the people glaring, the colours of everything turned dark and inhospitable.

According to the information I'd been given, the week before the course started was supposed to be a time to sign up for clubs and hobby groups, get acclimatised, attend social events and meet people. But as soon as I got back to my room, the idea of venturing out again became paralysing. What made things worse was listening to the other two students in the house – a girl and a boy – getting to know each other. The walls were paper-thin and I could hear it all. The girl was well-to-do, with a musical laugh. Though the boy wasn't as posh, he was still well-spoken, with a soft accent that washed over his rounded vowels. I lay on my bed, tears dampening my cheeks, alone and desperately sad. I waited until the house fell quiet before creeping down to use the bathroom or make some toast. It was pathetic and I hated myself.

On the fifth day, listening to the other two talking outside their rooms yet again, I swore quietly and forced myself off the bed. It was getting ridiculous. I had to go down and say hello. I walked to the door and reached for the handle, but as soon as my hand touched the cool brass, I froze. I couldn't do it.

'For God's sake,' I growled. 'You're Vikki Fisher. You study architecture at the prestigious Queen's School of Architecture. People want to be friends with you.'

I opened the door, at first just a crack, then enough to allow me to creep out of my room. The two of them were on the landing below. I held my breath and listened. The girl was talking about India, spewing a deluge of words about a Himalayan mountain trek and a woman she'd met who made jewellery from coconut shells. She spoke at ninety miles an hour, barely stopping to draw breath. 'So so talented. Seriously. I told her she could easily sell it in England and America. I've never seen anything like it.'

I inched closer to the banister and peered down through the stairwell. Though I couldn't see their faces, I could see parts of them. Her hands, pretty and slight, were decorated with jangling bangles and silver rings on her fingers and thumbs. She wore brightly coloured trousers, voluminous and loose, and flip-flops on her conker-brown feet, with more silver rings on her toes. I couldn't see much of him, only a flash of blue jeans and brown boots.

My heart was pumping so hard. I tried to take a step towards the stairs, but I couldn't do it. Dejected and angry with myself, I slipped back into the quiet solitude of my room. I thought of Mum then. Of how annoyed I got when she wouldn't leave the house, my patience thin as she peered nervously in the direction of the windows, before shaking her head and stepping backwards. Tears welled in my eyes. I missed her. I missed Mikey too. But though I ached to hear their voices, I couldn't call home when I was feeling so sad. I didn't want them to know how unhappy I was. I wanted them to believe I'd made hundreds of friends and was living my very best life, having an amazing time. I collapsed onto the bed and pulled my knees up to my chest. I was a coward, skulking in my room like a troll, too scared to breathe. I deserved to be miserable.

A little while later, the sharp *rap-rap-rap* on the door made me jump. I sat up on the bed, gripping the blanket, staring at the door as if someone might burst in with a weapon. The *rap-rap-rap* came again.

'Victoria?' It was Mrs Drummond. 'Are you in there?'

I went to the door and opened it.

'You're alive, then? We weren't sure if you'd died up here.'

I didn't ask who *we* were. 'I'm fine.'

'Just a little mouse then.'

'I've … I've been working,' I mumbled, then was struck by the sudden fear I was about to cry.

'Do you need to call your mum?' She smiled kindly. 'You won't be the first homesick student I've had here.'

I bit down on my lower lip. 'I'm fine,' I said again.

She moved to go, but then hesitated, and for a dreadful moment I thought she might try and hug me. I stepped back from the door, and thankfully she got the hint, gave a slight nod and left.

As I rested my palms flat against the smooth beige gloss of the door, it crossed my mind that now I'd assured her I was fine, if I did happen to die in her attic room, nobody would think to check on me until the smell of rotting Victoria drifted under the door and down the stairs to alert them. How long would that take? I could be lying dead for weeks. Months, even. It was a grim thought and one that only added to my unease. To try and take my mind off my dead and forgotten body, I retrieved my sketch pad and pencils from the desk, and sat on my bed to draw.

I began to sketch. A self-portrait. With my hair and clothes but then the face of a mouse. Beady eyes. Sharp protruding teeth. The face elongated to grotesque proportions.

'Hello Victoria,' I whispered as the foul-looking hybrid took shape. 'Squeak, squeak.'

As I sketched the whiskers, I pressed harder and harder, until the marks became angry slashes across the face. I lifted the pencil and jabbed it into one of the ugly eyes, over and over. *No, no, no*, a voice in my head screamed. The lead snapped.

I threw the pencil and sketch pad down and put my hands against my face. How could I let this happen? What was wrong with me? The thought of scurrying back to Knutsford with my tail between my legs made me sick.

There was another knock. Had Mrs Drummond come back to tell me it might be best to pack my bags and go home? Could she tell I wasn't cut out for university life? As I clambered off the bed again, I realised I wouldn't be unhappy if this were the case.

My breath caught in my throat when I opened the door.

It wasn't Mrs Drummond. It was the boy with blue jeans and brown boots. I wondered for a moment if he might be a hallucination, concrete evidence that my self-imposed isolation had sent me loopy. When he cleared his throat, I realised he was real. Not only real, he was possibly the most beautiful boy I'd ever laid eyes on. Tall, with light brown hair that fell over green eyes, and clear skin, his loose-fitting T-shirt revealing a perfectly defined collarbone. Around his neck hung a leather cord with a Celtic cross suspended from its centre. On his middle finger was a wide silver ring. As we faced each other, I had the peculiar sensation of knowing him, as if from a past life.

'Are you busy?' he said. 'I can come back.' He gestured over his shoulder towards the staircase.

I shook my head, and he smiled, which magnified his beauty a hundred times.

When he stepped into my room, I noticed a slight wrinkling of his nose, and I remembered the half-eaten Pot Noodle from the day before was still on my desk. My cheeks flushed.

'You sure I'm not disturbing you?'

'I'm sketching.' *What?* Shit. Why the hell did I say that? 'I mean, I'm … No, I'm not busy …' The rest of my words got stuck in my throat. I coughed to dislodge them.

'Sketching what?'

I glanced over at the sketch pad. 'Pigeons.' I swallowed, praying he wouldn't ask to see.

'Crazy birds.' His smile was like the sun coming out. 'I kind of like them, though. You know they're clever enough to read the alphabet?'

I didn't know what to reply, so I stayed quiet.

'Anyway, I wanted to come up and say hello, because we haven't met yet.'

We held each other's eyes, and in that split second, something passed between us. A connection. Two jigsaw pieces slotting together.

'Hello.' It was all I could manage. I worried he might drift away once he realised I was incapable of talking, but he stayed, rubbing the back of his neck, blushing slightly. 'Yes, exactly that.' He dipped his head. '*Hello.*'

I became painfully aware of my unbrushed hair and how in need of a bath I was. I'd only had one since I arrived, and that was three days earlier, past midnight, when the chance of coming face to face with anybody was negligible. But now I felt sticky and dirty, the stale air of my room coating my skin like a layer of clothing.

'Mrs Drummond says you're studying architecture at QSA?'

I nodded.

'Me too. I did better in my A levels than expected and got a late place. By then halls were full, though they said a room might come up as people drop out.' He smiled again. I hadn't noticed his perfect dimples before. 'Anyway, me and Mia – the other girl here – are heading to the pub. Would you like to come?'

My heart was racing. Though I wanted to say yes more than anything, I wasn't sure I could do it.

'Unless you're busy?'

'I ... um ... I need a bath.' My cheeks flushed with heat as I waited for him to show his disgust. But instead he smiled again.

'We don't have to leave for an hour or so. You have time. We're hooking up with some other architects and a couple of guys from UCL.'

How was he so at ease and confident? I'd never seen someone as comfortable in their own skin before. My body tingled with desire. It was an unfamiliar feeling and made talking even harder. But as I remained silent, he shifted his weight, his brow furrowing slightly, awkwardness thickening the air between us.

I didn't want this beautiful boy to leave. I had to speak.

'Yes,' I managed. 'If you're sure?'

'Of course.' He grinned. 'The more the merrier. We're housemates doing the same course, after all. We'll be spending a lot of time together.' He held out his hand. 'I'm Nick.'

Warmth spread through me. 'I'm ...' I hesitated. This was my chance to ditch the little mouse. It was time to cut Victoria loose. 'I'm Vikki,' I said.

His expression took me by surprise. He appeared puzzled. 'Really? You don't look like a Vikki.'

'Oh ... right.' I paused. 'What does a Vikki look like?'

He shrugged. 'There was a Vikki at school. She was pretty weird, actually.'

I didn't know what to say.

'Sorry,' he said. 'I've no idea why I said that. Ignore me.'

But I couldn't ignore him. I didn't want new me to be like the weird girl at his school.

'What would you call me?'

He laughed. 'What?'

'It's just I never liked Victoria. Or Vikki.'

'You want me to give you a nickname?' He laughed and pushed his sleeves up his arms. They were toned and tanned, the muscles well defined. I wanted to reach out and stroke them.

'What about Vix?' He smiled. 'Vix is pretty cool.'

Vix.

Vix was perfect. It felt like he'd given me the most beautiful gift.

'But if you want to stay as—'

'I don't.' Vix Fisher was the type of girl who had the strength to interrupt people. 'I like Vix.'

'I like Vix too. Vix …' I watched him turning the name over in his mouth as if tasting. Then he nodded, his face breaking into a grin. 'Vix suits you.'

A smile spilled out of me. It was as if I'd finally stumbled out of a cave. This radiant boy – Nick – had drawn me into the light.

He left my room with a raised hand. 'See you in a bit.'

I closed the door, walked over to the bed and reached for my sketch pad. I tore off the page with the monstrous mouse and ripped it to pieces. Then I dropped the pieces into the bin, smiling as I watched them fall.

'Goodbye little mouse.'

An hour or so later, the three of us walked down Frederick Street in the direction of college. Mia made me uneasy. Not only did she speak like actual royalty, but she was extremely pretty, and apart from A-level art, we had nothing in common. She was studying fine art at Central Saint Martins. She hadn't heard of Knutsford. She rode horses. At one point she asked me what school I'd been to. The question puzzled me. How would she know the schools near Manchester when she'd grown up in Hampshire?

'One in Northwich,' I said.

'A private school?'

'A normal one.'

She groaned and rolled her eyes. 'I *wish* I'd gone to state school. I hated my school. It was a hellhole. Everybody had to be the best at absolutely everything. It was exhausting. I didn't find my crowd at all, you know? Then I screwed up my A levels – well, apart from art – and my parents *totally* freaked out. They wanted me to do PPE at Oxford. *Ugh*. Can you imagine? Anyway, I couldn't wait to leave school. I was *so* envious of the day girls. Did you love coming home each day? When you board, there's no getting away from it all, you know? Thank God I got to go travelling. Anyway. School is over and here we are.' She smiled. 'Isn't college amazing? I did a foundation course at Farnham, but had my heart set on London. My parents are so unhappy I'm doing art, but I *love* it. Mummy's come round a bit because now she's worked out she can combine visiting me with a shopping trip. She'd live in Selfridges if she could.' She looked at me then. 'Do you miss home?'

I had no idea which of her barrage of questions I should answer first. Was she even expecting answers? I glanced at Nick, hoping for help, but he was looking ahead, hands in pockets, so I just shook my head.

'No, me neither. I travelled around Asia for three months after I finished at Farnham and didn't miss home one bit. I think travelling prepares you for life, you know?'

Nick asked what her favourite country was, and she babbled on in her regal voice, talking about places I didn't even know you could visit. Vietnam, Cambodia, India, Nepal, Laos. Throughout her manic monologue, Nick remained serene and patient. I was in awe of him. If he found her chatter bizarre, he didn't let on. My brother would have told her to 'shut the fuck up' before we'd even got out of Mrs Drummond's.

The Lord Challoner was heaving. Drinkers spilled onto the pavement, enjoying the late-September sun. Window boxes with pink and white flowers decorated the black-painted woodwork. The head of a moustachioed man with a military hat swung on a pub sign attached to the brickwork above. Men in shorts and shirts stood in groups holding pints, businessmen in suits drank spirits, a group of women in tiaras and pink feather boas popped champagne and laughed. We pushed inside and made our way through the crowds, the air thick with cigarette smoke and raucous laughter. I'd been to the Black Horse a couple of times for Sunday roast with my family before Dad went to prison, but other than that, I'd never been to a pub before. It was beyond thrilling to walk through the low-slung doorway into this secret buzzing world.

'They're over there,' Nick said.

I followed the direction he was pointing and saw a group of very beautiful people sitting at a table in the centre of the pub. When we reached them, there was a flurry of exuberant hellos as everybody jumped up, obviously pleased to see Nick. Judging by their excitement and the empty glasses littering the table, they'd been there a while. Had Nick delayed leaving the house to let me have my bath? I felt a rush of warmth towards him.

Nick introduced Mia and me. Mia barrelled into the group like an excitable puppy, kissing everybody on both cheeks, brimming over with enthusiasm, while I hung back, unsure if I was expected to greet them in the same over-familiar way. From that moment on, it was clear I was a fish out of water. These people and I were different breeds. They were breathtakingly gorgeous for a start. Especially the girls. I curled my fingers into my hands to hide the bitten nails and cursed my lacklustre mousy hair, still damp from the bath, in need of a cut to get rid of split ends. Dressed in shapeless jeans, scuffed DM boots with yellow laces, and a misshapen sweatshirt, I felt like an exhibit from a freak show next to their sparkling jewellery and achingly trendy clothes. My earring studs were plain and boring, and my make-up – a lick of cheap mascara – was babyish compared to their artfully applied liner and blended shadow. I stared with envy at their lip gloss in perfect shades of pink. The Vaseline I'd dabbed on my own lips was hardly worth it. I was nondescript and drab, a female blackbird at a table of peacocks and birds of paradise.

Mia fitted in perfectly, with her polished beauty, cut-glass accent and eye-catching outfit, a pair of Bohemian trousers she'd bought on a beach in Thailand, a woollen cardigan she'd swapped for two bangles in Kathmandu, her silver bangles clinking as she drank. But despite looking the part, I noticed how quiet she'd become, her attention drifting away from their chat, tapping the table as if she were bored or anxious. When she'd finished her first drink, she stood and said she was going to head back.

'Feeling OK?' Nick asked.

'Oh yes. Fine,' she said. 'I fancy a walk. Soak up the vibes of the city, you know?'

Two of the girls exchanged a look.

Mia saw it and stiffened a little. 'I guess I'm kind of over the pub thing after travelling.'

Nick didn't seem to pick up on the tension. 'Sounds nice. Enjoy,' he said. 'See you back at Frederick Street for a nightcap?'

She smiled softly and slipped away. None of the others said goodbye to her. Part of me – the part that felt as awkward in this group as she did – considered going with her. If we had this in common, maybe it meant we could be friends. But the other part, the stronger part, wanted to stay with Nick.

As I nursed a pint of beer, I listened to them with fascination. I'd never been anywhere near people like this.

The loudest and brashest was Julian, ruddy cheeks, brown hair parting over his forehead like curtains, not handsome exactly, but with an inner confidence that gave him an attractive air. He was wearing a collared shirt, neatly pressed cream trousers, leather shoes and an expensive-looking watch. Everything about him screamed wealth. When he spoke, he made no effort to keep his voice down, dominating the conversation as if born to be listened to.

There was Giles, with curly ginger hair and freckled skin, studying law at UCL, who knew Julian from school and declared everybody in his halls was 'bloody awful', all of them obsessed with 'hanging Maggie'. Apart from Giles and Julian, the rest of them had only known each other for a day or two, but I'd never have guessed that. They acted as if they'd been friends for years. Fraser, another architect at QSA, was the easiest to be with. With olive skin, black hair and unfeasibly white teeth, he exuded a laidback vibe and a generous smile. Then there were the two girls who'd exchanged the look when Mia left. Camilla – 'Call me Cami' – and Tilly, who were also at QSA. Another girl – possibly Alice, or maybe Alicia – was reading English at UCL, and told us numerous times that she'd missed out on Oxford by only one grade.

Though all of them glittered, it was Cami who shone the brightest. I found it hard to look anywhere else. Her auburn hair was thick and gleamed with hairdresser highlights. Her skin was creamy and her hazel eyes large and dewy. She could have been a sixties model, with her immaculate sweeping black eyeliner, long curling eyelashes and lips smeared with an elegant hint of bubble-gum pink. Her luminescence burned me.

I was mesmerised by how easy they were in each other's company, laughing with abandon, throwing back their perfect heads, their chat a mixture of gossip and wild exclamation, liberally scattered with swear words and excitable whoops. It was obvious they wanted people to notice them. And how could people not? They were dipped in varnish. Kings and queens. Self-assured, beautiful and without inhibition. The world was theirs and they knew it. They were everything people like me should have despised.

But I didn't despise them.

I wanted to be them.

I wanted to be the type of person Nick would be friends with. I'd stepped out of the cave and into the light, and now, with the sun on my face, there was no way I wanted to return to the lonely darkness. So as I sat quietly at the table, I observed them, taking in every detail, studying how they spoke, their subjects of interest, the way they smoked and held their glasses. I memorised their mannerisms, knowing later, in the privacy of my room, that I'd mimic the way they talked, their gestures and affectations, practising until I became fluent.

Nick made frequent attempts to draw me into the conversation. Each time he did, I caught Cami and Tilly exchanging half-smiles, somehow amused. I answered with single words, not wanting to reveal myself as an imposter, knowing that as soon as I did, I'd be out.

'Your accent is cute,' said Alice or Alicia.

'My accent?'

'Yes, I love it. Where's it from?'

'I'm ... I'm from Knutsford.'

'*Knuts*ford?' Julian laughed, but I wasn't sure why.

'It's near Manchester.'

'Manchester?' Tilly's brow wrinkled as if she'd never heard of it. Then she nodded slowly, casting another brief smile at Cami. 'Actually,' she said, tapping the table a few times with a perfectly manicured finger, 'now you mention Manchester, you sound *exactly* like Noel Gallagher. I couldn't place it before.'

There was general nodding, and Cami batted Tilly, crooning, 'You're so right. Close your eyes and she could actually *be* Noel.'

I didn't know how to reply.

Tilly smiled. 'So tell me, what does your father do up in ...' she paused, 'Knutsford?'

My heart skipped a beat. The table fell quiet and all eyes locked onto me. There was no way I could tell the truth. I knew from bitter experience that my dad was social suicide.

'It's OK,' Nick said. 'You don't have to answer.'

My eyes welled with tears and I dropped my head, my hair falling over my face to shield me. There was muttering. Then Nick rested his hand on mine and gently squeezed. I felt a rush of heat, and when he loosened his grip, I wanted to reach out and snatch his hand back.

Tilly cleared her throat. 'Another bottle of wine?'

Everybody agreed, and thankfully attention moved swiftly and effortlessly away from me.

When last orders were called, Fraser raised his glass. 'You know, I think we're going to have an awful lot of fun over the next few years. Here's to London, this fine group of people and as much bad behaviour as we can get away with!'

Everybody laughed and clinked glasses. 'To London.'

We walked out of the pub and joined the throng of people milling about on the pavement. A vague plan was made to meet for lunch the following day, then the others drifted off until it was just Nick, Cami and me. She stepped close to him, ignoring me, her eyes fixed on him, pink lips parted a little, her fingers toying with a strand of coppery hair. My hand went to my own hair involuntarily.

'Walk me back to halls?' Her words were sticky with honey and spice.

'I'll see you back at Frederick Street,' I mumbled, then started walking, even though I had no idea how to get there.

'Wait, Vix,' he called. 'We'll walk together. Cami's halls aren't too far out of the way.'

I glanced at Cami and noticed her smile had fallen away.

She hooked her arm through Nick's. 'So you must absolutely *loathe* living out of halls. It must be so boring. Halls are a riot.'

'Much better than I thought it would be, actually. My room's big and the landlady's nice. A bit uptight when it comes to music.' He smiled at me. 'Early days, but it's not bad, is it?'

'I like it.' I kept my reply brief. I was conscious I needed to sort my accent out.

'Back at the pub,' Cami said, looking at me, 'what was the thing about your father?'

My heart skipped a beat. I thought I'd swerved the subject of my dad, and found myself blindsided by her question. Vivid flashes from the day my father was arrested came at me. The way his face had fallen when my mother said the police were at our door. My mother's horror as he was pushed into their car. The awful sound of her begging them to let him go. The neighbours watching on their front lawns.

'I'd rather not talk about it,' I said.

'Ooh, keeping things mysterious,' Cami said with a sharp-eyed smile. 'I like it.'

My stomach twisted in knots as we walked. I listened to them chatting, heat burning my cheeks and the back of my neck. I wanted Cami to evaporate. She set me on edge, as if any moment she was going to put me under the spotlight. It was ten excruciating minutes before we finally arrived outside an austere Victorian building with music blaring out of a number of windows.

'Well, this is *moi*.'

'See you tomorrow,' Nick said.

'Sleep tight,' she replied. She only had eyes for him.

As we walked away, I knew I needed to say something about my dad. I'd seen Cami's face. Her quizzical look. The suspicion. If I didn't address it, they'd start discussing it behind my back – *Honestly, she was so shifty. I don't trust her, she was definitely hiding something. She's not one of us* – and that was the very last thing I wanted.

'My dad,' I said quietly. 'He … he, er …' My voice faded.

'You don't have to talk about it.'

I recalled the days and weeks and months after his arrest, the hatred and disgust from everybody we'd ever known, the way people stared when I walked into a classroom or assembly. The loneliness of those lunches alone. The judgement on my teachers' faces. Then my mother's desperate voice.

It would be better for us if he'd died.

That man had ruined Victoria's life. I wasn't going to let him ruin Vix's too.

'It's just he ... Well, my dad. He's ... he's dead.'

Once I'd started, the lies slipped out relatively easily. I told him how my dad had been walking home from the train station. 'There was a car. A hit-and-run. He was killed instantly.'

'Jesus,' said Nick. 'That's awful. How old were you?'

'I was ten.'

I'm not sure why, but I began to cry then. Real tears, not crocodile ones. Was it his sympathy? His expression of horror? Or was I crying with relief? That he'd bought my lie and I no longer had to fear him discovering our family's shame.

Nick put his arms around me, and we stood on the street while I cried. When I stepped back from him, I wiped away my tears with the flats of both hands, as if sloughing away the final remnants of my discarded skin.

'I'm fine, honestly. It happened a long time ago.'

'I hope you don't feel we were prying.'

'No, I'm glad. I feel better for telling you.'

Lying in bed later, too wired to sleep, my ears ringing with the noise of the pub, I couldn't quite believe what had happened. I tingled with the thrill of it. First thing in the morning I would go shopping for hair dye, make-up and clothes. I had some money saved from my summer of working, plus a bit Mum had given me for emergencies. And this was definitely an emergency. If Vix wanted to be friends with Nick and his crowd, she needed to look the part.

She also had to sound the part.

I practised all night, talking into the darkness, repeating words and phrases over and over until I was sure I'd rubbed the worst of my accent away.

'You,' I said into the darkness, 'are no longer a scared little mouse. Victoria is gone. You are Vix. You are confident. You are pretty. And you have shiny new friends.'

I grinned and pulled the duvet up to my chin.

This was it.

My new life had started.

CHAPTER FOUR

Coco

Coco took care not to make too much noise as she closed the front door and walked along the side return to unlock her bike. Although still early, not yet seven o'clock, it was already warm. The breeze blew through her hair as she freewheeled down the empty road, the seagulls calling casually overhead, the smell of summer in the air, the tang of salt as she neared the sea.

Stack Point had been her favourite thinking spot for years and was the ideal place to start her birthday. When her mum had first brought her up here, aged about eight or nine, she'd warned her to keep away from the cliff. A fall would be fatal, which, she'd then told her earnestly, was exactly why so many people went there to kill themselves. She described how they would walk right up to the edge and launch themselves onto the blackened rocks below. Coco had been fascinated by what her mother had said; the words interwoven with the dark thrill of death had set her pulse racing. At that age she hadn't understood why anybody would want to take their own life, but as she grew older, she got it, and, she reasoned, if you'd had enough of it all, Stack Point was definitely the place to go. A beautiful last image to take to your sticky end.

She laid her bike on the grass and walked towards the edge and peered down. The surface of the sea was calm and still, shining like a polished mirror. The cliffs were bathed in sunshine. She sat on her rock, wide and flat and charcoal grey, and stared out over the vast stretch of water. She wondered, as she had done a thousand times before, about the girl on the other side of the sea. A few years earlier, Coco had researched the area of coastline across the Channel, pulling up a map on the internet and working out the direction she was facing when she sat on her rock. She then traced a straight line with her finger, following the direction of her stare. The line landed on a place in France called Trégastel. When she googled it, the town sounded exactly like Falmouth, and in her head she'd built a picture of a girl her own age, with her own dreams and frustrations, sitting on a replica French rock staring right back at her. She found the thought comforting, and whenever Coco went to Stack Point, she always made sure to say hello to her twin in Trégastel.

She lifted her arm and waved. 'Happy birthday!' she called.

She held her breath and listened for a reply. A few seconds later, it came across the sea like an echo.

Joyeux anniversaire!

Coco smiled and drew her knees up to her chin, hugging them tightly. Birthday wishes all the way from Trégastel.

Something caught her eye then, a shadow moving beneath the surface of the water. She squinted and stared down. Could it be a basking shark? It was! A birthday gift from the sea. She grinned as she watched the prehistoric creature drifting across the bay, its dorsal fin cutting through the water, the tip of its tail fin swaying left and right as it powered through the blue. She pictured its mouth, a gaping cavern, swallowing thousands of gallons of seawater and filtering its breakfast, a billion minuscule flecks of zooplankton suspended in the water, all contentedly hanging about absorbing the sunlight, minding their own watery business. She imagined herself diving off her rock to swim alongside the shark in the turquoise silence, submerged in the peace, the sun making shapes as it hit the water and splintered.

How free she'd feel.

When the creature moved slowly out of sight, Coco climbed to her feet and stretched her arms out wide. She let out a warrior cry, which reverberated through her body, making the tips of her fingers tingle with a rush of adrenalin. A gull screeched above her. She tipped her head back and cried out again, louder this time, folding to bend at the middle to force the noise out of her as if every cell in her body might shatter like glass.

An hour or so later, she was home. The smell of fresh coffee and bacon hit her as soon as she walked back into the house. Her mother appeared from the kitchen, a worried look on her face. 'I didn't know where you were. Everything OK?'

'I fancied a breath of air to wake me up.' Coco slipped off her trainers and placed them side by side on the shoe rack.

Her mother seemed happy enough with this, and any concern was quickly forgotten. 'Happy birthday, princess!' Her face broke into the widest smile as she shook her head in disbelief. 'My baby. Sixteen years old! Can you believe it? Seems like only yesterday you were a precious little doll in my arms.' She pulled Coco in for a suffocating hug. 'I love you so much, baby.'

They sat at the small laminate-top table in the corner of the kitchen and ate bacon with the rind cut off, egg-white omelettes and black coffee. As a special birthday treat, her mother had bought orange juice. They had half a glass each. Coco stared at her mother as she sipped her juice. Something was up. She couldn't keep still, bobbing about on her chair like a bouncy ball, every sinew in her body pulled tight, fingers drumming excitedly.

'You OK?' Coco eyed her warily as she swallowed the last of her juice.

'Couldn't be better!'

Her phone buzzed on the table. A message from Shannon.
Hbd lysm babe see u later

Coco hearted the message. As she ate, she absently scrolled, acknowledging the stream of messages that lit up her phone.

'Lovely you've so many friends,' her mother said. 'But then again, you've always been popular.'

'Mm-hmm,' Coco replied.

'Sooooo ... *presents!*' her mum cried the moment Coco finished her last mouthful and set her knife and fork together.

'You didn't have to get me anything.'

'What? Of course I did!' She jumped off her chair and rushed out of the kitchen, returning a few moments later laden with beautifully wrapped gifts in gold paper with bright red ribbons. Clutched in her hand was a gold-foil helium balloon in the shape of a star. She handed Coco the balloon. 'Because you are one.'

Coco forced a smile.

Her mother put the presents on the table in front of her and Coco carefully opened each one, taking time to separate the Sellotape from the paper so as not to tear it. She'd been spoiled again. Her mother's extravagance always made her uneasy. They didn't have the money for all this stuff, and she worried how many extra hours she'd had to work to be able to afford it. There was a cashmere shawl, dove grey, soft as rabbit fur. A pair of Chanel sunglasses with tortoiseshell frames and some silver high-heeled sandals.

'Mum, honestly, you've bought too much.'

'Nonsense, princess! That's what credit cards are for. And anyway, as soon as you're discovered, you'll be able to buy everything you've ever wanted yourself. You won't need me any more!' She patted the sandals. 'And I've booked you a birthday pedicure. Can't have grotty toenails with a pair of shoes like this.'

Coco wrapped the shawl around her shoulders. The fine fibres stuck uncomfortably to the hot skin on her neck. The sunglasses were too large and slipped down the bridge of her nose. She pushed them up and smiled at her mum.

'Oh sweetheart. You look like a film star. A Golden Age one, like Sophia Loren or Lauren Bacall. The shawl is the same one Eva Mendes wore on a flight to LA in February. The magazine said she never flies without it. That and a tube of Eight Hour Cream.'

'Thanks, Mum. You've been really generous.'

Coco removed the sunglasses and put them back in their protective case, then folded the shawl and hung it over the back of the chair.

'I got you a cake, too. A small one. Only two hundred and twenty-seven calories, so you can enjoy every bite.'

Her mother opened the fridge and retrieved a plate on which was a single cupcake with no icing. She pushed a pink candle into its naked top, then lit it with a box of matches she fished out of her pocket. As the flame burned, she sang 'Happy Birthday'. When she came to the end, she rested her hands on her daughter's shoulders and kissed her cheek. 'Go on,' she urged. 'Make a wish.'

Coco watched a globule of wax roll down the length of the candle and plop onto the cake, solidifying on impact and turning opaque. She blew the flame out.

'What did you wish for?' Her mother giggled as she shook her head. 'Sorry. *Sorry.* I know! You're not supposed to tell me. But I've got a surprise for you and I'm thinking how good it would be if you wished for it first and I made your wish come true!' She grinned. 'Guess then … Go on!'

'What is it?'

'You'll never guess.'

Coco glanced up at her mother, whose eyes were popping out of her face like marbles. She imagined them flying out and bouncing as they hit the floor and rolled away. 'What?'

'Could you be a little more excited?'

She furrowed her brow. 'I don't know what I'm supposed to be excited about.'

'*Guess* then!'

The way her mother's body tensed with excitement meant

that whatever she was surprising Coco with was almost certainly something to do with acting or modelling, which was pretty much the only thing her mum ever got truly excited about.

'An audition? For an advert?'

Her mother beamed, delighted to see Coco finally engaging. 'Better!' She was flapping her hands at her sides like a penguin.

'Better than an advert ...' Coco glanced around the room and her eyes fell on the framed photograph nestled on the mantelpiece between her certificates for drama and ballet and the numerous medals she'd won in dance competitions. It showed her aged four – blonde hair set in perfect ringlets, a big blue bow pinned to the side of her head, her lips the colour of red roses, a white dress and blue sandals – holding a beach ball and beaming. The photo was cut from a catalogue. It was her first paid job. Her mum still talked about the thrill of receiving that call from the casting agent to say she'd got the contract. 'Modelling?' Coco guessed.

Her mum shook her head then nodded for her to try again.

'I give up.' Coco's patience had worn to nothing. 'Tell me.'

'OK ... well ... it's a ... Waitressing job ...' Her mother waggled her eyebrows and stepped closer to her. 'At Lowencliffe Hall!'

Coco wrinkled her nose as if her mother's words smelt bad. 'Waitressing? I don't want to do a waitressing job.' She didn't want to do a modelling job either. Or an advert. But they were both a lot more appealing than delivering food for a pittance to a load of posh drunk idiots at the stuck-up hotel where her mum's weird boyfriend worked.

'I haven't finished. There's more. It's not any old waitressing job. It's for a private function. A *wedding*!' Her mum grabbed Coco's shoulders. 'Julian Draper's.'

'Who?' Coco wriggled free of her mother's grip.

'Julian Draper,' her mother squeaked, almost on the point of combustion. 'He's marrying Ingrid Olsson!'

'What? The *real* Ingrid Olsson?'

Her mother couldn't contain her feverish delight and nodded so violently Coco pictured her head falling off. 'The one and only! All top secret, so you can't tell a soul, and I mean that. They'll put me in prison if the tabloids get hold of it. Sounds like the place'll be filled to bursting with every big name in Hollywood. Darren has promised me you'll be out front and not stuck in the kitchen. You'll be serving drinks and food to – oh my *God*, seriously, I can't believe it – Ingrid herself, and more A-list stars than you can count. Darren was saying they've got their own security and they've booked every room in the hotel. For the whole weekend! Can you imagine? How the other half lives, eh? That'll be you soon, princess. I *know* it.' She beat her chest with her fist. 'Right here, in my heart. Darren says there's going to be a champagne reception on the terrace, dining in the ballroom, then some fancy tent on the lawn for dancing. He says they've got a famous DJ and the type of singer who sells out arenas. He hasn't been told who yet, but from what the lady was saying, he's almost certain it's Harry Styles. She mentioned feather boas. They've had some fancy London florist come down. Darren says he's pretty sure it's the same florist who did the King's coronation. And if *that's* not enough, the exclusive rights to the whole thing have been bought by some fancy magazine. There'll be photos, Coco. Sent to all four corners of the world.' Her eyes glistened with tears. 'Oh baby, this is your chance to get *noticed*. It's the moment you've always dreamed of.'

Though Coco didn't actually want to get noticed by anybody – that was her mother's dream, not hers – she had to admit this was pretty big. Ingrid Olsson wasn't a fake or a wannabe; she was the real deal. A proper superstar with an Oscar nomination, three Golden Globes, countless BAFTAs, over thirty million Instagram followers and hundreds of millions of likes on TikTok, and the album she'd dropped last year had stayed at the number one spot in both the UK and US charts for six consecutive weeks.

Her friends at school were going to lose their shit.

But then a feeling of dread crept through her veins. What did her mum expect her to do? Deliver a bowl of soup and refuse to put it down until Ingrid cast her in a movie? Coco knew enough about the casting process to know this wasn't how it worked. Not any more. Now it was all agents and a hundred thousand auditions and battling the nepo babies for every single role. Maybe now was the moment to tell her mum she didn't want to be an actor. Coco had no desire to be extraordinary or shine the brightest. No desire to be on the front cover of *Vanity Fair*. Especially if it meant eating egg-white omelettes and icingless cupcakes for the rest of her life.

But as she stared at her mum's face – glinting eyes, huge smile, flushed cheeks – she realised she couldn't do it. Not now. Not while she was so fired up. Ever since Coco could remember, she had been primped and primed for the big time. Fame was all her mother had ever wanted for her. It would break her heart to discover her daughter had other ideas, and Coco didn't want to break her mum's heart. Anyway, it was almost pointless to try. The last time she'd said something, her mum had laughed. 'Don't be silly,' she'd trilled. 'You were *born* to be a star. You're far too beautiful and talented to do anything else. And what on earth would you want to do anyway?'

'I like writing,' Coco had replied quietly.

'Writing? Writing what?'

'Stories?'

'*Stories?* How will you make money writing *stories*?'

'I like writing poems, too.'

Her mother had snorted with laughter. 'Oh sweetheart, nobody ever bought a house rhyming cat with mat.'

Coco had let it go. The truth was, she couldn't imagine herself doing any job. The world seemed so big and confusing. Why did she have to know now what she wanted to do for the rest of her life? It was much easier to know what she *didn't* want to do. And what she didn't want to do was acting or singing. But her mum had had her future mapped out since birth. Her life was something she was strapped to, an out-of-control car hurtling forwards in a direction she didn't want to go, hands tied so she couldn't free herself, mouth gagged so she couldn't yell *Stop!*

'Oh princess. I can't read your face! Tell me what you're thinking. Surely you're excited to be going to Ingrid Olsson's wedding?'

Coco gave a half-hearted shrug. Her mum stiffened.

'You know, I can't believe you sometimes.' Her words were clipped and had a sharp edge to them now. 'This is a *huge* deal, Coco. Everybody who's anybody will be at Lowencliffe Hall on the twenty-seventh of July. You can be there too. Where you belong.' Then she softened and reached out to tuck a strand of hair behind her daughter's ear before cupping her cheek. 'Sweetheart, you're so beautiful. One of the most beautiful women ever born. You deserve to be adored. You deserve to be worshipped by the world.'

What would her life be like if she'd been born ugly? Would her mother have admired her brain instead of her looks? Would she have been as passionate about university? Forced her to be a doctor or a lawyer or a banker?

'*Coco!*'

The shouted word made Coco look up. 'I'm sorry,' she said. 'But I'm not sure I want to do a waitressing job.'

Her mum shook her head with frustration. 'Do you *know* how spoilt you sound right now? Do you *know* how much I've done for you? How much I've given up?'

Coco breathed in deeply; she'd heard what was coming next a thousand times.

I've driven you up and down the country. Spent hours of my life. God knows how much money. Clothes and haircuts and petrol. Speech lessons. Acting lessons. Ballet lessons …

'I've spent hours – *hours* – of my life taking you to auditions. Driven miles. Spent all our money on clothes and haircuts and drama lessons. All I want is what's best for you. All I want is for you to have what you *deserve*. And you deserve more than this.' She gestured around the kitchen, a look of disdain dirtying her face. 'I want the world for you, Coco. I want you ... I want you to have the very best life you can ...'

Then emotion got the better of her.

As her mum's face crumpled, Coco's stomach turned over. She couldn't bear seeing her upset. She knew how much her mum cared and how much she loved her. She only ever did what she thought was best for Coco. Coco's father – a boy her mum had met aged sixteen in a dive of a club in Plymouth – had disappeared 'like smoke up a chimney' when Debbie told him their grubby sex in the ladies' toilets had led to a positive pregnancy test. When he'd told her where to stick the test, she'd promised her unborn baby she'd be the best mother she could be. It was obvious how hard it had been. Sleepless nights, worries over bills, extra shifts at the pub, as many hours as they'd give her at the surgery, cleaning germs and sickness off the waiting room floor and walls and toilets. Dead on her feet. Dark bags under her eyes. Fifteen-hour days. Seven days a week. Every penny she earned going towards her dream of seeing Coco posing on a red carpet, dressed head to toe in Versace and Chanel, in front of an ocean of clicking cameras.

The waitressing job at the hotel was only for a few hours ...

'I'm sorry. You know, yeah, it's *brilliant*. Thank you for sorting it. And I can't believe I'll get to meet the *actual* Ingrid Olsson.'

Like the sun coming out after a storm, her mother's eyes started shining and a smile crept onto her face. 'You'll do it?'

Coco smiled. 'Turn down an opportunity like that? I'd be mad.'

Her mum hugged her, kissed the top of her head, then leant back and put both hands, callused from chemicals and scouring cloths and hard graft, on her face. 'You're a star. I knew it when I chose your name. I knew then you'd be a one-word icon like Cher, Bono, Madonna. Soon *Coco* will join them.'

'Is it OK if I go up to my room now?'

Her mum's face fell. 'Oh. I thought—'

'I should probably post a TikTok. There's a new dance people are doing on their birthdays. Mira Farhi got nearly a hundred thousand views when she did it.'

Her mum immediately nodded. 'Oh God. Yes. Of course. Good idea. Want me to film it?'

'I'll use the tripod you gave me.'

'OK, well shout if you need any help and I'll be right up.'

Upstairs, Coco closed the door to her bedroom and lay on her bed. She took her phone out, clicked on the TikTok icon and began to scroll. Her thumb moved with a mind of its own, scrolling and scrolling and scrolling, through millions of videos, strangers performing choreographed dances from kitchens, bedrooms and gardens all around the world. Everybody chasing a million likes. Everybody wanting their moment of viral fame.

'Happy birthday,' she whispered, her thumb moving faster and faster, the faces blurring like a wheel of fortune.

Darren had tried to close the computer screen when he'd noticed Debbie reading the booking sheet.

'*What?* Jesus, Darren! Show me!' She'd pushed him aside and jabbed manically at the keyboard in a futile attempt to restore the page.

'You shouldn't have seen that. It's confidential.'

She snapped her head around to look at him. '*Ingrid Olsson* is getting married here? Are you serious? Why didn't you tell me?'

He rolled his eyes. 'I didn't tell you because I knew you'd get all overexcited. And also I had to sign something that said if I did tell you they'd sue me for every penny.'

Darren and Debbie had met online. He was married but he and his battleaxe wife hadn't had sex in years.

'If you don't mind the wife, let's give it a go,' he had said after their first meet-up.

Debbie didn't mind at all. It suited her to have a no-strings-attached relationship. She didn't have time for a full-time man, not with Coco to think about.

A year later, they'd fallen into a routine. Saturday afternoon hook-ups after she'd finished cleaning at the surgery while Darren's wife was playing golf. A few weeks before Coco's birthday, he'd texted to tell her to meet at his office as he had a few bits to finish up.

He'd tried to close the screen before she saw, but it was too late.

Debbie stared at him. 'You need to let Coco work that day.'

'Don't be silly, Deb. I can't. She's fifteen—'

'She'll be sixteen.'

He shook his head. 'It's against hotel protocol. Waitresses have to be trained up. I mean, what if she's useless? These guys aren't mucking about. I've doubled the rate I'd usually charge and they didn't even blink. They'll want the best.'

'She is the best. The last place she waitressed at begged her to go full-time.' This was a lie, but Debbie would give Coco a crash course in waitressing. It wasn't brain surgery. Take an order. Deliver food. Clear plates away. Smile and don't spill anything on anybody. 'Plus, come on, she's a stunner. You know that. They'll be over the moon to have such a beauty looking after them. These types of people like to be surrounded by beautiful things. Including waitresses. Ugly waitresses make them feel bad. It puts them off their lobster.'

'They aren't having lobster.'

'Give her the job, Darren.'

Darren still looked doubtful. Debbie softened her face and put her arms around his neck. She planted a kiss on his ear lobe. He was weird about ear lobes. Having them touched sent him nuts. He moaned slightly as she took the fleshy lobe between her teeth and nibbled gently.

'Please?' she whispered. 'I've never asked anything from you. And, well, I've never said anything to Susan.'

Darren sprang back, his face a picture of pantomime horror. 'Are you …? You wouldn't … Why would you?'

She quickly kissed him. 'Tell her? Goodness, don't worry,' she said, between kisses. 'As if I'd do anything like that without good reason. I wouldn't want to cause any kind of bother. I imagine she'd be pretty angry, wouldn't she? But I've never said anything, even though it would be easy to …'

Darren was still hesitant.

Debbie smiled through half-lowered lashes and slipped her hand down the front of his trousers, hovering over his cock, flaccid and soft beneath the polyester. She rubbed a little and felt a slight stirring.

'We can't do this here,' he rasped. 'I'm not off work for another—' He groaned as she rubbed harder, her eyes on his face until she saw the familiar glassy look settle over him. When his eyelids closed like window blinds, she stopped abruptly.

'Carry on!' His voice was dry as crackers.

She moved her lips close to his ear. 'Coco will be a perfect waitress, Darren.' She nibbled his lobe. 'She just needs you to give her a chance.'

Darren moaned, then nodded.

Two minutes later, she was wiping her hand clean on a tissue from the box on his desk and watching over his shoulder as he typed Coco's name into the work roster.

Now, in her kitchen, birthday presents given, Debbie felt warm with anticipation of what this was going to do for Coco. She took a cloth and went over to the mantelpiece, where she carefully dusted the photographs in their frames. Coco had been an exquisite child, all soft golden curls, blue eyes and creamy skin. Debbie picked up one of the photos. It showed her baby when she was six years old. Soft pink leotard trimmed with royal-blue satin ruffles, a gauzy skirt of pink and blue organza, false eyelashes accentuating her eyes, rosebud lips perfectly painted in opalescent pink, silver sequinned shoes with cute high heels that slipped onto her feet like Cinderella's slippers. Clutched in the crook of one elbow was a huge silver trophy, almost as big as she was, and across her chest the winner's sash. Debbie loved Coco with all her heart, and if she had to choose a best day, when mothering her had felt like the biggest prize in the world, the regional qualifiers of Little Miss UK 2014 would have been it.

She stroked her fingers over the picture. 'You're going to be a star, baby.'

CHAPTER FIVE

26 July 2024

I'd told Celeste I'd make my own way to Lowencliffe Hall. I needed the option to change my mind at any point, and it would have been considerably harder if trapped in a moving limousine with another humourless chauffeur.

When I got off the train at St Pancras, the first thing that struck me was how much it had changed. The grot and grime had been replaced by a gleaming palace of smart shops and eateries, seemingly more upmarket shopping centre than train station. I tried not to dwell on where I was. I'd vowed I'd never return to London, and as I wove my way through the hordes, anxious energy crackling through me, I reminded myself over and over that I could turn back at any time.

At the entrance to the Underground, I stopped in front of the map to check my route to Paddington. As I stared at the tangled web of colours, the Central Line shone out like neon. I couldn't stop my gaze travelling to White City. The words struck me in the gut. I squeezed my eyes closed, trying to force out the image of him hitting the tracks, the thud of the impact, the screams that must have followed. I turned quickly and hurried away. There was no way I could take the Tube.

For a moment or two I stood on the street, blinking into the sunshine, trying to get my bearings. I'd forgotten it was possible to cram so many people into one place. All shapes and sizes, from every corner of the globe, dressed in every type of clothing one could imagine, coming and going, rushing, meandering, distracted, focused, all of them locked in their own small worlds. Scabby pigeons dodged the footfalls whilst searching for morsels of discarded food. Homeless people – more than I remembered – sat in doorways and beside cashpoints with cardboard signs and empty eyes. I gave the first one I passed a five-pound note. The next a few coins. The third I hurried past, like the stream of others who rushed on blindly, muttering apologetically that I was out of change.

I had an hour and a half until my train. Enough time to take a detour past a few old haunts. My first thought was Frederick Street. I recalled Mrs Drummond showing me around her home, pictured the discoloured bathroom suite, the oven with its layer of black grime, the pigeons cooing on the window ledge outside my attic room. I imagined knocking on her door. Would she remember me? The 'little mouse', innocent, wide-eyed, no clue how her life would unfold. If only I could have travelled back in time and persuaded that eighteen-year-old girl to make different decisions. I felt a sharp pang of sympathy for my younger self, a fugitive from an unstable home, craving friends and someone to love, desperate to experience new things, desperate for self-reinvention.

It broke my heart to remember the home I'd escaped. My mother, so affected by what people thought of her, ruined by the shame of my father. The change in her was hard on Mikey and me. When we were small, she'd been a good mother. Yes, she could be uptight, but she made sure we were cared for. We had six-monthly check-ups with the dentist. Polished shoes. Home-cooked suppers. She'd take us to the zoo and the pantomime. Our friends envied our packed lunches. Even at the tender age of ten, I understood how the rug had been pulled from beneath her. I did what I could to fill the gaps. I made our packed lunches. I cleaned up. I'd fetch a blanket and gently cover her when she fell asleep on the sofa, turn the TV off, remove the empty wine glass from her hand. But Mikey wasn't as understanding. He'd scream at her to get a grip. Tell her not to be so selfish. Tell her she was still our mother. Perhaps I was just better at adapting. Mikey lived in the past. The only mother he wanted was the in-control, chin-up-and-get-on-with-it, tidy-your-room mother he remembered. That mother had been able to handle his mood swings, but after our father left, she was too exhausted to deal with him. Mikey needed structure and routine. He needed Mum to carry him. Without her to keep him in check, he became a loose cannon.

Once, after he got in trouble for forgetting his football kit, he shouted at her then punched a hole through the wall. I told him to stop, that it wasn't her fault, that he should have remembered it himself. Mum had stared emptily, no apology, no excuse, just silence. It drove him mad. He stormed upstairs and slammed his door. Later he showed me the wall.

'Did it with my fist,' he said.

'But didn't it hurt?'

He held out his hand, the knuckles bruised and swollen, grazes on his fingers. I fetched the first aid kit from the bathroom and dabbed antiseptic cream on the cuts. 'Please don't punch walls,' I said.

'I'm sorry,' he whispered, eyes hollow now the rage had faded.

Though I was eighteen months younger, he was no protective older brother, no looming figure who looked out for me, who gave me advice or cared what I was doing. It was me who took on the older sibling role. Me who calmed him down and held him when he sobbed. I loved Mikey, but I was worn down by looking out for him. His relationship with Mum had been complicated from the start. A traumatic birth followed by what I now presume was undiagnosed postnatal depression.

'He's been hard work since the day he was born,' she used to tell anybody who'd listen: friends, the girl at the checkout in the supermarket, the other mothers gathered at the school gate. 'He's my devil child.'

I used to stiffen whenever she started her story, bracing myself for what was coming, knowing Mikey would be in my room later on, crying or sulking or stamping his feet.

'She means it nicely,' I'd say.

'Nicely? Her *devil child*? How is that nice?'

'Like calling you a terror or a monkey?'

'Eleven weeks old,' Mum would say. 'Face like a shiny red apple. Body stiff as wood, crying so hard he gasped like a guppy. Nothing would make him stop. People were staring – goodness *knows* what they must have thought – so I pushed his pram as fast as I could, practically running, even though my shoes were pinching, desperate to get him home.'

As she spoke, I'd watch Mikey, knowing he was trying to turn the volume down on her voice, knowing he never managed it. The pain on his face was obvious.

'Then this man, a filthy tramp, hair matted into rats' tails, clothes black with dirt – and God, he *stank* to high heaven – grabbed at my coat as I passed. Gave me such a shock. Oh, he was hideous. Lice crawling in and out of his hairline.' She would always pause here and lower her voice. 'He pulled me down to him. Breathing over me. It was like he'd swallowed something dead. "That baby," he said, "has a demon inside. A *devil* child." Then off he went, scuttling like a cockroach.'

Mum would smile and ruffle Mikey's hair as he dropped his eyes to the ground, his cheeks red and hot.

When I told them I'd accepted a place at university, I'd expected Mum to smile and offer congratulations, but she said nothing, her expression flat. Mikey, on the other hand, lost it, shouting, gesticulating, calling me every foul name he could think of.

'You're a rat! A dirty bitch rat jumping off a sinking ship. Selfish, selfish, *selfish*!' he screeched, storming upstairs.

Mum started to speak, but I saw red and tore out of the room after him. I was fuming. I'd never lost my temper with him before. I shoved open his bedroom door and let rip. As I railed, his eyes grew wide and his mouth dropped into an O of shock.

'It's not *me* who's selfish, it's *you*! Living in this house with you and her is *hell*. Don't you see that? I can't wait to leave. I hate my life here. You're both so *needy*. I *hate* you!'

If only I could travel back in time and take it all back. I should never have shouted. I should have held him and told him I loved him. I regret every one of those words I spat out.

Despite being only a stone's throw from Frederick Street, I decided not to go there and instead headed to Bedford Square. As I walked, things became more familiar, and by the time I arrived, I felt as if I'd stepped out of a time machine. I stood on the pavement looking up at the imposing row of grey-brick townhouses. The building had undergone a clean, the doors freshly painted in a slick of oily black, railings to match, neat window boxes, a polished brass plaque with the name of the college etched into it. As I stared at the building, I saw people from the past, holograms milling about on the chequerboard steps, spilling out of the door, talking and laughing, carrying portfolios and book bags. Some with headphones on. Couples holding hands. Chattering groups. I saw Fraser and Nick. Julian. Tilly and Cami. Dear Rav, then Julie Rainer. She raised her hand to me as she trotted down the steps, but as I watched, her smile faded, her eyes hardened and everything grew dark, as if a black storm cloud had rolled across the sky. Painful flashes of memory came at me. The whispering and staring. Everybody's eyes on me. The look on Nick's face. On Cami's. The horrified silence that still rang in my ears.

It was as if it had all happened yesterday.

I turned and hurried away, head down, fighting to keep my shoulder bag and holdall from falling as I jogged, desperate to put distance between me and those recollections. It was only when I was far enough away for the clamour in my head to quieten that I stopped to catch my breath.

I hailed a black cab and asked for Paddington.

'Praed Street OK?'

'Wherever is fine.'

The driver was a talker, asking me a variety of questions, which I answered with single words. *Yes*, I was visiting. *Yes*, I'd been to London before. *No*, I lived in France. *Yes*, I liked the French. He finally gave up on a two-way conversation and spent the rest of the mercifully short journey grumbling about the mayor of London.

My detour to QSA had eaten into my time and I ended up having to run to make the train. 'Sorry,' I said to the guard as I hurried past him. He gestured impatiently with his hand, but waited until I was on board before blowing his whistle. The doors closed in a series of hydraulic sighs, and I moved through the carriage to find my seat, the motion of the train pushing me side to side.

I lifted my holdall onto the overhead rack, glad to see the back of it, rubbing my shoulder where the strap had dug in. I was grateful I'd had the forethought to book a window seat, and as I rested my head against the glass, I wondered for the umpteenth time what on earth I was doing.

Somewhere between Reading and Swindon, the soporific noises in the carriage lulled me into half-sleep. The soft rumble of the train, the distant sound of a baby crying, a family laughing as they played Uno at a table behind me. I came to as we pulled into Tiverton Parkway and reached for my bag, stretching my back and shoulders as I rummaged for an apple. I hadn't eaten since the evening before. I should have been ravenous, but the constant gnawing anxiety had taken my appetite, and the first bite of apple sat leaden in my mouth, impossible to swallow.

The sea came into view as we approached Dawlish. It was

beautiful, with red cliffs on one side of the train and water on the other, its surface rippled by the wind as it lapped at the rounded pebbles which bordered the tracks. I thought about Marseille, about the concrete jetty where men sat on upturned cool boxes to fish and students ate their sandwiches and tourists wandered aimlessly.

As we drew nearer to Cornwall, I grew increasingly anxious. Feeling on edge, my nerves jangling, I instinctively reached into my bag for my sketch pad. I'd always found refuge in sketching faces. Perhaps it was linked to some deep-rooted desire to be somebody else. Like an actor or a novelist, portraiture allowed me to try on different skins. At my lowest points, drawing people, both caricatures and portraits, had been my salvation. It was meditative, releasing endorphins my brain so desperately craved. I looked across the aisle at a woman in a seat facing me. She was ten years or so older than me and was knitting, soft blue wool with large needles. She had kind eyes and clear skin, and I imagined she was travelling home from London after visiting her grandchildren. There was a contentment about her, as if she'd enjoyed her time but was now pleased to be away from the noise and chaos of young children. I drew her in sweeping sketched lines, making sure to keep her features soft. At one point she looked up and caught my eye.

'Are you drawing me?'

I hesitated. 'Do you mind?'

'Not at all. But I'm getting off at Plymouth.'

When the train drew into Plymouth, I tore the sheet of paper from my pad and handed it to her as she stood to retrieve her bag. She studied it for a moment or two, a slight smile forming.

'It's very good.' She offered it back to me.

'Keep it,' I said.

I watched her stop on the platform to sort herself out, buttoning her jacket, zipping up her bag, checking her phone then slipping it into her pocket. As the train pulled away, I saw her look at the drawing again, another smile, wider this time, lighting up her face.

When we neared Truro, I stood to get my holdall down. My back had seized up and I stretched, upwards and to the sides, the cracks of age rippling down my spine. I caught the connecting train to Falmouth, and finally, despite the undercurrent of doubt, I began to relax. Away from the hectic energy and biting memories of London, it seemed easier to breathe. I'd been to Cornwall once before, on holiday aged seven, to a campsite near Bude. I had hazy memories of icy water and big waves that tumbled us over and over, vanilla ice cream with chocolate flakes and sunburnt skin. Falmouth was nothing like the Bude I remembered, a rundown town with a few shops selling fudge and pasties and a Woolworths where Mikey and I had bought penny sweets in paper bags. There was an array of boutiquey shops with vibrant clothes hanging in the windows, galleries filled with colourful seascape paintings, cafés selling cakes and croissants that might even have impressed Fabian. Finally hungry, I walked into a café straight from the pages of an interiors magazine, with weathered driftwood, a jungle of pot plants, vintage leather chairs, and a glass counter displaying filled ciabatta rolls, lentil salads and home-made granola with creamy Greek yoghurt.

'What can I get you?' The girl behind the counter had a soft West Country accent and was fascinating to look at, with a shaved head, a tattoo covering most of her neck, and a slightly crooked nose, perhaps from a break.

I scanned the menu behind her. 'A latte?'

'Regular milk or plant-based?'

I smiled, imagining Fabian's horror at the question.

'Normal, please.'

'There you go, my love,' she said, handing me the coffee. She smiled again and her unusual face lit up. I'd have liked to have drawn her.

The Falmouth Sands Guest House was tired and dated, but inexpensive. As I pushed the door open and stepped inside, I was struck by the smell of wood polish and air freshener. The man on the reception desk was distracted, staring at a pile of papers in front of him, face tight, skin pale. It was only when I cleared my throat that he noticed me there. Fatigue was etched into his features, deep lines around his wide-set eyes, mouth turned down at the corners, his emotions and troubles fully on display. When I used to make a pittance drawing caricatures on the strip in Marseille, it was my job to study each face and select the features that best described the subject. I'd focus on these, exaggerating them enough – but not too much – to make the likeness instantly recognisable. Though I'd left the strip many years before, I still found myself assessing faces for a caricature. If I were drawing this man, I'd put extra shadow beneath his eyes, deepen his worry lines and stretch his lips tighter.

After I'd filled in the form he gave me, he pushed a key on a heavy brass fob over the counter. 'Room 3 is up the stairs, one flight, first door on the left.' He sighed, his brow knotting, the tension in his body turning his knuckles white.

'Are you OK?' I asked as my fingers closed around the cool weight of the key.

He seemed confused for a moment, as if I'd spoken in a foreign language. Then he attempted a smile. 'Business is tough.'

'I hope you sort it out.'

'Me too, love. Me too.' He sighed again. 'Let me know if you need anything.' His attention returned to the stack of papers before I could reply with a thank you.

Room 3 was small and clean, with white sheets, one pillow, and an orange waffle blanket folded over the foot of the bed.

There was a melamine chest of drawers with a mini kettle, a small jar of tea bags, a bowl containing capsules of long-life milk, and a twin packet of chocolate bourbons. My mother strolled into my head as I recalled her walking into our hotel room in Greece, four and a half weeks before the police knocked on our door and carted my father away. As she'd looked around, she'd lit up like a flare. 'Ooh, this is *lovely*.' She stroked her hands over the sheets – 'Has to be Egyptian cotton. So *soft*!' – then opened the minibar with an exclamation of joy. 'Goodness! They've stocked it with *everything*!' Her eyes flitted to the bathrobes folded on the bed. 'Fluffy gowns!' Then she walked over to the window and stared out, a happy sigh on her lips. 'And just look at that view.' She breathed in, as deeply as she could, her lungs expanding as her eyes closed in pleasure.

I never saw her that happy again.

I perched on the side of the bed, picking at the edge of a bourbon biscuit. Poor Mum. I should visit her, take flowers, but the thought of returning to Knutsford left me cold. Mikey's face appeared as it so often did. I thought about him and his 'black dog', a vile creature that had made him do that terrible, tragic thing. I never truly understood the tightrope he walked, constantly off-balance, constantly struggling not to fall. Back then, a child, I hadn't grasped the intricacies of mental health and vulnerability. Mikey was just my volatile nightmare of a brother, either consumed by wild rage or so depressed he couldn't form words. When I was revising for my exams, he'd often knock on the door and ask to be with me.

'I won't speak,' he'd say softly, walking over to sit in the corner, knees pulled into his chest. 'I just can't be alone.'

As I grew older and understood more about life, I reframed these memories and saw things with more clarity. Pieces of a complex jigsaw fell into place as I learnt about mental fragility, the long-reaching effects of a dysfunctional home, and how exhausting it was to keep demons at bay. I was haunted by all the times I'd muttered irritably under my breath as he sat in my room needing nothing more than somewhere to feel safe. I should have cherished my brother, not been frustrated by him. I should have made time for him. But retrospect wasn't a helpful lens. What had happened had happened and I couldn't rewrite history. There was no way to go back and give him the love and support that might have stopped him doing what he did. I'd abandoned him and I would carry the guilt at not being there when he needed me for the rest of my life.

CHAPTER SIX

October 1999

Julie Rainer, the head of first-year architecture at QSA, was a ball of nuclear energy. At points during her welcome talk she was so enthusiastic she actually left the ground, leaping and gesticulating and enthusing from one side of the room to the other. Looks of amused confusion were shared, subtle at first but then, as it became clear she didn't mind if we laughed, bolder and louder, filling the room with vibrant warmth. I liked her immediately.

'By the way, I meant to say earlier, I love your hair,' Nick had said on our walk from Frederick Street to the architecture school on Monday morning for our first lectures. 'The colour really suits you.'

I smiled shyly. Somehow he'd got even better-looking than when he first knocked on my door, as if he'd been marinaded over the weekend like a steak.

We lingered outside the lecture room, waiting to go in. 'Interesting shirt,' Tilly said. 'Where did you get it?'

'This?' I said as nonchalantly as I could, praying she hadn't seen it in Oxfam on Goodge Street, where I'd bought it for three pounds two days before. 'A boutique in Manchester. My cousin – she's a model – told me about it. I got it last year.'

'Oooo, new accent!'

I flushed with heat. Cami smiled at Tilly and batted her shoulder. I was about to tell them it wasn't a new accent, but Tilly spoke first.

'And new hair.' She said this in a strange way, as if it carried more weight than a simple observation. 'Looks nice, doesn't it, Cami?' They held each other's gaze for a moment, exchanging something unspoken.

Cami smiled fleetingly, then looked away, her thinly-veiled disdain as clear as day.

I followed them into the lecture room and watched their group grow bigger, as all the other confident, beautiful people were drawn to them like iron filings to a magnet. Their combined aura was blinding, and I noticed other students stealing glances at them as if they were freshly glazed cakes through a bakery window.

'So? What will you study over the course of the first year?' Julie Rainer clapped her hands together with glee. 'Well, you'll be getting to grips with the foundations of architecture – pun intended – and applying practical skills to the development of design. You'll begin to familiarise yourself with the formulation of projects, and the variety of ways you can communicate your architectural intention. You'll study light and space.'

There was a snort of laughter. I looked over at Tilly and Cami, who were whispering, writing notes to each other and giggling behind their hands like primary school children. I glanced at Julie Rainer, expecting her to tell them to be quiet or send them out, but she continued without seeming to notice.

'You'll become familiar with the varying structural approaches to building design. You will look at the history of architecture with reference to London specifically. We'll be privileged to have an exclusive preview of the Millennium Dome, which is due to open at the end of the year. You'll get to meet the architects and builders involved, study the full plans and scale models. Then you'll visit the site, have a good look round, and can ask questions about the construction processes. All whilst sporting a rather fetching hard hat! The project is incredibly exciting and we're lucky to have the opportunity to see it before it officially opens.' She smiled and scanned the room warmly, looking at us all as if we were already her pride and joy. 'By the end of this first year, you'll have developed the foundations of your future as architects, with a good understanding of the profession in both practical terms and aesthetic.' She beamed. 'Any questions?'

Nobody raised their hand.

'OK, well you can come to me at any time with questions or queries. The faculty are here to help and guide you, so please use us. Now, who are we and what do we teach? First up, we have Waylon Gorse, who some of you might have heard of. Waylon is a visiting professor from the University of Michigan and will be tasked with guiding you through the key elements and philosophies underpinning architectural design. Plus giving lectures in history of architecture and studying various design theories and movements, as well as the work of notable architects.'

I noticed that Julian had leant forward and was tapping Cami on the shoulder.

'Your technical studies module will be led by Neil Gilbert, covering structural and environmental principles, materials, fabrication processes, building components and assembly techniques. He's a very experienced and highly regarded tutor, having spent many years in industry, with a raft of impressive achievements and shelves of awards to his name.'

Cami smiled as she listened to what Julian whispered, then nodded and dropped her head to conceal a snigger.

'Alongside all this, you will develop your writing skills, and learn how to make scale models, use mood boards and illustrate your designs in ways clients can easily visualise. There will also be classes in analytical drawing. Then,' she went on, her beaming smile widening even further, 'there's what we call design studio. With me!' She stopped and made a comedic face of apology. 'Sorry about that.' She giggled and pushed her red plastic glasses up her nose. 'You'll split into three groups of twenty or so and meet twice a week. We'll start with the fundamentals of scale, architectural drawing and creative practice, followed by a four-week project. In the first term the task will be to design and construct a chair from four-by-two softwood and any other fabrics or materials you can find in the materials room. You'll design on paper, then build a model, source the materials you need, construct your chair and write an essay to support the practical element of the project.'

'Doesn't sound like architecture to me,' Cami said, supposedly under her breath to Nick, but with enough volume to be heard by most.

Julie Rainer didn't miss a beat. Cami clearly wasn't the first cocky student to question this project and the tutor appeared to relish the opportunity to address her comment, which she did with admirable patience. 'It might not seem it, but I promise it is. This project is about design and how we, as designers, implement our imagination and knowledge of engineering and materials. There's no point in coming up with a stunning and exceptional design if it isn't practical.' She then addressed the whole room. 'Architecture is the symbiotic marriage of aesthetics and function, and as future architects, future designers of buildings for human use, these are the most fundamental principles of our discipline.'

Cami smarted and I warmed to Julie Rainer even more.

'Coffee?' Fraser smiled, clapping Nick on the back as the lecture finished and we packed up our bags to leave. 'Or something stronger?'

Nick laughed and looked at his watch. 'It's not even midday.'

'It's always happy hour somewhere in the world.'

Everybody laughed. The group moved as an amorphous mass, like a shoal of fish or a flock of starlings. I stuck with them, keeping as close to Nick as I could, but then Cami skipped up with unnecessary bounce and pushed herself between us, thrusting her arm through his as if snapping him up in a clothing sale. She flashed me her fakest smile and tightened her grip on him. 'That woman. God, *how* weird?'

'Julie Rainer?' Nick asked.

'She's got a screw loose. I wouldn't be surprised if she's been struck off for a collapsed building or something.'

'I like her.' My heart fluttered as I let the words out.

Nick nodded. 'She's quirky, but at least she's not boring. I like the sound of making a chair.'

'Me too.' I smiled at him, inflating a little.

'Really? Christ. I think it sounds like a yawn fest. Anyway, whatever.' Cami looked at me. 'You know, your hair is a very similar colour to mine, isn't it?'

Tilly chipped in. 'They do say imitation is the sincerest form of flattery.' The two of them exchanged another look.

'People never quote that properly, you know,' said Julian. 'What Wilde actually said is: "Imitation is the sincerest form of flattery that mediocrity can pay to greatness."'

'I did *not* know that!' exclaimed Tilly with a laugh. 'Cami, your hair is clearly an example of greatness.'

'I … I wasn't copying. I already had the dye. It's what I usually use,' I stammered, floundering. 'I always—'

Julian laughed like a hyena. 'I don't think Wilde was talking about hair. You were in the Challoner with Nick. I've forgotten your name.'

'Vix,' I said quietly. 'Nick and I live in the same house.'

'Ah, yes. Vix. Nick says you're OK.'

Nick says you're OK …

And just like that, the sting of my mediocrity to Cami's greatness faded.

*

As the first week unfurled, I found myself accepted into this glittering group. Though it was everything I'd wanted, it was hard to relax in their company. There was a constant gnawing fear that they'd discover the truth: that I was an imposter, a different species, and however 'OK' they thought I was, the laws of nature dictated we weren't to mix. But until that moment I vowed to enjoy it.

While Julian appeared to be the lynchpin of the group, it was Cami who was the light at its centre. Everybody worshipped her. Except me. I could see through her. She'd make a big show of being friendly but it was all an act. It was obvious she didn't like me. She was a fake. I didn't trust her one bit. I didn't trust Tilly either. Tilly, who was sewn to Cami like Peter Pan's shadow. Sometimes I'd catch her staring at me, eyes cold, mouth set hard. I was under no illusion that if I ever did or said anything to upset Cami, Tilly would be the first to line me up against the wall and pull the trigger. But for whatever reason, they seemed to tolerate me in the group. Perhaps because I made them look shinier. I didn't question it too deeply. They let me sit with them in the department café, eating raisin scones and drinking Diet Coke. As I listened to them chat I'd watch, fascinated, as Cami removed the raisins using her pearlescent nails like pincers. She'd then meticulously pick off every crumb, before popping the naked raisin into her mouth and leaving the decimated scone uneaten.

All of the group had been to private schools. Tilly, Fraser, Julian and Giles had been to exclusive boarding schools, Cami to a girls' independent day school – whatever that was – in Surrey and Nick to a private school in Bristol on a sports scholarship. Nick gave me all this information on one of our walks back to Frederick Street, when I asked why everybody kept asking what school I'd gone to.

He shrugged. 'I guess they're trying to work out mutual connections?'

I had no idea what he meant.

'But you're right, it's an odd question. I hadn't really thought about it before.'

'So am I your token state school friend?' I said with a smile.

'I've got lots of state school friends.'

'I bet Julian hasn't!'

Nick laughed.

None of them would have looked at me twice at school. I knew that. Victoria Fisher would have been a blurry nobody in the background, unworthy of their attention. I had to keep reminding myself that Vix was someone different. I continued with my homework. Every day I researched things they mentioned, music I'd never heard of, food I'd never tasted. I borrowed a book on skiing from the library after Tilly said she was spending Christmas in St Moritz. I tried not to look like a rabbit in the headlights when we went out and tried not to think about what it was costing. We didn't go to the student union or cheap pubs popular with the others, but to glamorous restaurants, exclusive nightclubs, and bars that sold cocktails and bottles of vodka in champagne buckets. Julian and Tilly were members of more private clubs than I could count. The subject of money rarely came up. Tilly, Julian or Fraser would more often than not settle the bill with a credit card. Though it made me uncomfortable, Nick told me not to worry about it. 'They aren't paying themselves,' he said. 'Their parents pick up the tab.'

'Don't their parents mind?'

Nick laughed. 'They're so rich they don't even notice. But if you feel weird, you can always buy a round in the Challoner.'

So that was what I did, my eyes watering as I handed over the money I'd worked all summer to save, returning with a tray of drinks that were barely acknowledged.

My attraction to Nick meant I looked past most of their behaviour. I worked hard to ignore what they did or said, their collective sense of superiority and entitlement, their oblivious disconnect from the world most people inhabited. I pretended to enjoy the drinking games and raucous screeching. I allowed the vacuous conversations about holidays I'd never go on, restaurants I'd never visit and clothes I couldn't afford wash over me. I put up with it all just to be close to Nick. Sometimes it was hard though. Especially when they eviscerated people they were nice to face to face. It made me uneasy. What did they say about me behind my back?

'God, the state of that girl's outfit today. The one who asked the moronic question about Frank Lloyd Wright. Do we think she scavenges clothes from a skip?' Tilly shuddered dramatically. 'Maybe we could stage a double intervention? One in the name of stupidity, the other for crimes against fashion.'

'Allie? Oh, she's harmless.' Cami said the word *harmless* as if it were the worst thing a person could be. She did this, pretended to be all butter-wouldn't-melt, but I could tell from the hateful glint in her eye that although her comment sounded nice, it was intended to give Tilly encouragement.

'She's amazing at drawing,' Nick said, expertly steering the conversation away from poor harmless Allie. 'Her sketches of St Paul's and Trafalgar Square are so good. And talking of Lloyd Wright, have you seen pictures of his house in the woods in America? Incredible. Would be brilliant to see it one day.'

'Fallingwater,' I said, thrilled that I'd remembered the name of the house. 'I think it's in Pennsylvania.'

Nick beamed. 'That's the one!'

'It's one of my favourite buildings,' I said.

'Ugh. I loathe brutalist architecture,' Cami said, rolling her eyes.

'It's not brutalist. It's Prairie style.'

Nick raised his glass in my direction. 'Impressive. And you've impeccable taste.'

Cami's face clouded over and she glared at me, but I couldn't have cared less. I reached for my drink and lowered my eyes, taking Nick's words and tucking them inside me, where they glowed like hot coals.

*

Mrs Drummond didn't allow guests, which suited me as it meant I got Nick to myself. Sometimes Mia would join us, and though Nick was polite, she and I had little to say to each other, so she usually headed back to her room pretty quickly.

After a night out, Nick and I would make tea and Marmite on toast in the kitchenette, then take it into his room. His room was a heavenly pigsty. At home, Mum liked everything immaculate. Even in her broken state, she was a clean freak. Shoes came off at the front door. Toys were tidied away after playing. Beds were made with hospital corners and plumped pillows. Stepping into Nick's chaos was like visiting an exotic country. Clothes littered the floor. There were dirty mugs on every surface. Scattered papers. An empty pizza box with congealed strands of cheese. He never made his bed, and the room smelt musky and boyish, thick with the smell of his sports clothes, deodorant and unwashed sheets. If I closed my eyes and breathed deeply, I could even pick up a hint of his hair gel. These were my favourite times, sitting on his crumpled bed, clutching mugs of tea.

Talking to Nick was so easy. It was as if we'd known each other all our lives. Of course, I read up on things he mentioned, listened to Led Zeppelin and Pink Floyd on repeat, made sure we had plenty in common. One evening we chatted about the places we'd love to visit. Nick was shocked when I said I'd been abroad only once.

'Once?'

I nodded.

'Where?'

'Greece? Before my dad—' I stopped myself and dropped my head, pretending to be choked with emotion.

He smiled softly. 'Don't talk about it if you don't want to.'

'It's fine,' I said quietly. 'I like talking about it. When I do, it's like he's not really gone, you know?' I didn't feel bad for not telling the truth. If anything, it felt good to believe he was dead. 'It was a great holiday.'

I remembered every detail about the hotel. The smooth coolness of the marble floors. The never-ending buffet breakfast spread over three huge tables like a royal banquet. The sea so clear, like turquoise glass, the water silky on my skin, umbrellas and sunloungers and men in white shirts who'd bring ice-cold Cokes and slices of watermelon. I remembered the satisfaction on my father's face as he stretched out in his robe, my mother sipping a cocktail next to him, designer sunglasses perched on her head, Gucci beach bag birthday present beside her.

'Get used to this, my loves,' Dad said, eyes closing in the sunshine. 'The good life.'

Less than a month later, he was led away in handcuffs.

I thought of that beach, the sea with its sensuous water, and imagined Nick emerging from it. The Greek sunshine glinting off his wet, chiselled body, his perfect shoulders...

'Do you still miss him?'

'Yes,' I said, reluctantly leaving my fantasy. 'I do.' This wasn't a lie. I did miss my father. I missed the man who made jokes as he carved the Sunday roast, the man who sang Queen songs as he drove, drumming on the steering wheel and caterwauling at the top of his voice, the man who was the life and soul of any social gathering. Until he wasn't. 'But I've got used to him not being here.'

Nick put his arms around me.

I let him hold me, breathing him in, allowing his body to warm mine. I'd have given everything for us to stay like that for ever.

'Thank you,' I said when he finally pulled away. 'I don't have anybody else I can talk to like this.'

He smiled. 'Right. Something happier. Guess what my favourite country is?'

I didn't want to get it wrong and let him think I didn't know him. 'I'm useless at guessing.'

'France. It's amazing. The food, the history, the language. Paris is beautiful. Have you been? Oh, no, sorry. You said you'd only been away once.' He smiled. 'Honestly, you'd love it. The buildings are mind-blowing. And the art. We saw the *Mona Lisa*, which was a bit shit to be honest, but in the same museum there's this amazing painting by Delacroix called *Liberty Leading the People*. Do you know it?'

For a moment I considered lying and exclaiming, 'Yes, I know it! I'm desperate to see it in real life,' but I worried he might ask me what I liked about it and I'd tie myself up in knots, so reluctantly I shook my head.

'Hang on.' He jumped off the bed and grabbed a heavy book from the middle shelf above his desk. Then he sat back on the bed, his body pressed close to mine, and flicked through the glossy pages, which were filled with photographs of paintings.

'Here.' He put the book on my lap and tapped the page a couple of times. 'I was twelve when I first saw it, and I'll never forget how it made me feel. Like someone had lit a fire inside me.'

I glanced at his face. His eyes shone. Seeing him so excited by a piece of art was incredibly sexy, and it was all I could do to stop myself grabbing his face in my hands and kissing him.

'In real life it's huge – like, I don't know, over three metres long. I mean, look at her. Like she gives a shit about anything? Hard as nails. No shame. No fear. She's amazing. I love her.'

As I stared at her, I fought back a violent, unnatural stab of jealousy for the painted woman, *Liberty*. Statuesque, one muscular arm raised, the French flag clutched in her fist. In her other hand she held a musket. Her dress was torn and had slipped from her shoulders to reveal her glorious breasts. Despite her bare chest, there was nothing sexualised about her, nor was there anything maternal or nurturing. It was all about power, as if her strength lay in her femaleness, in her naked bosom itself. She led a group of men forwards, clambering over a heap of fallen corpses. Her feet were bare. Her body toned and solid. She was magnificent, fierce and strong. There was nothing in the way the artist had painted her to suggest she cared about beauty or what men – or anybody – thought of her. She was a warrior, and I loved that Nick loved her and admired her so passionately.

'I'd like to see her one day.'

'Maybe we could see her together? Plan a trip to Paris. Walk around Montmartre and along the Seine. Visit the Louvre and the Renoir museum.'

'Really?' I was breathless at the thought.

'Yes, why not? You know you can get the train straight from London to the centre of Paris now? It's so easy. I know some great hotels in the city too. My favourite overlooks the Arc de Triomphe and has incredible Eggs Benedict for breakfast. Seriously, everybody should go to Paris. It should be the law.'

That night I lay in bed and went over everything he'd said. I recalled the way he'd touched me. The way his eyes lit up when he spoke to me. Was it possible he felt the same as I did? He had to. Surely. Why would he talk about taking me to Paris – the most romantic city in the world – if he didn't?

Nick and me. Me and Nick.

I tingled with the thrill of it.

CHAPTER SEVEN

26 July 2024

I hung my dress in the guest-house cupboard and placed my shoes beneath it. I had no idea if it was right for the dress code, but trusted Anne-Marie who was by far the most stylish person I knew. When I'd asked her to look at the outfit I'd originally planned to wear, she nearly fainted in horror.

'*Chérie?* Are you out of your fucking head?'

'Oh God. Why? What's wrong with it?'

'*Merde!* What is *right* with it?'

I'd laid out a cotton dress in a shade of light blue that I'd convinced myself was a watery colour, and a pair of beachy espadrilles. I'd also put out my denim jacket, but as I looked at it with Anne-Marie tutting under her breath beside me, I noticed a smear of paint on one cuff that I hadn't realised was there.

'This is what you wear to buy fucking *pommes de terres* at the market! Not for a Hollywood wedding.'

'I don't do glam. I never have.' I wondered vaguely whether I should have told Anne-Marie any of it, and whether in doing so I'd broken the NDA and would find myself sued for everything – not much – I had in my bank account. 'God, I'm not sure I want to go.'

'Enough with this. You're going.' She huffed again. 'And you are *très glamour*. You're an artist, for fuck's sake. An artist who lives in Marseille and wins awards. Come with me, to my place.

I have dresses. *Mon dieu, chérie,* you give me an attack of the heart.'

Anne-Marie's apartment was straight out of the pages of an interior style magazine. Pot plants, modernist Swedish designer furniture, double-height windows with louvred shutters, and of course the artworks were stunning and lit to perfection. The entire flat exuded cool, and whenever I stepped through its front door I was reminded – as if I could ever forget – how deeply uncool I was.

She led me to her bedroom and flung open the wardrobe doors. She flicked through the rails and grabbed four or five dresses from the thirty or so that hung there.

'This one is the best.' She thrust forward a shimmery silver dress. 'But these are OK too. You are fatter than me, but these have, you know …' she thought for a second, 'a shape with space for you.' She gestured with her hands.

'Space for me?'

'*Exactement.*'

I went into the bathroom and undressed. The whole room was ceiling-to-floor mirrors and it was impossible to escape my reflection. I turned and stared at my body, stomach not as taut as it used to be, skin marked with moles and sunspots and beginning to crêpe around my neck. I cupped my hands under my breasts and lifted them, sucked my tummy in and allowed a moment of mourning for my passed youth. If only I'd known back then how good I looked. Beauty – not only youth – was wasted on the young.

The silver dress slid onto my body and was like nothing I'd ever worn before. A silk slip with delicate spaghetti straps and a fold of material that fell in a loose cowl at the neckline. The hem came to my ankles and the silken fabric skimmed my hips and followed the curves of my body. 'I think I'm too old for this,' I called through the bathroom door. But as I studied myself in the mirror, a frisson of pleasure wriggled through me. If I was going to see Nick, if I wanted him to notice me, this dress would definitely help.

Anne-Marie laughed as she opened the door. 'Too *old*? Crazy lady!' She whistled. 'You look *incroyable. Parfait!* Maybe the extra weight is better for this dress. Keep it. *Voilà!*' She held out a pair of silver sandals. '*Trente-neuf*. I think we are the same size?'

As I slid my feet into the shoes, Anne-Marie's face broke into a wide smile and she clapped her hands as if applauding a play.

'You look like a … What's this called when it is part of woman and part of fish?'

'A mermaid?'

'*Oui*. A mermaid! You must wear this.' She stepped close to me. 'You are *très belle, chérie*.' She spun me around and regarded me over my shoulder in the mirror. '*Vraiment* this is the perfect thing.' Then she grinned mischievously. 'It's good for your breasts. Shows them off, *oui*?'

I couldn't stop myself laughing at the irony of this. Jesus, if only Anne-Marie knew.

'Why is this funny?'

I shook my head, wiping away the tears that rolled down my cheeks. 'It's nothing.'

But the laughter felt good. Usually when I thought back to that day, I cringed and pushed the recollection away so violently I got whiplash.

She shrugged in her Anne-Marie way and put her hands on my upper arms. '*Alors*. It is *magnifique*.' She kissed me on both cheeks. 'And you should laugh more, you know?'

Now I closed the cupboard and walked over to the guest-house window, which looked over the Falmouth roofs. There was a slice of sea visible beyond, a deep gunmetal grey, its waves tipped white. From nowhere, a shot of horror flashed through me. The wedding present.

'Shit,' I whispered.

I'd forgotten to buy one. I looked at my phone. It was four o'clock. Would Falmouth have anything? I didn't have any other option.

By the time I reached the high street, I was out of breath and a sheen of sweat had gathered beneath my clothes. I jogged along the street, staring in the windows of the arty boutiques, shops selling joss sticks and tie-dye and galleries displaying colourful artworks. The next shop I came to had a pretty yellow and white candy-cane awning. Through the window I saw that the woman behind the counter was reading a book. When I pushed open the door, she looked up with a smile. She was a similar age to me, with dyed black hair held back by a paisley bandana and clear skin with no make-up. Her smile was relaxed and easy-going and gave her beautiful laughter lines. I thought about sketching her, how I'd add extra shine to her irises and deepen her wrinkles. The drawing would be a study of her smile, and her friends and family would nod and say, 'Oh, well done! You've captured her perfectly.'

'Let me know if you need help.' She smiled, then went back to her reading, licking her finger lightly before turning the page.

I picked up a scented candle. The label read *Sea Salt and Thyme*. It smelt of the sea and French cooking. Was it unusual enough to satisfy Ingrid's demand for originality? No, of course not. A candle wouldn't do. I placed it back on the shelf and ran my eyes over some painted ceramics, platters and bowls, in rich bright colours. 'You've got some lovely things.'

The woman looked up with another bright smile.

I glanced at her. 'Actually, I'm looking for a wedding gift. It needs to be unusual. And ideally connected to the sea?'

She closed her book and placed it on the counter as she stood up. 'Do you have a budget?'

'I don't want to spend a fortune. But maybe more than the candle.'

The woman thought for a moment. 'You know, yes, I've an idea. Just a sec.' She went to the back of the shop and unlocked a glass cabinet, then returned with a small bowl. 'This was made by a potter from up the road. Trudy Greenmore. She combs the beach for sea glass and drops it into her bowls before firing. They melt and form a layer. I think this looks like an all-seeing eye, don't you? It's definitely unusual.'

It was beautiful. A small, delicate bowl with a layer of shining turquoise that looked like water. 'It's perfect.'

'She's an up-and-coming young artist. She studied fine art at Falmouth, then did ceramics at Central Saint Martins. Lovely girl.' I had a brief flash of Mia and wondered what she was up to.

When she told me the price of the bowl, I baulked. Eight caricatures. I took a breath and let it out, reminding myself that I earned more now, and didn't need to price things in caricatures. Even so, it was a habit I found impossible to quit. A decade or so after my final night on the strip, and I still caught myself costing things out this way. A week's food shopping? Five caricatures. A demi-carafe of wine and some olives in the bar with Anne-Marie? Half a caricature. Eight for a present to celebrate the happiness of a man I wished dead was a lot. But then again, I couldn't go empty-handed.

'Thank you. I'll take it.'

The following morning I woke with stiff joints and a dull ache behind my eyes. I'd slept badly. The room was hot and stuffy and my mind had whirred chaotically all night at breakneck speed.

I stared at the woman in the bathroom mirror. What would I exaggerate if I were drawing her face? The tiredness in her eyes. The lack of spark. The fermented damage. People would look at the drawing and wonder what tragedy had stolen the light from her eyes.

'Stop feeling so sorry for yourself.' The woman in the mirror grimaced back.

Of course, everybody at the wedding would be blessed with money and good fortune. Stylists and beauticians on the payroll. The best clothes and shoes. Nourished by face creams and fillers. There was no way I could compete with that, and in a way, this meant the pressure was off. None of the glittering starlets would even notice me. I reached for my large tub of Nivea, still going after three years, dabbed my finger into the unctuous white and rubbed it briskly onto my face. This was the extent of my skin-care routine. Luckily, I'd inherited good genes from my mother. I might have been an emotional fuck-up, but at least I was an emotional fuck-up with half-decent, uncomplicated skin.

I dressed in jeans, a T-shirt and espadrilles, and packed my tote with Anne-Marie's dress and silver shoes, a hairbrush, some make-up and the wedding gift, which I swaddled in a sweater in the hope it would survive its time in the bag. Celeste had asked me to come early to choose the best position to display the portrait. I'd told her it would be fine anywhere, but she said Ingrid was insistent.

'She says that as the artist, you will know what light works best.'

As she'd spoken, impatient and brusque, it had dawned on me that it might be better to be *in situ* before the horde arrived. That way I could suss out escape routes and hiding spots and find a suitable vantage point to watch for Nick. The idea of walking into a crowd on my own and being scrutinised by the QSA clique was hideous.

The man on reception looked no less stressed than he had done the day before, but when he saw me, he smiled. 'Off somewhere nice?'

'Wedding.' I lifted the tote. 'Don't worry. I'm changing when I get there.'

'If you're back late, the code is twenty twenty-three. Help yourself to your room key.' He turned and hung the key on a peg behind him. 'I hope the happy couple enjoy their day.'

The happy couple. Ingrid and Julian. And then Julian's leering face pushed into my head and I felt the weight of him bearing down on me. I winced. My therapist would have a field day on why the hell I'd said yes to this wedding.

'I won't be late.'

'Sometimes the things we're not looking forward to turn out to be the most interesting.'

A man walked through the door, short and stout, a checked shirt straining over his belly, a small goatee stuck to his chin. 'Taxi,' he grunted.

I nodded, and he reached for my bag. 'I can carry it,' I said.

'Suit yourself.'

The man on reception smiled. 'Have a good time, love.'

I followed the taxi driver out of the guest house, dread building with each step. Was this what it felt like to head off to a firing squad?

'So,' the driver said, dark eyes looking at me in his rear-view mirror, 'Lowencliffe. Heard there's a fancy wedding up there.'

The nerves juddering away in the pit of my stomach flared. 'I'm hanging a painting,' I mumbled.

'But there's a wedding, yes? That young slip of a thing? Ingrid Olsson?'

He glanced at me again, willing me to say yes. What would he do if I nodded? Sell the info to the paparazzi? I imagined Ingrid's fury when I was discovered to be the rat. 'I'm not allowed to talk about it.'

I must have sounded snooty, as he narrowed his eyes and reached forward to turn the radio on. 'Have it your way.' The sounds of Pirate FM filled the car. He didn't speak again, which might have felt awkward if I wasn't so grateful for his silence.

It wasn't long before the taxi slowed and the indicator ticked on. The hotel entrance was grandiose, with stone pillars and huge wrought-iron gates tipped with gold detailing. There was a slate plaque with *Lowencliffe Hall* ornately carved into it and immaculate mature shrubbery with bursts of pink either side of the pillars. The taxi drew to a halt beside a hut at the gates. A man in smart black uniform, a touch too big for him, peaked hat shadowing his eyes, stepped out, clipboard in hand.

'Good morning,' he said to the driver, leaning in towards the car. 'Dropping off?'

'That's right,' the driver replied gruffly.

The man on the gate peered into the back seat. 'You're attending the private event today?'

'I'm here to hang a painting—' I stopped myself adding *for Ingrid Olsson* and glanced at the driver, who was staring at me in the mirror.

'Staff?'

I hesitated. 'I guess so.'

'Name?' He lifted his clipboard, pen poised with an air of impatience.

'Victoria Fisher.'

He consulted the clipboard, moving his pen down the paper. He got to the bottom, then flipped the page and did the same again. Then he shook his head. 'No Victoria Fisher on my trades list.'

'Oh, right. Well, I'm also a guest. Maybe I'm on that one?'

'So are you trade or a guest?' His brow was furrowed.

'Both?'

He eyed me suspiciously. Then he flipped over another page and searched two more sheets. Another shake of his head. 'You're not on either list.'

'I've got the email they sent when I accepted the invitation.'

He straightened his shoulders. 'Anybody could have forwarded an email on to you. You could be a terrorist.'

The taxi driver sighed heavily. 'Could you hurry this up? I've got another job.'

'I promise I'm not a terrorist.'

'If you're not on the list, you're not getting through these gates.'

I chewed my lip as the burning heat of embarrassment crept over me. Maybe this was for the best. I could run away, and when Ingrid demanded to know why I hadn't shown up, I could tell her the gatekeeper wouldn't let me in. But then the taxi driver rolled his eyes, and he and the man on the gate exchanged a look, clearly thinking I was a criminal here to take illegal pictures or blow the place up. Indignation set in.

'Hang on,' I said. 'Let me make a call.'

As I dialled Celeste's number, both men stared at me and my cheeks grew hotter. No answer. I hesitated. Should I call Ingrid? Sod it. This wasn't my error. It was Ingrid who'd begged me to come.

The phone answered on the second ring.

'What is it?' She sounded flustered and angry.

'It's Victoria … the artist who did your painting. I'm at the gate. I can't get in. My name isn't on the list—'

'For fuck's *sake*, are you serious?'

'I'm sorry—'

'Put the idiot on. Like I don't have more on my plate than manning the fucking *gate*.'

I lowered the window and offered my phone to the man with the clipboard. 'She wants to talk to you.'

He reached for the phone warily, his puffed-up superiority deflating fast.

'Yes, this is front—' He cleared his throat. 'We're under strict— Yes. Of course. I see. She didn't say.' His face flushed puce. 'No problem.'

He handed my phone back, his expression one of a man who had clearly been reminded of his place in the world. 'Your name is Vix?'

My stomach turned over. 'A nickname. I don't use it any more.'

His eyes narrowed, mouth tight with loathing. 'Clearly you do.'

He scanned his multiple sheets of paper, then made a point of writing something down – presumably a big warning sign next to Vix Fisher's name – before retreating into his hut. The gates crept silently open. The gatekeeper waved the taxi in, pointedly avoiding my apologetic stare.

'If you do end up killing somebody,' the driver said with a chuckle, 'I've a top-class story to tell.'

The taxi drove slowly up the driveway, which cut through an immaculate lawn flanked with perfectly trimmed yew balls, towards the imposing brick building that loomed over a gravel turning circle, a fountain with a lichen-patched Neptune holding a trident aloft at its centre. Double-height windows with curved tops punctured the walls. Four steps adorned with red carpet led to a porticoed entrance with heavy oak doors. Wherever I looked there were billowing arrangements of flowers, a mass of white, blue and cream with accents of fiery pink. The lawn rolled down to the cliffs and the sea beyond in perfect stripes. Every flower bed was an explosion of colour, not a leaf or a petal or a blade of grass out of place. It was an oasis of manicured glamour amid the rugged Cornish coastline.

The hotel was buzzing with activity. Frantic people ran in all directions, some drowning under flamboyant floral arrangements, others carrying crates or pushing trolleys laden with sacks of ice and boxes of wine. There was a group of men dressed in black, with tattoos and piercings, unloading sound equipment and lighting from a large white van. It was a frenetic scene, everybody intent on the last-minute preparations for the wedding of the Hollywood Beauty to the Beast.

The taxi driver sat for a moment after I'd handed him his money, craning his neck to get a good view of the goings-on. I spotted Celeste hurrying down the steps, walkie-talkie in hand. She made a beeline for the driver, shooing him away with three quick flicks of her hand. Then she turned to me, her face puce with anger.

'You called *Ingrid*?' The words exploded out of her.

'I tried you. There was—'

'What the hell were you thinking? Christ, she's in a rage.'

'I didn't know what—'

She closed her eyes and raised her empty hand, palm outwards, as if stopping traffic. 'I'm not interested. It's done now. Let's get this damn picture up.'

Despite being over forty, I felt myself welling with tears like a chided child.

Celeste rolled her eyes. 'It's fine,' she said, though clearly it wasn't. 'I couldn't take your call because I was dealing with one of the chefs, who managed to drop a tray of bruléed choux buns that were destined for the cake. Apparently there's no time to make more. I've told them to sort it any way they can. But it's one thing after another. Honestly, this wedding feels cursed.' She took a sharp breath in. 'I'll show you roughly where the painting is going, then leave you to it.'

'Is Ingrid not coming to OK it?'

Celeste gave an explosive snort of laughter. 'She's having her hair done, and frankly, that's the best place for her this morning. She doesn't seem to care too much about the painting today.' She gave me a meaningful look. A look that said, *That's Ingrid for you.*

She lifted the walkie-talkie and pressed the button. Static crackled. 'Gino. Cake? How's it going? I only want good news.'

'All good,' came a crackling reply.

She swore and bustled onwards, beckoning me to hurry. I followed her along a path to the back of the building. The gardens were breathtaking, and as we rounded the corner, I took a sharp intake of breath. On the lawn was a cavernous marquee, with open sides and swags of cream silk that hung in loops and framed the view down to the sea like theatre curtains. There were tables with exquisite flower displays, comfortable white sofas dotting the grass. Yet more staff were busying about the marquee, tweaking, pruning, polishing, picking up bits of twig and leaf from the seagrass flooring. There was a raised area, half concealed by orange and lemon trees in oversized terracotta pots, decorated with matching swathes of silk. In front of it was a vast dance floor, black and white checks, the darker squares flecked with specks of silver.

'It's beautiful,' I breathed. 'I've never seen anything like it.'

Celeste ignored my comment. 'The speeches are happening in the ballroom, where the guests will be dining. The lawn is for the champagne reception. The after-dinner entertainment and dancing will be in the marquee.'

I followed her through French windows into the most incredibly ornate room. Inside there were at least thirty tables, with twelve chairs at each, laid up with white tablecloths, seashells scattering the surfaces, displays of flowers in sea blues and white, crystal glasses, plates with gold rims piled on top of each other signifying a number of courses. There were sea-green napkins on each place setting, rolled uniformly and secured by silver napkin rings. Waiting staff in sandy linen uniforms, faces flustered, were polishing knives and forks as if their lives depended on it, checking them, then repositioning them. As I walked past one of the tables, I noticed the napkin rings were engraved with a logo, two capital letters entwined, a *J* and an *I*. The menus in silver stands on the table carried the same intricate monogram.

Celeste came to a halt beside a low stage at the front of the room, which held a rectangular table with two place settings, one at each end, in front of which were two seashell- and mother-of-pearl-encrusted thrones, emerald seaweed draping them, with rich turquoise-upholstered seats, any visible frame glinting gold.

'Ingrid wanted the thrones to look as if they've been stolen from Atlantis.'

They were obscene and I couldn't bring myself to say anything good about them, so I stayed quiet.

'The painting is to go there.' She was pointing to the oak-panelled wall behind the stage.

'I'm not sure I needed to be here to hang this. It has to go in the centre of the panel or it'll look odd.'

Celeste sucked her teeth with an aggressive click. 'Yes, well, you're here, aren't you? Get the painting up. Then the silk curtain.' She pointed to a folded piece of fabric on the stage. 'There's two hooks to screw in and a golden rope you need to attach to pull it open.'

I bit back telling her where she could stick her golden rope.

'Do you need a helper?'

'If you can spare a few minutes, that—'

She barked a laugh. 'Christ, not *me*. Are you clinically insane? I'll find you a minion.'

She clicked her fingers and pointed at a young girl near us. 'You. Yup, yup, *you*. Come here now. Come on, come *on*. God, *please* walk like someone who isn't dying in a desert.'

The girl was slim, nothing to her, with defined cheekbones, a wide mouth with full lips, and thick blonde hair tied up in a ponytail, two curling tendrils framing her heart-shaped face. Her body was in the twilight zone between fully grown woman and girl. She wore too much make-up, resembling a Barbie doll, a child cosplaying an adult. Her expression, however, was in perfect keeping with her age, a dark, surly frown that did nothing to dilute her beauty. I loved her obvious displeasure. It was oddly reassuring. Someone else who was completely unimpressed with this extravagant pantomime.

'Hi. I'm Victoria,' I said, as Celeste hurried off, firing clipped words into her walkie-talkie.

'Coco.' She glanced over her shoulder, then made a face. 'I heard that woman speaking to you, by the way. She's a total bitch to everyone. It's not personal. Something about a cake set her off. She's a fascist.'

'I'm sure she's not a fascist. Just stressed. I imagine she's feeling the pressure.'

Coco shrugged, her interest in me waning.

It took about five minutes to hang the portrait. I stood on a dining chair and adjusted it. 'What do you think?' I asked Coco. 'Straight?'

'Straight enough. Did you paint it?'

I nodded.

'It looks like her.'

'That was the aim.' And it was. Painting portraits was different to drawing caricatures. When sketching a caricature, a cartoon, speed was imperative, exaggeration employed to give an instantly recognisable but not faithful representation of the sitter. For a person to be happy with a portrait, they had to perceive not only a physical likeness, but also their character. It wasn't as simple as reproducing the version of themselves they saw in the mirror; their personality had to shine through. Whether it was nobility or command, compassion, kindness or icy cool, the portrait had to reveal the person within. With Ingrid I'd focused on her beauty, but also that ethereal quality that made her so mesmerising on screen, as well as her inner steeliness and desire to get her own way. 'It's a wedding gift for her husband.'

'I heard he's a prick.'

I snorted with laughter. 'He is.'

'You know him?'

I nodded and climbed down from the dining chair, sliding it back into place at the table we'd borrowed it from. 'I was at college with him.'

She gave a disinterested shrug and watched in silence, boredom all over her pretty face, as I hung the curtain, the golden rope ready to be pulled to reveal the portrait.

'You still need me?'

I shook my head.

She started to turn away.

'Actually, do you know if there's a room I can change in?'

She shrugged again. 'This morning I used the ladies'. If you don't mind changing in the toilet. Though it's not a normal toilet.' She wrinkled her nose with disdain. 'It's *gold*.' She shook her head. 'Pricks,' she muttered.

I liked this girl.

CHAPTER EIGHT

Late October 1999

The course was even more enjoyable than I'd hoped it would be. Much of this was down to Julie Rainer. I adored her lessons. Sometimes I allowed myself to daydream she was my mother. What would it have been like growing up in a house with someone so sunny and warm, so filled with passion and purpose, so creative and full of joyful enthusiasm? She was completely unbothered by what other people thought of her, and after my mother this was a breath of fresh air. I wanted to please her. When she praised my work, I'd swell with happiness. I'd have done anything for her.

The same, however, could not be said for Waylon Gorse or Neil Gilbert.

Listening to Gorse was like injecting liquidised sleeping pills into our veins. On and on he droned, his monotone Texan drawl peppered with dull anecdotes about people we didn't know and situations we didn't care about. His lectures became more about trying to stay awake than learning about important architects and philosophical movements. Neil Gilbert was an utter jerk. He appeared respectable, with an open-necked shirt and smart trousers, dark hair greying at the sides, round rimless glasses and a pallid complexion. Though his content was fine, it was hard to stomach his lechery. He'd stare in a way that creeped us out, looking the girls up and down as we walked past him, undressing us with vampire eyes, making no attempt to conceal his gawping. It soon became obvious that he had his favourite, and of course, it was Cami. He was obsessed with her chest, ogling shamelessly as he rambled on about steel and carbon and the load-bearing properties of reinforced concrete. Sometimes his tongue would caress his lower lip. Cami didn't seem bothered. After all, she was used to the attention and, watching her, I wondered if she secretly enjoyed it. Rather than turn away or look embarrassed, she'd lift her chin and push her shoulders back, giving him permission to stare, as if it were no bother to her either way. If it was mentioned outside of class, she'd laugh and make a face. 'He's just a sad old man who gets his kicks where he can.'

The end of October gave us the extravaganza of Cami's birthday. It took days of planning. Where we were going. Who was invited. What time we'd be meeting. Organising her present was an epic mission. In the end, Tilly chose a vintage *Breakfast at Tiffany's* film poster. She asked all of us to chip in. I gave her ten pounds, which was way more than I could really afford.

'The rest of us have done fifty, but ten's fine. I'll put the extra in to cover your share. Here,' she said, passing me a birthday card. 'For you to sign.'

Tilly had written an essay. Surely she didn't mean it all?

'Don't take up too much space. The others have to sign it too.'

I nodded. I had no idea what to write, so went with *Happy birthday from Vix* in the bottom left-hand corner.

Tilly laughed. 'You can write more than that!'

'I'll say a proper happy birthday when I see her,' I mumbled.

Nick was in the hall, ready to leave, his jacket on. 'You look great,' he said, and I smiled with relief. Then he hesitated. 'Should we ask Mia?'

'To Cami's birthday? I thought it was only a few of us.'

'To the club, yeah. But loads of people are meeting at the Challoner first.'

'Are you sure Cami likes her?'

'Mia? I mean, yes? There aren't many people Cami doesn't like. I'm sure she'd say more the merrier.'

I didn't understand how Nick could be so blind. There were loads of people Cami didn't like. He was incapable of thinking badly of anybody. Of course, that was a good thing, but it was also annoying. I wanted to shake him. Why couldn't he see beneath Cami's pretty outer shell to the ugliness inside?

'I'm not sure she'll want to come,' I said.

'Nice to invite her?'

I didn't agree. I didn't trust Mia. I'd seen the way she looked at him and knew if the opportunity arose, she'd shove me away and keep Nick to herself without a second thought.

But I didn't want him to think I was a bitch.

I nodded. 'I'll go ask.'

Mia answered the door in her pyjamas. Watercolour paraphernalia was laid out on her desk along with a mug of tea and a packet of chocolate digestives. The desk lamp threw out a pool of soft light, making the rest of the room seem darker. My mum would have loved her room. Nothing was out of place. There were embroidered cushions on the bed, a string of fairy lights, and a thriving pot plant on her windowsill beside a burning joss stick, a wisp of smoke rising gently and releasing the scent of sandalwood. On the wall around her bed were photos of friends and family, Mia hugging two big dogs, another with a fluffy white cat, then another with her smiling from the back of a horse.

'Oh, hey,' she said. 'Everything OK?'

'Nick and I are heading to the Challoner. Want to come?'

Her face broke into a smile. 'Sounds nice.' Then she hesitated. 'Actually, are the others going? Julian and Tilly and that crowd?'

I nodded. 'It's Cami's birthday.'

Her face fell and she withered a little, shaking her head. 'I think I should probably stay back and work. I've got an evaluation to write up and I'm a bit behind. And, well, to be honest, that lot aren't really my kind of people. But if you and Nick want to have a drink when you get back, knock for me. I'm planning an all-nighter, so would love a break.'

I ran back down the stairs. Nick was waiting by the front door, coat on. 'Is she coming?'

'She's got to work.'

As I reached for the door handle, the payphone in the alcove beneath the stairs began to ring. Nick bounded over to answer it.

'Yup. I'll grab her, she's right here. Can I ask who it is?' He nodded, then held out the receiver. 'Your brother,' he mouthed.

My heart sank. Having to listen to Mikey moaning was the last thing I needed. 'You OK to wait a sec?' I whispered, making an apologetic face.

'Sure. No hurry.'

I took the receiver and leant back against the wall. 'Hey. You OK?'

'No, *Victoria*. Of course I'm not.'

Even in those few words I could tell he'd been drinking. I banged the back of my head gently against the wall. He only ever phoned when he was in a bad place. His negativity was exhausting. Why couldn't he call when he was happy? I covered the receiver with my hand. 'I'll catch you up,' I whispered to Nick.

'Sure?'

I made a face and gestured at the phone, rolling my eyes with a what-can-you-do smile.

As I watched him leave without me, resentment towards my brother mushroomed. 'So then?' I said, unable to hide my irritation. 'What is it?'

'Everything.'

I slid down the wall as he launched into a rant, and rested my chin on my knees. I zoned out for much of his tirade. There was nothing new. This time it was all about Mum. Since I'd left, she'd been on his case the whole time. Nagging him to get out of bed, to shower, to stop smoking weed in his room. She didn't understand him. She didn't listen. He was done with it all. I'd heard it all before. Nothing I said ever made any difference, so there was no point trying any more.

'Hello? Fucking hell. Are you even there?'

'I'm here.'

'You didn't say anything.'

'I'm not sure what I *can* say. I'm not there. I'm miles away. Can't you find a way to work things out without me? And ...' I hesitated, 'maybe she's right about getting out of bed and showering.'

'You sound funny.'

'What?'

'Your voice. You don't sound like you. Sounds like you've got a poker up your arse.'

'Nice. Thanks, Mikey. Look, I've got a party to—'

'I can't take any more of her. She's doing my effing head in.' His voice dropped to a sad, faraway whisper. 'It's all doing my head in.'

I glanced at the clock on the wall. I wanted to go. This wasn't my problem. Mikey was twenty-one, Mum was forty-six. They were adults. They had to be able to find a way to get along without me there to mediate. I didn't want to be micromanaging their relationship from the payphone in the hall at Mrs Drummond's, I wanted to be in the pub with Nick, choosing tracks on the jukebox and drinking tequila shots. 'Try to remember she loves you.' My voice sounded doubtful, but surely it had to be true? She was his mother, and all mothers loved their children, even if they didn't like them. 'Don't let her get to you. Get on with your life.'

'I have no life.'

'Of course you do.'

'Not one that's worth it.'

'Don't be stupid.'

There was silence from the other end of the phone. I heard rustling. The sound of a lighter. An inhale. I pictured a spliff and a two-litre bottle of Strongbow. His go-to when his mood was low.

'Come home,' he said.

'I can't.'

'Please? I need you.'

'I'm studying.'

'Even on the weekends? You can't have one night away?'

I didn't want to be having this conversation any more. I didn't want to feel guilt-tripped into going home to glue my brother back together. 'Sorry! Yeah, I'm coming!' I called to an imaginary Nick. 'There in a sec!' I lowered my voice again. 'I have to go. Try to be kind, yeah? Maybe watch a film together or something. She'd like that. I think she's lonely.'

'Oh? And why's that?'

I didn't rise to the accusation in his voice.

'Watching a film sounds shit anyway. I'd rather stay in bed.'

I closed my eyes. 'I've got to go,' I whispered. 'I love you.'

'Whatever.'

The phone went dead.

'Jesus, Mikey. For fuck's sake!' I said to the receiver in my hand.

Tilly's dad had booked a table in the VIP area of a club called Rayaana for Cami's birthday.

'Dress up,' Tilly had told me. 'They don't let everybody in just because. Hilarious, but can you *imagine*? They refused one of Atomic Kitten once because she turned up without brushing her hair. And you can sometimes look a little, well, scruffy?' I swallowed the insult and didn't reply, focusing instead on putting together an outfit in my head. My pink tartan miniskirt. Tan-coloured nylon tights. The suede heels I'd found for fifty per cent off in Barratts and a white vest top. I would buy some earrings and maybe another necklace.

'Oh, *sweet*,' Tilly said when I arrived at the pub. 'Love the skirt. I had one just like it when I was younger.' She was wearing a red sequinned dress, short and backless, held up with spaghetti straps, and a gold choker. 'I'm sure the club will let you in. If they don't, I'll call in a favour.'

We jumped in cabs from the pub to the club. They dropped us right outside. Everybody waiting stared as we got out of the cars. We didn't join the queue, but instead walked right to the front, which made people grumble. My stomach churned as Tilly greeted the doorman.

'What if they don't let me in?' I whispered.

Nick laughed.

The doorman looked us up and down. I stood mute and terrified I'd be turned away for wearing the wrong skirt, while Cami, in sequin shorts and a camisole top that was sheer enough to show her bra beneath, smiled and flirted, told him it was her birthday, rested a hand on his arm and giggled. My heart hammered. I could hear his voice in my head. 'Not you. The others, yes. But you? No way.'

But instead he unhooked the velvet rope and stepped aside. 'Have a nice evening,' he said, and winked at Cami as she tottered in.

The club was dark and hot and like no place I'd seen before. Red and black and mirrored, with velvet sofas and red beaded chandeliers and muslin drapes. There was a DJ behind some decks on a platform, and a glittery dance floor where the world's most beautiful people danced, holding drinks and clutch bags, some wearing sunglasses, a number of men wearing slick suits with no shirts, some women wearing nothing but hot pants, bikini tops and stilettos.

Tilly led us towards a roped-off area. A woman in a sleek black dress, her hair piled up to show off long gold earrings, greeted Tilly with three kisses on her cheeks, then opened the rope to allow us through. As we walked in, Tilly raised a hand to a girl on the dance floor, who smiled and blew a kiss then swirled a circle.

'Home sweet home!' she said as we reached a section with two low tables and three sofas.

On one of the tables was a gold ice bucket and glasses, and a small gold sign reading *Reserved*. Julian cracked open the bottle of vodka in the bucket. Fraser lit a cigarette. He leant close to Julian and gestured towards the dance floor. I followed their gazes and saw a model I recognised from the newspapers.

I excused myself and went to the toilets. They were kitted out in black stone and gold. The basins had pebbles in them. There was a lady on a stool beside a tray set out with perfumes and hair clips, a hairbrush, mints, and a small pot with coins in. I said hello and she smiled emptily. When I came out of the toilet, she turned the tap on for me.

'Oh, I'm fine,' I said.

But she ignored me and handed me a folded black hand towel. I took it, and she glanced at the pot of money. 'I … I don't have change,' I muttered.

She glared.

I turned to escape and bumped into a couple of women as they rolled in, laughing and chattering and bundling into a cubicle together.

Back in the VIP area, Fraser handed me a vodka. Nick lit a cigarette for me, then passed the packet to Giles. As I sipped my drink, I listened. They were talking – their voices raised to be heard over the music – about Neil Gilbert.

'You know he was some high-up materials expert in Geneva? He worked for the government too.' Fraser's admiration was obvious. 'He's won loads of awards.'

'He's a pervert,' Cami said, leaning forward and gesticulating wildly with her cigarette, her voice loud and slurred. She shook her head.

'He's so *gross*.' Tilly wrinkled her nose. 'A total creep.'

'Is he?' Nick pressed his cigarette out in the Chinese-style ashtray. 'Why?'

Tilly laughed. 'You haven't seen him? All he does is stare at us with his tongue hanging out. Like, literally, *all* the time. He has a thing for Cami's tits.'

'What?' Nick said, putting his hand to his ear.

'He has a *thing* for Cami's tits!' Tilly shouted. 'Whenever she asks him something, his eyes are like, you know ...' She held her hands up either side of her eyes and jabbed the air with both fingers at Cami's chest.

Cami gave a shudder, overly dramatic, all for attention. 'He's *disgusting*,' she said. 'Can you imagine running into him in a deserted alleyway?'

'He wouldn't do a thing. He likes pretty girls, that's all,' Fraser said.

'What, because he isn't going to *rape* us, he can be as gross as he likes?'

'He's irrelevant!' Julian reached for the bottle of vodka and laughed. 'A nobody.'

'He's a *lech*.'

'You do wear pretty tight tops.'

Julian pointed a finger at Fraser and stabbed the air between them a couple of times. 'Exactly. The guy's only human.'

At the same time, Cami and Tilly rounded on Fraser. '*Excuse* me?'

'Are you serious?' Tilly said, leaning away from him, her arms crossed.

Fraser raised both hands and bowed his head. 'Whoa, whoa. OK, sorry. I retract!'

'Too late, mate!' Julian snorted and knocked back his vodka.

'So let me get this straight,' Tilly went on, tapping her glass for Julian to fill. 'Women need to cover themselves up because basement-dwelling paedos can't help drooling over us?'

'Paedo?' Julian laughed as he poured her the last of the vodka. 'That's a bit strong!'

I noticed Giles and Nick shifting uncomfortably. Giles stood and gestured in the direction of the bar. 'I'm going for another bottle. Anybody want anything else?'

Tilly lifted her chin in defiance. 'He's vile and you shouldn't defend him.'

'I get it,' Fraser said. 'He shouldn't be doing that. All I'm saying is you are all very good-looking, and when you wear—'

'Fraser! You're being a fucking *dick*,' Cami shouted. 'It's my birthday. I don't want to talk about Neil fucking *Gilbert*. He's an A-grade arsehole and you can't see it because you've crawled up his backside because of some stupid award in thermo-crappy-plastics. Defending him makes you sound like an arsehole too!'

Julian snorted with laughter. 'Bloody hell. Forget Gilbert. It's you who's terrifying.'

'Only if someone's being an arsehole.' She tipped her head and flashed him a challenging half-smile.

'I'm not saying he's right,' Fraser continued. 'I'm offering an explanation.'

'You're making this worse,' Cami said. 'Please stop talking.'

Nick held up his hands in an attempt to calm the situation. 'Look, come on, Cami's right. If she says he's staring, then he is. And if he is, he's a twat.'

Cami smiled at him, and I noticed they held eye contact for a second or two longer than they needed. Winded by a sharp stab of jealousy, I shifted closer to Nick.

Fraser faltered. 'I'm not saying he's not. I'm just saying—'

'I don't care what you're *just saying*.' Cami had got into her stride now and I almost felt sorry for Fraser, who was right in her firing line. 'You know the perv is married with two teenage daughters? He has a *wife*.'

'Can you imagine having to *shag* him?' Tilly pretended to make herself vomit. 'Poor bitch.'

'Stop making excuses for the arsehole,' Cami said.

'I wasn't—'

Cami interrupted Fraser with a clap of her hands. 'I'm not letting that prick ruin my birthday. I don't give a shit about him. He's pathetic. And boring. Let's dance!'

She jumped up and pulled Nick with her. We all stood and followed her onto the dance floor. Julian dropped an arm around Fraser's shoulders and whispered something. Fraser made a face and shook his head. He looked pained, as if he regretted what he'd said. I felt for him. It was obvious he wasn't supporting Gilbert, just making the point that if Cami was going to wear tops that showed off her figure, she couldn't expect people not to stare, but Cami and Tilly had deliberately chosen to take it that way. They didn't need to give him such a hard time. I gave him a smile so he knew I didn't think he was an arsehole too, but I'm not sure he noticed.

Cami threw her arms above her head, her hips gyrating to the beat. Her flimsy camisole rose up to reveal her washboard stomach, a diamanté stud glittering in her belly button like treasure in the sand. We circled her like moons orbiting the sun. What must it be like to have that power? I watched as Fraser danced close to her, mouthing, 'I'm sorry.' She laughed and flung her arms around his neck, her eyes drunken and sultry. The matter of Gilbert was clearly forgotten and Fraser visibly melted with relief.

I tried to copy the way she danced, but I felt awkward, my limbs not doing what I wanted, my brain unable to keep them moving in time with the rhythm. I felt absurd. Back home I'd dance in my room, the door wedged closed to stop Mikey barging in. I'd draw the curtains and turn off the lights, put my music on loud, then go wild, punching the air, kicking out, spinning around and around until my frustrations eased. But that was alone. I'd never danced in public, and the pressure of being with these people was paralysing. I imagined them whispering behind my back, 'Oh my *God*. Did you see her? She looked *ridiculous*!'

I slipped away and returned to the table. Pouring a vodka, I watched them. Everything around the group faded to a blur. They were all I could see, the six of them, lit as if they were on a stage under spotlights. They moved as one, beautiful, mesmerising, touching each other provocatively, uninhibited, unbridled. Nick's hair was damp with sweat, shirt undone to his stomach, skin glistening in the rainbow lights. I watched how he pulled everybody in, smiling, looping his arms around them, leaning in to talk, laughing. He was so fucking sexy. My body ached for him.

He must have felt me watching him, because he turned and caught my eye. He smiled, then jogged off the dance floor and collapsed with a laugh onto the sofa beside me. 'Love this place. Jude Law and Kate Moss are here. Mad!' He took my glass and had a swig of the vodka, grimaced slightly, then smiled. 'You OK?'

'Mm-hmm. A bit hot.' I watched him swallowing some more of my drink, his Adam's apple rippling, and imagined leaning over and licking the curve of his neck, the salty taste of his skin.

'Hey.' I looked up. Cami was standing in front of Nick, staring down at him, tucking her hair behind one ear. Then she reached for his hand and pulled backwards, smiling at him from under her eyelashes. 'It's my birthday,' she crooned. 'You're not allowed to sit.'

He fanned his face with his free hand. 'Just taking a minute to cool down.'

She made a cartoonish sad face, lips pouting, head tipping to one side.

He smiled, but didn't move. He stayed sitting. With me.

She began to move back to the dance floor, her eyes fixed on Nick, arms raised in the air, her top riding up to reveal that glinting diamanté. She turned a circle. The others gravitated back to her, everybody's focus. She smiled. She was an attention addict.

We left around three. I was exhausted and wanted to be back at Mrs Drummond's eating toast and drinking tea in the quiet of Nick's room. The late-October air was damp and cold. Giles had already left with a girl. Fraser and Julian were going on somewhere.

'Are you going to a strip club?' Tilly asked, laughing.

Julian laughed. 'Of course not.'

'They are, you know. I heard them talking about it,' Tilly said. 'You're not going with them, Nick?'

He shook his head. 'Not my scene.'

The four of us bought chips and walked up Shaftesbury Avenue, lights and traffic and people still keeping it awake. Cami and Tilly reached the turn-off to their halls.

Cami smiled at him. 'See you tomorrow,' she whispered, standing on tiptoes and kissing his cheek.

'Goodnight,' I said.

Thankfully, the two of them turned to leave, walking away from us, arms linked.

As we started to walk, Nick draped his arm around my shoulders and I tensed, inhaling, not wanting to speak or breathe in case he pulled away. He didn't, so I cautiously leant into him, the heat from his body warming me.

'That was a brilliant night,' he said.

'It was.'

'Vix?'

'Mm-hmm?'

'I have to tell you something.'

'Go on,' I said.

'I'm in love.'

My heart stopped.

'Jesus!' He grinned at me, tightening his arm around my shoulder. 'Seriously. Shit. *Shit!* I'm actually in love.'

My heart started up again so suddenly it caught my breath. 'Who with?' I managed. 'Someone I know?'

'Someone you know very well.' He stopped walking and turned to me. His eyes were twinkling in the street lights. 'It's hit me out of the blue. I mean, I knew I felt something, but tonight ... I don't know. It's mad. Completely mad.'

Was this happening? Was he about to tell me he loved me? Should I take his face between my hands and kiss him before he said anything more? *I love you too*, my voice whispered in my head.

'I'm going to ask her out tomorrow. For dinner. Somewhere nice. Where do you think?'

'What? Sorry?' My vision wavered. 'Who?'

'Cami!' He smiled widely. 'I didn't realise how much I liked her until this evening. I've not felt like this before. Not ever. I thought I'd been in love, but not even close.' He paused. 'Shit, Vix. Do you think she likes me too? I mean, I hope I'm reading it right, but I could be wrong. God, what if she doesn't?'

My liquefied heart dribbled through my body to form a puddle at my feet. I forced a smile as she danced into my head, hips swaying, hair shimmering, the stud in her belly button shining like the North Star to guide Nick to her.

'You two are friends,' he said. 'Do you think she feels the same?' His sweet face was twisted with sudden fear.

'Do I think Cami likes you?' My throat was dry and my voice sounded hoarse. 'Of course she does.'

'Really?' His face exploded with childlike excitement. 'Why do you think that? Has she said something? About me? Did she talk to you about me?'

I used all my strength to keep my smile from slipping down to join my puddled heart. 'Who wouldn't like you?'

His brow crinkled. 'I mean, romantically. Do you think she likes me like that?'

This hurt so much. I wanted to turn and run as far away as I could and cry for ever. 'I've seen how she looks at you.' I started to walk again, hands shoved deep into the pockets of my coat. A vice had tightened around my chest, making it hard to breathe. He jogged to catch up. I bolted my eyes to the pavement. 'You're the perfect couple,' I said. 'She's beautiful.'

And so are you.

'She is, but it's not only that.' Nick looped his arm through mine and electricity flickered sadly where our bodies touched. 'She's so much more than beautiful. She's amazing. She has this strength. This fierce, brave power. She doesn't care what people think. She's a force of nature.'

I didn't want to hear how perfect Cami was. I pulled my arm from his and picked up the pace.

'Cup of tea?' he said quietly, as we walked up the stairs.

'It's so late and I'm knackered. I'll see you in the morning,' I whispered back.

In my room, I lay down on my bed, covered my idiotic, undesirable face with my unmanicured hands and sobbed. My mind went over every signal he'd given me. There was no way I'd misread them. We had a connection and it was real. But he'd been tempted away from me like a hapless sailor to a siren. With her willowy legs and honeyed skin, her mane of shiny hair, her perfect figure and immeasurable confidence, Cami was glorious, while I was a dull little mouse in the shadows. I hated her. She'd stolen him from me, all the time pretending we were friends. She knew I loved him, but rather than letting things grow between us, she'd bewildered him with her charm and those puppy-dog eyes and that ridiculous pout. She could have chosen anybody, but she'd chosen Nick. Just because she could.

She was greedy and she was selfish.

She was a fucking bitch.

I hated her more than I'd ever hated anybody in my life.

CHAPTER NINE

27 July 2024

I lifted my hair up and away from my neck and studied myself in the mirror. Should I attempt a style? A sophisticated chignon? Pretend I was classier than I was? I let it fall back down and ruffled it with my hands. No. I wasn't that person any more. I wasn't going to pretend I was someone I wasn't, however scared that made me. Therapy had helped me come to terms with who I was and why I'd kept my true self hidden, fearful of rejection. My therapist said it was to do with my father. I'd smothered a laugh when she'd said this. It didn't take a degree in psychotherapy to work that one out. But over time, she helped me separate myself from his crime. She helped me see I wasn't responsible for my brother.

Or for what Julian had done to me.

Their actions didn't make me who I was. Yes, they contributed to my life's tapestry, they shaped me, but they didn't define me. Even though I knew this, the impulse to reach for a mask to hide behind, to construct a version of Victoria Fisher who was happily married with children and a dog, a vibrant social life and a lovingly renovated house overlooking the sea in Cassis or Bandol, was strong.

I handed my bag to the bored-looking girl at the cloakroom. 'Is there somewhere to leave wedding gifts?'

'Table in the reception hall,' she said. 'I like your dress.'

'A friend lent it to me.'

'Nice friend.' She smiled.

The wedding didn't officially start for another hour. I decided to find a quiet spot where I could be alone, away from busy people running this way and that, faces tight with concentration. My nerves were raging, but it was with anticipation rather than dread. Now that I was here, sheathed in silver silk, my fear of facing Julian had paled beside the realisation that I'd soon be reunited with Nick.

As I walked back into the reception area, I spotted a crowd of official-looking people with walkie-talkies and clipboards, so I turned around and walked back down the corridor in search of a back door. I turned again and found myself in another corridor, narrower and darker, lined with stacked crates and boxes, and at the end an open door to outside. I passed a room with lots of staff busying to and fro and spotted Coco, surly-faced, placing champagne flutes on a tray. I smiled at her, but she either didn't see me or, now that I was in Anne-Marie's silver dress, my hair loose, make-up done, didn't recognise me. I slipped outside and found myself in a parking area, rammed with cars, vans, trolleys and yet more crates. I walked across the tarmac, through a gap in the hedging, and out into the gardens.

The day was perfect – Ingrid would be pleased – blue skies, salt-scented air, still and hot but not stifling. 'With weather like this,' I heard my mother say, her tone disingenuous, 'who needs to go abroad?'

The lawn sloped gently away from the hotel towards the cliffs and led to a folly overlooking the sea. There was a stone terrace shielded by shrubbery and a pergola entwined with honeysuckle, which threw dappled shade over two sumptuous sunloungers with soft linen cushions. I lit a cigarette and sat down, closing my eyes, the sunlight dancing across the backs of my eyelids, warming my skin. The tension in my body melted away in the heat. The sounds of a string quartet tuning their instruments floated down from the terrace whilst the waves crashed against the cliffs below and the seagulls sang to each other in a lazy way. This would be the perfect place to spend the day. Tucked away. Safe and peaceful. I imagined getting a message to Nick. Telling him to meet me here. I pictured us lying together, sharing cigarettes, talking about art and music and travelling. I heard him telling me how much he loved me. His hands pushing the silk dress up over my thighs. Tearing at my underwear. Fucking as the wedding guests drank champagne and ate canapés on the lawn above.

A screech interrupted us. I opened my eyes, turned my head in the direction of the noise and listened. The musicians were now playing Vivaldi. There was a rumble of voices. The slam of a car door. Another scream. I stood up and walked to the edge of the hidden terrace, peering through the shrubbery, back up towards the marquee. The first guests had begun to arrive, milling on the grass, waiters in black and white handing them flutes from silver trays. The string quartet was arranged in a semicircle on the terrace facing the lawn. Nobody seemed concerned. Had I imagined the scream? It was then that I saw a pair of peacocks, both males, luxuriant tails folded up like umbrellas behind them. One of them stopped to rustle his feathers before giving another almighty shriek. A blue and turquoise feather fell onto the grass from his quiver. He moved on, oblivious. Two guests, a woman with a pixie cut wearing a shimmering blue dress, a man in Bermuda shorts and a white linen shirt open to his navel, laughed and looked at the bird. Their eyes found me then, peering out from behind the hedge. I inhaled sharply and pulled myself back behind the greenery.

A path skirted the lawn and led to a thick forest of rhododendrons. I followed it, relieved to be hidden by the dense bushes, and found myself in a large, slightly sloping field, which appeared to be the car park. There were a number of vehicles in neat rows, among them a red Ferrari with a personalised number plate, G0LD3N, a Range Rover with blacked-out windows, a handful of Teslas, and several limousines, their drivers leaning against their cars and chatting.

I passed a stretch limo, its driver lying back in his reclined seat, eyes closed, mouth open, hands folded over his chest. Would he wake if I climbed into the back of his car and hid?

'Vix?'

I turned, squinting, shielding my eyes from the sun. 'Nick,' I breathed.

He stepped towards me, arms open wide. 'Oh my God, I didn't know you'd decided to come!'

'It was last-minute really.'

'I'm so glad! Wow. You look stunning.'

Though he was obviously older, his hair a touch greyer at the sides, deep laughter lines written into his face, Nick looked exactly the same, and every cell in my body leapt in joyful recognition. He wore a well-cut light blue suit with sand-coloured leather deck shoes and a soft linen shirt, white as a sail. He was tanned and healthy, lithe and fit, his hair lustrous. He could have stepped straight out of a fashion magazine. He was perfection.

He grasped my shoulders and kissed me on the cheek. 'Seriously. Look at you! What a dress!'

I was conscious I must smell of smoke. 'Sorry, I've just had a sneaky cigarette to calm my nerves.'

He laughed. 'God, I haven't smoked in years.' There was a pregnant pause, then he smiled. 'It's good to see you.'

'It's nice to see you—' I didn't get to finish my sentence as a sudden swell of horror swept the rest of my words away. A figure was approaching. A woman. Greeny-blue satin dress. Dark honey hair with auburn highlights that caught the sun and shone like burnished copper. A superficial smile and a haughty glare.

What?

No!

'I thought she couldn't make it?' I whispered, maybe to myself, maybe to Nick.

'Her plans changed a couple of days ago. Thankfully Ingrid was happy for her to join last minute.'

'Vix.' Cami stretched my name out like it was elastic. The long, slow drawl made my skin crawl. 'How lovely to see you. You look so *well*. God, it's been years, hasn't it?' She kissed me on both cheeks. Despite the fact she'd had three children, she'd maintained her slim figure, though her dress hinted at a delicate rounding of her belly. If anything, this heightened her sexual allure, an outward display of fertility that made my childless body feel dry and withered. She smelt of expensive perfume, her skin was soft, her make-up flawless, shimmering green eyeshadow and a perfect sweep of blue eyeliner. Two delicate plaits lifted the front of her hair from her face, and through them were woven tiny mother-of-pearl shells, glinting purple and green. Dangling pearl earrings. A matching necklace with a drop-pearl pendant. Around her shoulders was a net shawl, more shells and silver sequins sewn to it. Silver rings on her fingers. A shell bracelet. She was an ethereal creature, a sea goddess, straight from the ocean. Cami the siren.

Why are you here?

Go away. Go away!

'Hi, Cami. I like the shells in your hair.' It was all I could manage.

Her hand went to one of the plaits and she smiled. 'Our daughter Connie did it,' she replied. 'She'll plait anything she can get her hands on.'

Our daughter. Nick's daughter.

One piece of the family he couldn't walk away from.

There was a moment of silence, but then Cami gave a tight smile. 'Was your journey easy?'

I nodded.

'And your hotel?'

'It's fine.'

She forced another smile.

Having to make conversation with the woman who'd stolen

Nick was torturous. I despised her to my core and the hatred was mutual, yet there we were pretending to be interested in each other.

'You could have stayed with us if we'd known you were coming.'

'That's kind.'

'Next time.'

I smiled.

'What did you make of the *unusual* gift request? We thought that was a little odd,' Nick laughed. 'Talk about ramping up the pressure!'

'Oh, I found a bowl made by a local potter in Falmouth.'

'Nice,' Nick said. 'I was stumped, but luckily Cami thought of a binary star.'

'A what?'

'Two stars that constantly orbit each other,' Cami said. 'You can name a pair. So they're up there for ever, Julian and Ingrid, tied to each other in space.'

I felt like running into the hotel, grabbing the bowl and hurling it over the cliff into the sea.

'A bit naff, but honestly, what do you give the world's most influential couple?'

Another silence settled over us. Nick cleared his throat and clapped his hands, rubbing them together. 'Into the fray?'

As we walked, I hung back a little. I had a powerful urge to reach forward and grab Cami's shell-studded shawl and pull it tight around her neck until she choked. I dug my nails into my palms to banish the thought, hearing my therapist's soft-spoken words. 'Holding on to hatred solves nothing.'

Nick turned and smiled at me, then at Cami. 'This is mad, isn't it? Brought together at some swanky hotel to watch Julian bloody Draper marry a Hollywood film star.' He laughed. 'Today is going to be wild!'

Everything about this was wrong. I closed my eyes and swore silently.

'It's a shame Fraser can't make it,' he continued. 'He's best man, too. I think he's doing the speech by video link.'

'Why can't he come?'

'Some meeting in LA with a bigwig director. Gerwig. Or maybe Nolan.'

'I read he's a film agent?'

'Biggest in the business,' Nick said. 'Homes in LA, Monaco, Lake Como and London. Julian actually met Ingrid at Fraser's villa in Italy. She was dating Fraser at the time, but ditched him for Julian.'

'Poor Fraser.'

Nick laughed. 'You don't need to feel sorry for Fraser. He's living his best life, as far as I can tell.'

This didn't surprise me. Fraser had been good-looking and charming. He was the only one of that group, apart from Nick, who was ever interested in me. His main fault was being friends with Julian, and he'd always been better company when Julian wasn't around. Julian was like rot, infecting anything and everything he came into contact with.

As we reached the hotel entrance, Nick held out his arm as a signal for me to go ahead. 'You OK?' He smiled kindly.

'I'm fine. I feel out of place, I suppose. I'm not used to events like this.'

'None of us are used to events like this. Let's just go in with no preconceptions and enjoy it. You really do look great, by the way.'

Heat flooded my body as a vivid memory thrust into my thoughts. Nick and me in my bed at Mrs Drummond's. His lips on mine. His hands all over me. Finally – and desperately – together.

CHAPTER TEN

An ogre of a man in a black suit with the features of a heavyweight boxer waited like a statue at the hotel doors. I wouldn't have needed to do much to turn him into a caricature, though for extra flavour I'd have added a jagged scar to one stubbly cheek.

'I need to check your bags.' His words were without intonation, robotic and faintly comical.

'Do you think they're expecting an assassination?' Cami whispered to Nick as she opened her turquoise clutch.

A young woman was standing in the lobby. She had a tight brown ponytail and neatly manicured fingernails slick with clear varnish, and was wearing a navy-blue suit and holding a walkie-talkie.

'Hello!' She flashed us an alarming smile. 'I'm Flick. It's lovely to welcome you to Julian and Ingrid's special – *special* – day.' Her voice was bright and cheery with the sing-song notes of a holiday rep. 'I believe you're Cami and Nick.' She looked at me quizzically. Her eyes narrowed to suspicious slits but her smile didn't waver. 'The gateman didn't mention a third person in your car.'

My cheeks warmed. 'I came in earlier.'

'Ah, yes, that makes sense.' Her relief was palpable. She glanced at the bouncer and gave a nod, as if telling him to stand down. 'You must be the artist?' She winked. 'Mum's the word. I know Ingrid's keen for it to be a surprise!' She gestured a zipping motion over her lips. 'Thank you for letting us peek in your bags. Now if you could kindly give your phones to Keith …' She gestured to the man behind the reception desk, who was distractedly writing something with a Sharpie. He looked up and put the lid on the pen. He was dressed in an immaculate burgundy jacket with the hotel's name stitched onto the pocket of his lapel. In his gloved hand were small plastic bags, our names now scrawled on them.

'For your phones,' he said, holding out the bags.

'Is this really necessary?' Nick asked. 'Can't we swear scout's honour we won't take photos?'

'Oh goodness, that's so *sweet*!' Flick's voice was saccharine. 'I'm afraid – scout or not – it *is* necessary. It was in the Ts and Cs of your acceptance.'

'What if we need to call home?'

'Oh, it's not like prison!' Her melodic laugh was as grating as her ever-widening smile. 'You can use your phone whenever you want. Keith will be here and he'll show you to the guest comms room.'

'Seems a bit over the top,' Nick said as we watched Keith seal our phones into the bags.

'It's standard nowadays. You can't trust anybody not to post all over their socials. Plus, this way everybody gets to enjoy themselves, however they want, without fear of finding their faces all over the front pages.'

'You mean their powdered noses,' Nick whispered.

'Sorry?' Flick smiled.

Nick smiled back.

Flick's walkie-talkie crackled. She put it to her mouth and pressed the button on the side. 'Just a sec, Martin.' She pointed down the corridor. 'If you could head to the end, through the Red Room, the reception drinks are on the lawn. There's a cloakroom for bags and jackets halfway down the corridor, and a table by the entrance to the Red Room for presents. Have a lovely day!' She lifted the walkie-talkie. 'The Right Honourable Jonty Harries-Pick and his wife Marguerite? And Mr Giles and Mrs Arabella Clark.' She turned to Keith and raised her eyebrows to make sure he'd heard the names. He gave her a thumbs-up and began naming bags. 'Thank you, Martin.'

'Giles,' Nick said. 'Excellent. Let's wait for him.'

'Could you please move on down?' Flick's smile was stretched to its limit. 'We're trying to avoid gridlock.'

'I imagine she was a very important monitor in her primary school,' Nick said as we started walking down the wood-panelled corridor. Paintings of ancient seascapes, fishermen in storms, sunrises over turquoise waters lined the way, and on every available surface were lavish floral displays. My mother would have called it classy, but to me it felt brash, the type of hotel you went to be seen, where an Instagram shot of a cocktail on the terrace was the holy grail of #Blessed.

We stopped and waited. The Right Honourable Whoever-he-was came in first, dressed in a striped blazer, greying hair swept over his bald spot. His younger wife was bedecked in gold jewellery, her enhanced breasts standing proud like two buoyancy aids, which, I thought with a smile, suited the coastal dress code perfectly. She wasn't happy about giving her phone to Keith and gesticulated aggressively at Flick, whose smile didn't falter despite the air-jabbing.

There was a loud exclamation from Cami as two more couples walked in. I recognised Giles immediately, but it was only when one of the women echoed Cami's cry and they ran to each other that I realised it was Tilly. She looked impossibly glamorous in a tailored naval-style jacket with gold buttons and a short flared skirt.

'Oh my *God*!' Cami said. 'You look younger and younger every time I see you.'

Tilly laughed. 'What can I say? I've an incurable addiction to fillers and a jar of every face cream on the market. If Simon knew how much this witchcraft costs, he'd die on the spot.'

She turned her gaze on me and I watched her sift through her memory bank until her mouth fell open in surprise. 'Oh my God. *Vix?* I didn't know you were coming. How lovely to see you!'

'Hello, Tilly.' She was prettier than I remembered, having grown into her features. If I was drawing her, she'd be all Cupid's-bow lips and elfin chin, with blemish-free skin and eyes cool as ice. 'I'm actually Victoria now.'

Giles approached me and said hello stiffly, no outstretched hand or kiss offered. There was an honesty in his stand-offishness that I warmed to. He wasn't going to pretend we were all still best friends. He embraced Nick and gave him two firm pats on the back. 'Hey, buddy. Good to see you.' Then he turned to Cami, arms spread, head cocked to the side. 'Darling Cami. Stunning as ever.'

Cami smiled and batted away the compliment, then kissed his cheek.

'Simon, this is Vix. She was with us at QSA,' Nick said.

'Oh dear,' laughed Tilly. 'I don't think we're going to manage Victoria, are we? You might just have to be Vix today.'

I was about to protest, but then realised she was right. Correcting people all day long would be tiresome.

'I understand your group ruled the roost in London back then,' Simon said as he shook my hand.

'Definitely not me,' I replied flatly. 'So you're married to Tilly?'

'I am.' He smiled at Tilly. 'The man she hides the Crème de la Mer receipts from.'

Tilly rolled her eyes. 'You'd *loathe* me old and wrinkled, darling.'

Giles grabbed the hand of the other woman. 'My wife, Arabella. Bels, meet the gang.'

Arabella was demure and understated, traditionally dressed for a wedding in a navy suit, a scarf dotted with white seagulls, and a navy fascinator pinned to the side of her head, with smart navy court shoes, and very little make-up.

'Giles has told me all about you.' Her voice was aristocratically posh. 'And if I fall asleep on you, I can only apologise. We had surprise twins three years ago and I'm *exhausted* to the bone. They're literally feral.'

Giles grinned. 'Boys will be boys!'

We were interrupted by Flick, her smile finally failing. 'Could you *please* move on down?'

'Of course,' Nick said. 'I'm sorry, we appear to be causing a jam.'

'You are rather,' she said. 'I know it's hard to follow instructions when we're excited, but if you could?' She turned her smile back on.

The others went ahead and left me with exhausted Arabella. 'So,' she said, to break the silence, 'where do you live?'

'France,' I said. 'Just outside Marseille.'

'How terribly glamorous!'

I thought of my small flat in the attic of Monsieur Timon's decrepit building. The paint on the floor and the radiator that wheezed every winter. Fabian's café with its simple tables and basic menu. 'Yes,' I said. 'I suppose it is. Do you have other children, or just the twins?'

Arabella beamed, clearly not too exhausted by her children to talk about them. 'We have two daughters,' she said. 'They're thirteen and fifteen, and are *beside* themselves we're here. I'm half expecting them to appear having stowed away in the boot of the Jag.' She grinned. 'Do you have children?'

I shook my head.

'Oh *dear*,' Arabella said sadly. 'Did you not want any?'

'Never.' This wasn't the truth. I'd often thought about having a baby, but only ever as part of my fantasy life with Nick. In Paris he'd shown me a photo of his children and I'd been struck dumb with jealousy. The love in his eyes had scorched my heart. Of course I'd smiled and told him how beautiful they were, resisting the urge to snatch his phone and hurl it into the Seine.

Exhausted Arabella appeared taken aback by my abruptness, so I added, 'I'm sure if things had worked out differently, I'd have loved them.'

Her shock switched to an expression of regret. 'Oh Lord. I'm *so* sorry.'

Two beefy security guards stood sentinel either side of the large double doors at the end of the corridor. I stared at their jackets, trying to work out if they had guns tucked away.

'Evening, officers,' Nick said. Neither man cracked a smile.

Nick lifted his eyebrows and smiled as we walked through the double doors into an Aladdin's cave of opulence. The walls were blood red. The triple-height windows were draped with heavy scarlet curtains. The room was filled with fake trees. A pathway scattered with petals wound its way through the pantomime forest to giant French windows opening on to the lawn. Six waiting staff lined the way with silver trays of champagne. One of them was the girl I'd met earlier, that delicious scowl still welded to her face.

I grabbed a glass of champagne and took a generous swig as I followed the others outside. The temptation to grab a bottle and disappear to a quiet corner to get drunk was overwhelming. The sunlight was blindingly bright, and Tilly and Cami slipped their sunglasses on in perfect synchrony, as if they'd been rehearsing for weeks. The young and beautiful were gathered on the lawn, the salty air heavy with confidence and charisma. Dotted around was a smattering of bulbous politicos, identifiable by their sun-starved skin and crooked teeth, which only accentuated the tans and dental perfection of the gleaming stars around them. As I scanned the perfect faces, I cursed myself for thinking this was a good idea. It was a terrible idea. One of my worst, and there'd been a lot of terrible ideas that had come before this. I noticed Giles and his exhausted wife talking, heads close. She nodded, then cast me a glance, looking quickly away when she caught my eye.

I tried not to worry about what he'd told her, sipping my champagne as Cami and Tilly chatted about the achievements of their respective offspring.

'Well, hey, hey, Nick!'

I turned in the direction of the booming greeting and saw a man in sunglasses bounding down the step onto the lawn, arms outstretched in greeting.

'*Fraser?*' Nick said. 'What the hell? I thought you couldn't make it?'

The two men hugged warmly. Fraser grinned as they separated. 'As if I'd miss the event of the century for a poxy meeting. Greta can wait.'

He had got better-looking with age, now noticeably attractive with the air of a matinée idol. Smartly dressed in an expensive suit and crisp shirt with no tie. Around his neck, in a nod to the dress code, hung a shell necklace, the type a surfer might wear. His skin was evenly tanned and wrinkle-free, dark hair swept back and long enough to give him a chic continental feel, whilst his teeth were Californian-white.

'Heff, darling. Gorgeous to see you.' Fraser laughed as Tilly kissed him on both cheeks. 'You remember Simon?'

'Of course.' Fraser shook hands with Simon before moving on to Giles, hand extended. 'Good to see you, mate.' Then he turned to Cami. From the look on his face and the change in his body language, it was immediately obvious he still had feelings for her. This didn't surprise me one bit; Fraser had always loved her. 'Darling Cami, as exquisite as ever.' He leant in to kiss her cheek.

Did I imagine his thumb lingering on her shoulder? A subtle caress? Cami drew away from him, glancing at Nick, a flash of guilt blowing over her face like a breeze. Her cheeks flushed pink. Something had passed between them. I could see it in her eyes.

'We thought you couldn't make it,' she said. Her words sounded staged, as if she'd known all along he'd be there.

'How could I stay away?' His eyes were locked on hers. His words carried an undercurrent of flirtation.

I glanced at Nick to see if he'd picked up on the tension, but he was oblivious, looking at Fraser and Cami with a wide open smile.

'You remember Vix?' Cami said.

He leant back, studying me for a moment, before his mouth opened with surprise and he laughed. 'Well now, if that isn't a blast from the past! I'd no idea you were coming. You look gorgeous. What a dress!' He bent to kiss me. He smelt incredible, scented with some no doubt extortionate designer aftershave. 'How have you been?'

'Fine. I mean, you know, it's been …' I tried to find a few words to describe the last twenty-five years. 'Fine.'

'So tell us,' Nick said then, jumping in to save me as he always had, and sweeping a hand over the lawn, 'are all these glamorous babies in Versace your very best friends?'

Fraser laughed. 'Yes. All of them. Of course.'

'Honestly.' Tilly sipped her champagne, lazily scanning the lawn, then shrugging. 'My children are spitting tacks I'm here, but I don't recognise anybody. The fiasco is *wasted* on me.'

'The champagne isn't, though, darling.' Simon smiled at a waiter and raised his glass. The man hurried over and refilled us.

'Is Julian here yet? I can't see him.' Giles craned his neck to search the crowd. 'It would be nice to say hello.'

'There's some grand entrance planned,' Fraser replied. 'We were at the registry office this morning. Ingrid wore a silver cowboy hat and matching boots and the shortest pair of silver sequinned shorts you can imagine. You'll like her. She's got a real spark. In fact, she's quite a firebrand.' He turned to me and smiled. 'A bit like you.'

My stomach clenched as I forced a smile, sipping my champagne, the hairs on the back of my neck prickling as Neil Gilbert wormed his way into everybody's thoughts. I glanced at Tilly and Cami. Did I catch a shared smirk? But then Tilly lifted her sunglasses and leant close to Cami. 'Oh Lord, I think I *do* recognise that one. Isn't she from that thing on Netflix?'

I pressed my fingers to my temples to release the building pressure.

'So, Vix,' Fraser said. 'What are you up to now? Doing something worthwhile, no doubt. You always had such passion.' He smiled.

Everybody's eyes turned to me. 'Nothing like that,' I said, my throat tightening. 'I'm an artist.'

He raised his glass, seemingly impressed. 'Well, you were always very good at art—' His attention was caught by something behind me. I turned to see Celeste frantically punching her watch and gesticulating from the terrace. He smiled and clapped his hands together. 'Well, if you'll excuse me, I believe I'm required by that woman with the clipboard.'

'Where do you sell your work?' Tilly asked after Fraser moved away.

I thought about the scores of unsold canvases gathering dust in my studio, but then Anne-Marie bustled into my head with a stern glare. 'Out of a gallery in Marseille, but I also take commissions.'

'She's playing it down,' Nick said, smiling. 'She's just won a prestigious award.'

'How incredible. You clever, *clever* thing!' Tilly's over-the-top reaction felt false, as if she were teasing me, and I was grateful we were interrupted by a waitress holding a tray of canapés.

'Mmm,' Simon said, pushing a miniature Wagyu beef Wellington into his mouth. 'Delicious. I'll take another of those,' and he reached for two more.

'I heard what you did, by the way.' I realised exhausted Arabella was addressing me. 'At university.' She spoke quietly, conspiratorially, so nobody else could hear.

Though there was no sign of unkindness or judgement, her comment skewered me. I had a flash of Giles and her talking earlier and bristled at the thought of them gossiping.

'That tutor sounded awful.' She shook her head. 'Men are such bastards.'

I smiled tightly. 'Not all men.'

'No, I didn't … Of course not *all* men. I mean, I managed to find a lovely one.' She laughed nervously and lifted her hand to show me her wedding ring, wiggling her fingers like a child. I noticed her nails were bitten to the quick. 'He's a wonderful father.' Her eyes found Giles and settled on him with relief, then flicked back to me. 'Sorry if I said the wrong thing.'

'It's fine.'

'It's, well, you've … You've turned a touch pale.'

An awkward cloud settled over us. She cleared her throat and gestured back at the hotel. 'If you'll excuse me?'

Her escape was interrupted by a loud gong. The string quartet fell silent and the crowd turned in the direction of a podium that had been placed in front of the marquee. Flick was handing Fraser a microphone. He stepped up onto the podium and surveyed the guests with a beaming smile. As he opened his mouth to speak, a screech of feedback blasted out of the speakers. He made a face and handed the mic back to Flick, who made an adjustment before returning it to him.

'Well,' he said, patting his heart. 'You are all a sight to behold. And what a day for it, hey?' The crowd responded with a ripple of agreement and a clink of glasses. 'I'm not going to say much now, as you'll be hearing from me later and I don't want to use up any of my precious jokes. All I ask is for you to raise your glasses to our fabulous newly-weds … Mr and Mrs Olsson-Draper!'

He held his champagne out in the direction of the right-hand side of the lawn, and the string quartet started up with Handel's 'Arrival of the Queen of Sheba'. The crowd swivelled en masse like a flock of starlings to watch Julian and Ingrid appear from the side of the hotel. There was a collective intake of breath, soft oohs and aahs and whispers. Ingrid was astride a magnificent white horse. Its coat glistened like polished marble, its silky mane and tail fluttering in a barely detectible breeze. She wore a white dress of the finest organza, which fell over the back of the horse, translucent and studded with a million diamanté beads. Her hair was long and wavy, a silver crown encircling her head. In one hand she held a bouquet of flowers and trailing silver ivy.

But all I could focus on was the man leading the horse.

Julian.

My throat constricted, skin prickling. It was hard to look at him but impossible to look away. He wore a sandy suit flecked with gold, an upright collar like a Chinese emperor, golden buttons, white patent-leather shoes. He looked older, skin pallid, tinged yellow, with dark puffy pillows beneath his eyes. He'd thickened around the middle and was shorter than I remembered, though perhaps this was an illusion created by Ingrid and the horse towering over him.

When they reached the corner of the marquee, they stopped, and a man in cavalry attire ran forward to take the horse. Julian stepped to the side and held out his hand to help Ingrid down. As she dismounted, the train of her dress got caught on the horse's rump, and she stumbled on landing. Somebody behind me smothered a laugh.

Ingrid recovered herself, gave a small curtsey with a girlish giggle, then took Julian's hand. Together they beamed and waved. The lawn erupted, as everybody cheered and raised their glasses, and a snowstorm of golden confetti fell around them, shot behind from a blower.

'Oh my *God*, she's stunning,' breathed Arabella, her exhaustion temporarily replaced by wonder.

As Julian and Ingrid moved through the crowd, greeting their guests, warmly shaking hands and kissing cheeks, guffawing, clapping people on their arms and back, memories from that night pummelled me. His breath. My head swirling. His hands on my throat. The purple bruising on my thighs. My pounding head. Mrs Drummond's voice as I huddled in my bed later.

Your brother's on the telephone.

I watched, frozen with horror, as Julian caught sight of us and came barrelling over, his face twisted into a rictus grin, arms outstretched in greeting.

'My oldest friends! The true VIPs amongst these …' He lowered his voice and made a show of checking over his shoulder, '*dreadful* wannabes.' He winked. 'Bloody *brilliant* to see you all!'

There was a rumble of congratulations and kisses and excitement. I felt sick, desperate to turn and run. Julian said hello to everybody in turn. He kissed Cami. 'Just *look* at you, gorgeous creature.' He put his hands together in prayer and mouthed a thank you to God, before turning to Nick and shaking his head. 'How a schmuck like you snared a goddess like this confounds us all.'

Nick laughed and gave an exaggerated shrug. 'Unlucky at cards, I guess.'

Everybody tittered with laughter.

Cami kissed Julian on both cheeks. 'Congratulations, darling.'

Then he looked at me. 'And Vix! QSA's very own feminist superhero. Or should I say heroine? I'm never quite sure these days.' He roared with laughter. 'Anyway, what a coincidence you're a friend of Ingrid. Something to do with the art world?'

My tongue was tied in knots.

'Ingrid loves her art, doesn't she?' Nick said, jumping in. 'And Vix is one of the hottest new portraitists in France.'

'That makes sense. My beloved wife has something of an eye for a mover and shaker. Considers herself a patron of the up-and-coming creatives.' He smiled. 'I'm delighted to see you. I trust this means you've forgiven me. Thank Christ for *that*!'

Before I realised what was happening, he'd lunged forward

to kiss my cheek. He smelt exactly the same – of aftershave and arrogance – and my insides curdled.

'Congratulations.' It was all I could manage to get out.

'Ingrid said you encountered an idiot on the gate. He'll be fired, don't worry.' He laughed.

'What? No. He didn't—'

'Your *face*! I'm joking. I won't fire him. Well, not today, anyway.' He winked and his face twisted into a smug grin.

'Right then.' He patted Nick's shoulder a couple of times. 'Enjoy, and please eat and drink as much as you can. This wedding's costing me the GDP of Albania.' He laughed.

Mrs Drummond's voice echoed in my head. *Your brother's on the telephone ...*

I stared at Julian's face and began drawing him in my head, my hand twitching involuntarily at my side, as if sketching.

Round, spongy face.

Receding hairline.

Horns and a background of flames.

CHAPTER ELEVEN

November 1999

From the moment they strode into the studio, hand in hand, faces radiant, Nick and Cami were the ultimate golden couple. By coming together, they'd managed to create something bigger than the sum of their parts. They had become our luminescent centre.

Despite being hollowed out by heartbreak, I stayed part of the group. Self-preservation would have had me put as much distance between them and myself as I could, but as masochistic as it was, I had to keep near him. Even the thought of the alternative was agonising. Since he'd told me he loved Cami, my feelings for Nick had become a thousand times stronger. Though I couldn't explain why, I became obsessed with them. I watched them talking and touching and laughing. I studied the way she tipped her neck to one side to let him stroke her with his finger. I'd stare at his hand caressing her thigh beneath the table in the pub. Alone in bed I'd think about them, whispering the words she said to him, practising over and over until I had the pitch and intonation perfect.

'Nick, *stop* it,' I'd say into the darkness. 'Don't *say* things like that. Not in *public*.' Then a peal of childlike laughter.

Nick and Cami getting together was written in the sand from our first day at QSA. I was an idiot for being so blind to it coming. Popular, beautiful, symmetrical and shiny, two of a kind, destined to marry and spawn a litter of shiny, symmetrical children. But despite this inevitability, it was obvious to me it was contractual, nothing more than an arranged marriage. It wasn't true love. They had no interests in common. Not like Nick and me. I knew their relationship couldn't last. One day he'd get bored of her, and when they broke up, I'd be ready. In the meantime, I'd show him I was desirable; not only pretty, but the type of girl he wanted, a force of nature. Not a friend, but a lover.

I stared in the mirror for hours trying out sophisticated hairstyles. I bought glossy fashion magazines and pored over make-up tutorials. In a copy of *Cosmopolitan*, I found an article titled: '9 Ways to Get Men to Notice You'. It was like I'd struck gold.

Most of the list was embarrassing, and as I read it, I cringed. Was this where I was going wrong? Was I dismissing the obvious stuff because it made me uncomfortable?

9 Ways to Get a Guy to Notice You

1   Smile! Light up when he looks your way!
2   Make eye contact and hold his gaze for a few seconds!
3   Play with your hair. Push it behind your ear or flip it over your shoulder!
4   Throw him a glance. Let him literally turn your head!
5   Get close to him. Look for excuses to be near him!
6   Looking good (and yes, girls, we mean sexy!) will catch his attention!
7   Be unexpected. Don't be afraid to do something out of the ordinary!
8   Speak up. How will he notice you if you keep your head down?
9   Relax and be yourself. Don't try and be someone you're not!

Apart from number 9, which clearly hadn't worked, the list looked straightforward enough, and when I read it, I tingled with excitement.

I found a skirt that finished mid-thigh, and as the shop assistant handed it to me in a carrier bag, a thrill wriggled through me. I then splashed out on a soft cream sweater, a pair of heeled wedges with ballerina tie-ups like Cami wore, and a denim jacket I'd spotted in the window of a second-hand shop. I shaved my legs and rubbed in some fake tan, and plucked my eyebrows.

My nerves hammered as I walked into the studio. The words of the article ran through my head on a loop. *You want to make him notice you? Step out of the shadows! Once you have his attention, you're halfway there. Good luck!*

We were due to present our material design projects that morning. They counted towards our end-of-year exams, and everybody was more tense than usual. We'd been given a list of building materials and asked to choose one to form the basis of a design. The project had been set a month earlier and required us to research the material, write a design statement, draw a plan, and create a mood board with sketches, paintings, photos and drawings. I'd chosen glass. My favourite part of the project had been creating the mood board. I'd designed a glazed beach house and illustrated the inside of the main living area, which looked out over the sea. I'd created it with Nick and me in mind. I'd imagined us standing in front of the S-shaped glass wall, discussing Delacroix and Lloyd Wright. I saw us sitting together on the white leather sofa in the expansive room with its limestone floor, glasses of wine on the glass-topped table beside a vase of fiery, passionate tulips. I gave us a cat, grey, long-haired, asleep on the Eames chair, which was positioned on a cream seventies-style shag-pile rug, something I was particularly pleased with when I drew it. I knew my design was good – both aesthetic and practical – but when Nick had strolled over, studied it for a moment or two, then whistled quietly through his teeth and said,

143

'Wow, that's amazing. It's like my perfect house. I can see myself living somewhere like that one day,' I'd nearly died of joy.

Fraser was first up. He walked to the front of the studio, smiling as everybody whooped and cheered. His design was dreadful, but his presentation was incredible. Instead of doing drawings, he'd gone to a run-down area of east London and used students from the drama society to make a five-minute film about a girl being hunted by a pack of zombies. Everybody was in fits of laughter watching it, even Gilbert. At the end of the film, the girl ran into a lock-up, and over the racket of bangs and crashes from outside, out of breath and panting heavily, she looked to camera and said with a wink, 'Everybody knows zombies can't eat through sheet steel.' Then came a still of Fraser's model, a basic hut roughly covered in tin foil with some bloody handprints dotted around. Pinned up on the board beside the projector screen was a sheet of paper with a scruffy pencil sketch of the four-walled hut.

Neil Gilbert clapped loudly. 'Highly inventive, Mr Jenner! The building lacks the imagination of the film, of course, but yes, very entertaining. I'm impressed with your creativity. Maybe next time put as much energy into the design as the presentation? Next we have ...' he consulted his sheet of paper, 'Camilla?'

Nick mouthed, 'Good luck.'

Cami smiled at him. Before she picked up her portfolio, she squeezed his shoulder. Why did she always have to touch him so publicly? It was as if she had to remind us *all* the time that he belonged to her.

Julian cheered. 'Go, Cami!' He laughed, then whispered something to Giles, which, annoyingly, I couldn't hear.

Cami set out her mood board, drawings and artist's impression. She was wearing tight jeans and low-heeled cowboy boots, a vest top and no bra, which left little to the imagination. She oozed sex and my heart sank. Despite my new outfit, I felt frumpy and dull. How would Nick notice me now?

Her design was solid but dreary, a timber-framed building in a forest, traditional with stone piers and cedar cladding, one half a mirror image of the other. She wasn't a gifted artist and her painting was flat. However, what she lacked in artistic flair she made up for in presentation skills, clear and confident without any stumbling or hesitation. But a few minutes into her talk, one by one we began to notice Neil Gilbert. His chair was behind the desk, but in view of at least three quarters of the room. His mouth had opened slightly and he was staring at Cami in his usual creepy way.

'Oh my God,' Giles whispered to Julian, this time loud enough for me, and most of those around us, to hear. 'Has he got a *stiffy*?'

Julian snorted. 'Jesus, he *has*!'

My eyes shot to Gilbert's crotch, and I was horrified to see the fabric of his trousers straining. He moved his hand and pushed the heel of his palm against the bulge to readjust himself. I looked back at his face. His eyes didn't waver from Cami.

'*Psst*, Nick,' Julian whispered, leaning forward to tap Nick on the shoulder. 'You going to stop Gilbert eye-fucking your bird?'

'Fuck off, you dick,' Nick hissed back, his cheeks flaring with colour and his jaw clenching.

'Bit tetchy, mate.' Julian laughed and sat back, grinning at Giles.

Cami seemed oblivious to Gilbert as she described how she'd used heavy timber pillars to mimic the pine trees surrounding the building. But as more people began to notice him, she seemed to realise something was up. She turned to look at Gilbert and did a double-take as she clocked his hand on his crotch. Her cheeks flared red. She glanced around and realised others had noticed too. An uncomfortable atmosphere settled over the room. She angled herself away from Gilbert, hunching her shoulders slightly in an attempt to hide her chest. Was Fraser's voice ringing as loudly in her ears as it was in mine?

You do wear pretty tight tops.

Her voice faltered. She tripped over her words as she lost her train of thought. Tilly was clearly fuming, glaring at Gilbert, arms crossed aggressively, eyes needling him with disgust.

Though I hated Cami, this wasn't right. Gilbert was disgusting and I felt for her. As I stared at him, he began to rhythmically press his trousers, a small movement, hardly noticeable, his tongue lightly touching his upper lip.

Nick rubbed his temples as if he had a migraine. He shifted in his seat, looking distressed, unsure what to do. My heart broke for him.

Julian gave a half-suppressed snort of laughter. Cami visibly winced. She looked at Tilly, the expression on her face saying: *Help me.*

I was bombarded with images and snippets of thought, as if someone had upended the contents of a shopping bag in my head. The image of Liberty. Her raised arm. Her strength. Her courage and her bravely bared chest. The words of the magazine article. *Don't be afraid to do something out of the ordinary!* Nick's words from the evening he shattered my heart. *She has this strength. This fierce, brave power.*

Then some unknown force took hold of me.

I stood up.

'Mr Gilbert?' The strength of my voice surprised me.

He looked at me, straightening his shoulders, shifting back in his seat, his hand falling from his crotch.

'What? Is this important? Camilla hasn't finished her presentation.'

'It's just you seem more interested in her breasts than in what she's saying.'

A collective gasp rang around the room.

Gilbert's face crumpled in astonishment. 'Excuse me?'

I moved swiftly, pulling my new cream sweater over my head and dropping it on the floor. Another gasp from the room. This one louder. For a moment, I wondered if the other girls might follow my lead, and we'd all, one by one, stand up and take our tops off. The thought spurred me on. The buzz was incredible. I felt strong and empowered.

I heard a few people whispering to each other, quiet swearing, words laced with disbelief.

'Oh my God ...'

'Jesus Christ ...'

'Fucking hell ...'

'Victoria!' shouted Neil Gilbert. 'What on *earth* are you doing? Put your clothes on!' Flustered, he glanced hurriedly at the door. Low murmurs and stifled laughter began to grow around me.

'Yes, Vix! You *go*, girl!' cried Julian.

Gilbert's look of panic mixed with my own surging adrenalin propelled me onwards. I saw Liberty smiling, applauding our victory. I tipped my chin upwards, blood pumping, and unhooked my bra. I slipped it from my shoulders.

The studio fell silent.

'Is this what you want?' I said. 'You want to look at breasts?'

Gilbert froze as if someone had pressed pause.

The shocked silence in the studio thickened, and then as suddenly as it had appeared, my bravado started to fade. What was I doing? Why was I standing there in full view of my peers half naked? I closed my eyes for a moment and tried to conjure Liberty, but she'd left me.

Jesus, what had I done.

I'm sorry, I wanted to say. *I'm sorry, I don't know what came over me. Please wipe this from your memories.*

When I opened my eyes, Gilbert had galvanised himself and was marching towards me, his face clouded with rage. He bent to pick up my sweater and thrust it out towards me. 'Put your bloody clothes on!' he snarled. 'Unless you want to look like a prostitute while you're explaining yourself to the vice chancellor?'

I slipped my sweater on and tucked my bra into my back pocket like a slingshot. Mustering the last bit of strength I had remaining, I stared at him and said, in as clear a voice as possible, 'It's not me who needs to explain myself.'

The room exploded with cheering and clapping; a few people chanted my name.

Gilbert turned and shouted at them. 'For God's sake, shut up!'

The laughter and cheering grew louder as he bundled me out of the room. I looked at Nick as I walked past, but when he caught my eye, he turned away.

The vice chancellor appeared confused and asked me to explain for a third time. 'I'm sorry, I still don't understand.'

'He was staring at her.'

'Staring.' She took a steadying breath. 'But not at you?'

I shook my head. 'Another girl.'

'And that's why you stripped?' She had a sharply cut bottle-blonde bob, and fuchsia-pink lipstick, which shone out of her face like a high-wattage lamp. 'Because you wanted him to stare at you not her? You didn't like her getting the attention?'

'No! God, *no*. That's not it.' My cheeks burnt red and I had a flash of unhooking my bra and the feeling of air on my breasts. I cringed. 'And I didn't strip. It wasn't like that. I ... I took my top off.'

It was clear from her platinum-framed face that she saw little difference between her definition of stripping and my explanation of what I'd done.

'Like *Liberty Leading the People?* The painting. Do you—'

She raised a hand and nodded wearily, as if she'd heard a hundred girls before me tell her the reason they'd taken their bra off in class was because of Delacroix's *Liberty*. She leant forward and steepled her hands on the desk in front of her. 'Listen, Victoria. You cannot take your top off and show your body in that way in a classroom. If nothing else, it's disruptive. Have you been drinking?'

'Drinking?' I shook my head, tears prickling my eyes. I'd never been sent to anybody for any sort of bad behaviour before, yet there I was, in front of the head of QSA, trying to explain why somebody sober would strip off in front of their peers and a member of staff in a presentation. A wave of nausea barrelled through me.

'So you took your top off because Mr Gilbert was staring at another girl. What did you hope to achieve?'

Perched on the edge of the leather chair in her office, feeling small and silly and ashamed, I realised I needed to think carefully about answering her question. Was I going to get myself into a sticky mess? I couldn't tell her I'd done it to make Nick see me as a force of nature. But if I accused Gilbert of something serious, this wouldn't go away. I'd be stuck reliving it over and over as we went down a treacherous route of he said/she said. If I apologised, however, and said I had no idea what had come over me, would she send me away with nothing more than her disappointment? I thought about the way Gilbert had touched his cock through his trousers as he leered at Cami. The way he'd licked his lip. The unbridled anger that had burned in his eyes as he marched me out of the studio.

Liberty gave a rousing battle cry from the far reaches of my head.

'Neil Gilbert had an erection.'

'*What?*'

'And he was touching himself.' With the dam breached, my words came out in a torrent. 'I know it might seem weird, what I did, and I can see there might have been better ways to handle it, but it sort of happened. I got angry. We all knew what was happening. I wanted to stop it. What he was doing wasn't right.'

The vice chancellor leant back in her chair and clasped her hands, putting them up to her lips. It was clear from her face, from the narrowing of her eyes and the set of her mouth, that things had shifted up a gear. Ten seconds earlier, this had been nothing more than student skylarking, but now, with the mention of an erection and touching, it had become a serious accusation, something she would need to address with due care and attention with fallout she'd need to manage.

'Right, so we're both clear, what you're saying is that Mr Gilbert was masturbating in class?'

I hesitated. 'No, he wasn't doing *that*. I mean, not exactly. He was sort of ...' Again I hesitated, trying to find the right words to describe what it was he'd been doing, 'pressing it.'

'*Pressing* it?'

I nodded.

'*It* being his penis.'

The word *penis* sounded out like a klaxon in the room. I swallowed and nodded again.

The vice chancellor scribbled something on a piece of paper. 'And others in the class can corroborate this?'

'I think so. I mean, yeah. People were whispering and pointing. Maybe not everybody. But some.'

She lifted her hand to stop me, then wrote something else. Then she sat back and looked at me for a moment or two. 'I need to look into this properly. I'll get in contact if I need to speak to you again.'

'Am I in trouble?'

'Well, you certainly can't go around taking your clothes off every time you want to highlight a problem.'

'I feel a bit sick about it, to be honest. I don't think I'll do anything like that again.'

She smiled then, her face cracking with unexpected warmth. 'I understand. Off you go now,' she said. 'Unless you have anything else to add?'

I shook my head.

'Obviously I need to think about how best to handle this. You'll have to face some sort of disciplinary action. You understand why, yes?'

I nodded and pursed my lips as I tried to hold back tears. Was she going to ask me to leave? Send me back to Knutsford under a dark cloud of shame? My poor mother. This might be enough to finish her off.

'Don't look so crestfallen, Victoria. It won't be anything serious, but you've got to promise me that you won't do anything like this again. Keep your nose clean and your body covered.'

I nodded quickly.

'But off the record?' Her voice softened. 'I think what you did is rather marvellous. The type of thing I would have wanted to do when I was your age but would never have been brave enough to.' She smiled. 'Off you go now.'

Later that night, we were due to go to a pub in South Kensington with live music. I didn't want to go, but hated the thought of everybody talking to Nick behind my back about what I'd done.

'Will you stay in with me?'

'I'm meeting Cami there.'

'I'm not sure I can face people.'

'You'll have to eventually.'

He barely spoke on the way to the pub. I tried to talk to him, but each time I asked something, he answered in only a few words.

'Are you OK?' I said.

'Fine.'

'You're being very quiet.'

'Tired, that's all.'

We walked via Cami's halls and picked up her and Tilly.

'So? What happened with the VC?' Cami asked, as soon as she saw me.

'Not much,' I said with a shrug. 'She told me not to do it again. There'll be some sort of disciplinary action, but I don't think it'll be too bad.' I paused as the implications of what I'd done tightened like a clamp. I put my hands over my face. 'God. How am I going to face everybody?'

Tilly grinned. 'Are you *serious*? You're a bloody hero! Literally everybody is talking about it.' There was a new look in her eyes. For the first time she seemed interested in me, as if I'd hatched from a dull-coloured egg she hadn't noticed before and become an exotic bird with rainbow feathers. She laughed and shook her head. 'God, the look on that creep's *face*! What you did was *so* cool.'

I groaned quietly. 'I'm not sure it was *that* cool. Everybody's seen my boobs.'

'If I had tits like yours, I'd have stripped off too.'

I looked at Nick, but he was staring at the pavement, hands in his pockets, expression fixed. Why wouldn't he speak? Why didn't he tell me what I'd done was brave and I was a force of nature?

I got separated from him almost as soon as we walked into the pub. I pushed through the crowd, trying to find him, but the pub was too rammed, so I went back to the bar to join Tilly and found her with Fraser and Julian.

As I stood with them, I noticed people pointing me out to each other, staring, talking behind raised hands.

'This is awful,' I whispered. 'I'm so embarrassed.'

'Honestly, don't worry about it!' Tilly said. '*Everyone* I've told thinks it's amazing. You're a local legend!'

Fraser thrust a glass of wine into my hand. 'Tilly says you're not sure what the college will do?'

I shook my head.

'Hope they don't kick you out. If you do, we'll have to protest. Stage a naked sit-in or something.' He grinned.

I kept scanning the pub for Nick. I was desperate to talk to him.

When I finally caught sight of him, I waved to get his attention. He nodded his head, but didn't make a move towards me, stayed chatting to Cami and Giles. I sipped my wine, watching him, waiting for the right moment to grab him. Finally he said something to Cami, gestured in the direction of the toilets and moved away.

I followed, pushing into the men's toilets after him. He looked surprised, glanced at the man using the urinal and furrowed his brow. 'This is the gents,' he said, rather dimly.

'What's wrong?'

'What?'

'You're being off. Since the studio?'

He shook his head, unable to meet my eye.

The man at the urinal washed his hands and moved past us. 'Maybe have this conversation outside?' he said as he left.

'Are you angry?'

'Of course not.'

'You seem it.'

He hesitated. My stomach turned over. 'Not with you. With that piece of shit Gilbert. Maybe with myself. I just sat there. Did nothing. I should have stood up to him like you did, but I sat there like a dick.' He slammed his hand against the wall and swore.

I watched in horror as his eyes welled. This wasn't what was supposed to happen. He was supposed to think what I did was brave, not be consumed by self-loathing.

I didn't know what to say. He dropped his head and walked past me without another word.

I followed him out of the toilets, my eyes smarting with tears. I needed to leave the pub. I needed to be away from these people.

Two boys were standing in the corridor. They saw me coming, behind Nick, and nudged each other.

One smirked. 'Nice tits,' he said as I passed.

Nick turned and pushed the guy up against the wall. 'What the fuck did you say?'

His friend tried to step between them as Nick pressed in close to the boy. 'He didn't mean anything. It was a joke.'

'It wasn't funny.'

As I watched him squaring up to the other guy, his mouth set hard, his eyes burning, I felt a surge of pleasure. Nick had jumped to my defence. Nothing like this had ever happened to me before. It was like something from a film. My heart swelled.

'Nick?'

I turned to see Cami.

'It's OK. You don't—' I began.

She spoke over me. 'What are you doing?'

Nick hesitated, closing his eyes, mouthing something. He stepped back, nodding, then dropped his head.

The guy walked off, scowling, shoving Nick as he went. 'Wanker,' he said over his shoulder.

Cami put her arms around Nick. She stroked his back. He leant his head against hers. 'Can we get out of here?' I heard him whisper.

'Of course,' she said. She looked at me then. 'Don't worry,' she said. 'It's fine.'

But as I watched them walk away, his hand in hers, I wanted to shout after her, scream until my lungs turned inside out, that nothing – nothing at all – was fine.

CHAPTER TWELVE

Coco

The morning of the wedding, half an hour before Darren had asked Coco to arrive, Debbie had stopped in the hallway and turned to face her daughter. She'd unscrewed the mascara and touched the wand lightly to the tips of Coco's perfectly mascaraed eyelashes, just as she'd done a thousand times before.

'Remember, baby, these people aren't any old people, they're *important* people. People who can make things happen. Assume everybody in the room has connections and turn your charm on them all, yeah? And don't be scared of them. They shit like you and me.' She took Coco's chin in her hand and tipped her face one way, then the other, checking to make sure everything was perfect. She then applied a lick of pink pearlescent lip gloss, as if putting the finishing touches to an oil painting. 'Smile, hold your shoulders back, and when you walk, shimmy those hips and flick your hair, like you would at a pageant. Got that, princess?'

Coco rolled her eyes. 'I know what to do.'

'Sure, sure, but what kind of mother would I be if I didn't remind you? What if I assumed you'd remember to smile and shimmy and flick but you didn't, and Ingrid Olsson didn't notice you, and you didn't get offered a part in her next Hollywood film? Because this is real, Coco. These people are—'

'Important. Yes, I know, you've told me a hundred times.'

'And they—'

'Shit just like us.' Her mother's face fell. Coco laughed and kissed her cheek. 'I'm joking. I know. These people can make things happen. Don't worry, I've got it.' She turned to check her appearance in the mirror, and Debbie watched as she touched the tip of her finger to her tongue, then carefully wiped upwards under her eye, smoothing away a slight smudge of eyeliner. She swelled with pride. Her baby, all grown up and heading off to work at the swankiest gig of the decade.

Coco fixed her eyes on her mother's reflection in the mirror. 'You know, I don't think this is the opportunity you think it is. I'm going to be serving drinks and clearing plates, not dancing on a stage.'

Debbie rested her hands on Coco's shoulders and leant forward, her face next to her daughter's. 'Baby, you're sixteen now. As you get older, this business will become even harder and more competitive. You make your own luck in life. You make the most of your chances. You know that, don't you? This wedding is one of those chances. They might not offer you a job tonight, but if you make an impression, let people know what you do and how well you do it, you've no idea what doors might open in the future. Your face has got to stick in their heads, so when they're chatting with one of their big-shot director mates, over a round of golf or at a meal in some fancy-pants restaurant, and they mention they're looking for an unknown teen beauty to star in their next blockbuster, Ingrid Olsson – or one of her Hollywood friends – will say, "You know what? I know the *perfect* girl."'

Coco shook her head and smiled.

Debbie stared hard at her. 'You're looking at me as if I'm bonkers, but I'm not. Take it from me, I know how the world works. People like us, we have to graft for our chances, graft then make the blinking most of them.'

Coco sighed.

'You understand, don't you? I haven't cleaned blood and shit off surgery toilets and pulled a hundred thousand pints to watch you fade to nothing. This beauty of yours' – Debbie stroked her fingers down Coco's cheek – 'is your ticket to the moon. But it's up to you to drive the rocket to get you there.'

Later, as they passed through the grand gates of Lowencliffe Hall, Coco's tummy had tingled with nerves. Swarms of people buzzed about and the atmosphere was charged with electricity.

Debbie tapped her hand and pointed out of the windscreen at the hotel. 'See that window there? The one on the far left. That's the fanciest suite. Huge bedroom, sitting area, its own terrace overlooking the gardens and sea. I bet my last penny that's Ingrid's room. I bet she's in there right now with a football team of stylists and make-up artists and hairdressers. One day it'll be you up there, baby. And I'll be with you. Getting our hair done for your wedding. Drinking champagne and staring out over the glittery sea.' She took a breath and patted Coco's knee. 'Diamonds,' she whispered. 'One day, baby, you'll be just like the sea. Covered in glimmering, shimmering diamonds.'

Coco was polishing glasses in the kitchen when her phone vibrated in her pocket. Her heart skipped a beat and she prayed nobody else had heard the faint buzz. She was supposed to have given her phone to the terrifying man on the door when she arrived. But there was no way she was handing it over – screw *that* – so she'd lied, switched it to silent and told him she'd left it at home.

'Left it at home?' he'd grunted suspiciously.

'I knew we weren't allowed them.'

He'd stared at her, hesitating.

'Frisk me if you want.' She narrowed her eyes and set her mouth. I dare you, her expression said.

For a moment she wondered if he was going to. What would he

do if he found the phone? But he didn't; he just waved her through with a glare.

Now she mumbled an excuse and ducked out of the kitchen, concealing herself behind a stack of crates, and pulling her phone from her pocket. She was hoping it was Jamie. She and Jamie had kissed at Shannon's last night, and though she'd messaged that morning, he'd left her on read. Shannon said he liked her, but if that was true, why was he ghosting her?

The text was from her mother. Shannon was full of shit.

Good luck baby!

Coco gave it a heart then went back into the kitchen, wondering if she should message Jamie again. Why were boys so rubbish?

Darren – her mother's on-off boyfriend – rushed into the kitchen clapping his hands like he was having some sort of fit. 'Right, half an hour until the guests arrive! I've had a message from Mr Draper. He wants a bottle of champagne and three glasses sent up.' He scanned the kitchen, which was a hive of frantic activity, with head chef Barry and three sous chefs, Fred and Gina and one other whose name Coco didn't catch, busily preparing the scallop starters, and about twelve waiting staff – including Coco – milling about polishing glasses, arranging canapés and chopping herbs. 'Maeve, can you sort that out? Andre has the champagne in the fridge ready to go.'

'They're a bit up against it with the starters, but if someone's around to take over shucking these scallops …' Maeve was about her mum's age with a neat bun, tightly pinned and slicked down with hairspray, and a starched shirt, her sandy linen skirt without a crease. Coco had overheard her earlier telling another waitress that this was her twentieth year working at Lowencliffe Hall. 'Nobody knows this place better than me,' she'd said, with obvious pride.

'I've nearly finished here, so I'll get back on them.' Gina wiped her hands on the cloth draped over her shoulder and walked over to where Maeve was working.

Maeve nodded, rinsed her hands beneath the tap and dried them, then marched off, serious and focused, as if going to defuse a bomb rather than deliver champagne.

'Do you want me to help?' Coco asked Gina. 'I've finished those glasses.'

'*You?* Help with the scallops?' Gina laughed, then gestured dismissively at the sink. 'Wash that lot up if you've nothing to do.'

Coco shrugged. Screw Gina and her vile scallops. She walked over to the sink. Washing up suited her better anyway; she could drift off, keep herself to herself. She retrieved her AirPods from her pocket, surreptitiously slipped one into her right ear and pressed play on her phone.

It wasn't long before Maeve bustled back in, calling for Darren. She was clearly agitated, huffing and puffing, her face a deep puce and fit to explode.

'Calm down, Maeve, for goodness' sake. What is it?' Darren's voice was clipped with impatience.

Maeve blinked slowly, her hands clenched together in front of her, her lips tight. 'He doesn't want me serving drinks. Or food. At all. For the rest of the day. He said if there's anybody else *like me* then he doesn't want them front of house either.'

'What?'

'He wants staff who are …' She cleared her throat and took a deep and laboured breath, 'different.'

Another woman burst into the kitchen then. She carried a clipboard and a walkie-talkie and spoke as if she were firing bullets from her mouth.

'I found a smear on one of the knives,' she barked. 'All the laid-up cutlery needs to be checked and polished.'

'I checked it already.' Darren's hackles were up.

The woman turned steely eyes on him. 'Not well enough. I suggest you get some of your people in there with cloths quick-smart.'

'I don't have any spare—'

'Just do it.' She turned on her sensible navy heel and was gone.

Darren looked up at the ceiling and shook his head. 'What am I doing?' he muttered. 'What the hell am I doing?' He took a deep breath and refocused on Maeve. 'What did he mean, different?'

Maeve stared at the space above his head. 'He didn't say. Just different. To me.'

Darren growled under his breath. 'Jesus, Maeve. I haven't time for this! How can I sort it out if I have to use telepathy to understand? Hmm?'

Maeve sniffed, then her face hardened. She lowered her gaze and fixed her eyes on him. 'His exact words were, "Tell that useless twat of a manager I want more decorative staff."'

There was a smothered snigger from the kitchen area. Coco saw Fred drop his head and Gina smack him on the arm.

'He asked for a second bottle, but not served by me. He doesn't want to see me again. And you know what?' Maeve sniffed loudly. 'Suits me *fine.*'

Darren turned red, his eyes grown wide and round. 'He called me a *what?*'

Fred coughed to hide another snort of laughter.

'He can't dictate my staffing. You'll take the champagne up and tell him you're employed by the hotel to serve, and that's what you'll do.'

Maeve shook her head and crossed her arms. 'I'm not going up there again. If he wants someone more decorative, find someone more decorative.' Her eyes flicked over to Coco, which sent a flash of heat shooting up Coco's neck.

'She's got no experience.'

'Well I have, and experience isn't what this man wants. He wants *decorative.*'

Darren shook his head and swore again as he turned his gaze on Coco. He hesitated, then sighed, throwing his hands up in the air in defeat. 'Do you know how to pour champagne?'

Was it any different to pouring anything else? Coco had no idea, but she assumed it was nothing more complicated than aim bottle at glass and fill glass, so she nodded.

'Tuck your shirt in, then go and fetch another bottle of champagne from Andre in the bar and take it up to the Princess Suite. After that, get back down here quickly and start polishing the goddam knives and forks for the meal. You'll be taking Maeve's place on the floor today, too. She'll run through things with you.'

Coco felt like a lamb on its way to the abattoir.

Darren's face softened. 'Smile. Pour the drinks. If he gives you any trouble, come and get me. He might be Julian Draper, but he's not in charge of this hotel. *I* am.' He walked away, muttering under his breath. 'Useless twat. How dare he ...'

Coco found Andre at the bar and asked him for another bottle for Mr Draper.

'Don't spill it.' Andre gave her a wink. 'This is Louis Roederer Cristal 2002. This lot clearly have more money than they know what to do with. They've got a hundred of these ordered. Imagine having that kind of cash. Can you put some olives into one of those dishes?'

As Andre slipped the bottle into a silver wine cooler with the hotel's name and logo engraved on its side, Coco spooned olives from a large glass jar into a white dish, then carefully wiped a splash of oil off the china with a cloth. Andre shook some almonds into another dish, set the two dishes and the cooler on a silver tray, then draped a starched napkin over the neck of the bottle.

'Which is the Princess Suite?' Coco asked.

'Up the main staircase to the first floor. Turn left. All the way to the end of the corridor.'

Why was her tummy such a ball of nerves? She was only delivering a bottle of stupid champagne, not about to do brain surgery.

'Hey.' Andre placed a hand on her arm. 'Don't look so worried. You'll be fine.'

Two security guards stood motionless at the foot of the staircase. They resembled futuristic statues with their matching dark suits, earpieces, and stony expressions of don't-even-try-it. 'I'm taking this up to Mr Draper.' Coco projected her voice like she would if she was acting to try and sound confident.

They nodded like automatons, and she walked past them and up the stairs. At the end of the corridor, she set the tray down, knocked on the door and waited. After a moment or two, another member of security with uniform dark suit and earpiece opened it.

'I have Mr Draper's champagne.'

The man stepped aside and she walked into the suite. The room wouldn't have looked out of place at Buckingham Palace, with oak panelling, and velvet sofas set either side of a marble coffee table holding a huge arrangement of vibrant orange and red flowers resembling flames.

There were three people in the sitting room, but Coco only had eyes for one. Ingrid Olsson. Right there. In front of her. On film she was stunning, but in real life she was totally lit.

'Thank fucking *God*. The service in this place is glacial.' The man – who looked vaguely familiar and who she assumed to be Julian Draper – wore a hotel dressing gown and beige socks. His face was pale and puffy, and his eyes a little beady.

Coco looked at Ingrid, who was sitting on one of the sofas in an ivory silk dressing gown. Her make-up was done, silver eyeshadow, perfect blusher, her hair a tumbling mass of golden curls. Her feet were bare, smooth and tanned, and freshly pedicured. Her manicured fingers held a diamanté-encrusted phone – surely they couldn't be real diamonds? – and she stared at the screen, scrolling with the edge of her thumb.

Coco cleared her throat, hoping Ingrid would look up so she could smile at her, make eye contact, but she didn't lift her gaze from the screen. How on earth was Coco supposed to get her attention? Her mother was delusional.

'Thank God they've got rid of that old witch they sent up before,' puffy Julian said. 'I mean, you spend over half a mill on a wedding, the very least you expect are staff who are easy on the eye.'

Coco felt his gaze on her like every pageant judge or casting agent or leering old man before him.

'We learnt that at college, didn't we, Fraser? Aesthetics are everything.'

The other man in the room – Fraser – smiled at Coco. 'I promise he's not as bad as he comes across.'

Julian laughed. 'No, I'm probably worse!'

Fraser laughed too. 'I can't argue with that.'

Despite Fraser seeming relatively normal and quite friendly, Julian gave Coco the creeps. Not just the way he was talking, but as he moved, his dressing gown cord was loosening, and she worried it might fall away at any minute. Desperate to escape, she smiled tightly and gestured casually at the door behind her, signalling her need to get back to work. 'Do you need anything else?'

'I'd like you to pass on a message to the sommelier – who I'm not sure knows his arse from his elbow – and tell him the champagne isn't cold enough.'

Ingrid groaned and rolled her eyes, without looking up from her phone.

'This bottle is *warm*, and it won't do. Cristal should be served as cold as a prince's knob at his brother's wedding.'

'Don't be a prick.' Fraser looked at Coco. 'Ignore him. The champagne is delicious.'

'Was it even in a fridge?' Julian went on.

Coco thought back to the bar and recalled Andre getting it out of the fridge. 'Yes, but I'm sure he'll swap it for another bottle if you want.'

'From the same fridge?'

Coco had no idea. 'I guess so?'

Julian rolled his eyes. 'No point in swapping the bloody bottle then, is there? It'll have to do, but I'd have thought a sommelier at a joint like this should know better.' He flicked his hand a couple of times, dismissing her. 'Off you trot.'

Coco turned and made for the safety of the door. Fraser followed. 'The champagne's fine,' he said quietly as she stepped out of the room. 'I think he wanted to use the knob joke.'

Coco fought hard to keep from saying what she wanted to say, which was *He's a prick*.

'Top marks for keeping your cool. He'll be impressed. He likes people who can take a bit of banter.'

Coco nodded. 'I'll tell Andre to make sure the champagne is as cold as it can be.'

CHAPTER THIRTEEN

'You still see Rav?' Nick asked as we stood on the edge of the lawn.

'Gosh, no. I've not seen him since I left.' Hearing Rav's name was like finding an old photo, and brought forgotten memories of him – his smile, his kindness, his enthusiasm – flooding back. But then the horrors of the night of the rag dance swept the sunny stuff away. 'Do you?'

'We bumped into him a few years ago at a design show in London.'

'I didn't recognise him. He's incredibly good-looking now,' Cami said.

'Rav Rani?' Tilly interjected. 'Presumably he's cut his hair, then?'

'I quite liked his long hair,' Cami said.

Tilly wrinkled her nose.

'Anyway, yes. Hair cut, taller and slimmer. Looks like he runs marathons. Oh, and cheekbones you could cut paper on. Very successful. He designed the new British Arts building. He's married to the most glamorous woman I've ever seen. An architect too. Mina. They set up together. In fact, Rani & Rani was named one of the twenty most influential Asian businesses in the UK a few years ago.'

Hearing Cami talk about Rav stirred up an array of emotions. I'd often thought about him over the years. Would things have been different if I'd spent more time with him instead of latching on to Nick and the others? Rav had been there for me and I knew I hadn't been kind enough back. It wasn't a surprise he was now a success. He'd been head and shoulders above the rest of us. Naturally gifted. Hard-working. Top of the class from the start but never too busy or too self-involved to help. Our first project was to design a chair, and he had stepped in when it became obvious how useless I was at joinery.

'It's awful,' I'd moaned, as I regarded my rickety construction. 'A kids' TV presenter could do better with a cereal box and some sticky-backed plastic.'

'It's not awful. You're so creative. I love it.'

'It'll collapse as soon as somebody sits on it.'

'So let's make sure it doesn't.'

Rav spent two days patiently helping me. At the end of the second day, he'd told me he liked me. He'd looked at his hands, muttering the words, shifting his weight awkwardly like an embarrassed child.

'Oh,' I'd replied, glancing over at Nick, crossing my fingers that he hadn't heard. 'Right.'

'Can I take you for a coffee?' His voice was so quiet I could barely hear him.

'Just the two of us? With nobody else?' I'm not sure if I managed to conceal my feelings of shock. I had a feeling not, as he mumbled something unintelligible and scurried out of the studio.

Nick wandered over and ran his hands over the thrift-shop fabric I'd unholstered the seat with. 'This looks great.' I'd beamed, Rav's invitation forgotten.

How many chances of happiness had I thrown away by loving a man I couldn't have?

'God, I still remember your costume at the rag dance,' Tilly said. 'It was incredible!'

My heart skipped a beat. Had she forgotten what happened that night?

As if summoned by demons, Julian reappeared. My breathing grew shallow. Fear crept instantly over my skin once again. This was the man who'd lived in my nightmares for twenty-five years. The gall of him to act as if nothing happened. I searched his face, hoping to detect even a flicker of remorse or shame, but there was none.

'Why is my wedding full of these deathly dull people? How the hell can you moan for half an hour about a writers' strike? Thank *fuck* AI has come in to execute the shit ones. Don't tell the new Mrs Draper I said that.' He rolled his eyes. 'Jesus, look at your glasses. Where's the bloody staff?' He clicked his fingers at Coco, who was passing with a bottle of champagne. Before she affixed her radiant smile, a fleeting look of contempt passed over her face, and I warmed to her even more.

'More Cristal.' Julian pointed at our glasses. 'And make sure to keep this lot topped up, there's a good girl.'

My body tensed as I braced against the memory of his weight on me, the sound of his breathing, the smell of him.

Fraser smiled genially as Coco filled him up. Julian thrust his glass out. As she poured, her face a picture of concentration, he shifted his hand a few inches to one side so the first drops of champagne spilled onto the grass.

'Careful!' he barked.

She paused, lifting her head to stare at him, her eyes hard as rock. Then she reached out to hold his glass as she filled it.

Julian laughed. 'I like this one!'

Coco filled my glass, then Tilly's. I thanked her, but she didn't acknowledge it. I didn't blame her. If I were her, I'd think we were all a load of arseholes too. As she turned away, her mouth re-formed into a perfect glower, twisting her face into something beautifully grotesque. I decided there and then that my favourite of all human expressions was a teenage girl's scowl. If only I had my sketch pad with me. Drawing Coco would have been a joyful escape.

'Anyway, Ingrid's asked me to come and remind you we have to go and pose for that bloody photographer before we can eat,' Julian said to Fraser. 'The magazine's paid a million for the photos and she says we can't be drunk or they'll refuse to cough up.'

'Can I pay you two million to get out of it?'

Julian threw his head back and laughed. 'Only if you can face the wrath of Bridezilla.'

Fraser opened his eyes wide and shook his head with mock fear.

Julian looked at Giles and Nick with a sudden air of smug satisfaction. 'Speaking of which, what do you think of Mrs Draper two point zero?' He might as well have been asking them to admire his new Ferrari.

Tilly pushed him. 'Jesus, Julian. You really are a wanker.'

He laughed. 'You know I'm joking. I am – as the romantics might say – head over heels in love.'

'With yourself or Ingrid?' Fraser raised his eyebrows.

Julian roared with laughter.

Giles saw something over my shoulder then and exclaimed loudly in surprise. He waved a hand. 'Noah? God, Noah Buckley!'

Two men were striding towards the group. I didn't recognise either. One was grinning and opening his arms to hug Giles. He was tall, his Nordic blonde hair cut across his forehead in an extravagant sweep, his chiselled jaw reminiscent of a Disney prince. His trousers were too tight, or his thigh muscles too large; either way, he was like the Hulk, about to burst out of his clothes.

He seemed vaguely familiar. 'Who's Noah?' I asked Tilly.

'He was at university with us. He joined the group after you left. Always had a bit of a crush on Fraser, actually. A total rugby bore. Had a trial for England under twenty-ones or something like that, but fractured a couple of vertebrae when he got pissed on a yard of Long Island Iced Tea and jumped off a chairlift whilst skiing.'

Having said hello to Giles and Julian, Noah smiled at the rest of us. 'So good to see you all. This is my husband, Colm.' He reached for the hand of the man he'd walked over with, who was gentle-looking, with dark-framed glasses, blue eyes and sandy hair.

'Great to meet you,' Colm said, in a soft Irish accent. 'What a party, eh?'

Noah turned to me then. 'Hi,' he said. A peculiar look settled over his face, and a sense of awkwardness that contrasted with the jovial man who'd arrived. Presumably, like exhausted Arabella, he'd heard the stories.

I offered my hand. 'I don't think we've met. I left before the end of the first year.'

'Vix, we did know each other. Well, kind of.' He smiled. 'I actually owe you an apology, though I'm going to plead being led astray by Julian.' He glanced at Julian and shook his head. 'Honestly, I don't think I've ever behaved more badly with any other person in my life. Including my brother. Though maybe my mother wouldn't agree.'

For a moment or two I racked my brains trying to place Noah, but nothing came to me. We'd certainly never had a conversation and I had little interest in starting one now.

'Julian was a bad influence on all of us,' said Fraser.

I didn't want to stand there and have the past raked up so Noah could apologise for whatever he thought he'd done wrong. Whatever it was didn't matter now. The only people who should have to apologise were Julian and Cami. They were the ones who'd ruined my life.

'I've just remembered I … I have to … Excuse me …' I turned and quickly walked away, pushing through the guests as they laughed and shrieked and drained their glasses. The French windows into the hotel were blocked by Ingrid, her dress perfectly arranged to trail around her, flanked by a group of young and instantly recognisable Hollywood stars posing for a man with an oversized camera and a handlebar moustache. I switched direction and followed the path around the hotel, breathing out with a sigh of relief as I made it to the back of the building, finally out of sight of the reception, the noise of the gathered guests fading as if someone had turned the volume down. I walked left, between two tall yew hedges, hoping to find somewhere quiet and concealed where I could hide away. As I walked through the gap, I saw the waitress, Coco, leaning on a pile of upturned crates, vaping and scrolling her phone. It was hard to tell for sure, but it looked as if she might have been crying.

'Oh fuck. Sorry.' She jumped to her feet, hurriedly hiding her phone and vape behind her back, her face turning white with panic. 'The phone ... I'm ...'

I laughed. 'God, I don't care. Well done for smuggling it in.'

She tucked the phone into her pocket and started to walk away.

'Don't leave on my account.' I reached into my clutch and took out my cigarettes. 'I'm hiding too.' I noticed a bottle of champagne at her feet, a white napkin around its neck. 'Is there anything in that?'

She bent to pick it up and held it out towards me.

I took the bottle and tipped it to my lips. The bubbles erupted, spilling out of the top. I bent at the waist to avoid being soaked.

Coco laughed.

'Probably not the stuff to be drinking from the bottle.' I smiled at her. 'My name's Victoria.'

'I remember. You painted the portrait. I helped you hang it.'

I lit my cigarette and smiled at her. 'I'm sorry about Julian earlier. Did he upset you?'

She furrowed her brow.

'When he moved his glass?'

She made a face and waved my concern away. 'Dick move, but that shit doesn't bother me. It's his money he's wasting.'

I smiled.

She gestured at the champagne. 'You know that stuff is a thousand pounds a bottle? They've got, like, ten crates of it and each crate has twelve bottles in.' She whistled through her teeth.

Six thousand caricatures.

She shook her head. 'It's mental.'

I hesitated, drawing on my cigarette again. 'So,' I said carefully, 'if it wasn't Julian, did something else upset you?'

She looked at me blankly.

'You look like you've been crying.'

She shrugged. 'It's not him.' She took a puff on her vape. For a moment or two the air was filled with a white cloud of vanilla.

'Smells like ice cream.'

She held it out to me. 'Want to try?'

'Is it nice?'

'Better than that stuff.' She gestured at my cigarette with a flick of her fingers.

I trod the cigarette into the gravel and took the vape. It was smooth and as sweet as it smelt, like smoking candy floss.

'You can tell me if someone's being mean, by the way. I think they're all arseholes.'

She did a double-take.

I handed the vape back.

'It's not them. It's … God. No. It's silly.' She nodded her head in the direction of the party beyond the yew hedge. 'I'm supposed to talk to Ingrid Olsson, right? But she won't even look at me and I can't see how I'll get a chance.'

'Supposed to?'

'My mum got me this job so I could meet her, because she thinks Ingrid can make me a *star*.' She splayed her fingers and traced an arch with her hand.

'Oh, I see. I imagine Ingrid has a lot on her mind today. Maybe it isn't the best time to talk to her. Can't you tell your mum you tried but Ingrid was too busy?'

Coco made a face. 'Mum isn't really like that. She's one of those, you know, grab your chances and make your own luck kind of people.' She inhaled her vape and blew out vanilla. 'The world is your oyster, Coco,' she mimicked. 'You've got to *make* things happen. She'll be angry if I don't talk to her.'

'Could you pretend you've spoken to her?'

'The woman is a human lie detector. I swear to God. It's a gift or something.'

'Or maybe you're a bad liar?'

She shrugged. 'Anyway, me being famous is pretty much the only thing she wants.'

'Is that what *you* want?'

She took another puff on her vape. The cloying vanilla reminded me of the custard Mum used to make us for Sunday lunch before Dad left. Bird's from a tin. The starchy powder mixed to a bright yellow paste, stirred into sweet warm milk, then left to cool so a gelatinous skin formed.

I missed her custard.

'I don't know. Maybe?' Coco didn't sound convinced. 'All I do know is that Mum wants the best for me. She wants to have nice things and an easy life.' She tucked her vape into her pocket. 'I should get back to work or they'll start stressing.'

'You've a smudge of mascara.'

She lifted her finger to the eye I'd pointed at and scrubbed beneath. 'Gone?'

I shook my head. 'Want me to?'

She stepped closer and tilted her head back, and I gently worked at the mark with the pad of my thumb. 'There. All gone.'

She regarded me carefully, a hint of mistrust still clinging on. 'Thanks. You're definitely nicer than the rest of them in there.' Then her cheeks reddened. 'Sorry, I shouldn't have said that.'

'It's fine. I agree.' I was pleased to see her smile. 'Don't let them get to you, OK? If they do, come and find me and have a bitch.' I'd never been particularly maternal, but there was something about Coco, a sweet vulnerability hiding beneath the make-up and the womanly figure, that made me want to wrap her up and keep her safe. 'And keep snarling at Julian Draper. He deserves it.'

She laughed, and it was such a genuine, open sound I felt honoured, as if she'd unlocked a door to a private room and welcomed me in. 'Is he an ex?'

'Julian? Why do you ask that?' It was hard not to sound defensive.

'You hate him, so he's got to be an ex, right?'

I hesitated. 'Not an ex. Far from it, actually. But yes, I do hate him.'

'Dick moves?'

Dark memories snapped at me, and I nodded.

She stared at me, briefly searching for the story behind my nod, before giving up with a small shrug. 'I should get back or Darren'll be on my case.' She paused at the gap between the hedges. 'I like your dress.'

CHAPTER FOURTEEN

Late December 1999

'You're going back today?' Mum took another egg out of the carton and cracked it into the bowl. I'd told her I didn't want any breakfast, but she'd said she'd scramble some eggs anyway. When I arrived back from London she said I'd got scrawny, and she been trying to feed me ever since. 'Do you have to?'

'I said, remember? There's a New Year's Eve party.'

I'd dreaded coming home at the end of term. I knew it would be a quagmire of emotional blackmail and guilt, and it was as bad as I'd feared, if not worse. Mikey spent most of his time in his room, and if he did emerge, all he did was glower. Mum was fixated on making this 'a Christmas to remember', and strapped us to a manic Yuletide roller coaster of paper hats, charades and Quality Street, insisting the three of us gather around the tree singing carols from an A4 printout. By the time we got to 'In the Bleak Midwinter', I was ready to scream.

'But you can't leave today. It's still Christmas.' She beat the eggs with a fork so fast her hand blurred.

'It's the twenty-ninth.'

'The bit between Christmas and New Year is still family time. What will I do with the turkey? Especially with your brother turning vegetarian. Oh God,' she muttered, rubbing her forehead. 'There's shell in the eggs.'

'Pescatarian. He still eats fish fingers.'

She picked out a fragment of eggshell, then wiped her hands. 'It's a bloody nuisance. I've still got a kilo of leftover bird.'

'I could take some back to London?'

She sighed heavily. 'I'll put it in the freezer. I still don't understand why you have to go today.'

'We're going to help prepare for the party.'

'*Two days* to prepare for a party? I suppose things are different in *London*. And you with your accent and fancy new clothes.'

I didn't reply.

'I don't want to be alone on New Year's Eve.'

'You won't be alone.'

She scraped some butter from the dish into a saucepan on the hob. It sizzled as it hit the hot metal. 'You know full well Michael will be in his room and I'll be having beans on toast and a nine o'clock bedtime. Happy Millennium to me.' Her voice was quiet and faraway, muffled by a veil of sadness. She sniffed and fixed her gaze on our silver tinsel tree. It was the same one we'd always had and had seen much happier times. The four of us sitting around it opening presents, eating smoked salmon – 'because it's Christmas' – on brown bread with the crusts cut off, listening to our favourite *Classic Christmas Tunes* CD and singing along.

The smell of burnt butter hit my nose. Mum swore and grabbed the pan, slamming it into the sink then dropping her head, shoulders slumped.

I crept out of the kitchen to escape the cloying guilt. I couldn't wait to get back to Frederick Street. I'd lied to Mum. We weren't preparing for two days, but I needed to sort out my outfit and get ready. I wanted to look my best. Though it still made me cringe, the now infamous incident with Neil Gilbert seemed to have made me more interesting to the others. They noticed me. Engaged me in conversation. People who'd never given me a second look now approached me as if I were a strange creature they'd discovered under a lifted rock. If they referenced what happened, their comments were laced with a mixture of disbelief, admiration and amusement, and though reliving it was excruciating, I'd be lying if I said I didn't enjoy the attention.

When Fraser invited me to his New Year's Eve party, I finally felt like one of them. I'd never been invited to a party before, so the affirmation that I was truly part of the group meant everything.

'They sound like wankers,' Mikey had said when I told him about them.

'Well they're not.' His dismissive contempt punched me in the gut. I wanted him to be impressed by them and by what I was doing. I think there was a part of me that wanted him to be a little bit jealous. 'And they're way more cool than anybody *you* know.'

'Everybody *I* know is a cunt.'

Kew was nothing like central London. It was green and peaceful, sparkling clean, as if somebody had run over the streets with a vacuum. Fraser's house was a magnificent red-brick mansion with five floors, elegant sash windows, and a gleaming black door with a polished brass doorknob. It fronted on to a green across which wandered smartly dressed people, some walking miniature dogs in tiny coats.

'It's *huge*.' I was unable to keep the awe from my voice as I stood on the pavement and stared up at the house.

Nick jogged up the stone steps and rang the doorbell.

Fraser answered with a big smile. 'Well, happy bloody New Year, my friends! Come in, come in.'

We walked through the front door into a hallway with black and white tiles, white walls, a towering pot plant in a shiny black pot, and a chandelier the size of a small car. Everywhere I looked were striking bits of antique furniture and sumptuous sofas, sculptures, art and expensive-looking rugs.

'There's no way Mum would let me have a party if we lived here,' I said.

'My parents are pretty cool. But they're in Barbados, so they won't even know.'

'Is his dad a prince or something?' I whispered to Nick as we followed Fraser through to the expansive kitchen.

Nick laughed. 'Plastic surgeon to the stars. Fraser's mum comes from an old banking family. They're loaded. How do you think he affords all that camera kit?'

Cami squeezed between us and passed her arm through Nick's. 'I'm so glad you're finally here,' she crooned. 'I've missed you *so* much.'

I was careful to hide my irritation. How did she not drive him mad? She was so clingy, always pawing him, talking to him in that annoying sing-song voice.

In the kitchen, Tilly and Julian were mixing vodka and strawberry jelly, flirting and mucking about as they drank from the bottle and danced to the Charlatans.

'To the party kings and queens!' Julian cried as he offered around shots of unset vodka jelly.

That evening, we ate pizza, smoked spliffs and watched a pirate copy of *The Talented Mr Ripley* in a windowless room off the kitchen. The walls were painted deep red and hung with an array of electric guitars and framed photographs of famous rock stars, signatures scrawled across their sweaty faces in thick black marker pen.

'Dickie reminds me of you,' Cami whispered to Nick, as Jude Law lit up the screen.

'If Nick's Dickie, which one of us is Tom?' Tilly exchanged a look with Cami, and both of them smothered a laugh.

I was sleeping in a small bedroom on my own on the third floor. Cami and Nick were in the room next to mine. Tilly was sharing with Freya, a friend of hers who studied history at Cambridge.

Freya had no interest in me, but buzzed around Cami, laughing and cooing at everything she said. Julian and Giles had a room one floor below next to Fraser.

Whilst I was getting ready for bed, I could hear muffled voices from Nick and Cami's room. I pressed my ear to the wall ineffectually, desperate to know what they were talking about. As I was drifting off, I heard different noises. It took me a moment to realise it was them having sex. I listened to her crying out quietly, the rhythmic rock of the bed, him moaning. Tears welled in my eyes. I stared at the ceiling, praying they would stop.

They finally fell quiet, but I couldn't get the image of them out of my head. It ate me up from the inside out. Giving in to it, I slipped my hand inside my pyjama bottoms and thought of Nick fucking me instead.

We got up late, past midday, and gathered around the expansive kitchen table. Cami made bacon sandwiches for everybody and refused to let anyone help.

'Honestly, I *love* cooking. You lot chill. I'll shout if I need a hand.' Nick came up behind her as she was laying bacon on a tray and kissed her neck. She giggled and kissed him back. She was wearing thin cotton shorts and a camisole top, no bra, bare feet, her toenails painted a soft pink. Her skin was make-up-free, her loose hair tousled, but rather than looking as if she'd just got out of bed, she looked relaxed and sexy, as if she'd had a day on the beach. She padded about the kitchen without a care in the world, not a self-conscious cell in her perfect body, as she effortlessly rustled up breakfast. There was no way I was sitting around in my tired old pyjamas, so I'd dressed in jeans and a sweater before I came down. I needed a shower, but was too shy to ask Fraser for a towel.

'Oh *fuck*,' Fraser exclaimed. 'I totally forgot. Did you hear about Neil Gilbert?'

My body tensed at the mention of his name.

'What about him?' Cami picked up her mug of black coffee.

'His wife called the police on him. Last week. Said he got violent after they had a row about, you know …' he paused for a moment, 'what happened. With Vix.'

Heat radiated up from my chest to my cheeks as I shrank into my chair.

'How do you know that?' Nick asked.

'Robbie.'

'Robbie knows shit,' Nick scoffed, shaking his head.

'No, seriously, he's shagging one of the women in admissions who's friends with Gilbert's wife. Or maybe a friend of the wife's friend.' Fraser shook his hand, as if trying to wave Nick's scepticism away so he could finish the story. 'Whatever. She knew about it and told Robbie.'

'Interesting pillow talk,' said Julian, sniggering. 'How old is this bird?'

'Does that matter?'

'I'm interested—'

Nick interrupted them. 'I bet Robbie's not even shagging her. Or anybody, for that matter. It's bullshit. I mean, how would anybody know—'

'Shut up! Let me finish. There's more.'

I thought about slipping away, sneaking upstairs to hide. Just the mention of Neil Gilbert made me queasy.

'The police knock on his door. Wife answers. They ask to speak to him. And according to Robbie' – Fraser took a swig of his coffee – 'the guy freaks the fuck out and runs upstairs. Wife's screaming. Kids are screaming. The police find him in his study, tearing his computer off his desk and chucking it at the wall.'

'Why did he throw his computer at the wall?' Cami asked.

'Holy *shit*!' Julian snorted with laughter. 'His hard drive?'

Fraser clapped and pointed a finger at him. 'Exactly, my friend.

Turns out our award-winning plastics and concrete tutor with a penchant for breasts has some pretty interesting pictures stashed away.'

'Jesus,' Nick whispered.

Bile burnt the back of my throat.

'What were the pictures?' Cami's face was twisted with disgust.

Fraser shrugged. 'No idea, but bad enough to make the wife pack up and leave with the children.'

'Grim.' Tilly shuddered. Then she turned to me. 'Thank *God* you did what you did, Vix. If you hadn't, the bastard might still be at it and nobody would know.'

'Did they arrest him?' Nick's face was ashen.

My mind drifted to thoughts of his wife and children and the pain they would be in. I thought of my mum, of Mikey and me, the nightmare of living in a town obsessed with our father's shame.

'You OK?' It was Nick. He put a hand on my arm and smiled.

I shrugged, pulling my knees up to my chest and resting my chin on them. 'I feel bad for his family. And it's because of me.'

'God, Vix, you did them a favour.' Tilly spoke with no hint of sympathy. 'You probably saved his children from their abuser.'

Cami nodded. 'If I was his wife, I'd want to know. Wouldn't you?'

I wasn't sure I agreed. Having seen what public humiliation had done to my mother, I reckoned she would disagree as well.

'Seriously, don't sweat it. He deserves what he gets. If he was into bad shit, he should rot in prison.'

'Enough about that twat,' Julian said. 'I'm going for a fag if anybody wants to join.'

Fraser nodded and got up to follow him. 'Thanks for breakfast,' he said, and squeezed Cami's shoulder as he passed. She smiled at him and gave his hand a stroke.

Neil Gilbert was forgotten.

'Right,' Fraser said. 'All hands on deck. Four hours to get this place ready for a party.'

Freya and Tilly hung strings of fairy lights. Julian and Giles moved furniture and set up the speakers. Cami and Fraser unpacked boxes of wine and set the bottles out on the worktop in the kitchen alongside mixers and spirits.

'Can you go to the garage and grab the large grey plastic bin?' Fraser asked Nick. 'We need to empty the ice bags into it – there are five or six in the chest freezer – then put the lagers in to get cold.'

'I'll help,' I said. 'Sounds like a two-person job.'

I followed Nick through the kitchen and into the garage. There was a navy car, like something out of a Bond film, not a speck of dust on its gleaming bodywork.

'Wow,' I breathed.

'De-wrinkling Hollywood royalty is clearly a licence to print money. Apparently they jet in from all over to see him. Right ...' he scanned the garage, 'grey bin ...'

'There!' I pointed at it, a touch too triumphantly. 'Shall I get the ice?' I lifted the top of the chest freezer and reached in for a couple of bags. Nick came up beside me, so close we were touching. When he leant in to grab another few bags, I could smell him, his hair, his deodorant, a musky fragrance that made my body twitch.

'I never said thank you for what you did in the pub,' I said. My heart hammered. I'd wanted to talk to him about it since it happened, but the timing never seemed right.

'The pub?' He closed the lid of the freezer and looked at me.

'When that guy said that thing about me?'

'Oh, yeah. My head was all over the place. He pissed me off.'

'Well, it was really nice of you.'

He laughed. 'I'm not sure about that.' He hesitated. 'Look, are you OK? About Gilbert?'

'I guess. It feels weird. Like it's my fault. If I hadn't—'

'Listen.' Nick put down the ice and placed his hands on my shoulders. 'You didn't put that shit on his computer. *He* did.'

By eight p.m., the house was heaving with people, music was pumping and alcohol was flowing. The party poppers Fraser had bought for midnight had already been popped, and their rainbow spaghetti innards scattered the immaculate house along with empties, mud from the garden and discarded coats. My mother would have been horrified.

'Where are the bin bags?' I asked Fraser, shouting to be heard above the music.

He laughed. 'Fuck bin bags! Just enjoy yourself. We'll deal with the mess tomorrow.'

Julian strode up to me and whistled. 'You look great,' he said. '*Love* the dress.'

I blushed. I'd found it on the sale rail in Top Shop. It was short, tight and black. I'd dithered about buying it, and nearly hadn't worn it. Julian's comment made me happy I had.

'Party time, boys and girls,' Fraser said, waggling his eyebrows with a mischievous grin. Julian rubbed his hands together, and as they walked through the kitchen, Fraser beckoned at Cami and Nick to follow. Cami made a grab for Tilly.

'Where are we going?' Tilly said, as we passed two boys I didn't recognise tipping spirits into a saucepan and scooping the cocktail out with mugs.

Cami giggled.

Fraser led us to the room with the guitars and closed the door. He reached into his pocket and pulled out a plastic pot of pills, which he shook like a maraca. 'Benzos, baby!'

'How we love Daddy's medicine cabinet!' Julian laughed.

'And let's not forget the prescription pad lying on his desk,' Fraser said. 'Having a doctor in the family has a lot of perks.'

Everybody but me and Cami held their palms out. Even Nick. Fraser deposited a white pill into each of their hands as if he was doling out sweets. Cami stuck her tongue out and stared suggestively at him. He grinned and placed the pill on the tip of her tongue.

'Vix?'

Everybody was looking at me. 'I'm not sure.'

'They're fine,' Fraser said. 'My mother takes one every morning with a double espresso and half a grapefruit.'

'You don't have to,' Nick said.

I shook my head. 'Sorry. It's—'

'Not your thing?' Tilly said, then shared a look with Cami.

'I've done drugs. At home. Everybody in Manchester does drugs. It's no big deal.'

But nobody cared. They were laughing, piling out of the room, forming a group, backs to me as they danced, reaching for each other's hands and singing along to the music. I stood in the doorway and watched them, the outsider looking in.

'Hi,' said a voice. There was a girl standing next to me. She tipped her head close and spoke loudly over the music. 'How do you know Fraser?'

'I'm at college with him,' I shouted back.

She nodded. 'Cool.' Then stared at me, waiting for me to speak. 'What about you?'

She smiled. 'We met in Barbados. When we were six. Do you know the Royal Westmoreland?'

I shook my head. The silence between us turned awkward. 'Did you go to a private school?' I asked, dredging my brain for conversation.

'Excuse me?'

'Did you go to a school that costs money?'

She stared at me as if I was talking in tongues, then pointed at something vaguely. 'I've just seen a friend.' She moved away before I could say anything else.

Nick and Cami stopped dancing and walked over to a couple of boys, back-slapping, kissing, laughing and launching into animated chat. I took a breath and headed towards them. As I joined them, Cami glared at me, then grabbed Nick's hand, winding her fingers through his, watching me as she did. 'Come upstairs?' She tipped her head coquettishly to one side, her thumb stroking the inside of his wrist as if he was made of the softest velvet.

My skin flushed with heat as I caught his reply, soft and raspy. 'Yeah.'

Cami giggled and walked backwards, eyes sultry with lust and alcohol and pills, pulling him with her, glancing at me and smiling with smug unkindness.

I picked up two vodka shots from the table and knocked both back.

Tilly ran into the kitchen screeching. Fraser and a group of boys roared and started chanting. Giles was kissing a girl. She was sitting on the kitchen worktop, legs around him, a bottle of beer casually held in her hand as they devoured each other. Everything grew loud and intense. The noise and heat mixed with alcohol and jealousy made my head spin. Though I was surrounded by people, I'd never felt so alone and out of place, a stranger in a hostile land.

I made for the guitar room and pushed open the door. As I walked in, I saw Julian. He was sitting on the edge of the sofa, leaning over a line of white powder on the low table. I tried to back out, but it was too late. He'd seen me.

'Sorry,' I said. 'I'll leave.'

'You want some?' He gestured at the table.

I shook my head. 'I just came in for a bit of quiet.' I pointed back towards the door and the noise of the party beyond. 'But I'll leave you to it.'

He put a finger over one nostril, then snorted the line, sat back and sniffed loudly, shaking his hands out theatrically. 'Stay for a bit, if you like.' He reached for a large bottle of cola. 'That cocktail they made is rank. I found some Coke to have with my coke.' He drank, then passed the bottle to me.

The sugary sweetness was like nectar. 'Thanks,' I said, taking another swig.

There was a brief lull in the music between tracks. The next one to come thumping in from the kitchen was 'Missing', by Everything But the Girl. 'Oh, I love this song,' I said, the words slipping out before I realised I'd said them aloud.

'Dance, then.'

'Sorry?'

'If you love the song, dance. I don't mind.'

I shook my head and smiled. 'I don't dance.'

'Everybody dances.' He laughed as he fell back against the sofa and rubbed his face. 'I'm too fucked to do anything. But you could dance and I can watch.'

'No, I can't …'

'You look fucking hot tonight.'

I stopped dead. Heat flashed over me. I stared at him. Was he teasing me? I'd never been called hot before. I had no idea what to say. Maybe I should—

'Shit, you have *incredible* tits.'

My heart stopped.

'When you got them out for us – fuck *me* – that made me rock hard.' His eyes locked onto my chest, stripping me naked.

He pushed himself up from the sofa and came towards me. 'Can I touch them?' His eyes glazed over.

I wanted to say, No, *fuck off, keep your hands to yourself, you arsehole.* But would that make him angry? Would he say bad things about me to Nick? Was I supposed to be flattered by this? Before I had a chance to say anything, he grabbed my left breast, kneading it like dough, squeezing so hard it hurt.

'Don't,' I stammered. I stepped backwards, but he moved with me, kneading harder, his other hand grasping my right breast.

'Oh Jesus,' he rasped. 'These are seriously great tits.'

'Let go!' I pushed his hands off me.

'Hey,' he crooned. 'Don't be like that.'

'You're hurting me.'

'Take the dress off.'

'Please …'

'I want to see them again.'

Tears welled in my eyes. I felt dirty and grubby. The music and laughter was white noise in my ears. I thought of Nick and Cami, oblivious upstairs.

Julian made another grab for me. At last I found some strength and shoved him with force. 'Get *off* me!'

He laughed and held up his hands as if I were pointing a gun at him. 'OK, OK, I get it. I'm high as fuck. I misread the signs.'

'There weren't any signs.'

At that moment, a couple barged into the room.

'Oh shit,' the boy said when he saw us. 'Sorry, mate. You guys getting busy?'

Julian laughed. 'Not really. I was hoping Vix might give me a show.'

'A show?' The boy looked momentarily confused, then light dawned on his face. 'You're the one from Fraser's course?' He grinned. 'The one who stripped?'

'Slut,' muttered the girl.

I'd died and gone to hell.

Then another girl – Lottie, who I knew vaguely from evenings out – sauntered in. She stopped abruptly, and I watched as her brain whirred to make sense of the scene. 'What's going on?' She was petite and blonde, like a china doll.

'Julian was about to have a private show.'

The first girl giggled.

'Jesus, Julian. I was only gone ten minutes.'

'You're not jealous, are you?' He laughed.

Lottie looked me up and down and made a face. 'As *if*.'

Heat rose over the back of my neck. And then to make everything a thousand times worse, Tilly appeared, flanked by Cami and Nick, Cami's hair mussed up, Nick's shirt untucked.

The atmosphere in the room was palpable, and I watched Nick's face fall. 'What's up?'

Lottie crossed her arms and set her mouth. 'Julian's a two-timing prick is what's up.'

I shook my head. 'It's not like that.'

'Come on, let's go get a drink.' Cami's voice was slurred, drunk and high, as she pulled on Nick's arm.

Nick ignored her. 'Julian?'

'It's nothing.' Julian sniffed and wiped his nose. 'Everything's fine.'

'She was going to strip for him.' The boy spoke with salacious glee.

Tilly's eyes shot wide and she glanced at Cami.

'I wasn't!' I cried. 'I would never—'

Nick's eyes flashed with thunder. 'For *fuck's* sake, Julian.' He turned to me, his voice softening. 'Are you OK?'

'She's fine. Nothing happened.' Julian sounded cross. 'We were mucking about. Why the fuck are you so uptight anyway?'

'I'm not uptight.'

Cami rolled her eyes. 'Jesus, Julian said they were mucking about, and it's not like she doesn't have form.'

'What?' Cami's comment pierced me.

'Oh, don't look so offended. What do you expect? You *stripped* in class.'

'She did that for you!' Nick cried out.

I wanted to run into his arms and beg him to take us back to Frederick Street for Marmite toast and tea.

Cami stifled a bitter laugh. 'For *me*?'

My voice failed me as a clamp closed around my throat and tears began to roll down my hot, embarrassed cheeks. An image of Gilbert tumbled into my thoughts. His erection pushing against his trousers, his eyes fixed on Cami's chest. Then me, breasts bared, everybody staring as shock and whispers filled the air. I swiped at the tears. I didn't want to cry in front of them.

'She didn't do it for me. She did it for attention, and it worked, didn't it? I mean, she got Julian's attention.' Cami crossed her arms. 'And yours.'

'Cami, stop it. This—'

'No, *you* stop it. You talk like she's some kind of folk hero. She didn't find a cure for cancer. She didn't bring world peace. All she did was take her clothes off in front of everybody and now she's crying because Julian got the wrong end of the stick?' Cami's words flew out in an angry, drunken torrent.

'Why are you being such a *bitch*?'

There was a stunned silence.

Cami stared at Nick, eyes blinking, mouth aghast.

My heart thumped and I swallowed.

Her eyes narrowed to hard slits. 'You know what? Fuck you, Nick. You want to take her side? Then *fuck* you. In fact, if you like her and think I'm such a *bitch*, why don't you get it together? See if I care.' She snapped her head around and glared at me as if I was something nasty on the sole of her shoe. 'There you go. You've got him.'

Nick opened his mouth as if to speak, but before he could, I pushed through them and ran, out of the room, through the dancing crowd in the kitchen and into the hallway. I yanked open the door and ran down the steps and onto the green.

Nick's voice called to me from the house. I slowed to a walk, but kept going, wiping away fresh tears. I couldn't face him. I couldn't bear to. Hot shame scorched my skin.

He caught up with me and grabbed my wrist. I snatched my arm away, throwing both hands up to cover my face.

'I'm so sorry. That was awful. All of it. I can't believe Julian. And Cami … They're drunk and high on those pills, and … God, I know that's no excuse. But Cami didn't mean it. I promise. I don't know why she said that stuff.' He sighed heavily, then growled with quiet frustration. 'I'm so ashamed of them.'

'It's fine,' I muttered, lowering my hands. I kicked the grass with the toe of my shoe and wiped my face.

'I think they might also be arseholes.' He paused. 'Jesus. Am I an arsehole too?'

I laughed through my tears. 'Maybe?'

He took hold of me, his hands on my upper arms. 'Cami isn't like that usually. I don't know why she kicked off. Maybe she was embarrassed?'

'*Embarrassed?* Why would she be embarrassed?'

'When I said you did it for her, I saw her face. It was as if I'd accused her of not standing up for herself. She hates the idea of being weak. But what she said … what Julian did …'

'Forget it,' I whispered.

'You should have lamped him.'

I laughed again. 'If I did that, he'd hate me.'

'So?'

I hesitated, unsure if I should give my thoughts a voice. 'If Julian hates me, and Cami hates me, then Tilly and Fraser will too. And Giles. And then—' I stopped myself saying anything more.

'And then what?' He smiled.

'And then I'd have to stop being friends with you, and … I couldn't cope with that—'

He laughed and interrupted me. 'Don't be daft. I'm not friends with you because they like you. I'm friends with you because *I* like you. I don't care what they think.'

'But Cami said—'

'Cami will be fine. She's drunk. She knows you and I are friends.'

'That's what we are?' Every part of me willed him to tell me he loved me.

'Friends? Of course. Honestly, you idiot, you're awesome and I love being friends with you. Let's go back and sort things out. We can't see a new millennium in by fighting.'

I wanted to curl up on the ground and stay there until I froze to death.

He took my hand. 'Come on, let's get inside.'

'I can't go back.'

'Of course you can.'

'I'm going to get my stuff and head to the station.'

'Now? There won't be any trains.'

'I'll walk, then.'

'The streets will be full of drunk people. What if you get raped or murdered?'

'Then everybody will have something else to gossip about instead of my breasts.' I tried to smile, but it fell flat.

'Come back to the party.'

'I can't.'

'You'll be fine. You're with me. Let's find Cami and sort things out.'

I shook my head. Didn't he realise that Cami and I would never sort things out? I would hate her for eternity. Just as she hated me.

But, of course, I let him lead me back to the house.

Julian and Lottie were in the hallway, kissing, her skirt pushed up around her thighs, his hand inside her knickers. The sight of them made me want to vomit.

'You seen Cami?' Nick said to Tilly.

Tilly shook her head, eyes unfocused.

'I'll check our room.'

He took the stairs two at a time, and I stood staring at a bookshelf, pretending to read the titles of the books, until he returned a few minutes later and shook his head. I followed him through the kitchen, watching him scan the faces. Then he opened the door to the guitar room. Cami and Fraser were on the sofa. His arms were around her. As we came in, they pulled apart quickly. Cami jumped up, smoothing her hands over her hair.

'What the fuck?' Nick said.

Fraser stood up. 'It's not what it looks like.'

'No? What the fuck is it then?'

'Nothing.' Cami's voice was higher-pitched than usual. 'I was … I was upset …'

'Jesus Christ,' Nick said under his breath as he turned to leave.

Fraser grabbed his arm, but Nick shook him off.

'Don't go! Nothing happened,' Cami pleaded, sounding every bit as guilty as I knew she was.

'Because I came in!' Nick shouted. He rounded on Fraser. 'How dare you?'

'Nothing happened.'

'But you want it to, don't you? I know how much you like her. You told me at the beginning of the year. I see you looking at her. All the fucking time!'

Fraser shook his head. 'She's your girlfriend, not mine. She was upset and I was comforting her. As a *friend*.'

The guilt was written all over Cami. I'd known it all along. It was all I could do to stop myself punching the air with vindication. At last Nick would see her for what she was. A two-faced, heartless cow.

'How is this any different to you and Vix?' Fraser said then.

Horror skewered me. What? Why was Fraser bringing me into this?

'Vix likes you. You know that. But you still went to check she was all right. And – presumably – nothing happened, yeah?'

Nick opened his mouth, but then hesitated. He was wrong-footed. I wanted to run to him and throw my arms around him, tell him not to doubt himself, that his instinct was right, Cami and Fraser had been doing things behind his back. I glanced at Cami, who was staring at me with pure loathing.

Outside the room, the New Year countdown began.

'Nothing happened,' Cami said again, stepping towards Nick, her voice quieter now, faint and childlike. She reached out and put her hand on his cheek. 'I love you, OK? I love *you*.' She had started to cry, deceitful tears coursing down her face. 'You have to believe me.'

Nick shook his head, then his whole demeanour softened and, as the house erupted in cheering and fireworks exploded outside, he took her face in both hands and kissed her tenderly, while Fraser and I looked on, his expression of broken-hearted rejection mirroring my own.

CHAPTER FIFTEEN

27 July 2024

A gong rang out over the reception lawn and Celeste stepped onto the podium. She'd ditched the clipboard and walkie-talkie but none of her tightly wound efficiency. 'Dinner is served. Please now make your way to the ballroom. We have a lot of people to seat, so do be patient with us.'

I hovered at the French windows, staring into the panelled room at the galaxy of starry guests, now well lubricated with Julian's champagne. The rumble of voices – the chatter and laughter, exclaiming, kissing, whooping and squealing – was overwhelming. The room shimmered with silk and organza, sea-greens and sea-blues, silver, diamonds, gold, beaded headpieces, translucent slips that revealed too much, unnaturally white teeth beaming out of smooth, tanned faces. The atmosphere was charged with success and back-slapping confidence – *we are the players, the winners, the beautiful people* – reminding me of those London evenings behind the VIP ropes at Rayaana.

The circular tables were set for twelve and each one was named after a famous beach. I'd heard of four – Bondi, Copacabana, Santa Monica and Cap d'Antibes – but none of the others. We were on Spiaggia Grande, which – I learnt later – was in Positano in Italy and was where Julian had proposed to Ingrid. Each table was set with an abundance of ivory candles, flowers in clusters of silver vases, starched napkins with monogrammed napkin rings. In the centre of each gold-rimmed dinner plate was a pearlescent oyster shell with our names written on them in hand-painted calligraphy. Nestled beside each oyster shell was a muslin bag. While everybody else talked, I picked up my bag and untied the silver string. Inside was a pearl on a silver chain. Colm made a noise of appreciation and reached for his. He tipped it up and a pair of pearl cufflinks fell into his hand.

'I know the designer who refurbished this place,' Tilly said as she sat down.

Cami moved the muslin bag off her plate without looking inside and reached for the bottle of water to fill her glass and those either side of her.

'Awful woman, but it's an incestuous industry, so as far as everybody else in London is concerned, we're interior design's very best BFFs.'

I'd hoped I'd be seated next to Nick, but I wasn't; exhausted Arabella and Tilly had that pleasure. But I was next to Fraser, which was preferable to Giles, as I was pretty sure neither of us would have a clue what to say to the other. On my other side was a man I didn't recognise. 'Andrew,' he said, beaming as he offered his hand in greeting. He wore a gold signet ring with a lion's head pressed into it. 'Jolly nice to meet you.'

'Vix, how lovely.' Fraser smiled as he took his place. 'We've a lot to catch up on. Twenty-five years is a lifetime.'

Another gong sounded and a man in a black tailcoat and white tie stood to the side of the platform and the hideous thrones, the curtain concealing the portrait behind. 'Please stand for your bride and groom!' Celeste made a hand gesture. The man nodded, then turned in the direction of the doors to his left.

Some people stood, though not everybody. Those who did craned their necks for a glimpse of the couple; those who didn't carried on chatting, pouring drinks, giggling.

'Could this be any more tacky?' Tilly made no effort to keep her volume down. 'I think the woman might be stark raving mad. I suppose most of these Hollywood types are.'

Simon gave her a hard stare and put his finger to his lips.

'What?' Tilly smiled. 'I'm not saying anything that isn't in the pages of the dreaded *Daily Mail*.'

Julian and Ingrid walked in hand in hand and climbed the steps onto the stage as if ascending to collect an award. They stopped in front of their thrones and kissed. When they separated, Ingrid smiled, one hip jutted out, head tipped, a red-carpet pose, and everybody clapped. Then the couple moved to their thrones at either end of the table and Celeste handed Julian a microphone.

'Welcome!' His voice boomed out of the speakers surrounding us. 'Well, haven't you scrubbed up well? It's like you all do it professionally.' A titter of self-congratulatory laughter rippled around the room. 'Ingrid and I have decided to go against tradition and get the speeches out of the way now. This way I can get riotously drunk and not make a fool of myself.' He smiled at Ingrid, who dropped her eyes coyly on cue. 'My beautiful wife, Mrs Draper the second ...'

Ingrid made a face of comedic shock and the guests laughed again. As I stared at him, a sheen of sweat coating his face, bloated with conceit, these obsequious people applauding jokes that weren't funny, my hatred congealed to a solid mass inside me. I took my eyes off Julian and instinctively found Nick. He was listening to the speech. Smiling. Leaning back in his chair. The fingers of one hand caressing the rim of his wine glass. I dropped my gaze.

'... this one is certainly an improvement on the last. So far at least ...'

What would happen if I stood up now and told everybody what he was really like? Would the brainless hulks at the door blow me to bits with their badly concealed guns? Would I manage to get the words out before I was bundled out of the room? I held onto my chair to stop myself moving.

'… Banter aside, I want to thank this beautiful woman. I might finally have found the one human being who can keep me in check. Ingrid, darling, I love you with all of my heart.'

Heart? What heart? All Julian Draper had in his chest was a hard black stone.

'Now, before I hand over – with trepidation, I'll admit – to Fraser, I'd like to thank him for inviting me to his birthday party and letting me swipe Ingrid from under his nose. I'm sorry, but on this occasion, clearly the best man didn't win. I did.' Then he pulled a black box from his jacket pocket. 'For my love.' He handed the box to Celeste, who walked it to the other side of the table and passed it to Ingrid. 'Almost as beautiful,' Julian said. 'But not nearly as expensive.'

Ingrid opened the box and gave another show of shock as she removed what was within. Even from our table towards the back of the room I could see how gigantic the diamonds were. She threw a kiss to him, then dabbed beneath her eyes with a bent finger, before beckoning him to her. He handed the microphone to Celeste, then walked over to his new wife and fastened the bracelet around her wrist, where it sat like a string of ice cubes. Then he kissed her again and returned to his throne, lifting a hand to the crowd, who obliged with a round of applause.

Celeste passed the microphone to Ingrid. She stood and sent a smile around the room. 'Well, what can I say? I'm the luckiest girl in the world.'

I bit down on my lip and gripped my chair harder.

'And to remind you of this, I have my own gift.' She turned to face the curtain, then nodded at Celeste, who stood poised with a hand on the golden rope. Celeste tugged and the curtain fell away to reveal the painting.

Oohs and aahs filled the room, then everybody cheered and clapped.

'I love it!' shouted Julian. 'Now I don't need Google to remind me what you look like!'

Ingrid looked out across the room, hand over her eyes, searching the tables. 'Thanks go to award-winning artist Victoria Fisher for painting it. She's based in France and is one of the most exciting up-and-coming painters in Europe. One day this will be worth millions, which will please Julian no end, I know.'

I flushed with heat as the roomful of people turned in my direction, muttering, asking their neighbours, 'Which one is she?'

Fraser stood and faced me, holding his hands out towards me and clapping. The room followed with muted applause. I wanted the floor to open up and swallow me whole.

I glanced at Nick. His face was alight. 'Well done,' he mouthed.

'And now,' Ingrid said, 'tradition dictates that my husband be roasted by his oldest friend.'

Fraser laughed and nodded and waited for Flick, who trotted over with another microphone.

'Enough of the oldest, thank you, Ingrid,' he said with a laugh. 'Now, contrary to expectation, I'm not going to roast Julian. The tabloids and keyboard warriors do that for our enjoyment on a daily basis. I'm also going to keep this mercilessly brief as I'm keen to crack on and get wildly drunk. What I do want to say is that Ingrid Olsson, who I've known for ten years now, since she was a seventeen-year-old firework in the making, might well be one of the most talented and beautiful actresses in the world, also happens to be one of the worst judges of character I've ever come across, and it appears dear Julian has very much benefited from this tremendous flaw.' Everybody laughed. 'Please raise your glasses and join me in wishing the happy couple congratulations and a long life together. And best of luck, Ingrid. You'll bloody need it!'

The room erupted with good wishes and clinking glasses. Ingrid laughed, then walked across to Julian and kissed him. My stomach heaved.

Andrew put his glass down, then turned in his chair. 'Stunning painting! I'm looking forward to a closer inspection after the meal.'

He beamed and leant forward for a bottle of wine. 'I understand you're another Queen's student? I did law at Cambridge for my sins but was at school with Julian. This is my wife, Esme.'

The woman next to him smiled. She was rosy-cheeked with a mousy bob, wearing a white silk kaftan. 'I can't believe I'm here!' she squealed.

I raised my eyebrows and reached for my glass. 'Me neither.'

'Well, I'm just a housewife while you're a famous artist. You fit in far better than me.'

I cleared my throat to conceal a stifled laugh.

'Ingrid said you're based in France? You didn't happen to train at the École des Beaux-Arts in Paris after QSA, did you?' Andrew asked. 'I had a girlfriend – Kinny – who studied there.'

The echo of 'What school did you go to?' made my skin itch. 'No, I left QSA after one year, then hitchhiked to Marseille and scratched a living drawing caricatures for tourists whilst constantly on the brink of being homeless.' Though the homeless bit wasn't true, I enjoyed watching Andrew's face fall.

'Really? You mean on the streets?' The touch of revulsion turned me sour. Were any of them aware of what lay beyond their ivory towers? I ignored his question.

Esme rested a hand on his knee, perhaps a gesture of comfort, perhaps control. 'By caricatures, do you mean cartoons of people?'

I nodded and refilled my glass.

'How did you get into that?' Andrew had managed to regain his composure.

'I fell into it. I met a girl in Marseille, Nicole, she said it was easy cash. She taught me.'

'Is she a famous artist now as well?' Esme smiled.

'She's dead.' I reached for my wine. 'An overdose.'

Andrew and Esme exchanged a look.

'You say it was easy cash,' Andrew said, ploughing on admirably. 'Was there much demand?'

'Sure. Honeymooners mostly.' I thought of my spot on the strip and the way I would lure couples in. Smile. Give a compliment to the young wife. Tell the sex-drunk husband he needed a memento of this beautiful evening. Offer a seat in front of the easel. Another compliment. Draw her in sweeping black lines, magnifying her beauty. Never ridicule. If it were him on the stool, a little ridicule was expected, guaranteed to make his wife laugh and beg to buy it. But as smartphones took hold, demand for caricatures declined. They belonged to a different time, when people cared less about being laughed at.

'Were you good?'

'Good enough.'

'Do me!' he said then, exploding with laughter, any residual discomfort vanished.

'A caricature?'

He nodded enthusiastically.

'Now?' I shook my head. 'I don't have any paper or anything to draw with.'

Andrew reached into his pocket and pulled out a pen, then took the ivory card the menu was written on and turned it over, lying it flat on the table, banging the pen down on top.

'I can't,' I said. 'Honestly, I need—'

'One quick sketch?'

'Oh *do*,' Esme said. 'And don't be kind.'

I looked over at Nick, who smiled, amused, then gave a conspiratorial why-not shrug. I picked up the pen.

Despite his wife's instruction, I wasn't unkind. I could have expanded his forehead to epic proportions and deepened his jowls, made his piggy eyes rounder and smaller, but I didn't. It took me a few minutes, and as I worked, I was aware of Nick watching. It had to be good. I wanted to impress him.

When I'd finished, Andrew clapped. 'Bloody *brilliant*! Seriously good. I'm framing this!' He tucked the drawing into his jacket. 'Maybe I've the next Michelangelo in my pocket.'

'You really don't,' I said. Then a movement caught my eye. Cami pushing Fraser's hand off her knee below the table. She stared at him, gave an imperceptible shake of her head, then a glance at Nick, who was now talking to Arabella.

Cami excused herself from the table. Fraser watched her go. Noah said something to him. Fraser laughed and nodded but was distracted. Then he stood, dropping his napkin on the table, and followed her. I thought of them at his Millennium Eve party, the way they'd jumped apart when Nick and I disturbed them.

'I might just nip to the ladies' before the food arrives.' I vaguely directed my sentence at Andrew, but he didn't hear me, too focused on Esme, who was excitedly pointing out celebrities.

Fraser and Cami had stopped to talk halfway down the corridor. Cami was agitated. Fraser's body language appeared relaxed, as if reassuring her. Fraser caught sight of me and smiled. Cami followed his gaze and when she saw who it was, drew in a breath then lifted her chin and walked back towards the ballroom, eyes fixed ahead as she strode past. Without Nick around, there wasn't even a pretence of friendship.

'All good?' I asked Fraser.

'Of course. Great wedding, isn't it?'

'Is Cami OK? She looked annoyed.' My heart thumped in my chest. I willed him to confirm my suspicions.

'Annoyed?' He laughed. 'A little. She thinks I was mean to Julian in my speech. But hey, what did everybody expect?' He grinned, but I could see the lie in his eyes.

I forced a smile. 'You let him off easily.'

He laughed. 'True. But I'm not a total arsehole and it's supposed to be a happy day.' Then he gestured in the direction of the ballroom. 'See you back at the table?'

The first course was waiting when I returned. I wrinkled my nose. According to the menu it was scallop ceviche on charred brioche with fermented lemons and a kimchi foam, but what sat on the plate was a gelatinous slop on burnt bread with a dollop of dirty spume. I loathed shellfish, salty and slimy, with the looming threat of food poisoning. I picked at the edge of the brioche whilst the others shovelled the marinated scallops into their mouths, washing them down with copious amounts of wine as they laughed and talked. The only other person who wasn't tucking in was Cami. Of course she didn't eat. Nobody could keep that slim and eat actual food. I imagined she lived on celery and tissue paper.

The ceviche was followed by flash-fried venison, barely cooked and bloody. It was tender and soft, but I was too tense to swallow, and in the end I laid my cutlery together and pushed my plate away, the juices swilling around the fine bone china. As more wine was consumed, the table grew louder and more animated. Every now and then I'd steal glances at Nick. He seemed uncomfortable, looking at Cami, obviously having noticed her mood as well. Despite him mouthing, 'Are you sure you're OK?' a couple of times, she did nothing to reassure him, just sat there in stony silence, resolutely ignoring everybody.

'Good evening, all!' The voice cut through me. I looked up from my bloody plate to see Julian pulling up a chair and squeezing himself between Cami and Fraser. 'Hope you're having fun?' Words of appreciation flooded the air. He filled his glass with wine, then raised it. 'To my dearest friends. What stories we have, eh? I'm hoping most stay safely buried today.'

I bet you want them to stay buried, you fuck.

He settled in, holding court like some medieval gout-ridden king, knocking back wine, mopping up venison blood from Fraser's plate with a torn-off corner of sourdough, braying loudly with his mouth full. When he tried to pour more wine and found the bottle empty, he turned in his chair and aggressively clicked his fingers at Coco as she passed.

'Wine,' he barked.

'Yes, sir,' she said, a superficial smile only thinly masking her glower. 'I'll be right back.'

'Chop-chop.'

As Julian drained the last of his glass, I stared at the knife on my plate and wondered how easy it would be to drive it into him.

Coco reappeared with two bottles, one red and one white.

'You look like a dancer,' Julian said as she put them down in front of him.

'Sorry?'

'Are you a dancer?' He enunciated his words as if he thought she were stupid.

'A dancer?' She furrowed her brow in confusion.

'Dancing? You know? Moving around to music on stage.'

'On stage? A bit. I won a couple of competitions when I was young, but mostly I act—'

'A couple of *competitions*?' Julian laughed and leant back in his chair. Then an idea apparently came to him. He reached into his gold-thread jacket and out came his wallet.

'For God's sake, behave, Julian. Why are you carrying a bloody wallet on your wedding day?' Fraser tried to grab it, but Julian snatched it out of his reach, then laughed as he opened it. He pulled out a note – a pink fifty – and held it between forefinger and thumb, smiling at Coco. A few guests on the tables nearest ours had stopped talking, their attention grabbed by what was unfolding.

'How about a little pre-pudding entertainment?'

Coco's eyes stretched wide with horror.

'Leave the poor girl alone.' Fraser smiled at her. 'Ignore him. He can't hold his drink.'

Nick and Cami also started to intervene. But rather than backing off, Julian ignored everybody and pulled a second fifty-pound note out of his wallet. 'Come on,' he cajoled, waving the money in front of Coco. 'A hundred pounds for one dance?'

'Jesus,' I whispered under my breath. 'She's trying to do her job—'

I was interrupted by Ingrid, who sashayed up to our table and rested both hands on Julian's shoulders. 'Julian?' she said. 'What are you up to?' She squeezed his shoulders, her fingers digging into him, and looked at Fraser for her answer.

Everybody else had fallen quiet.

'All under control,' Fraser said.

'Apparently this young lady has won competitions for dancing, darling. You're always looking for new talent to champion,' Julian said, winking at Coco. 'We talked about entertainment during dinner; well, isn't this a marvellous coincidence? A trained dancer right here.'

Coco shook her head vigorously. 'I'm not trained. I don't want to dance.'

'Of course you don't have to dance.' Ingrid laughed then, ruffling Julian's hair. This defused the tension, allowing Coco to visibly relax. Julian gave a sad shrug and made a show of tucking his money back into his wallet. 'The fun police have spoken. Perhaps later.' He tapped his glass. 'For now, just some wine.'

Coco filled his glass, eyes smarting with tears, cheeks burning. I dug my nails into the table, forming eight little moon shapes in the cloth. I felt her pain as if it were my own all over again.

As soon as his glass was filled, she bolted from the table, making a beeline for the door. I jumped up and went after her. 'Coco?' I called as I followed her through it.

'I'm fine,' she said. 'Honestly.' She pressed the sleeves of her shirt against her eyes, smearing the cotton with smudges of mascara and orange foundation. 'You were right about him being a prick.' She shook her head and looked up at the ceiling. 'The worst thing, though? Mum will be cross that I didn't dance. She'll say that was my moment to shine. Was I wrong to say no?'

'Are you serious? *No.* Absolutely not. He humiliated you. I know how that feels.' I hesitated, then reached out and rubbed her arm. 'Do you think you should talk to your mum and tell her how you really feel? I'm sure she'll understand.'

Coco's eyes fired. 'What are you talking about? You don't know anything about her. Or me. Just mind your own business, yeah?' The hard teenage scowl that had so endeared itself to me a few hours before was back. As she turned her anger on me, I realised how much she reminded me of Mikey, and the weight of responsibility – heavy with tragedy – bore down on my shoulders with a desperate urge to protect her.

The door to the dining hall opened and with it a blast of hubbub from the guests on the other side. It was Fraser. 'I want to apologise for him. He's drunk and got carried away. I think he thought it was all a bit of fun, but he misfired. Are you OK?'

Coco nodded and sniffed, her glower darkening.

'I think I heard you say you act?'

She hesitated, then gave another nod.

'And you want to do it for a career?'

She shrugged.

'I understand. Look, I don't know if you know, but I'm Ingrid's agent, and to make up for Julian's behaviour in there, if you'd like a few tips on getting a foot in the door, I'd be happy to chat to you.'

'For real?' Coco's face lit up like the Christmas lights on Regent Street.

'The least I can do.' Fraser smiled kindly. 'Grab me after dinner.'

'Thank you!' Coco beamed at him, then at me, before running down the corridor and through the door into the kitchen.

'That's kind of you,' I said. 'It'll mean a lot. I think her mother's quite pushy.'

'All the mothers are pushy.'

'Fraser?'

'Yes?'

'Why do you always make excuses for him?'

'Excuses?'

'For Julian. He didn't get carried away. He's always like that.'

'Not always.'

I took a breath and closed my mouth. There was no point in arguing. Fraser was Julian's best friend and would always have his back. I wasn't going to change that, no matter what questions I asked.

'It's good to see you, Vix. I'm sorry we lost contact. I always liked you. In fact, I'd go so far as to say I had a crush on you.' Then he flashed me a different kind of smile. Was he flirting? 'Are you with someone?'

I shook my head.

'Surprising. I always imagined you'd be snapped up.' He stared at me then, eyes boring into mine. 'You were always very desirable. We all thought that.'

There was something odd about the way he was speaking to me. It wasn't flirting. It was darker. Something underneath his words. The way he looked at me made me feel vulnerable and exposed.

Then it hit me. Julian and Fraser were best friends. They always had been.

Oh my God.

Fraser *knew*.

He knew what Julian had done to me.

CHAPTER SIXTEEN

Mid-January 2000

Nick went up to the studio ahead of me. My shelf in the fridge at Mrs Drummond's was empty and I hadn't had breakfast. Things between Cami and me had been openly difficult since Fraser's New Year's Eve party, the string that held us together, ensuring we remained civil, on the point of snapping.

I'd hoped that after the party, when they discussed what had happened, she'd confess her feelings for Fraser, and Nick would find himself free from her perfect pink talons and realise what he felt for me. But this wasn't the case. It was like none of it had ever happened. Cami and Nick were still together. Nick and Fraser were still friends. Nobody said anything to Julian about what he'd done. At points I wondered if it had all been a drunken hallucination and maybe I'd lost my mind.

I bought a Coke and a flapjack, then ran up the stairs to make it in time for class. When I pushed through the doors, the atmosphere hit me like I'd run into a wall. Nobody spoke. A couple of people were crying. There were lots of drawn, pale faces, mouths open in shock. There was no sign of Julie Rainer and no evidence of anybody thinking about work. As I walked in, attention gradually focused on me, everybody staring, a few whispers, a few people dropping their eyes. Nick had his arms around Cami, her head buried in his chest, his expression tight with concern.

'What is it?' I mouthed.

He said something to Cami, then walked over to me.

'What's happened?' I whispered.

He glanced back at Cami, who was being comforted by Tilly, before returning his attention to me with a heavy frown.

'Nick?'

'It's Neil Gilbert.'

'What about him?'

'He's … Christ … Look, he's … he's dead, Vix.'

'*Dead?* How?'

Nick hesitated, then shook his head, his kind eyes hooded with regret. 'He killed himself.'

It took a while for his words to sink in, and when they did, a wave of nausea swept through me. 'Oh my God,' I breathed. The studio began to spin. The heat of everybody staring burnt into me. I focused on Nick, reached for his hand, held onto him as if he were a life raft. 'How?'

'He threw himself in front of a Tube at White City.'

Julie Rainer walked in, ashen-faced, her eyes puffy and red from crying, and stood solemnly in front of us. Without her usual lightness and enthusiasm, she was a different person. She looked around the room, and when her eyes landed on me, she held my gaze for a moment.

Was that blame in her eyes?

She took a minute or so to compose herself, then cleared her throat. 'In light of today's tragic news, we've decided to close the department for the rest of the morning. You're welcome to use any part of the building, but there'll be no staffing until after lunch. If you need to take the day to be with your thoughts, the teaching faculty understand. The … the, er …' her voice cracked, 'welfare officer is on duty if any of you need support at this time.'

A loud sob came from Cami. Tilly put her arm around her and the two of them walked out of the studio. My horror thickened.

Students fell into groups. Some hugged. More began to cry. The grief was catching. Were these the same students who only days before had been daubing breasts on the whiteboard and calling him Gilpervert behind his back?

'I'm going to take Cami back to her halls,' Nick said. 'She's too upset to be alone.'

'Because of Gilbert?'

He nodded.

'But why?'

'Why what?'

'Why is she so upset?'

Nick appeared confused. 'Because of what he's done?'

'But she hates him. She was always bitching about him. She thought he was a creep.'

'Come on, Vix. You know it's not that straightforward. She didn't want him staring at her, but nobody – Cami included – wanted him to kill himself.'

I didn't say anything.

'She thinks it's her fault.'

'Her fault he killed himself?'

He nodded.

And then the realisation dawned on me that if Cami – and Nick and the others – thought it could be her fault, then it stood to reason that really they all believed it was mine. It was *me* who'd escalated it. *Me* who'd taken my top off. *Me* who'd told the vice chancellor about Neil Gilbert's erection. If I'd sat there silently and left him to do whatever he was doing, then he'd still be alive. That was what they all thought. That was the blame in Julie Rainer's eyes.

I followed Nick out of the studio and down the stairs and out to the courtyard garden at the back of the building. Cami was huddled on a bench, sobbing, as Tilly rhythmically stroked her back. When Nick approached, he and Tilly exchanged a look of mutual concern. He sat down and Cami threw herself into his arms. A small crowd gathered around the bench, everyone murmuring sympathetically.

I stared at the scene with bitter disbelief. Cami had managed to do what she always did and insert herself into the centre of the story. The whole mess was a prime-time drama with her in the leading role. I wanted to scream.

'It's not your fault,' I heard Tilly soothe. 'You can't blame yourself.'

Then she looked up, directly at me. It's not Cami's fault, her eyes said.

It's *yours*.

Guilt grew like mould. Neil Gilbert consumed my thoughts. His expression when I'd stood up to him, the way he'd marched up to me, rage written all over his face. Had he known then that the police would find his computer and uncover his perversions? Had he known he'd inevitably lose his family and face public humiliation? Had he known as he led me to the vice chancellor's office that he'd have no other choice but to end his life at White City Tube station? I had no idea what was on his hard drive, or what horrors lurked in his closet, but I knew it was my stunt that had set this sorry mess in motion. I might as well have pushed him in front of that train myself.

I turned and went back through the doors, through the foyer and out onto the street. Tears blurred my vision as I walked. London traffic hummed around me. Buildings loomed tall. The smell of pollution made me dizzy. I felt as if I was shrinking, smaller and smaller, an insignificant speck of nothing in this monstrous city. I leant back against a wall, sliding down until I was sitting, and covered my face with my hands. As I breathed slowly and deeply, I recalled my mother's slack-jawed shock when the police knocked on our door and marched my father away.

'What on earth for?' she'd cried. 'You've got the wrong man.

He's done nothing wrong!' Then she turned to my father, her voice a feeble whisper. 'What did you *do*?'

But my father said nothing. He walked out with the police, silent, staring straight ahead.

It was the lawyer who told her about the money he'd stolen from the charities. After the phone call, she'd sat in the kitchen, mouth ajar, eyes wide and unblinking. 'What will people *say*?'

I don't know how long I'd sat on the pavement before Nick said my name. I opened my eyes and looked up. He was crouching in front of me, his hand resting on my knee. I saw his face and burst into tears. He put his arms around me and rested his chin on my head, and I cried. He didn't hurry me; he held me, stroking my back, until gradually I ran out of tears.

'What makes someone do that?' I whispered, wiping my eyes on my sleeve, when he finally let go of me.

Nick stood and stared upwards, then shook his head and looked back down at me with a slight shrug. 'I don't know, but I reckon there must have been some proper evil stuff on his computer, and everybody knows what happens to sex offenders in prison. Better dead, I guess?'

He held out a hand. I took hold of it, my skin crackling where it met his. He pulled me up. My body had stiffened in the cold.

'Want to go back to Frederick Street?'

I nodded.

'Come on, I'll walk you.'

'What about Cami?'

'Tilly's with her. I'll go back in a bit.'

He looped an arm around my shoulders, and as we walked, I pressed myself close to him so the warmth of his body seeped into mine.

'Do you think it's my fault?' I asked him as we waited at the pedestrian crossing.

'Jesus, no. It's nobody's fault but his. He made that decision.'

We crossed the road into Brunswick Square. The noise of traffic faded as we walked through the park, the leafless winter trees and the Georgian buildings behind, our footsteps echoing slightly on the cold tarmac path, which glistened with winter dampness.

Nick stopped and bent for something on the edge of the path. When he stood, he was holding a small stone, snow white, between forefinger and thumb.

'It's almost perfectly round,' he said. 'It was right there, lying on the path, as if someone had put it there for us. Surely that's a sign?'

'A sign? Of what?'

'My grandmother used to say white pebbles were lucky. She'd say God left it for us.' He held it out for me to take. It was hard and cold. I stroked my finger over its smoothness. There wasn't a blemish on it. I passed it back to him.

'Do you believe in God?' I asked.

'Believe? I don't know. I mean, I don't go to church – apart from Midnight Mass but we're usually hammered – and I don't believe in virgin births and Jesus coming back from the dead, but there has to be something, don't you think? Something bigger than us.' He smiled and shrugged slightly, then tossed the stone in the air and caught it. 'It feels a bit bleak to have nothing to believe in. What about you?'

'When I was little. But then Dad went—' I managed to stop myself mentioning prison. 'I prayed and asked God to make Mum smile and stop my brother being so angry, but they both got worse, so I guess, if there is a God, He isn't interested in me.'

Nick held the white pebble out towards me. 'Keep it. For luck.'

'Really?'

He smiled.

As my hand closed around the stone, everything inside me inflated. It was like he'd given me a part of himself. We walked the rest of the way in contented silence, the smooth white pebble now warm in my hand, as if not just good luck but love too was radiating out of it.

As we turned onto Frederick Street, my smile was impossible to contain. Nick got his key out of his pocket. I stood close to him, resting my forehead on his shoulder as he opened the door.

'Nick?'

I turned to see Cami on the pavement, huddled in her coat and scarf, her face stormy.

No, no, not now. Go away. Leave us alone. I squeezed the pebble hard in my hand, but it didn't feel warm now. 'Hi,' I said. 'I thought you were with Tilly?'

She didn't reply, but looked at Nick, her cheeks wet with tears, her nose red from the cold. 'We need to talk.' She looked at me then, eyes mean and icy. 'Alone. If that's all right with you?'

My cheeks flared. 'I'm going inside anyway.'

'I honestly don't give a shit what you do.'

'Cami—'

She rolled her eyes and lifted a hand to stop him. 'Leave it, Nick. Our tutor fucking killed himself. I'm not in the mood to be kind right now.'

A vivid image of Neil Gilbert lying mashed up on the tracks at White City barrelled into my thoughts, a bloody mess smearing the front of the Tube, his glasses smashed to smithereens beside him.

'You'll be OK?' Nick said to me.

'For fuck's sake! She's not a child.' Cami wrapped her arms around herself and turned on her heel, marching back down towards the end of the road.

'I hope things are all right.' Then I thought of the pebble. I held it out to him and smiled. 'Here, have it for luck.'

He nodded, rubbing the stone, then slipped it into his pocket.

*

I sat on my bed, waiting, drumming my fingers to ease my worry as I listened for footsteps, the door, his voice, anything that would tell me he was home. It wasn't until six o'clock that I finally heard him on the stairs. I jumped up and opened my door, ready to sprint down to his room, but he was already climbing the flight up to mine.

My heart lurched when I saw him. He was in a terrible state, unable to focus, hair in disarray, swaying, blinking slowly, reeking of alcohol.

'What's happened?' I asked.

'Cami and I ... Jesus, I can't even ... Cami and I. We're ... we're over.' His words poured out in a drunken slur. 'It's over.'

I tried to keep my voice level and my excitement hidden. '*What?* Are you sure?'

His face was twisted in anguish. He was chewing his lip. His eyes wavered left and right as if searching for something. 'She ... er ... she thinks something's going on with us. You and me. She was so upset. I've never seen her like that.' He raked his hands against his scalp so hard I thought he might gouge himself. 'But there isn't anything going on. I told her that. I told her ...'

Was now the time to say that Cami was right? That she could see the truth; that – *yes* – there *was* something going on with us.

'She didn't believe me.' He winced and banged his head with the heel of his hand. 'She said she can see it.'

My pulse had gone crazy. I wanted to reach out and pull him close, kiss him over and over, tell him everything was all right and I'd look after him. 'What did you say?'

'I said she was wrong, but she kept saying she knows what she can see. Everybody can see it. Tilly, Fraser, everybody.' He began to sob, shaking his head, wincing as if in pain. 'She ... she wouldn't ... listen.'

I took a deep breath. 'Do you think,' I said quietly, 'she might be right?'

His face registered confusion. 'About what?'

'About us.' I pictured Liberty and her bare-chested bravery, forging onwards as she clambered over the pile of corpses. 'Because I think she might be. I feel something. And I think you do too. Maybe she's just seeing the truth.'

'No, no.' He shook his head, his body swaying. 'You and me are … are friends. I don't feel … that way.'

I laid the flat of my hand on his cheek. 'Are you sure?'

He pulled away from me. His eyes blinked slowly and finally focused on me, his brow furrowing slightly.

Emboldened, I stepped closer, stood on tiptoe and gently, very gently, I kissed him.

He drew back, stumbling a little. 'I can't. Cami—'

'But it's over. You said so. And … Nick, nobody needs to know. It's only us here. I won't tell anybody. Maybe she's right. Maybe there is something.'

I kissed him again, and this time he gave in a fraction. With my other hand I took hold of his and brought it to my breast. Again he resisted, but only for a few seconds. I kissed him again and again, little butterfly kisses on his lips and cheeks.

'I love you,' I whispered. I pulled him into my room and pushed the door closed. 'I love you so much.'

There was a final moment of hesitation before he leant down and pressed his lips to mine, and as he kissed me, he released a sob of relief.

He was gone when I woke the next morning.

I would have been disappointed if I wasn't so elated. I lay in bed and hugged myself, smiling like a lunatic, every part of me buzzing. Sex with Nick had been better than I'd dreamed of. It was every love song and sonnet ever written all in one night. A couple of times he'd cried, and I'd kissed his cheeks, licking the salty tears from his skin. 'It's OK,' I'd whispered. 'I'm here now.' And he'd kissed me harder.

I dressed and brushed my hair and teeth. I put some lip balm on, my fingers lingering on my mouth, remembering him kissing me. I grinned and reached for my mascara and applied a little, then ruffled my hair for that post-sex, beach-babe look. Skipping down to the kitchenette, I made two mugs of tea and a plate of toast, then stood outside his room, my tummy a riot of joyful butterflies.

'Hey,' I said through the door. 'It's me.'

There was no answer.

I put the plate and mugs on the floor and knocked lightly.

Still no reply.

'Nick?' I opened the door. 'Are you awake?'

He wasn't in his room.

Everything was still. The bed made. Curtains open. No sign of him.

It was Saturday, so there were no lectures or formal studio time, but maybe he'd headed to the department to work on his bridge. They were due to be weight-tested on Monday and he was miles off finishing.

'Yes,' I whispered. 'That's where he'll be.'

I walked to Bedford Square briskly, pushing open the main door and running up the stairs. I could hear the radio, and my heart leapt, but when I opened the doors, it was only Rav in the studio. He was carefully glueing a toothpick to his bridge.

'Hey, Vix.' He put his glue gun down and smiled brightly. 'You here to work?'

'I thought Nick might be here.'

Rav turned the radio down. 'I've not seen him and I've been here since eight.'

It was hard to contain my disappointment. 'If he shows up, can you say I'm looking for him?'

'Sure. Have you called his mobile?'

'Oh. I don't have one. And I don't know his number anyway.'

'Borrow mine?'

As he rummaged in his bag for his phone, I stared at his bridge. It was a breathtaking structure, two sweeping curves crossing in the middle, connected by a latticework of gardener's twine and an intricate toothpick buttressing system. It was in a different league to everybody else's. 'Jesus, Rav. This is incredible.'

'Thanks,' he said brightly as he handed me his phone. 'That's his number. Press the green button.'

I did as he said, but it went straight to a recorded message. *Leave a message. Or, you know, don't.* Hearing Nick's voice made my heart skip.

'Hi. It's me.' I turned away and shielded my mouth. 'Not sure where you are. Hope you're OK.' I wanted to say more, but with Rav there it felt awkward. 'Bye then.' I handed the phone back. 'Can you write his number down for me?'

Rav scrawled Nick's number on a corner of paper he tore from his sketch pad. I clutched it as if it were a lifeline, willing Nick to call back and ask to speak to me. But the phone stayed silent.

I walked the streets, scanning left and right, popping into any cafés and pubs I passed, desperate for a glimpse of him. As I searched, my worry multiplied. I had to find him. I kept reminding myself what an amazing night we'd had and that there was bound to be a logical reason for him vanishing. Back at Frederick Street, I waited in his room, sitting on the edge of his bed, picking at my nails, eyes bolted to the door. At seven o'clock, I couldn't take it any more, and knocked on Mrs Drummond's door. The television fell quiet, then I heard her footsteps.

'Everything all right, Victoria?'

'Sorry. Yes, I'm fine. It's … well, I haven't seen Nick today. I've checked everywhere. I'm a bit worried.'

'Oh bless you. Don't worry. I saw him early this morning. He's gone home for a few days.'

'Home?' Why would he have gone home without saying anything? 'Did he say why?'

'Obviously everybody is terribly shocked about Mr Gilbert. Goodness, what a business. His poor wife. I imagine Nicholas needs some space to process it all. At times like this it can help to be with Mum.'

I hadn't even thought to call my mother after the news about Gilbert.

I rang Nick's mobile from the payphone a few times, but it kept going to his recorded message.

'Please, Nick? Please call me.'

That night I slept in his bed, wrapping myself up in his musty duvet. I needed to feel held by him, to smell him, and I wanted to know the second he got back. He didn't return that night and he was gone the whole of the next day too. I called his phone every hour. Each time I got his voice telling me to leave a message. Fear dissolved my insides as if I'd swallowed sulphuric acid.

By the early evening I couldn't bear it any more, and in desperation I jogged over to Fraser's halls.

He seemed surprised to see me. 'Vix? Jesus. Are you OK? You look ... well, you look a bit rough, to be honest.'

'Do you know when Nick will be back?'

'Oh, right. I'm not exactly sure. They went to his parents' for the weekend.'

'They?'

'He and Cami.'

'*Cami?*' I shook my head. 'No, they've split up.'

'Not any more,' he said, with a rueful shrug. 'Didn't even last twenty-four hours apart. They're like Romeo and Juliet—' He stopped himself. 'Are you sure you're OK? You're looking pretty pale.'

'I'm ... I'm fine. Yeah. No. I'm fine.'

'Do you need to sit down? Come in if you like. Have a beer? Or I've got some wine?'

I shook my head. 'No, I ... I need to ...' As I turned and walked away, my head swam, the corridor floor listing like the deck of a ship. Fraser had to be mistaken. There was no way Nick and Cami were back together. Not after the night he and I had spent together. The way he'd touched me. The way he'd become overwhelmed with love and cried when he kissed me.

Back at Frederick Street, the house was silent. I trudged up the stairs and opened the door to his room, sat down on the floor and pulled my knees into my body.

An hour or so later, I heard the front door.

I stood up and held my breath, listening to the footsteps. 'Please be you,' I whispered. 'Please. Please be you.'

When he opened the door and saw me, he jumped with surprise. 'Fuck, Vix. What are you doing in here?'

'Where were you?'

He dropped his gaze.

'Nick?'

At last he lifted his head and stared at me. His eyes were hard and glassy. His fists clenched at his sides. 'You can't be in my room.'

'Tell me it isn't true? About you and Cami?' My voice cracked as I forced her name through my lips.

'Vix, please—'

'Is it? Fraser said she went home with you. But he's lying, isn't he? He must be.'

Nick was silent.

'How could you?' I whispered. 'After what happened …'

'What happened was wrong.'

'*Wrong?* No! No, it wasn't *wrong!*' I spat each word out like a dart.

He said nothing.

Tears sprang to my eyes and I looked up at the ceiling. 'What happens with us now?'

'There is no *us.*'

'But the other night. When we … I … Oh God. I …' I clutched my stomach as it cramped in pain. 'I don't understand.'

He paused, hesitating. 'I'm sorry,' he whispered. 'I really am. It shouldn't have happened. I was all over the place. Upset and drunk.' He shook his head. 'None of this is an excuse for hurting you. I shouldn't have let it happen.'

My world was crumbling. 'But it was special.'

'I want to make it work with Cami. And ... Look – shit, this is hard – there's something else. You and I ...' His voice tailed off.

'You and I what?'

'We can't be friends any more.'

Everything around me melted.

'Cami can't handle it. If I want to be with her, we can't be friends. It's her or you.'

'And you ... you chose her?'

'I love her.'

I shook my head, tears rolling down my face.

'I realised that when we ... It's only ever been her.'

'Don't ... do this,' I said through my racking sobs. 'Please, Nick. Don't. You're ... making a mistake. What we have is ... is special.'

'I'm sorry, Vix. But you need to go.'

CHAPTER SEVENTEEN

Coco

Have you spoken to Ingrid??? Whats happening? Tell me!

Coco hesitated. Maybe she could do what that woman – Victoria, was it? – had suggested and lie, but there was no way her mum would fall for it. She'd keep probing and Coco would slip up. No. She'd stick to the truth but keep it brief.

Not yet but her agent said hed talk to me

A split second after she pressed send, she saw her mum was typing a reply.

Her AGENT??? Omg! Show him your reel!!!! U got to. He wont mind its his job to find new stars. Yr doin him a favour!!!

That was a lot of exclamation marks. Coco swore under her breath. If it wasn't for the fact that she'd already worked ten hours and wanted her money, she'd have got the hell out of there. Though maybe ditching the wages was a better idea. She could head up to Stack Point and watch the sunset on her rock, wave at the French girl across the sea, maybe see the basking shark again.

From her spot outside the back of the kitchens, concealed from view behind the refrigeration truck, she could hear them all inside, those glossy stars, laughing and crowing, knocking back wine like water in a desert. She thought of Victoria then. Awkward and jittery, a million miles out of her comfort zone, that thunderous look on her face when Julian got his wallet out. She took a drag on her vape. How could a man so old and gross fancy himself that much? He was delusional. Just a bloated prick who thought he was so much better than everybody else.

Another text arrived.

Call me!!!!

Coco rolled her eyes, dipped back around the corner, hiding herself behind a thick rhododendron bush, and dialled her mum's number.

'Oh my God, oh my *God*. It's too exciting. Tell me *everything!*' Debbie's voice was staccato with excitement.

'I can't,' Coco whispered. 'I'm supposed to be working and I'm not allowed my phone. I'll talk to you later.'

'Give me a taster.'

'There's nothing to tell.'

'What's she like? Ingrid. And her dress? Who's there?'

'I need to go.'

'Her agent, though. I mean. Her actual agent! Smile at him, yes?'

Coco rolled her eyes. 'Mum, this is a *wedding*. They're all busy. I might not even get to talk to him.'

There was silence from the other end of the phone.

'Mum?'

'Please, love,' she said. 'Don't muck this up.'

Coco didn't say anything.

'Talk to the agent. Show him your reel. You're a pretty girl, and pretty gets you far in life.' Her mum laughed. Did that mean she was joking? 'Use those feminine charms of yours. Be nice. To the agent, to Ingrid, her husband. To all of them.'

Coco recalled the way Ingrid's vile husband had pushed his grubby money into her face, and shuddered.

Her mother squealed then, as if she'd suddenly been branded with a hot iron. 'You know what? When this agent sees your reel, I wouldn't be surprised if he signs you on the spot! Oh Coco, baby. I *knew* you could do it.'

'He's not going to sign me tonight.'

'Get rid of that negativity right now. He doesn't have to sign you tonight. Ask for his business card. We'll follow it up with an email on Monday. All you need is a way in.'

You mean, all you need is a way in. Coco sighed. It didn't matter. Her mum was trying to help. She had to keep reminding herself that. It would be fine. She'd talk to the agent. Get a couple of useless tips. Her mother would email him on Monday and get no reply. Done and dusted.

'Yeah, OK.'

'My beautiful girl.'

'I should get back to work before Darren notices.'

'Love you, baby.'

'Love you too.'

'Right,' the woman with the clipboard was saying as Coco walked back into the kitchen. 'They're about to cut the cake.'

'Fucking cake,' Gina whispered under her breath.

The 'cake' was like no cake Coco had ever seen. It was a six-foot tower of choux buns draped in hardened caramel and decorated with thousands of edible flowers.

'Took us over eight hours to make,' Gina said to her. 'You know there are two thousand and forty-four choux buns on that monstrosity? Each of them filled with hand-made *crème pâtissière*. Jesus, what a faff.'

'It's a masterpiece,' said the clipboard lady without any hint in her voice that she actually believed her own words.

Andre was giving the waiters and waitresses bottles of cognac, which they were to take out with a tray of brandy glasses for each table. 'Quick tasting notes,' he said. 'This is Courvoisier Mizunara cognac. Aged in French oak to develop its flavour. Transferred to a cask made from a species of oak tree called Japanese mizunara. Exciting, exquisite, and the same price per bottle as a holiday to Tenerife for a family of four. Don't spill any, and for God's sake don't drop the trays. Put one bottle on each table and a brandy glass at each place setting.'

The lady tapped her clipboard. 'We need staff out there to take portions of the *croque-en-bouche* to the tables. After that we'll be moving people back out to the marquee for the entertainment. I know rumours are flying about as to who the singer is, but we'll be keeping this under wraps until the moment he – or she – appears. Whatever happens, whoever it is, you all need to maintain your professionalism. Poker faces, people. Poker faces.'

'She means don't cream your pants when you see Harry Styles strut out,' Fred whispered to Gina.

Gina giggled and the clipboard lady glared at them.

Holding her breath, Coco carried her tray of cognac and glasses to Copacabana. Everybody was up on their feet watching Ingrid and Julian, who were on the platform in front of their obscenely decorated table, on which had been placed the skyscraper cake. They moved together to the caramel-cloaked mountain, clasping an enormous sword, his arms encircling her from behind. Screeching with laughter, they pushed the sword through the caramel, which splintered like glass. The structure wobbled and they both made faces of mock panic. The room gasped as three sticky balls broke free and tumbled to the floor. Ingrid laughed and reached up to stick her finger into the creamy inside that had been revealed, then dabbed it on Julian's puffy nose.

Gross, thought Coco, as the arsehole wiped his nose with his own finger then offered it to her to lick. Grosser than gross. Thankfully Ingrid agreed with Coco and pushed his hand away.

Coco turned and noticed Ingrid's agent, Fraser, taking his seat at Spiaggia Grande with a couple of others, including Victoria, who sat staring at nothing, mouth set, hand tapping the table as if agitated. He'd said he'd chat to her after dinner, but not given a time. Maybe he'd forgotten? She heard her mum's voice loud and clear: 'Coco, baby, you've got to *hustle*.'

Once laden with small plates of pretty cake, the caramel and cream oozing onto the white china, she walked up to the table. 'Wedding cake?' She smiled the widest and brightest smile she could muster.

Victoria gave her the briefest of looks and a quiet thank you.

'Can I get you anything else?' Coco asked after she'd distributed the choux balls. 'Something else to drink? More to eat?'

'We're fine, thank you,' said the man next to Victoria. He smiled and raised the glass in his hand. 'I'm sorry our friend was so badly behaved earlier,' he said after a brief hesitation.

'*Your* friend,' Victoria muttered, reaching for her wine.

'It's fine,' Coco said, though she had to bite her tongue. She couldn't understand why anybody would be friends with that man. 'Are you sure I can't get you anything else?' she repeated.

Fraser reached for the Courvoisier bottle. 'I'm very happy with this rather special cognac.'

A woman joined the table whose name Coco didn't know. Coco smiled at her. She'd been lovely to serve, kind and polite, making eye contact and being helpful. She was incredibly beautiful and very serene. Everybody in the kitchen had been discussing how it was possible to get so many wankers in one place, but this woman wasn't one of them.

'Ah, Cami,' Fraser said as she sat down. 'You know,' he turned back to Coco, 'these two got together in the first term of university. Broke a few hearts.' He gestured with his glass at Cami and Nick. The brandy sloshed around the sides. 'Isn't that right, Vix?' He looked at Victoria, who bristled visibly.

'Fraser ...' Nick said his name with a warning tone.

The beautiful woman, who Coco now knew was Cami, stared at Fraser with cool eyes and shook her head. It was brick-in-the-face obvious these two had history. Coco thought it was hilarious when people at school tried to keep relationships secret. The signs were always so easy to read.

'Ah, come on. It's important to celebrate true love. Especially today.' Fraser beamed. 'Imagine finding your soulmate at eighteen. Amazing.' He lifted his glass. 'To Nick and Cami.'

Coco noticed that Cami's fists were balled tightly on her lap. The others at the table lifted their glasses to toast the couple. All except Victoria. There was a scrape of a chair as she pushed back from the table and walked off.

Nick looked at Fraser and shook his head with a sigh. 'Did you have to?'

Fraser laughed. 'She can't still be in love with you, can she?' But then he turned to Cami and smiled. 'Or maybe she can?'

Cami whispered something to Nick, who nodded, then sighed and rubbed his face.

Coco watched with wry amusement. It was like a soap opera. There was so much drama bubbling under the surface of this group. It would make a brilliant short story, or even a stage play. She wondered what kind of ending she'd give them.

She cleared her throat and addressed Fraser. 'You said you might chat to me. I wondered if that was still OK. I mean, I know it's a party, but if you're happy to, I've a showreel ...'

Fraser seemed to take a breath, his eyes falling to the swilling brandy in his glass. She'd obviously said the wrong thing.

'I'm sure Fraser can give you a few bits of wisdom,' Nick said.

Fraser smiled at him, but Coco could tell it was fake. She was an expert on fake smiles.

'Sorry. I shouldn't have bothered you.' She picked up some empty glasses to clear away. 'It's not the right time.' There was nothing for it but to lie to her mum and be done with it.

'No, Nick's right. It's a daunting industry. Trying to break in can seem impossible. You said you've got a copy of your showreel?'

Coco broke into a smile. 'Yes.' She hesitated. 'I mean, not here. Obviously I don't have my phone, because, you know, the NDA thing. But it's on YouTube. Mum set up a page for me to share performances and things.'

'I'm happy to take a look if it's not too long.'

She beamed. 'For real? Seriously, that would be amazing. Do I email it?'

'Or show me now?'

'Now?' She looked over at the stage and caught the eye of the woman with the clipboard, who motioned aggressively at the cake then made a hand gesture that roughly translated as *get your arse back over here and deliver more caramel balls.* 'I'm supposed to be working. I'll get in trouble.'

He laughed. 'A little bit of trouble isn't always a bad thing. When you find a convenient time later, come and find me.'

'Yeah, OK. That would be great.' As she left, she smiled at Nick. 'Thank you,' she mouthed.

'No problem,' he mouthed back, before leaning over to whisper something to Cami, who nodded. He kissed her cheek, then stood to walk away.

Coco returned to the wedding cake table with a spring in her step. If Ingrid's agent watched her reel, her mum was going to spin backflips.

CHAPTER EIGHTEEN

Nick found me in the corridor. I was leaning against the wall, head back, digging my nails into my palms and cursing Anne-Marie for encouraging me to come to this bastard wedding. My skin burnt with the humiliation of Fraser turning a spotlight on my feelings for Nick in front of everybody.

Especially Cami.

'You don't need to check on me,' I said as he approached.

'Fraser shouldn't have said that.'

I swallowed and shook my head. 'It's fine. I shouldn't have come. I'm going to call a cab.'

Nick was holding a bottle of cognac and two glasses. He lifted them. 'Have a drink with me first? Somewhere we can talk.' He smiled kindly, and my heart started punching dents in my ribcage as if I were eighteen all over again.

There was a group of people on the terrace, sitting around two tables pushed together, snorting cocaine off bar menus, screeching like banshees, completely off their faces.

'There's a place down there.' I pointed to the far side of the lawn. 'Past the marquee. I found it this morning.'

We walked down towards the folly, and he made appreciative noises as we stood on the paving and took in the view. The sea was a silvery pink in the setting sun, the sky a soft apricot. Nick perched on one of the loungers and poured two glasses of cognac.

It was delicious, smooth and smoky, and slightly sweet like honey. I looked at Nick as he savoured the drink, holding the glass at arm's length to admire the caramel-coloured liquid inside. How was it possible for him to be even more beautiful? It pained me to think of all our lost years, all those days, hours, minutes I should have been looking at his beautiful face.

'You know this stuff is over two grand a bottle? There's a bottle on every table and there's, what, thirty tables?' He looked at me when I said nothing, then gave a quiet laugh. 'Ah yes, of course. But is he *happy*?'

I put my glass on the low table between us. 'Nick?'

'Mm?'

'Are *you* happy?'

'Right this minute or in general?'

'Both.' I watched his face carefully for clues to his inner thoughts.

He hesitated, studying his glass as if looking for his answer. 'There are ups and downs. Nobody can be happy all the time. But Cami and I, yes, for the most part we're happy.'

His words sounded forced and it hurt to think he was papering over his sadness. If he were with me, I'd want to him answer, 'Happy? Of course. Every second of every day.'

'What about you?' His question was followed by a soft smile. 'Are *you* happy?'

I surprised myself with my honesty. 'No,' I said. 'I'm not.'

'Never?'

'I'm content, I guess. But happy? I don't know. I'm not sure I was destined for happiness.'

His mouth opened as if he was about to speak, but then closed. He looked at the floor.

'Go on,' I said.

He let out a slow breath. 'I think perhaps happiness is a choice.'

Happiness is a choice? Like choosing whether to have milk in your tea or which pair of shoes to wear? I shook my head. 'I wish it was that simple.' I thought about my father, my brother, Nick, Julian. All of them had made choices, choices that were beyond my control, that had affected my ability to be happy. 'Do you ever think about sliding doors?' I asked then.

'Sliding doors?'

'Wondering what your life might look like if you'd chosen a different fork in the road.'

'No, never. When people do that, they assume the other path would have led to an ideal outcome. Who's to say had you chosen the other way it would have been better? It might have turned out worse. Regret is pointless. We make decisions based on information available at the time, on a specific set of circumstances. Hindsight is a glorious thing, but you can't go back, you can only move forward. Yearning for a fantasy life will drive a person mad.'

He gave me a soft smile and I recalled the pain in his eyes when he'd said we weren't allowed to be friends. Then that same pain magnified when he'd walked out of our hotel room in Paris.

'I miss you.' My mouth was running away from me, but I couldn't help it. This was most likely my last chance to tell him how I still felt. 'Every day.'

'Oh Vix.' His brows knotted, and he placed his glass on the table. 'Please don't do this today. It's not the right time.'

'But when *is* the right time? I can see how unhappy you are. Your children are grown up, so you don't have to stay now.'

'They're fourteen and sixteen.'

Desperation reared its angry head and all my emotions rushed to the surface. 'But I love you. And in Paris—'

'Nothing happened in Paris.'

'That's not true. You came to me. You didn't have to.'

'You said you needed me.'

'I did. And you came.'

'I was worried.' He leant over and took my hand. 'Cami and I are happy.'

I shook my head. 'You're not. She's so bitter and sour. She hasn't smiled once. I've never seen you so tense.'

He dropped my hand and looked out across the sea, which had turned a fiery red now the sun had fallen lower. 'There's something's wrong with Cami, but it's not to do with her and me.'

I hesitated. 'It's to do with her and Fraser.'

His head snapped round. 'What?'

'I saw the way he touched her. She pulled away, then immediately checked if you'd seen. I saw them talking. They jumped away from each other, just like they did at that party on New Year's Eve.'

'That was twenty-five years ago.' He stood, shaking his head. 'I need to get back.'

'No, don't. Please stay. I'm sorry, Nick …'

But he had already walked away from me and was heading across the lawn, towards the hotel. I followed him, trotting to catch up, but then, as if black magic had a hand in it, Cami appeared through the French windows. Nick broke into a half-run towards her, and I swallowed the urge to scream.

'I'm the one who can make you happy,' I whispered as I watched her face show no pleasure to see him.

I continued walking, stopping a few metres from them. His hands were on her shoulders. 'Are you OK?' he asked her.

'I'm not feeling well. I'd like to go home.'

He put his arms around her, but she stepped away from him, unable to meet his eyes.

'We should say goodbye to the others,' he said.

'Can't we just slip away? I don't want to ruin the party.'

I couldn't help my snort of laughter.

Cami shot me a look over Nick's shoulder. 'Something funny, Vix?'

'Maybe Nick doesn't want to go. Maybe you could think about what he wants for once.'

'I'm happy to go home.'

I ignored him and moved closer to them. I'd waited too long for this; it was time I finally told Cami a few home truths. This was the last time I'd see either of them again. I knew that. I had nothing to lose. 'It's because of me, isn't it? That's why you're leaving. Somehow you always manage to find a way to stop Nick and me being together.'

Cami gave a low, guttural growl. She threw her hands up in the air and walked away from us, onto the lawn, shaking her head and muttering under her breath.

Nick moved to follow her.

'Stay with me,' I begged.

But it fell on deaf ears.

Though the two of them had walked out of earshot, I could watch their body language, both of them tense, her gesticulating angrily, looking at the sky, hands on hips, shaking her head. Him trying to reach for her, her knocking him away with obvious aggression. Cami would never change. She would always be the spoilt princess, always need to be the centre of attention.

Somebody came up beside me. It was Tilly, her face tight and anxious. 'Is she all right?'

'Of course she is,' I snapped. 'She's doing a Cami, that's all.'

'Doing a *what*?' Tilly's face was riven with fake horror. 'What does *that* mean?'

'Come on, Tilly. It's what she always does. Grabbing the limelight. Wanting everything to be about her. Inserting herself into the middle of everything. Even at someone else's wedding.' A dam had burst inside me. I didn't care any more. As I spoke, I felt a wave of euphoric energy charge through me.

'What an awful thing to say. You have no idea what's going on, so you're in no position to comment.'

'I know what's going on. She's been like this for ever. Maybe it's you who doesn't know what's going on.'

'Really?' Tilly raised a single eyebrow and crossed her arms. 'What's going on then?'

'Cami and Fraser are having an affair.'

Tilly scoffed. 'Jesus Christ,' she said under her breath, regarding me with unbridled contempt.

'I saw them together earlier.'

Her face set like concrete. 'You've got this very wrong and you need to be careful what you say.'

'Are you threatening me?'

She dropped the cigarette she was holding and trod it into the grass. 'I'm not *threatening* you, for God's sake. We're not in the bloody playground. I'm saying you need to be careful, because bandying around baseless accusations can be damaging.' She narrowed her hateful eyes. 'Now, I'm going to assume you've had too much to drink and put this nonsense down to that, but if I were you, I'd keep your nasty little thoughts to yourself.'

She walked away from me, down the steps onto the lawn, and over to Nick and Cami. When she reached them, she put her hand on Cami's arm. They spoke. I wanted to know what they were saying so badly it hurt. Cami nodded, then Tilly leant forward and kissed her cheek. Nick smiled at Tilly.

The scene made me sick.

I marched down to them. 'Tell Cami about Paris!'

'Jesus,' Nick said.

'Go on, tell her what happened.'

'*Nothing* happened.'

'Just stop this,' Tilly said.

I ignored her. 'Tell your wife you came to see me in Paris and we had a night together but you said you couldn't be with me because of the children.'

'Vix,' Cami's tone was irritatingly gentle. 'This isn't—'

'Nick and I love each other! We always have and it's only because of *you* that we aren't together.' I turned back to him, frustration and love burning in the pit of my stomach, firing every cell inside me. 'Tell her what happened in Paris.'

'I know what happened in Paris,' Cami said then.

I shook my head. '*What?* No, you don't—'

'You think he didn't tell me? He told me everything. I was there at home when you rang and said you needed to see him. And I was there, remember, when it happened. We went to the hospital with you. We took you to the mortuary. We both saw how traumatic it was. When you called, terrified, panicking, we couldn't turn our backs. Nick wanted to help you.'

I looked at Nick, desperate for him to speak up, but his face was impassive, eyes lowered.

'What else could he do?' she went on. 'What type of person would turn their back on an old friend in such a state? I *told* him to go to Paris. I *told* him to go to you.'

She stopped talking and sighed, tipping her head back to stare up at the dusky sky.

'But while we were there …' I swallowed and blinked back my tears. 'The time we had together. In bed. Holding each other. Crying because we couldn't be together.'

Nick shook his head. Then he looked at Cami. 'Nothing happened.'

'*No!*' I shouted, angry at his betrayal. 'That's not … that's not true. I was there. I know how it was. You said you loved me. You … you always have.'

'Listen to me. I love *Cami.*'

'But she's a bitch!'

Cami gave a snort of bitter laughter. 'I was *never* a bitch to you,' she cried. 'I tried so hard to be friends, but you hated me from that first night in the pub. Oh my God, the way you used to glare at me! At college, in the bar, *all* the time. Yes, I admit it, I was jealous of the friendship you and Nick had. I knew you loved him – everybody did – and even though he swore blind there was nothing going on, it got to me. I tried not to let it, but every time I made an effort, you bit me.' She stopped speaking and shook her head wearily before looking at Nick. 'I can't do this. I need to go home.'

'And what about you and Fraser?'

Cami's features crumpled in horror. The colour drained from her face.

'*No!*' Tilly cried. 'Stop this now, it's highly inappropriate. This is a wedding—'

'This isn't a wedding, it's a *farce*.' I looked at Nick. 'You've got to believe me. There's something going on with Cami and Fraser. Ask her. Ask her to tell you.'

Nick shook his head in disbelief. 'Christ, Vix. Why would you say something like that?'

Tilly put her arm around Cami's shoulders and began to lead her back over the lawn to the terrace, their heads tipped close together.

'I saw them! Cami and Fraser.' My stomach pitched as I watched Nick's face grow dark, any residual warmth and kindness dissolving to nothing. 'Nick, will you—'

'Enough!' His undisguised anger stunned me. 'Just leave us the fuck *alone*!'

CHAPTER NINETEEN

Mid-January 2000

I waited on the top landing, peering over the banister, until I heard his bedroom door open, then I jogged down the stairs as if we were bumping into each other by chance.

He didn't acknowledge me.

'Nick?' I followed him, but he didn't stop, not until I put myself in between him and the front door so he couldn't open it. 'Can we talk?'

'I can't,' he mumbled as he tried to push me out of his way.

'But it's only us here. She won't know.'

The sadness in his eyes cut into me. This was crazy. I was so angry. What kind of psycho asks her boyfriend to choose between her and his friend? It drove me insane with frustration. If I couldn't get close to him, how was I going to show him what a massive mistake he was making?

'A few minutes?'

He hesitated. Why wouldn't he look me in the eye? What had changed? It was as if I'd become invisible.

'I just can't see what you have in common. Does she love *Liberty* and Marmite on toast? Do you talk about travel and Lloyd Wright and the existence of God? Do you talk like we talk?'

He still didn't speak. I watched his face and imagined him considering my words, realising I was right, facing up to what we both knew was the truth. But if anything, he seemed to withdraw further.

Finally he took a breath. 'I love her, Vix.'

Jealousy squeezed my heart like a clamp. 'And I mean nothing?'

'It's not like that. When we …' He hesitated.

'Slept together.'

He recoiled from the words. 'It was a mistake.'

Emotion welled up inside me. 'No, you wouldn't do that. You're not that kind of person.'

His eyes flickered left and right. 'I don't want to hurt her.'

'But it's OK to hurt me?'

'That's not fair.'

'On *who*?' I hated the pitch of my voice, hated the way I was making him look so pained, hated how demanding I sounded. No better than her. 'I'm sorry.' I did everything I could to regain my composure, forced myself to sound calm in spite of my raging emotions. 'I don't understand why we can't be friends like before. You're the … the most important person in my life. How does staying friends hurt her?'

I hoped he would hear these words and soften, look at me tenderly, smile and say, 'You're right, of course we're still friends.'

But he didn't. 'I had no idea how much it was hurting her.'

I pictured her face, her puppy-dog eyes, her downturned Cupid's-bow mouth, playing the victim to get her own way. What a bitch.

'You understand, don't you?'

I couldn't speak, afraid of what might come out.

'Vix? Please. This is tearing me apart.' He looked as if he was about to cry. I hated to see him that sad.

'I understand,' I lied.

The relief on his face verged on comical.

'So how will it be at college?'

He frowned, as if not understanding my question.

'Now I'm out of the group and back to eating lunch on my

own?' I didn't care about sounding petulant. I didn't care how I came across. None of this was fair.

'Why are you out of the group?'

I laughed bitterly. 'Jesus, Nick. How do you think it will work if I'm not allowed to look at you, let alone talk to you? It doesn't matter anyway. It was always only a matter of time before I was sent back to the shadows.'

'The shadows?'

I rolled my eyes and shook my head.

'You're making no sense.' His undertone of irritation rankled. He didn't get to be irritated. Neither of them did. It was me who was the collateral damage. Me who got to be irritated.

I drew in a deep breath. 'You and Cami – the rest of them – you live in a world I don't belong in. I was no more than a tourist. Like visiting France or Greece.'

'You're talking like a crazy person. What does that even mean?' His volume rose as frustration gave way to anger. 'You know what? This isn't about *you*. It's about me and Cami. *Our* relationship.' They were her words he was repeating. I could hear her saying them. 'Please move out of my way. I don't want to be late for studio.'

I held his stare for a few moments before stepping sideways, unblocking the door. 'You go first. I'll follow in five minutes. I guess you don't want to walk in at the same time as me?'

'For God's sake,' he said, reacting to the note of childish spite I'd allowed to creep into my rhetorical question. He bent for his bag and walked out without saying another word.

I banged my fist against the wall. I'd sounded like a spoilt brat. No wonder he didn't want to fight for our friendship.

'I'm sorry,' I said into the quietness of the hall. 'Please, Nick, I'm sorry.'

I fumbled for the catch and pulled open the door, willing him to be standing there, regret and apology written all over his face, desperate to undo what we'd said and make up. But he wasn't there; he was at the end of Frederick Street, hurrying on without a backward glance.

On campus, everybody appeared to have forgotten Neil Gilbert's creepy perving and whatever nasty shit was on his computer. The vice chancellor had penned a letter that was pinned to the board in the department's reception. She talked about his awards and his services to education, about how he was a talented but ultimately troubled man, and ended with: *We must take heart in the knowledge that Neil Gilbert is now at peace.*

Good for Neil Gilbert, I thought as I turned away from the board and trudged up the stairs.

The studio was subdued. Class had started. People glanced at me as I snuck in quietly, but nobody smiled or acknowledged me. Julie Rainer's stare was flat, devoid of her usual warm welcome. Cami sat beside Nick. Around her neck, tied onto a leather cord, hung the white pebble. My breath caught in my throat. That was my luck she was wearing. I flinched as pain jabbed my stomach.

Between lectures, everybody clustered around her like wasps on jam. Nick, of course, Tilly and Giles, Julian and Fraser. Another couple of girls. All of them focused on Cami, generous with their kind touches and crooning words.

I'd felt lonely before, but never like this.

Our next class was materials. Neil Gilbert's class. The silence in the room was deafening. When the door opened, a short man in a ribbed sweater and jeans walked in. He had wild hair and a bow tie. He walked to the front of the studio and turned to face us.

After a moment of reverential quiet, he addressed the room solemnly. 'Good morning. My name is Fred Garson and I will be stepping in to take this class following the sad news about Neil Gilbert.' He paused. 'We're all shocked by what's happened. I will do my best to—'

238

I didn't wait to hear any more.

I grabbed my bag and fled. The stares, whispers and judgement were too much to take. As I hurried through the building, I could feel Gilbert everywhere, lurking in corners, behind closed doors, in every air molecule I breathed. I couldn't be there a moment longer.

I didn't stop running until I reached Frederick Street, panting and coughing, lungs burning. I tore up to my room and threw myself on the bed.

It was late in the afternoon when I heard his feet on the stairs. Then the door to his room opening and closing. I stood up from the bed.

'Don't go down,' I whispered. But it was torture. I was an addict and Nick was my drug.

I made two mugs of tea, then stood outside his door, my heart kicking my ribs.

'Nick?'

Nothing.

'Look, it's fine. I know we can't be friends in front of Cami. I get it. But I was hoping we could still hang out here?' I waited, my forehead resting against his door. 'I won't talk to you anywhere else.'

Still nothing.

'I'm going back up to my room. I've left a mug of tea outside your door.'

When I came down an hour later, the mug was still there, the tea untouched, cold, with a circle of grey skin floating on its surface.

At nearly midnight, I pushed a note under his door.

Missing my friend.

An hour later, another.

See you tomorrow?

'Hey,' said a voice behind me. I startled and whipped around. Mia was standing there in her pyjamas and dressing gown, her eyes sleepy, hair mussed up. 'Are you all right?'

Tears stung my eyes as I pushed past her and ran back upstairs.

I stayed in my room for three days. I didn't want to see anybody. It was like those first days of freshers' week. I'd wait until the house was quiet before sneaking out to use the bathroom. I ate dry cereal and baked beans from the tin. I lay on my bed and stared at the ceiling, half hoping it might collapse and bury me.

When Mrs Drummond *tap-tap-tapped* on the door, I dragged myself up. 'I'm not dead,' I said.

'I'm pleased about that,' she said with a smile. 'Your mother's on the phone.'

'Can you tell her I'm out?'

'She sounds upset.'

I nodded wearily and went down to the payphone. 'Mum?'

'Oh love. Oh God. I can't cope with him.' Her voice sounded shaky and high-pitched.

'I can't talk about this now.'

'I'm at my wits' end.' Her pitch grew even higher, as if somebody was tightening it like a guitar string.

'There's nothing I can do. I'm hundreds of miles away and late for class. Surely you can—'

'He won't come out of his room. He won't talk to me. He isn't bathing or dressing. I don't even think he's eating. He's like a troll.'

There was no space in my head for my mother and Mikey. I closed my eyes and leant back against the wall. 'Give him time,' I said. 'He'll snap out of it soon.'

'When are you coming home? I haven't seen you since December.'

'It's only January.'

'Nearly February.'

'Look, I don't know. I've so much work on. Are you getting out of the house much?' I asked, to change the subject. 'It might do you good. The two of you cooped up together is asking for trouble.'

'Weather's been bad.'

'That's the north for you.' My attempt at lifting her mood fell flat. 'I should go. I've got class.'

'I miss you, love.'

I thought of her then, pictured her sitting on the telephone stool, twiddling the cord around her fingers. It would be nice to be back home. Cosy in my room with my pretty pink bedsheets, my posters, my desk, and the comforting hum of the television downstairs. 'I'll try and get back in the next few weeks. Maybe we can plan a shopping trip? Get you out of the house. You need to try and find some joy in life, Mum.'

She was silent for a bit. Then she breathed in deeply. 'Thanks for chatting, love. Take care. If you can, phone Michael. I know that would make him happy.'

I wanted to tell her that nothing would make Mikey happy, but instead I said, 'I'll call him tomorrow.'

On Friday, there was a knock on my door. Despite being ragged with abandonment and lack of sleep, I leapt off the bed.

'Nick?' I said under my breath as I pulled open the door.

It wasn't Nick. It was Rav.

'Oh, hi. Hey …' He shifted awkwardly, reaching up to rub the back of his neck. 'Your landlady let me in. She said she was happy for me to come up as it would save her a trip to check you weren't dead. I think she was joking.'

'Still alive.' I managed a weak smile.

'Maybe this is silly. And sorry if I'm overstepping. But … I'm a bit worried about you. You haven't been in class since you ran out, and you seemed pretty upset.'

'Not feeling one hundred per cent,' I said quietly. 'Maybe a virus or something.'

I could tell by his face he wasn't falling for a mystery virus.

'Will you come into college with me?' He smiled. 'You can sit next to me. It'll be OK. I think you need to come back. You're missing quite a bit.'

I shook my head. 'I … I can't.'

'Everybody's forgotten about Neil Gilbert.' He spoke quietly, almost mumbling Gilbert's name. 'Julie was humming show tunes yesterday. Everything's back to normal.'

It might be back to normal for everybody else, but it wasn't for me. Gilbert was still with me, mashed up on the tracks at White City. I was haunted by the thought of his ravaged family as they mourned his death and reputation. The accusation in the eyes of my peers and tutors. Nick's rejection.

'Julie asked after you,' Rav said. 'She's worried too. If you don't come back, you can't pass end-of-years.'

I pictured Julie Rainer, her kind face, asking the class if anybody had seen me. I pictured Nick looking at the floor, his cheeks reddening. Cami glaring. As I thought about college and Julie, the reality of Rav's warning began to sink in. If I failed the year, what would I do? Return to Knutsford to rot in the house with Mum and Mikey?

'I can help you catch up what you've missed.' Rav paused and smiled gently. 'Don't let this thing with Gilbert ruin your life. You're a good architect and a very talented artist. One of the best. You worked hard to get here. Don't throw it away because of a creep like him.'

His words seemed to clear the fog in my mind. Throwing in the towel would leave me worse off than ever. I'd have nothing and nowhere to go.

I nodded slowly. 'I can't fail the year.'

Rav beamed. 'Good. Come on then. Pack your bag and let's head in.'

I started to protest. 'I'm not ready today. I'll come in tomorrow.'

But he was insistent. 'I'm not leaving without you.'

*

Though Rav promised that things at QSA were back to normal, I felt the atmosphere sour as soon as I walked into the studio. A hush settled over the room. Cami and Tilly didn't acknowledge me. Nick fixed his eyes resolutely on the desk. A few others smiled tightly. There were some quiet whispers. If it wasn't for Rav grabbing my hand, I'd have turned and run again.

After the lecture, I stayed sitting until everybody but Rav had piled out in a mass of chatter.

'Told you it would be OK,' he said, packing his drawings into his portfolio. 'Fancy a coffee?'

I hesitated.

'Friends only,' he said quickly, holding up his hands. 'Promise it's not a line.'

I laughed, which felt good. 'Why not?' I said, nodding. 'Coffee would be nice.'

'Well done for coming in,' he said as we sat at a table in the canteen. 'It can't have been easy.' He stirred three sachets of sugar into his milky coffee. 'Did you see the rag dance posters?'

A group of people walked in. I scanned them for Nick, but he wasn't amongst them.

Rav tapped my hand. 'Earth to Vix?'

'Sorry? What?'

He chuckled. 'The rag dance. For Comic Relief. It's fancy dress and the theme is famous couples. They've hired a barge down on Victoria Embankment. Looks really cool.'

My first thought was Nick. Was he going? I dug my fingers into my thigh. I had to stop this fixation or I'd send myself mad.

'Everybody's going,' Rav said, as if reading my mind. 'The whole department plus guests. I think they might open it up to other London unis as well. Tickets include a couple of drinks. I was thinking, maybe, if you didn't have other plans, you might go with me? I had this idea we could dress up as Leonardo and the *Mona Lisa*.' His face was alight with enthusiasm. 'I've got a design with a frame that would fit over you so you'd look like the painting.'

The thought of having to go to a party with everybody there made me weak. 'I don't think so. I'm not sure I'm in the mood. And I'm also pretty skint.' This wasn't a lie. The money I'd saved was now spent, and the cash Mum had given me for emergencies was almost gone too.

'I'll buy your ticket. It's for charity anyway.'

'I can't let you do that.'

'I'd like to. You'll be a brilliant *Mona Lisa*. She suits a low mood. You don't even have to smile.'

Despite myself, I laughed again. 'Can I think about it?'

Rav tried to cover his disappointment with a smile. 'Of course. No hurry. I can find someone else if you don't want to go.'

My attention was grabbed by a loud shriek of laughter from a huddle of girls on the next table. I noticed another pair, arms linked, chatting away as they queued. Then a boy laughing at something his friend had said. All these people, getting on with it, and there I was wallowing in the wreckage of Nick's rejection. I had to get a grip. If I didn't, I'd end up like my brother, festering in his room, every last drop of joy squeezed out of him.

I forced a smile onto my face. 'I've thought about it. Yes please. I'd like to go with you.'

'What? Oh wow! I didn't expect you to actually say yes.' His smile lit up the café like a flare. 'Amazing!'

I lifted my chin and took a bolstering breath. I didn't need Nick and the others. I was my own person. I was Liberty.

Screw the lot of them.

CHAPTER TWENTY

27 July 2024

My skin smarted from being dismissed by Nick. Righteous indignation magnified with every step as I stormed back into the hotel. How dare Cami twist history like that? How dare she say she tried to be friends and insinuate it was *me* – not her – who was the bitch? She was delusional. Playing the victim was bad enough, but pleading jealousy? Jealous of *what*? It was laughable. She had everything I wanted.

I was so angry with myself for coming to the wedding. I'd allowed my heart to be torn to shreds again. But what else had I expected? That Nick would take one look at me in Anne-Marie's shimmering dress and be overwhelmed with desire? That Julian would beg for forgiveness? I was pitiful, an idiot. As I walked along the corridor towards reception, I hated myself more than I'd thought possible.

There was a sudden roar of cheering from the ballroom behind me. I thought of him braying in there. Julian Draper, Hollywood starlet on his arm, a crowd of sycophantic caricatures patting his back, quaffing his drink and inflating his ego.

Disgust swept through me.

Fuck you.

Then from the murky pit of self-loathing, a spark of long-forgotten fire flickered inside me. I should have stayed away, but I hadn't. I'd come all this way, and while I might not have Nick,

I could still tell Julian exactly what I thought of him. Adrenalin coursed through my veins as I turned on my heel and strode towards the ballroom, through the doors and past those ridiculous bouncers pretending to be tough guys like extras from a low-budget action film.

Nick was talking to Giles and his wife in a way that suggested he was saying goodbye. He glanced at me, face falling, then turned away. Cami stood by the door on the opposite side of the room, arms folded, fidgety with impatience.

Julian was still seated at our table with Fraser. Two men and a woman were sitting on the opposite side cutting cocaine with a platinum credit card. Coco stood beside Julian and Fraser holding a bottle of cognac, engaged in conversation with the two men.

'Well, here she is!' Julian said as I approached. 'I was telling this young lady that with a bit of hard work she can do anything she wants. No need to be stuck serving arseholes like me for the rest of her life. I believe you were once a waitress and now look at you. World-famous artist!' He laughed.

Was he mocking me?

'I'm still a waitress, and there's no shame in that.' Despite my thumping heart, I managed to keep my voice steady.

Julian's brow crinkled as if surprised to hear my voice. 'But it's hardly what young girls dream of, is it? Most people aim a little, well …' he raised his glass and regarded it for a moment before fixing his eyes on me, 'higher?'

'I'd rather be a waitress than an arsehole.'

Coco's eyes snapped wide open in shock.

Julian did nothing for a moment or two, then he opened his mouth and howled with laughter. The noise of it wriggled into my veins.

'Touché!' He dabbed a tear from the corner of his eye with his finger. 'I've always had a soft spot for you.' He winked at me. 'I can't bear a wallflower with no *spunk*.'

Awful memories gripped hold of me, and though there were so many things I wanted to say to him, all my words now appeared out of reach.

'Bring us another,' he said to Coco, tapping the bottle in her hand.

'Andre ... I mean the sommelier, said to say there's only one bottle of the Corvoyser left.'

Julian barked with laughter and slapped the table, causing the man snorting coke to look up in surprise, a dusting of white beneath his nose. 'Cor *what* now?' he said, with undisguised amusement.

Coco's cheeks reddened.

'Now listen here, we can't have you going around mispronouncing the name of the best cognac you'll ever pour.'

She stepped back as if making an escape. 'I'll go and get another bottle.'

'Hang on, hang on. I want you to get it right,' Julian said. 'I'll help.' He beckoned her closer and gestured for the bottle, and she passed it to him. He turned the label towards her and jabbed it with his stubby finger. 'Go on, try again.'

Coco's skin deepened in colour as she stared at the label, blinking quickly, her jaw tensed.

Fraser pushed Julian's hand with the bottle, then looked up at Coco. 'Off you go. There's no need to indulge him when he's like this. None of us do.'

'But I'm helping her. I'm showing her how—'

'Leave her alone.'

Julian dismissed my interjection with a flick of his hand. 'Surely, you want to learn to pronounce it right, don't you?' he said to Coco.

Fraser opened his mouth to speak again, but Julian lifted a hand to silence him. One of the men who'd been taking cocaine had stopped to listen intently, as if interested in the lesson himself. The other got up from the table, obviously bored, waving at a young woman on a different table, who squealed in delight.

'Try again,' Julian said.

'Cor … erm, voy—'

'Vwah,' he said. 'Vwah, not voy. Then si-*ay*.'

'Cor … vwah …' Coco's voice faded.

My skin itched with the recalled humiliation I'd tried so hard to forget. Julian was a hateful, *hateful* man. 'Leave her alone.'

'Christ, you really need to calm—'

'Cor-*vwah*-siay,' Coco said quickly. 'Courvoisier.'

Julian beamed and placed the bottle down. 'Clever girl! That's it. See?' He turned to me, his expression cool. 'No harm done.'

I thought of Anne-Marie and what she would say to him. The way she would cut him down to size. When men like him came into her gallery, flashing their cash, talking as if they knew everything about art, she would turn to ice, glaring, nose wrinkled as if they'd walked dog shit into the space.

'And how about a French lesson for *you*?' I stepped closer and leant down near his face. '*Va te faire foutre.*' I paused and straightened. 'Go *fuck* yourself.'

Then I turned away, not waiting to hear his retort, and marched out of the ballroom, my chin held high, my legs threatening to turn to jelly as I walked out into the corridor.

'I need my phone and a taxi,' I said to the man behind the reception desk in his gold-buttoned coat. My whole body was trembling. 'As quickly as possible.'

There was a roar of cheering and clapping.

'Before the music starts?' he asked. 'You might not want to miss it.'

'I just need a taxi.'

CHAPTER TWENTY-ONE

Early March 2000

When Rav showed me what he'd created for my *Mona Lisa* costume, I was genuinely stunned. I touched the gilt-effect frame in wonder. It was tonally perfect, complete with intricate decoration, exactly like the real thing. 'Blimey, Rav, you could go into forgery!'

Canvas was stretched tight across the frame, stiffened somehow, with an opening cut into it.

'Your body goes through the hole. Fold your arms – like she does in the painting – over the support to stop it tipping backwards. Then you'll need to paint the canvas to look like the painting.'

'God, I don't think I can.'

'You're an incredible artist.'

'You're asking me to paint the *Mona Lisa*!'

'Just the background. I have faith.' He turned the structure around to show me the framework. 'These supports will sit on your shoulders. The frame is polystyrene and balsa, so it's pretty light. It's not that robust, but I didn't want it to be too heavy and uncomfortable for you.' He put the frame down and fished something out of a carrier bag. 'You don't have to wear this, but I spotted it in a charity shop.' He shook out a shapeless jacket made of heavy brown velvet. 'I've got some gold trimming that will add a bit of Renaissance detail to the sleeves. Maybe a black dress underneath it, and …' his excitement was palpable as he showed me a photocopy of the *Mona Lisa*, 'I found some fine black netting for this detail.' He indicated her hairline with his finger. 'See this? Your hair is the right length and colour. You'll need to wear it loose and parted in the middle, then a bit of gel to smooth it down? Though I imagine she used egg white.'

I laughed. Rav had been a wonderful friend over the last few weeks. He was gentle and caring and he'd been a refuge, not to mention very helpful when it came to catching up on lecture notes. 'What about you?' I asked him.

He bent down to rummage in his carrier bag. When he stood up, he was wearing a long grey beard and a large floppy hat. 'I'll wear a black smock and carry this,' he said, lifting an old-fashioned artist's palette. '*Al suo servizio, signorina.*' He flourished a bow, then grinned. 'What do you think?'

'I think it's amazing,' I said. 'You're a genius. Like actual Leonardo.'

The acrylic painting took me three days. It felt good to hold a brush again. I'd missed it. And as I pressed the muddy-coloured paint into the canvas, relaxed and at ease, I realised I was happy for the first time since Nick abandoned me.

When I finished the painting, I was like a small child, bouncing about, excited to show Rav. I set it on an easel in the studio and covered it with a sheet. He did a drum roll on the desk with his fingers as I laughed and pulled the sheet off. 'Ta-dah!'

'Vix, that's brilliant! You've got that background spot on. Seriously … Wow. If anybody's going to make a career out of creating knock-off da Vincis, it's you. This is so good!'

I smiled. Though I was trying my hardest not to think of Nick, I couldn't help recalling the time he'd told me about the *Mona Lisa*, and my body filled with warmth.

*

250

On the morning of the dance, I woke up buzzing. Enough time had passed. Though we weren't hanging out, tensions had eased in the department, and I was determined to build bridges. I would talk to Fraser and Giles and drop into conversation that I was over Nick and was happy he and Cami – 'Well, they're made for each other, aren't they?' – were together. I'd smile at Tilly, and though it would cut me to the core, I'd apologise to Cami. I didn't need to be Nick's girlfriend. I just wanted to be back in his life.

When I explained that we were creating a costume together, and the famous couple we'd chosen, Mrs Drummond said it was no problem for Rav to get ready in my room. 'As long as you promise to show me your costumes. I *love* dressing up. When I lived in Somerset, I was part of the local historical re-enactment group. Templecombe medieval pageant was the highlight of my year.' She smiled wistfully. 'Happy days gadding about in a wimple.'

Painting my face took a while. Turning myself into the *Mona Lisa* wasn't as straightforward as I'd hoped, but when we were finally dressed and ready, the frame positioned over my head and body, we stood side by side in front of the mirror.

'*Mamma mia!*' Rav gave an exaggerated chef's kiss. 'We look *favolosi!*'

He was right. The optical illusion he'd managed to create with the frame was breathtaking, and my reproduction of the *Mona Lisa*'s background was perfect. 'I think this might be the greatest costume ever!'

'You won't be too hot?'

'I'll put up with it for the art.'

'Very noble of you, *signorina*.'

I knocked on Mrs Drummond's door as we passed. When she saw us, she clapped her hands together and beamed with delight. 'Marvellous! If you ever want to join a re-enactment society, I'm sure your attention to historical detail would be welcomed.'

We caught the bus down to Victoria Embankment. Rav thought it was better for me to stand up rather than try and sit on a Tube or in a taxi. 'We want your frame in one piece. I'm not sure it'll survive a trip on the Circle Line.'

Everybody stared at us on the bus and on the street. We giggled together, enjoying the attention and confused looks. Locals and tourists alike wandered along the embankment, making the most of the balmy spring evening and the spectacular sight of the latest addition to the London skyline, the Millennium Wheel, standing majestic, an enormous Ferris wheel with capsules hanging like dragon eggs. The river glistened in the low sunshine, reflecting the buildings that lined its banks. The frame made walking hard. It was ungainly and awkward, and dug into my shoulders. With every step I worried a sudden gust of wind might pick me up and carry me off like a Renaissance kite.

As we approached the barge, adorned with strings of colourful lights, music pumping from within, there was already a buzz in the air. The gangway bustled with energy as people eagerly awaited their turn to board. Laughter and chatter and a palpable sense of anticipation filled the air like static. I was thankful to have Rav beside me. If I'd been alone, I might have bolted. I think he sensed it, as at one point he grabbed my wrist and held on tightly.

Everybody had gone to a lot of effort, but rather than admire the parade of characters, all I could see was how gorgeous the other girls looked in a kaleidoscope of sexy outfits, as if they'd misread the theme and come as soft-porn models rather than famous couples. As we joined the queue, a few people turned to assess us, some with nods of appreciation, some blankly, as if we were transparent.

'Don't forget your enigmatic smile,' Rav said with a wink.

The people immediately in front of us – a girl with a black and white wig, a white coat with black spots, leather hot pants and extremely high heels, and a boy in black jeans, black shirt and Dalmatian face paint – smiled.

'*Eccellente!* Cruella and a stolen puppy. *Bene!*'

I was mortified by Rav's pantomime accent and would have been quite happy for the boat to sink there and then.

'You look cool. Who are you?' the Dalmatian puppy asked.

Rav flourished a bow, his hand flying up to his head to hold his hat on. '*Buonasera. Mi chiamo Leonardo da Vinci.*'

The Dalmatian turned to me, 'So that makes you—'

'The *Mona Lisa*,' I said quietly.

Sexy Cruella smiled and gave us a thumbs-up. '*So good.*'

'*Grazie.*'

I glared at Rav.

'What?' he whispered.

'Stop speaking like that. People will think you're weird.'

'Who cares?'

I shifted the frame on my shoulders to make it more comfortable. The velvet jacket, dress and tights were hot, my skin clammy beneath, and as I focused on sexy Cruella's never-ending legs, I wished I'd worn a miniskirt and heels.

There was a desk set up at the end of the gangway with a girl sitting behind it. As we drew up in front of her, she gave us a smiley welcome. 'Names?'

She ticked us off, then beckoned for my hand and stamped the underside of my wrist with a navy star. 'I *love* this outfit! You've really got into the spirit of things! *Wonderful!* We're not doing prizes, but if we were, you'd definitely be in the running. Well done!'

She stamped Rav's wrist too. 'Three free drinks,' she said, handing us each a piece of flimsy card printed with three numbered boxes. 'The guys will stamp each box when they give you a drink. Have fun!'

'*Grazie!*' Rav held out his hand to me. '*Venite, signorina.*'

I didn't take it.

We carefully negotiated the stairs down into the bowels of the boat. The whole of the lower deck had been turned into a party room, with a low ceiling and areas of royal-blue upholstered seating around the edge. There was a mahogany bar with a mirror and a wall of spirits at one end, and a dance floor at the other with a door to an outside deck. The room was packed with partygoers and my nerves had grown unbearable. I wanted to rip the frame off and throw it into the Thames.

'I need to use the toilet,' I said as we reached the foot of the stairway.

'I'll wait for you here.'

'You don't have to,' I said quickly.

'Leonardo without the *Mona Lisa* isn't really a couple.'

The toilets were snug and everything was dark and clad in wood-effect laminate. There was a room freshener by the basin that smelt of pine disinfectant. I stared at myself and thought of sexy Cruella and all the other high-heeled legs, up-thrust cleavages and cinched waists, while here I was dressed head to toe in unflattering shapeless garments and DM boots, wearing a picture frame, my face painted in a mush of Renaissance yellows and browns. Why on earth had I come to a party dressed as a painting? And not just any painting. A painting that required my hair to be parted in the centre and plastered down with gel, my eyebrows camouflaged, no lipstick, no mascara, no jewellery, and wearing an old jacket that smelt of mothballs.

I tried to reach for a paper towel to dab the beads of sweat that were gathering at my hairline, but the frame made it impossible. I was close to tears.

The door opened and a girl walked in. She was dressed in a red T-shirt with yellow geometric shapes pinned to it, red tights, gold stilettos, a red cape, and a headband with cute little teddy ears. She was gorgeous. 'Let me help,' she said, pulling a couple of sheets from the dispenser. '*Mona Lisa*, right?' She smiled as she handed me the towels. 'You look so good!'

I pressed the wad of towel against my forehead. 'Thanks,' I muttered. 'I feel stupid.'

'Stupid? Why? God, no. I wish I'd thought of it. Do you know who I am?'

I stared at her, racking my brains, but there was nothing. I gave an apologetic half-smile.

'SuperTed.' She put her hands on her hips and struck a superhero pose. 'My boyfriend's come as Spotty, wearing yellow pyjamas with green splodges.' She laughed. 'The most famous couple *ever*, right?' She turned to check her make-up in the mirror, reapplied her shiny lip gloss, then winked at me before skipping back out. 'See you in there, Mona!'

I regarded myself in the mirror. 'Come on,' I said to my reflection. 'You're here now.' I had to remember how kind Rav had been over the last month. He'd taken care of me and made sure I was never alone in the department. He'd helped me catch up with my work. He'd thrown everything into this costume. If I did it for nothing else, I should do it to say thank you to him. I gave a decisive nod, formed my mouth into its enigmatic smile and walked back to the stairway clasping my hands in front of me.

Rav smiled. 'Ready?'

I nodded.

The party room was a frenzy. As I walked through the crowd I had to say 'Excuse me. Sorry. If I could just squeeze past' on repeat, carefully manoeuvring the frame through the maze of excited people. At the bar, we handed over our drinks cards and got two beers in return for two stamps. Then, as we clinked glasses, there was a sense of attention being drawn to the stairway. I knew who they were looking at before I'd even set eyes on them, and yes, there they were, four of the QSA elite, beaming and waving as if arriving at a film premiere.

Cami, Nick, Fraser and Tilly.

Nick was dressed in black tie and carried a toy gun. He stopped at the base of the stairs in a James Bond pose. Cami stood beside him, arm draped over his shoulder, hip jutted out. She was dressed in a gold catsuit, so close-fitting it could have been sprayed on, open to her chest, her rounded cleavage barely contained. Her hair was pulled into a high ponytail and she wore thigh-high golden platform boots. Every bit of her exposed skin glistened with gold paint, her perfect figure gilded as if she was the prize treasure from an Egyptian tomb.

She was breathtaking.

Tilly was giggling, pretending to be self-conscious, shaking her head. 'Oh my God,' she mouthed to a friend. 'I can't believe I'm dressed like this!'

Nor could I.

She wore a black corset and patent-leather high-waisted briefs, fishnet tights and black stilettos, a white collar with a bow tie, and black satin bunny ears. Next to her Fraser wore black silk pyjamas with a purple velvet dressing gown and a captain's hat, a pipe held to his mouth.

The entire room's attention focused on these four like a spotlight. The crowd parted as they walked through, glinting and gleaming, oozing sex appeal. Nick and Cami stopped to talk to a group while Fraser and Tilly continued onwards. Too late I realised that the line they were walking brought them directly to us. My first thought – as ever – was escape, but Rav sensed it. 'You'll be fine,' he whispered.

Fraser reached for Rav's hand and shook it warmly. 'Good evening, Mr da Vinci!'

'*Buonasera, signore* Jenner.' Rav spoke with an even more exaggerated accent. I wanted to die. 'Or should I say *signore* Heffner!'

Fraser laughed. Then he smiled at me. My stomach clenched with embarrassment, my cheeks flushing beneath the heavy layer of face paint. 'And the *Mona Lisa*. You both look incredible.' Though I searched for it, I found no hint of anything other than kindness.

'Is Julian here yet?' Tilly asked. 'I heard rumours that he and his rugby mate are planning something epic for their costume.'

'Do you know what?'

'No idea. The girlfriend of one of the other rugby guys said they couldn't wait to show everybody.'

'I heard the same,' Fraser said. 'I saw him a couple of days ago and he said it was hilarious. Not sure how they'll beat Hugh and his Playboy bunny, though.' He pointed a finger at Tilly, who pouted and bobbed a curtsey.

Cami and Nick appeared at Fraser's shoulder. I was expecting them to turn away when they realised the painting Fraser was talking to was me. But they didn't.

Nick smiled. I noticed a golden smear on his cheek as if she'd marked him as hers. 'Hi, Vix.' He and I were civil to each other at Frederick Street. He would nod when we passed in the hallway or met in the kitchenette. Occasionally he'd say hello or give me a tight smile in the department, but tonight there was something more open to his greeting. His smile was wider and warmer.

Instinctively I glanced at Cami.

She rolled her eyes with a smile of her own. 'Oh for God's sake, it's been weeks. Let's put all that behind us, shall we? Feuds are for school, and we're here to have fun, not fight.'

'Too right.' Fraser grinned at her, but she ignored him, cooling a little as she cast a guilty glance at Nick, the same guilt I'd seen flash across her eyes at the New Year's Eve party. But it wasn't my problem. If Cami was screwing around behind Nick's back, he'd have to find out himself. There was nothing for me to gain by accusing her and having her deny it.

'You look really good,' Tilly said to me. It was clear the group had unanimously decided to end my banishment. 'How on earth did you make it?'

'Rav did it,' I said, conscious of the river of sweat trailing the line of my spine and the frame digging into my shoulders.

She reached out to touch my hair, and when she found it rock hard with gel and spray, she tapped it with a single scarlet nail. 'Oh Christ!' She snatched her finger away with an expression of mild revulsion. 'That's going to take some washing. Right, who's for shots?'

She and Cami linked arms and pushed their way through to the bar. Fraser followed.

I gave Rav a hard stare, flicking my eyes at Nick a couple of times.

It took a moment or two, but thankfully he got the hint. 'Just going to … er … check out the dance floor. Don't go anywhere, though. I need my muse.'

He moved away, greeting a friend in his loud fake Italian, waving his palette about like a flag. Nick and I were left facing each other, and almost immediately everything else – the people, the music, the clamour – faded into the background.

'You look brilliant,' he said.

'Like the real thing?' I smiled.

'Way more impressive.'

'Does this mean we're friends again?'

He hesitated, his face twisting in discomfort.

'Sorry. I shouldn't have said—'

'No, no. It's fine. I should have spoken to you ages ago about it all. I haven't been kind, and I've been feeling really guilty about it. What I did – what I let happen – wasn't right.'

'It was horrible not knowing where you'd gone.'

'I know. I panicked. When Cami texted me in the middle of the night and said she needed to see me, I didn't think, I just went.

She was all over the place. I've never seen her like that. Fragile and withdrawn. Shaking. She could barely talk. It really scared me. I didn't realise my friendship with you was doing that to her. I came back and grabbed a few things, spoke to Mrs Drummond, then left.' He looked over at the bar, his eyes finding Cami. 'She seems better tonight. We haven't been hanging out with the others as much. She hasn't wanted to. Tonight she's back to the Cami we know and love. It's as if she's given herself a shake. Spending time just the two of us has been good for us. Anyway, sorry, I'm going on. But yes,' he said. 'If you still want to, and you don't hate me, I'd like to be friends.' Then his smile fell from his face. 'Just don't—' He stopped himself and glanced over his shoulder. 'Don't tell her, OK?'

'About what?'

'About what happened.'

I stared at him for a moment. 'You didn't tell her?'

'God, no.' He appeared horrified at the thought. 'She wouldn't understand.'

'That it didn't mean anything?'

He took a breath, his expression hardening a touch. 'I know it's difficult to hear, but it's the truth.'

It meant nothing?

That was the *truth*?

Something snapped inside me. I'd had enough. I was done with the lies. This emotional roller coaster was exhausting. 'You know what? I can't fucking do this any more.'

'Do what?'

'Be with you like this. Pretend I'm OK with it. Nod and smile when you tell me what happened didn't mean anything. Keep trying to be someone you might fall in love with.' I dropped my manufactured southern accent, shrugging it off like a heavy blanket. 'I'm not Vix. I'm Victoria. I'm from Knutsford. Manchester. And this is how I speak. Frank Lloyd Wright isn't my favourite architect.

I think Julian and Tilly, Giles and Cami, even Fraser are entitled twats who live privileged lives they aren't even grateful for.'

His mouth fell open in bewildered confusion.

'I was only friends with them because of you.' Before I could stop them, words I should have kept inside me tumbled out in a torrent. 'Cami doesn't deserve you. I'm pretty sure she's sleeping with Fraser and has been since New Year's Eve. And my dad didn't die in a car crash. He stole money from two charities he did the books for. Then one night he blew a few thousand at a strip club, got drunk, ran his mouth off and told the wrong person, and got sent to prison. My mother can't leave the house because of the shame and my brother has manic depression.'

And at that moment, just as I'd taken my mask off and revealed my scales, Tilly and Cami bundled back with a tray of shots.

'Hey, hey, hey! Party time!'

I turned and walked away.

It was strange. Despite my trembling body and the tears that prickled my eyes, I felt ten tons lighter. I looked back at them. Nick and Cami were talking, heads close. Her face was wrought with shock. She glanced my way, then leant in to whisper something to Nick. He nodded.

'Oh, just *fuck* off,' I mouthed.

'Oh my God!' Sandy from *Grease* stopped abruptly in front of me. 'You look like an *actual* painting. Careful someone doesn't steal you!'

I gave her a thumbs-up, laced with sarcasm, and she skipped away, throwing herself at a leather-jacketed Danny, who smoothed his quiff with a comb.

My shoulders were agony now. I found a seat in the corner, where I sat down and dropped my head into my hands, the wooden frame pinching my skin.

'Hey.'

I looked up.

It was Fraser. The pipe was tucked into his breast pocket and he held two plastic cups each with a pink cocktail umbrella. 'You don't look like you're having much fun,' he said. 'Want a drink?' He held out one of the cups.

I took it without saying anything.

'Fuck knows what's in it. I asked for something fun and tropical. Think they added a bit of pineapple and vile blue curaçao. Maybe some vodka. What's up?'

'I told Nick that my dad's in prison, not dead, and now he hates me.'

Fraser laughed. 'Your accent's gone full Gallagher again.'

'This is me,' I said bitterly, and tipped the drink he'd handed me back in one. It was warm and alcoholic and burned the back of my throat.

He held out the second. 'Another?'

I grabbed it and drank.

'Anyway, why would Nick hate you? I can see why you wouldn't want to tell people your father's in prison. Dead is easier. Fewer questions. No big deal.' He shrugged. 'What did he do?'

'Defrauded two charities.'

Fraser whistled through his teeth. 'Shitty.' Then he rested his hand on my knee and smiled again. 'You know, even with all that ugly face paint, you're very pretty.' I flinched, embarrassed at the unexpected intimacy. I looked up. Cami and Tilly were stealing glances at me and talking. When I looked up, they turned quickly away.

Fuck them.

I stood.

'Where are you going?'

But I didn't answer him. I pulled at the frame, trying to release the shoulder straps. One side of the polystyrene cracked.

'No!' Rav cried, running through a group of people towards me. 'What are you doing?'

'I'm hot. I feel … faint. This costume…' I clawed at the frame. I needed it off me. 'It's doing my head in.' Ripping the left strap, I tore the frame off and threw it onto the floor.

Rav stared at me, open-mouthed.

'I'm sorry—' But he didn't wait for me to finish. He turned and left with a look of devastation on his face.

'For God's sake,' I whispered. 'It's only a stupid costume.'

'I'll get us another drink,' Fraser said. 'Wait for me here?'

I stood in my brown jacket, thick tights and DM boots amongst all the Lara Crofts and She-Ras and Pamela Andersons, and heard an echo of everything I'd said to Nick. I recalled the way his face had fallen when I told him the truth about my dad. God, where was Fraser with that drink? Then I realised he was probably talking to the others. I pictured them gossiping, the looks and whispers. I had to get out of there.

But of course, as I made for the stairway, I ran straight into golden girl herself.

We stood in front of each other, her beautiful eyes staring out of her gilded face, her hair gleaming, her body catwalk perfect. As I stared at her, she wavered in my vision, the heat and shame and alcohol rushing to my head.

'Are you OK?' Her voice was distant, as if I were hearing it through water.

'We had sex.'

She flinched as if I'd slapped her.

'Me and Nick.'

She blinked slowly. 'You think I don't know that?'

I shook my head, which felt loose on my neck. 'He didn't tell you.'

'He didn't need to. I can read him like a book. What he did wasn't fair on either you or me, but it happened. Sometimes these things do. They just happen.'

Why wasn't she angry? Why wasn't she confronting him? But then I realised she was talking about her and Fraser and what had happened between them. That was why she didn't care about me and Nick. If she did, she'd be a hypocrite.

'I know you love him,' she said then. Her sudden softness disarmed me. 'But I love him too, and life can be really crap sometimes.'

Then she turned and faded into the crowd.

My head swirled.

The partygoers around me began to distort. Their features grew and twisted. The music seemed to rise in volume, and objects and people melded together like melting boiled sweets. My chest felt tight. Was I having a panic attack? Was I drunk?

The room was becoming hotter and hotter.

Shit. Was I going to throw up?

I ran for the nearest door. It opened onto the outside deck and the fresh air was like a tonic. I stumbled to the railings and gripped on, leaning my body against them as I breathed in deep slugs of air and watched the light making shapes on the water below. People chatted and smoked around me, their noise deafening.

'Hey,' said a voice.

It was Fraser.

'Sorry I took so long. The bar had run out of ice. Shit,' he said. 'Are you OK?'

'I feel faint. My head …'

'Hopefully the fresh air will help. Or I can walk you home?'

'I just need a moment out here.'

Nick appeared at Fraser's side. His face was torn up with worry.

'No,' I moaned. 'Please. Nick, I'm sorry …'

He took my hand and began to lead me to the other side of the deck. I leant into him and closed my eyes. I wanted to stay there, curled up like a cat.

'We need to leave.' He pushed through the door back into the party room.

'What's going on?' Fraser said from behind us. Then he smothered a gasp. 'Holy *shit!*'

'Keep your eyes closed.' Nick's voice was urgent.

I opened my eyes. Fraser was staring at something, his mouth open in amused shock.

Nick tried to pull me to the stairway. 'Come on. Let's get out of here.'

'I'm not feeling good ...'

'Please come.' His eyes were locked on something behind me.

Then Cami appeared. 'Nick's right. Let's go upstairs. We should talk.'

'Get off me,' I said, pushing her out of the way.

The clamour in the room ebbed as people began to notice something, craning their necks, whispering, some smothering laughter, others exclaiming wildly. Then the crowd parted, and through the channel waltzed Julian and another boy – his rugby mate, had the others said? – laughing and strutting.

My breath caught and my knees buckled.

What? Oh my *God*. Vomit rose in my throat.

Julian was dressed in a short black skirt, black tights with holes, DM boots with yellow laces, identical to mine. He wore a wig, copper-red, with an inch of brown root on show. Dark lines of badly applied eyeliner. Round circles of pink on his cheeks. And there, pushing out of a button-up shirt, open to the waist, was a grotesque pair of enormous rubber breasts. Pale and bulbous, with bright red nipples and huge pink areolae. Daubed across them in black marker were the words *Perv Slayer*.

His rugby mate sashayed beside him. His skin was coloured white, eye sockets charcoal-grey, lips purple. One half of his head was covered in red sticky gloop, fake blood, which poured down his face like melted wax. He wore round rimless glasses and a crumpled grey suit. The whole outfit was soaked with red. There was something down the front of his trousers. It pushed the fabric outwards as if he had an erection. Around his neck hung a piece of white card, and on it was written *Boob Man.*

The laughing started like distant thunder. Julian made a stupid face. Shrugged theatrically. Mouthed, 'What? *What?*' a few times with fake innocence.

The world around me swirled. I was floating away.

Someone cried out, 'Nice tits, Draper!'

And then the two of them were standing in front of me. I stared, my face paint running in the tears that poured down my cheeks. I had to get out of there. I stumbled as I made a break for the stairway. As I passed Julian, he grabbed my arm. 'Hey,' he said. 'It's a joke. We're just mucking about.'

I stared at him. He blurred and swayed. The vulgar breasts grew bigger and bigger, as if they were being inflated. 'A *joke?*'

'Hey, the joke's on Gilpervert, not you,' said Julian's rugby mate.

Something raw took hold of me. I turned and blindly grabbed the first thing to hand, a bottle from a table beside me. My fingers closed around it and I swung it at Julian's head with a roar. But I was too drunk, my vision tipped, and there was a dull thud as the bottle made contact with the shoulder of a She-Ra behind him.

She cried out. 'Jesus Christ!' She stared at me with sharpened daggers. 'You fucking *psycho.*'

The room fell quiet, as if a thick layer of snow had settled over it.

I ran up the stairs and past people talking on the upper deck, out along the gangway, my head listing, vision disintegrating as if moving through a strobe light. At the end of the metal walkway I tripped and fell, launching into the air and landing heavily, my head smacking the pavement. I cried out and my hand flew to my forehead. When I drew it away, it was dark with blood.

'Vix! Shit, are you OK?'

It was Cami.

'Go away,' my voice slurred.

'You're hurt.'

I dragged myself upwards, unsteady on my feet, and saw her, Nick and Fraser.

'I'll take her home …'

Everything became hazy as my mind floated away.

Then there was nothing.

I had no idea how long I'd been drifting around the hinterland between sleep and wakefulness.

Where was I?

In bed. Undressed. My head pounded and my limbs felt heavy. Nausea came in waves. I touched my forehead and winced. Everything ached. Memories returned in snippets. Arriving at the party. Cami shining like a golden beacon. The way Nick looked at me with disgust when I told him about my dad. Bile rose in my throat as I had a vivid flash of Julian and his friend in those costumes. People laughing. The thud as I hit the girl with the bottle.

How had I got home?

I had no proper memory of anything after my fall, just isolated flashes. Stumbling up the stairs at Mrs Drummond's. The softness of my bed. A glass of water tipped to my lips. Something cool – a flannel? – on my forehead. Cami's face near mine. Someone pulling my dress off. Voices talking quietly.

'Will she be OK?'

'She needs to sleep it off.'

Then silence.

I carefully eased myself upright. Pain pierced my head from temple to temple. I winced. I needed water. I managed to stand and stagger to the door. When I reached for my dressing gown, I saw my arm was covered in bruises. Purple and pink, blotching my skin.

My other arm was the same. Another flash of memory. A knock. A crack of light as the door opened. A figure walking in. Then Julian's voice.

Why was Julian in my room?

'Go away.' I heard my own voice in the darkness. 'Leave me alone.'

My head swirled. I looked around. My underwear on the floor. I bent to pick up my pants. They were torn.

Then a memory of his weight on my bed as he sat down.

His voice again. 'I'm sorry ...'

I closed my eyes and dredged my brain, desperately searching for lost pieces. The door opening and closing.

Someone leaving or someone coming in?

Nick again. Cami. Another door. It was all too fuzzy. Another vivid feeling of weight. This time on top of me. Struggling to breathe.

A hand on my mouth?

It was so hard to make sense of the fragments. I walked over to the mirror. My lip was swollen. There was a cut on my forehead. Falling off the gangway. I'd hit my head as I ran from the dance. But my lip? I peered down at my naked legs. More bruising on my thighs. Fingers digging into me. A hand pulling my legs apart. Tearing my underwear off.

Julian in my room?

'Oh my God,' I said, letting out a breath.

I collapsed on the floor in horror.

I couldn't say how much time had passed before a knock on the door made me jump. I tried to move, but I was cold and stiff. Everything ached.

'Vix?' It was Nick.

'Don't come in!' My voice rasped against my dry, painful throat. I pulled myself up and clambered into bed, pulling the duvet around me.

'Are you OK?'

Emotion welled and I swallowed back a lump in my throat.

The door opened a crack and his face peered around the edge. I burst into tears, the sobs magnifying my throbbing headache.

'Hey,' he said softly. He walked in and sat on the edge of my bed, and I had a violent flash of Julian doing the same. I recoiled and pushed myself away from him. 'Go away,' I said through my tears.

'Let me help.'

'Leave me alone.'

But he didn't move.

'Get out!' I cried, mustering all the energy I could to force my voice out. 'Get *out!*'

And he went.

The room fell quiet and still. I drew my legs into my body and curled up tightly, everything hurting, inside and out.

My heart, like my body, was broken.

Some time later, another knock on the door. I'd ceased to have any concept of time. I stayed curled up, pretending I hadn't heard, pretending I wasn't there, pretending the wetness that had seeped out between my legs was a figment of my imagination.

'Victoria? It's Mrs Drummond.'

Just a little mouse.

'Can I come in?'

'I'm sleeping.'

The door opened. I sat up, drawing the duvet to my chin. Every bone and joint and muscle was rigid from lying in the same position for so long.

'Your brother's on the telephone,' she said. 'He sounds rather desperate. He wasn't making much sense.'

'I'll call him later.'

'I wonder if it might be urgent?' She hesitated. 'He said everything was getting too much. The word he used was *unhinged.*

He didn't sound good, if I'm honest.' But then she looked at me, her brow knotted. 'You don't look very well either. Maybe too much to drink last night?' Surprisingly, there was no note of reproach in her question. I could see her mind whirring, wondering, her face setting with concern. 'You can tell me if something's happened. It's what I'm here for.'

'I'll shower, then I'll call him.'

As the door closed, I pulled the duvet over my head and breathed in the stuffy dark air. I couldn't talk to my brother. Not now. I couldn't cope with his misery on top of my own. I'd call him later. Or in a day or two.

First I needed to process what had happened to me.

CHAPTER TWENTY-TWO

Coco

Coco ran into the kitchen. 'Oh my God, this woman – one of the guests – just marched up to Ingrid's husband and told him to go fuck himself!'

'What?' Maeve said, a smile breaking out over her face for the first time that day.

Coco snorted with laughter as she regaled her and Gina with the full story, from the moment Victoria appeared looking like she was out for blood to her spitting out the words, then turning on her heel and leaving them all at the table, open-mouthed. 'Seriously, I wish you could have seen that spongey face of his, all gobsmacked with the shock of it!' She laughed again.

Gina sniggered as she carefully arranged some delicate petits fours on a small plate.

Maeve sucked her teeth and nodded. 'Good for her. He's a real see-you-next-Tuesday, no doubt about it. One of the worst I've ever met, and I've been in hospitality for over thirty years. More money than sense. Not all of them can handle being wealthy. Rots their brains. Andre reckons the alcohol alone is nearing a hundred thousand.'

'*Pounds?*'

She sucked her teeth again. 'It's a different world, love.'

Coco thought of her mother scraping and scrimping, taking job after job, working until she was dead on her feet. Yet here these people were, spending enough to buy a house and a holiday and a yacht on one wedding. She looked at the pile of plates on the trolley. They couldn't even finish the food. How much were these leftovers worth? Thousands of pounds destined for the bin.

It struck her then how unfair she was to her mum. All Debbie wanted was for her daughter to have a shot at an easier life. Coco pictured her back at home, staring at her phone, tapping her fingers whilst waiting to hear what Ingrid Olsson's agent had said. This was all Coco had to do to make her happy this evening. One conversation. That was it. There was plenty of time to tell her she didn't want to be an actress or go on *Love Island*. Plenty of time to tell her she wanted to sit her A levels and apply to college to study English or creative writing. And hey, maybe Ingrid's agent would have contacts on the other side of the business, a friend who was a writer who could give her some advice on writing screenplays.

The music had started and most of the guests had moved from the ballroom. Coco thought she recognised the voice. Was it Harry Styles? God, if it was, her mother would go nuts. She searched the ballroom for Fraser, but he wasn't anywhere to be seen, so she assumed he'd gone to the marquee. She stepped out onto the terrace and walked across the lawn. The sun had set and it was getting dark; the sea had turned black and twinkled with lights from Falmouth. She peered into the marquee. It had been completely transformed into a nightclub of sorts. Gone were the cream drapes and flowers and white chairs and tables from earlier in the day, and in their place black silk, disco balls, mirrored cube tables and stools, a black dance floor inlaid with glitter, and a huge stage at the end with high-production lighting.

Just as she was about to go into the tent, she caught sight of Fraser on the terrace. He was leaning against the French window frame, smoking a cigarette and nursing a cognac.

'Oh hey,' she said, walking up to him. 'I was wondering … well … it's just I'm about to finish my shift …'

'Shit. God, sorry,' he said, taking a puff on his cigarette. 'It slipped my mind. When are you heading off?' He squinted against the smoke that billowed out as he exhaled.

Coco shrugged. 'Soonish?'

Fraser looked over her shoulder into the marquee. 'I'm introducing Ingrid and Julian's spin on the dance floor; she's swapped first dance for showtime. But that's our Ingrid. She wants everybody warmed up before she performs. Think the band are supposed to finish their set first, so I have a little time to look at your reel. To be honest, showreels are important and it's easy for me to tell you what's working and what's not. You've no idea how many castings are lost because a director fell asleep during the reel.'

'That would be incredible.' She smiled.

'There's a television with internet in Julian's suite. The one you brought champagne to earlier?'

'Upstairs?' Coco's alarm bells jangled quietly. Going to a hotel room with a man she didn't know wasn't something she was comfortable doing. 'I'm not sure.'

Fraser picked up on her hesitation. 'Of course. Sorry, I wasn't thinking. You don't know me from Adam.'

'I'm just, well …' Her voice trailed away and she shrugged a little.

'You're right to be cautious.' He smiled and threw his cigarette into the flower bed. 'Though we won't be up there long. The first few minutes are the most important. They need to grab the attention. The hotel might have a business room downstairs we can use. Wait here?'

Coco stood on the terrace and watched people dancing in the marquee. They were really going for it, as if at a festival, which wasn't surprising given the amount of alcohol and drugs they'd stuffed into their bodies.

A few moments later, Fraser came back. 'The two conference rooms are being used for wedding prep and as a green room for the performers. But Ingrid's in her room getting changed for her dance, so you won't be alone with me.'

Coco hesitated. 'Won't she mind?'

'She pretends to be tough, but helping new talent is kind of her thing. She'll probably give you a few tips as well.' He put his hands against his chest and bowed his head. 'And I promise, hand on heart, I'm a man of exemplary manners.'

She pictured her mother beaming and applauding wildly. She would definitely be telling her to go, and as she followed Fraser down the corridor, she smiled, imagining how happy Debbie would be when she told her that Ingrid's actual agent had watched her showreel.

When they got to reception, Victoria was sitting on a chair, knees pressed together, hands in her lap. She looked up when she saw them. Coco gave her a thumbs-up and Victoria smiled, but the smile was weak and slipped off her face almost immediately.

'Good luck with everything.' She sounded tense and wobbly, on the verge of tears.

'Are you OK?' Fraser asked.

'I've a taxi coming.'

He went over to her and bent to kiss her cheek. 'You're not the first person to tell him to fuck himself, you know.'

Victoria sniffed.

'Safe journey.'

She nodded.

'Coco, shouldn't you be in the kitchen with Gina? They're trying to get the cheese and ham croissants cooked and ready for midnight.' Darren had appeared like an apparition.

'Oh, I'm …' Coco's voice trailed away.

'Ingrid asked me to find a female member of staff to help with her outfit. I grabbed this lovely girl, who said she could spare a moment.' Fraser nodded at Coco, who stared at him before glancing at Darren and smiling as best she could.

'I'm not sure we can—'

'You can speak to Ingrid if you want? Discuss it with her?' Fraser leant over the reception desk and took hold of the phone.

'No, no. Go on up. It's fine.' Darren shot Coco a look of exasperation, as if she'd been nothing but trouble all day, which felt unfair. Coco managed to hold back her glare.

Fraser started to dial.

'I said it's fine.' Darren's hand shot out and tried to take the phone. 'No need to disturb her.'

Fraser pulled it away. They held each other's gaze for a moment, before Fraser smiled. 'If it's all right with you, I'd like to speak to Ingrid to tell her we're on our way up. We don't want to walk in without warning, do we?'

Darren smiled insincerely, his mouth tight, nostrils slightly flared. What on earth did her mother see in this weasel?

Fraser dialled. 'Ingrid? Yes, it's Fraser.' Pause. 'Are you OK for us to come up?' Pause. 'Yes, of course. On our way.' He put the receiver back in the cradle. Then he looked at Darren. 'Sorry,' he said. 'Did you want to talk to her too?'

'I don't need to talk to Mrs Draper, no. Can I help with anything else, sir?'

Fraser clapped him on the back. 'The service here is top notch, no need to worry. I'll be popping a glowing review on Tripadvisor.' He winked, and Darren responded with a tightening of his mouth that Coco assumed was supposed to pass for a smile.

She followed Fraser up the stairs, past the thickset guards, who hadn't moved a muscle in hours. He turned to her as they reached the top.

'Number one rule of life? Never let a bellend like that tell you to go into the kitchen.' He laughed. 'And,' Fraser added, 'for what it's worth, I think you'll make a great actress. You've a good look and a bit of spice. That goes a long way.'

At the end of the corridor he stopped in front of the door,

reached into his pocket and took out a card, which he pressed against the entry pad.

The light turned green.

'You have a key?' Coco glanced back down the corridor.

'For best-man duties.' He smiled and pushed the door open. 'Wait until you see the view from the terrace. It's beautiful.' He stepped to one side to allow her in. 'After you.'

CHAPTER TWENTY-THREE

As I waited for the taxi, I couldn't clear my thoughts of what Julian had done to me all those years ago. I recalled what he'd said to me when we stood face to face earlier, the first time we'd seen each other since that horrific night.

I trust this means you've forgiven me.

Forgive him? How could I ever forgive him?

I cringed as I recalled the way I'd struggled to speak, managing to say nothing more than 'Congratulations.' And then later, sitting in silence, watching him humiliate Coco. Why hadn't I said something? Why did I stay so pathetically mute?

I became aware of people approaching reception. Fraser and Coco. She gave me a thumbs-up and I tried to smile. I told her good luck and I meant it. I wished she didn't feel the need to do what her mother wanted, and I hoped that sometime soon, maybe when she got home tonight, or over breakfast in the morning, she'd pluck up the courage to tell her the truth. Part of me wanted to speak to her mother myself. Beg her to let Coco make her own life choices. But it wasn't my place, and who was I to offer advice to anybody anyway.

Fraser was talking to the manager on reception. As they spoke, Coco threw the man one of her fabulous scowls. Fraser mentioned Ingrid's name. I strained my ears to hear what they were saying. Something about Coco going up to help Ingrid. Fraser then reached for the phone as the manager made a feeble attempt to stop him.

He spoke to Ingrid, and then the two of them headed towards the stairs. The man behind the desk mouthed 'Wanker' as they walked away, then straightened his jacket and checked his watch.

Through the window to the side of the main door, I saw car headlights and a small orange taxi light pulling up. As I stood, I glanced down the corridor towards the ballroom and those moronic bouncers. Who did Julian think he was? Sitting on a throne, drinking liquid gold, mopping up venison, treating everybody around him like shit on his shoe. Painful flashes of memory came at me again. His weight. My bruising. His hand over my mouth …

'Where to, miss?' said the driver, through the open passenger window as I approached.

I hesitated before giving him the name of the guest house.

He nodded and I reached for the door handle, but my hesitation grew stronger. Julian barged back into my thoughts, gurning and laughing. His smug superiority became exaggerated in my caricaturist's mind, his sickening smile stretching widthways, eyes narrowing to slits, cheeks puffing out.

'Actually,' I said, backing away from the taxi, 'I've changed my mind.'

'What? No, you've still got—'

I didn't hear the rest. I ran back into the hotel. The manager looked up from behind the desk. 'Can I help you?'

'I gave my purse to a friend to look after. He still has it,' I called over my shoulder as I jogged down the panelled corridor.

The bodyguards moved to block my entry. 'For goodness' sake,' I said. 'I was just in there. My friend has my purse.'

They exchanged a look, as if trying to decide whether to let me go in.

'I need my purse.' I spoke through gritted teeth. 'I've a taxi waiting.'

They stepped aside like pre-programmed automatons.

'Arseholes,' I breathed.

The room was mostly empty. A few scattered people at the tables. A couple were kissing, her straddling him with no care for who was watching, tongues moving like salsa dancers. I walked through the ballroom and out of the French windows onto the terrace. There was a small group sitting around a blazing fire pit, smoking and laughing. The music was loud. Lights flashed from the marquee. The air smelt of burning oil from the flares that dotted the flower beds and ran alongside the pathways.

Julian was on the lawn in front of the marquee. He was smoking a stubby cigar and holding a glass of that ridiculous cognac. Adrenalin pulsed in my veins. He stood in a circle with Simon, Giles and the other one. Noah? I stared at Noah. Something he'd said earlier rang in my head. He'd wanted to apologise. Why? He was definitely familiar. I knew him but why couldn't I place him?

I saw the moment he caught sight of me. There was a beat before he smiled. A glint of embarrassment? I focused on his features as I drew closer. I was good with faces. Faces were my bread and butter. I searched my mind as if flicking through index cards, desperate to find the one that matched him.

Then it hit me.

It was Julian's rugby mate. The other half of his hateful costume. The bloodied reincarnation of Neil Gilbert.

'You were on the boat,' I said quietly. 'The rag dance. You dressed up as ...' My voice faded.

Noah opened his mouth. Was he going to say sorry again? Tell me it was a joke? Tell me again how Julian had led him astray?

I raised my hand to silence him. 'I don't want to hear it.'

Noah was nothing to me. It wasn't him I wanted.

I turned on Julian. 'I should have gone to the police.'

He laughed. 'Because of our costumes?'

'I should have reported you.'

278

'*Reported* me? What on earth are you talking about? Reported me for *what*?' He looked at the others, baffled, making a face to insinuate I was insane.

Tears gathered in my eyes. I looked up at the sky, dark now, stars twinkling a million miles away, the music and cheering and dancing an inappropriate backdrop to the pain I felt.

Tilly stepped out of the shadows. I expected her to shout at me, but she didn't. She rested a hand on my arm. 'Vix, I think you should leave. For your own sake. This situation doesn't seem to be good for you.'

Her words were coaxing and kind. It felt like a trap. I pulled my arm away from her.

'No, hang on a minute. She's not going anywhere,' Julian said. 'You can't sling accusations like that around without explaining yourself. Why would you call the police for a fancy dress costume? It was a student prank. God, everybody's so bloody delicate these days. So bloody *woke*.' He pointed angrily at me with his cigar. 'It was you who hit that girl with a bottle. We should have called the police on *you*.'

My heart pounded. I heard his breathing in my ear. His hand on my mouth …

'You *raped* me.'

His mouth opened and closed like a guppy. 'What did you say?'

I stepped closer to him, my finger prodding his spun-gold suit. 'After the dance. You came into my room. And you raped me.'

'Are you out of your mind?'

Blood and adrenalin pumped through my veins. 'Maybe. But not about this.'

Julian looked back towards the hotel, and gestured with urgent flicks of his fingers at the bodyguards, who were now loitering at the French windows.

'I did nothing of the sort.' His face was twisted with malice. 'Why would I *rape* you? I never had any problems getting women.

279

I could get whoever I wanted, whenever I wanted. Have you seen my wife?'

'But you couldn't get *me*, could you? Remember New Year's Eve? I knocked you back. In front of people. I didn't give you what you wanted. So you came to my room that night and took it.'

Nick and Cami appeared next to Julian. Nick clapped him on the shoulder, 'Sad to say, we have to get home. We were going to slip away, but—' He caught sight of me and stopped speaking suddenly. 'Vix? I thought you'd gone?'

I ignored him and stepped closer to Julian. 'Did you hear me?'

Julian made some sort of communication with the bodyguards as they drew close, and they grabbed my arms.

'What are you doing?' Nick cried.

I pulled back from the men, managing to free one arm. In a repeat of history, I grabbed at something, Noah's glass of cognac, and hurled the contents at Julian's face. He blinked at me, brandy pouring down his cheeks and shirt, then slowly took the handkerchief out of his breast pocket and blotted the liquid from his face, lip curled with disgust. 'Get rid of her,' he said.

'It's OK, Julian,' Nick said. 'I'm sure this is all a misunderstanding—

'Get *rid* of her!'

The bodyguards began to drag me back towards the hotel. I tried to shake them off. 'Let go of me!' I looked at each of them in turn. 'Let *go!*'

But they didn't let me go. They bundled me over the terrace and through the French windows, people stopping to watch, whispering, alerting each other to the disturbance. A few jumped up looking shocked, backing away as if running for safety.

The manager bustled out, his face pale. 'Do we need the police?'

'No,' Nick called from behind me. 'Absolutely not.'

'Let go of her,' came Cami's voice. Then she was beside me. 'Did you hear me, for Christ's sake?'

'Let's all calm down,' Nick said. 'Everybody's had a bit too much to drink that's all.'

'I'm not drunk!'

Nick took a breath and tried to smile. The manager flapped helplessly, as if this was the most dramatic thing ever to have taken place at Lowencliffe Hall.

Cami stepped in front of the men. 'Let go of her. She's not going to do anything. Are you?' She looked at me with meaning.

I shook my head. 'Please. You're hurting me.'

They finally let go. 'If she's not off the premises in five minutes, Mr Draper will have her arrested,' the one on the left growled.

'Arrested?' I rubbed my wrists where the men had held me. 'What for?'

'Public disorder and assault.'

'*Assault?*'

'You threw a glass.'

'I threw brandy.'

'You were going to glass him, and that's what we'll tell the police.'

I swore under my breath.

As I walked back towards the main door, I passed the man who'd been on the gate earlier. When he saw me with the bodyguards, I watched him put two and two together, a victorious smile creeping over his face. 'Oh, go fuck yourself,' I said.

Nick and Cami followed me outside. I wanted them to leave me alone. A pantomime of care and concern was the last thing I felt like.

'What was all that about?' Nick said.

Every atom of my body and soul was exhausted. What was the point? Men like Julian Draper never had to face up to the consequences of their actions. They were always protected. 'It doesn't matter.'

'I think it might.'

I sighed and shook my head. 'Julian raped me,' I said, so weary I wanted to curl up on the floor and sleep.

'What? *When?*'

'After the rag dance.'

'Are you sure?'

I looked at him in disbelief. 'Am I *sure?*'

'Sorry. I didn't mean that. It's ... well ... Cami and I took you back in a cab that night. We put you to bed.'

Cami stared at the ground, rubbing her wrist rhythmically.

'It was after that,' I said. 'He came into my room.'

'I know. We were there. He came to apologise. Fraser made him. They came to Frederick Street to say sorry, but you were out of it. There was no way you were in a fit state to hear what he had to say, so he said he'd talk to you the next day. Cami and I went back to the boat with him. Cami made him take the costume off. He threw those breasts he was wearing into the river. He was with us all night. He and Lottie got back together at the dance. After the boat, a few of us went to hers and ordered pizza.'

Cami looked at me then. She held my gaze for a minute. 'It wasn't Julian.'

CHAPTER TWENTY-FOUR

'What do you mean?'

'What I said. It wasn't Julian.'

She was twitchy, on edge. What was she withholding?

'Nick's right. We were with Julian when he came to your room. We left with him and went back to Lottie's with him. We ate breakfast together.'

They were closing ranks to protect their friend. Why would they do that? Indignant rage bubbled up inside me. 'Don't tell me it didn't happen. He was in my room. I woke up with bruises. My underwear was torn. There was *semen*.' My voice cracked. Twenty-five years later and the pain of the assault was still raw.

'Julian was never alone with you. We were there when he tried to say—'

'You don't believe me?'

She stared at me. There was so much going on in her eyes. Too much to read. 'I believe you,' she said. 'But it wasn't Julian.' She glanced at Nick, grimacing as if something was piercing her.

'What?' Nick said, brow knotted with concern. 'Just tell me what's going on.'

We were interrupted by a car racing up the driveway, gears crunching, engine screaming. A small red Vauxhall slid to a halt on the gravel and the driver's door flew open. The woman who jumped out was white-faced, eyes shooting left and right as if searching for something.

'Coco?' Her voice was thick with panic. 'Have you seen her? The waitress? She's my daughter. I need to find her.'

'She's here,' Nick said.

'What's wrong?' Cami asked.

'I think she's in trouble. She sent me a text. Just now. I was waiting on the road by the entrance for her to let me know she'd finished work.'

I'd pictured this women so differently. Loud, brash, a bottle blonde whose ambition gave her a steely fire, but she was nothing like that. She was small and quiet, with a soft mousy perm, wearing a zip-up fleece over a light grey T-shirt and no make-up, which accentuated her pale-faced worry.

'What text?' Nick asked.

The woman pulled her phone from her pocket and turned it screen out.

Help mum in ind

'Please help me find her.' Then she grabbed Cami's arm, chewing her bottom lip. 'But, shit, don't let the manager know. We can't make a scene. I promised there'd be no trouble if he gave her this job.'

'She went somewhere with Fraser,' I said.

'Fraser?' Cami's face fell in horror.

'They went up to see Ingrid about something. I heard him talking to her on the phone in reception.'

'She's with Ingrid?' The woman smiled with relief. 'Oh goodness me. That's great! The text must have been an accident. Maybe she sat on her phone.'

'We need to find her.' Cami spoke urgently as she started to run back towards the hotel.

'Is something wrong?' Coco's mother called.

'We need to find her *now*.'

When we pushed through the door, the manager started to speak, then noticed Coco's mother. 'Debbie? How did you get past the gate?'

'What do you mean? I'm here all the time.'

'The night man should have phoned up.'

'It's Keith. He knows me. I'm only here to collect Coco.'

'Is everything all right?'

Debbie forced a smile. 'I'd like to be at home and in bed, that's all. Daft girl was supposed to meet me outside. Difficult to communicate without phones, and you know what teenagers are like.' She rolled her eyes and tutted, and the manager nodded in a way that made it clear he had no idea what teenagers were like.

'You,' he said as he noticed me. 'Get out.'

Cami and Nick protested, but Darren scooted back behind the desk and grabbed the phone whilst frantically beckoning the goons, who'd resumed their posts at the end of the corridor. They needed no persuading to start running back towards us, hands on earpieces.

I swore and looked at Cami. 'Upstairs. Ingrid's room.' I raised my hands, stepping back towards the door. 'I'm going. I'm going.'

As I retreated, I spotted the ballroom doors opening. It was Ingrid. She'd changed and was wearing shiny turquoise hot pants and a bikini top made from mother-of-pearl and shells that barely covered her breasts. Her face shimmered with glitter and metallic eyeshadow.

The security guards grabbed at me.

'Stop!' Ingrid yelled. 'What's going on?'

Debbie's face fell, her jaw slackening in surprise. 'Oh my God.' Her voice was breathless with awe, her panic momentarily forgotten. 'It's you.' Then her brow knotted in confusion. 'Aren't you supposed to be with Coco?'

'Who?'

'Oh God,' whispered Cami.

I looked at her face – pale and stretched – and my stomach clenched. But I'd heard Fraser talking to Ingrid on the phone in her room. Had he been pretending? The two heavies continued to push me backwards. Their hold on me was too strong for me to break free, their faces set with cartoonish menace.

'Stop right now. Let go of her,' Ingrid shouted again. The men hesitated, pushing against me still. 'Did you hear me?'

Their hands fell away from me as if they'd run out of batteries.

'Why are they throwing you out?' she asked.

'I chucked a glass of brandy over Julian.'

'Christ almighty, I do that every day. Leave her alone,' she said to them.

They stepped aside, glaring at me. I ran through them, back to Cami and the others, reaching them just as Ingrid did. 'He was on the phone to you,' I said. 'I heard him. Arranging for you to meet Coco and talk to her. In your room.'

'What? I haven't spoken to anybody. Who was this?'

'Fraser.'

The colour drained from her face.

'Coco sent me a text,' Debbie said quickly. 'It didn't make sense. It said *help*. Is she all right?'

'Ingrid!' came Julian's bellow from the end of the corridor. 'That woman wants us for the dance.'

'Key to our room. Now!' she called back.

Julian bustled up to us, steely eyes locked on me. 'What the hell is she—'

'Key!' Ingrid held out her hand. 'Hurry.'

'You have one, don't you?'

She fixed him with a look. 'Where exactly do you think I'd keep it in this outfit? Just give me the key.'

'Fraser has it.'

'We need to get up there.' Cami's fear was palpable.

Julian's expression changed, guilt slicking his face. We all saw it.

Ingrid turned to the manager. 'Duplicate key. *Now*,' she barked.

'Something's wrong, isn't it?' Debbie's voice trembled.

Ingrid grabbed the card from the manager's hand and started running towards the staircase.

As I moved to follow, Julian grabbed my arm.

'Get off me,' I said as I pulled away from him.

'It wasn't me.'

My stomach contracted.

'I came to apologise that night. Fraser said I had to. Said I'd taken things too far. He came with me. He and Nick charmed that landlady of yours to let us in. I came in to talk to you. But you were out of it, so I said sorry and left, then I went back to the party. I didn't come back. It wasn't me.'

I studied his face, the small changes in his expression, the flickering in his eyes. The bravado had gone. He was telling the truth. My world shifted as history began to rewrite itself.

'Fraser didn't leave with you, did he?' I whispered.

'He needed the loo. He said he'd catch me up. I just wanted to get back to the party and that girl I was seeing.'

The last bit of the horrific jigsaw puzzle slotted into place.

'Did you know?'

'Know what?'

'What he did to me?'

'He told me you had sex. He said you'd been after him all night. Said he went in to say goodbye and you made a move on him.'

I stared at Julian, this man I'd feared and hated in equal measure in all my waking thoughts and nightmares for over two decades; the man I'd wrongly accused. But then, as I watched his face, the twitches and tells, I realised that he knew what had really happened to me. Even if he hadn't known at the time, when I'd confronted him by the marquee, when I'd accused him of rape, he'd known then it was Fraser, yet he'd said nothing. He'd belittled me in front of the others and got me thrown out like some sort of criminal.

Had he known Fraser was taking Coco up to his room?

Had he known she'd be alone with him?

I turned and ran after the others.

CHAPTER TWENTY-FIVE

Early March 2000

It was a few days after the rag dance and I still wasn't able to leave my room. I'd removed my sheet from the mattress, bundled it up and thrust it to the back of my wardrobe, then moved my pillows and duvet to the floor. I couldn't sleep on the bed; if I tried, I was plagued by flashes of pain and glimpses of blurred memory. Nick had been up to try and talk to me a few times, but I couldn't face him. I couldn't face anything.

Mrs Drummond knocked on my door some time in the afternoon. I stayed quiet. Held my breath. But she kept on, her *tap-tap-tapping* getting louder and more insistent.

'Victoria, please open the door. It's urgent.'

I got up from the floor, ready to tell her I'd call my brother back, that I wasn't dead, that I was, indeed, just a little mouse. But her face stopped me in my tracks. It was pale, no colour at all, her lips tight. Something about the look in her eyes made my blood freeze.

'The police are downstairs.' Her voice cracked. 'They need to talk to you.'

'Do you know why?' My mind shot to the rag dance. The girl I'd hit with the bottle. Had she pressed charges? Or maybe someone had found out what Julian had done.

'They didn't say. They're in my living room with a cup of tea and a custard cream.'

I followed her downstairs, my mind turning over and over.

Dread filled me as I got closer to Mrs Drummond's door. As she reached for the handle, her words from the other morning rang like a tolling bell.

My brother.

The word he used was unhinged.

An image of Neil Gilbert flared in my head. His broken body on the tracks at White City. Smashed face unrecognisable. Grey suit and white shirt soaked in blood …

Oh Christ. Mikey.

No …

I didn't want to go any further. I wanted to run back upstairs, barricade the door shut and stay up there for ever.

The two uniformed police officers loomed large in Mrs Drummond's living room. The room was crammed full of stuff, like a bric-a-brac shop, with tapestry throws, tasselled cushions, spider plants, dark furniture, photographs of smiling children, and hundreds of little china ornaments. It smelt of potpourri, talcum powder and roast chicken. My stomach rumbled, despite my apprehension. I hadn't eaten since the day before.

'Have a seat, lovey.' Mrs Drummond gestured at a dark green velvet armchair with a crocheted blanket in all the colours of the rainbow draped over one arm.

She hovered for a bit; the officers smiled and waited until she got their hint. 'I'll be in the kitchen if you need me.'

The air hummed with foreboding. Even the ticking of the carriage clock on the mantelpiece sounded ominous.

'Victoria Fisher?'

I nodded.

'I'm afraid we're here with some bad news.' The policeman paused. 'There's no easy way to break this to you.'

'It's my brother, isn't it?' I spoke quietly, clutching my arms around my body as tightly as I could. 'It's Mikey. He's killed himself, hasn't he?'

CHAPTER TWENTY-SIX

Mikey didn't kill himself.

He killed my mother.

It was hard to make sense of what the police were telling me, and as they spoke, I drifted away. I retained slivers of information, but everything from the moment I walked into Mrs Drummond's room until the following day became a murky haze.

I would later find his scrawled note in my desk drawer. My name written in his handwriting made my blood freeze. I pictured him rolling a cigarette then sitting down to write, my mother's bloodied body motionless on the kitchen floor below.

Dear Victoria,

What happened? Right. So she's playing music, yeah? Fleetwood Mac. I'm sick of it. She's dancing. Why is she dancing? She says she's had enough of being sad. She says you told her she should be happy. 'Happy? Ha! That's dead nice for you,' I say. 'But this music is doing my head in. Turn it down.' She ignores me. I go back to bed. Put my head under the pillow but the music's like torture. I go down and tell her to turn it off. Doesn't even look at me. Just keeps dancing. 'Turn it *off!*' I'm dead angry now. They say it's a red mist, don't they? And this mist is like gas and I'm filling right up and any moment some twat will light me with a match and I'll explode. I turn it off myself. She swears and turns it back on. So I pull the plug out the wall. She shouts. Says she hates me. Says I bring her down. I tell her I'm feeling bad. I get these dark thoughts, you know? Sometimes I want to die. Dark, dark thoughts. Mum rolls her eyes and plugs the music in. I want to call you. You know how to calm me down. But you seem to hate me now. So I ask Mum again but she turns the music up louder. I snapped like a twig. Proper lost it. I grabbed a knife and told her to stop dancing. She ignored me so I stuck the knife in her. 'Turn the fucking music *down*!' Next thing I know she's not dancing any more. She's on the floor. There's blood. I turn the music off and ask if she's OK. She doesn't answer me. Anyway, I'm going now. Catching the bus to the police. Hope you're happy.

Your brother,
Mikey

His words crawled all over me like insects.

I closed my eyes. All I could see was the old tramp from Mum's story. His features amplified. Mad eyes staring. Lips pulled back to reveal yellowed teeth. Gnarled finger pointing at my brother in his pram.

Devil child.

Nick and Cami spoke to the coroner's office and arranged for me to see her body. They came to Manchester Royal Infirmary with me, and I was glad they did. It was hard enough to move, let alone get myself onto a train. I couldn't talk to them on the journey up – I was numb and dazed – but they sat with me quietly, and bought tea and fruit cake from the buffet car.

'Sugar helps with the shock,' Cami said, pushing the cake closer to me.

I wanted to tell her cake couldn't help when your mother had been stabbed to death by your brother whilst dancing to Fleetwood

Mac. I closed my eyes and allowed myself to inhabit a parallel world, one where she was still alive, standing in the kitchen smiling, holding a glass of Chardonnay and calling up to us.

'Dinner time, kids!'

I saw us tearing down the stairs, Mikey pulling my pigtail, me thumping him on the arm, both of us laughing as we piled into the kitchen and tucked into Mum's lasagna. Though she'd always been a dreadful cook, right then I violently missed the stodgy, flavourless food of my youth.

Nick chatted to the taxi driver who drove us from the station to the hospital while Cami held my hand, her thumb stroking back and forth like a metronome. I didn't have the energy to pull away from her. At one point, she stopped stroking and asked about the bruising on my arm.

I didn't answer.

'Maybe from falling off the boat the other night?'

I stared straight ahead, trying to keep from spinning out of control. I was all over the place. Emotions fired through me. My body ached. I was too shell-shocked to even cry.

The train pulled in to Manchester Piccadilly. People stood and stretched and retrieved bags. I didn't move. I was frozen.

'Vix?' Nick said.

The name sounded surreal, as if he was talking to a stranger.

When we arrived at the hospital, Cami had a conversation with the woman behind the glass screen on the reception. Their voices were low. The woman looked at me with soft sympathy, then gestured as if giving directions. My mother was on the third floor. We took the lift. The fluorescent light was harsh on our skin. Nick and Cami didn't look as shiny as usual.

'I hate hospitals,' Nick whispered to Cami.

'Me too,' she said.

I followed them down the corridor. The smell of disinfectant was strong, but not strong enough to cover the stench of death. At the double doors that led into the mortuary, I stopped. 'I think I'm going to faint,' I said.

Cami led me to a chair while Nick fetched a polystyrene cup of water. They sat either side of me as I sipped the water and waited for my head to stop whirling.

'Do you want us to come in with you?' Nick asked when I finally stood, my legs unsteady. The tenderness in his voice hurt like acid. All I wanted was for him to take me somewhere safe, but instead he reached for Cami's hand. Neither of them wanted to come in with me. I could see it in their eyes.

I shook my head.

'Are you sure you'll be OK?' Cami smiled gently.

What did she mean by OK?

With a dead mother, a murderous brother, a violated body and a shattered heart?

How would I ever be OK again?

Despite the circumstances of her death, Mum looked peaceful. I don't know what I was expecting. Maybe visible pain and trauma? Blood everywhere? Blame tattooed on her pallid skin? But it was nothing like that. She looked calm. Serene, even. As I stared down at her, I realised I'd never seen her look serene before.

Perhaps she was finally happy.

'I'm sorry,' I whispered. Then I collapsed on the floor, my head against the cold metal of the trolley she lay on, and cried.

As my crying ebbed, the bruising on my wrists came into focus.

You did this.

You.

If it wasn't for you, I'd have picked up the phone to my brother. I'd have talked him down. I'd have stopped it. But you hurt me and I didn't take his call.

Guilt and blame circled my head like prowling lions. I should have taken Mikey's phone call. I should have gone home to see my family.

I should never have left them.

He should never have hurt me.

It took a few weeks to sort out the funeral. It was small. Most of Mum's friends had drifted away after Dad went to prison, which wasn't surprising, as she turned down any invitation to see anybody and never left the house.

The service was held in the crematorium in Northwich. The vicar talked about creationism and how believing in Jesus would save our souls. He didn't seem to know much about Mum, so maybe he was just filling time.

Thankfully, Mikey wasn't granted permission to attend. Instead, he telephoned. I froze when I heard his voice.

'For God's sake, Victoria, *say* something!'

Still I couldn't talk. I felt sick.

'Talk to me.'

Finally I found the words. 'I have nothing to say to you. I *hate* you.'

'I can explain. When I'm out of this place, I'll explain. I'll find you and explain it all.'

'I never want to see you again.'

Then, with a flat tone, he said, 'You should have called me back.'

Later, I went home and packed my belongings – important papers, money, savings book, passport – knowing I'd never return. I'd assumed – vaguely – I'd go back to QSA, but when I got off the train at King's Cross, something stopped me heading out and walking to Frederick Street. Instead, I wandered through the bustling station, lost, alone and torn to shreds.

From nowhere, I heard an echo of Nick's voice describing Paris with such warmth and enthusiasm. Didn't he say you could catch a train there from London? The more I thought about Paris the more convinced I became. It was as if that was where Nick wanted me to go. As if he were guiding me. I caught the Tube to Waterloo and there I bought a ticket to Paris. My stomach buzzed with adrenalin. Another new start. Perhaps Nick would join me. Perhaps he would take me to the museums and restaurants he loved.

But the city was nothing like the sanctuary I'd hoped it would be. It was big and brash and I spoke only a little pidgin French. I managed to find a room in a youth hostel near the station. For three days I lived on a bag of brioche buns I'd bought for five francs and free instant coffee from the hostel's reception. I wandered the streets and slept. On the fourth day, I walked past the Louvre. Of course I thought of Nick telling me about the *Mona Lisa* and *Liberty*. I thought of them both in that building. In a trance I walked into the gallery. I stood in front of the *Mona Lisa*, but all I could see was my face in hers, as if it were me up there, nailed to the wall, doomed to hang for eternity, a mush of underwhelming browns and greys. I sat on a leather bench in front of the painting and watched the thousands of people who came and went in a continuous slow-moving queue. Some paused to take photographs, others filed past, glancing at her for no longer than a second or two. I thought of Nick in that same queue of people. Unmoved. Unimpressed. The painting too plain and dull to catch his eye.

A security guard asked me to leave at closing. '*Vous ne pouvez pas dormir ici. Il faut que vous partiez.*'

I didn't understand him, but I could read his face, his features, his expression. I hoped he might leave me alone and let me stay where I was. If he had, would I ever have moved?

I decided I'd save *Liberty* for when Nick could go with me. I imagined him asking if I'd seen her already. 'No,' I'd say. 'I was waiting for you. You said you wanted to take me, remember?'

The following day, I began my journey south in a traumatised stupor, stopping for a night or so in both Dijon and Lyon – I don't remember a single detail about either – then a small village outside

Montélimar, where I worked on a farm for a month in exchange for lodging and food.

Eventually I ended up in Marseille, where I met Jean with his rough Gallic charm, drank pastis, had dull sex, and ended up stuck, dreaming of Nick and what might have been, and battling my nightmares.

Fourteen years later, my brother was released, and that was when I decided to call Nick. I was terrified Mikey would come looking for me. Terrified he'd hurt me. It crossed my mind it might be better to kill myself than wait for him to find me. I became paralysed with fear. The only person I could think of, the only person I felt safe with, was Nick.

So I picked up the phone and called him.

'Please,' I'd said, between sobs. 'I'm so scared. I'm having thoughts … About killing myself. My brother, Mikey … He's out of prison … I think he's coming for me. Please help me, Nick. You're the only person I can trust. *Please* help me.'

CHAPTER TWENTY-SEVEN

Coco

The suite was insane. Bigger than her whole house. The sitting room had two sofas and a glass coffee table piled high with fancy-looking books, a vase of fiery red flowers and a bowl overflowing with exotic fruit. On the right, through a half-open door, was the bedroom. The bed was at least twice the size of her mum's, with a gold bedspread and a chandelier above it. In front of her was a set of double doors leading out to a balcony that had an array of plant pots with spotlit foliage.

'Ingrid?' Fraser called, hovering at the bedroom door.

When there was no answer, he went in. She heard another knock on a different door, which she assumed was the bathroom. He came back seeming confused. 'Strange,' he said. 'She was up here a moment ago. Oh, hang on, my phone just buzzed.'

Coco watched him retrieve his phone from his jacket pocket.

'I know, I know,' he said. 'We were supposed to hand them in. Naughty me.' He grinned and looked down at the screen. 'It's a text from Ingrid – she knows I kept my phone. She's gone down to fetch a bottle of champagne.' He slipped it back into his pocket. 'Said to make ourselves comfortable.'

'Couldn't she get room service?'

'Yes,' he said, his face registering confusion. 'You're right. Maybe she needed to talk to Julian. Anyway, I'm sure she won't be long. We'll watch your reel while we wait for her.'

The reality of actually having to watch the reel with him suddenly hit her. Her mum didn't have the five hundred pounds it would have cost to get a professional three-scene reel, so she'd stitched something together with the help of Darren, who'd clearly lied about being an expert with iMovie. She was pretty sure Fraser's advice would be never show it to another living soul.

'Can I take a look out there?' She gestured at the double doors and the balcony. Before he could reply, she walked over and cupped her hands around her eyes and leant against the glass, her breath making a cloudy circle on it. She looked out over the lights of Falmouth and the dark expanse of sea beyond, and was almost certain she was looking in the direction of Stack Point and on to France. She thought of the girl in Trégastel. Was she out there? Sitting on her flat rock, staring across the sea towards Coco and the lights of England?

'Drink?' Fraser asked. 'I'm going to have one. The minibar has pretty much everything you could want.' He hesitated. 'Except champagne, apparently.'

'Oh,' she said. 'Yeah, sure.'

'Vodka? Tequila?'

She wrinkled her nose and shook her head. 'A Coke?'

'Coming right up.'

While Fraser opened the minibar, Coco unlocked the doors to the balcony and stepped outside. It was a haven of plants and lights, a wrought-iron sofa with canvas cushions, and a coffee table, set up like a living room with ornaments and a large candle. She walked to the edge and rested her hands lightly on the top bar of the railings. '*Bon soir!*' she called softly to her French friend.

Good evening! came the distant voice across the sea.

The suite was at the back of the building, but from the balcony, she had a view of the gardens and marquee, which flashed with colourful lights like a spaceship on the lawn. Music blared loudly into the darkness. A nineties dance anthem. People singing along.

Fraser appeared and handed her an old-fashioned bottle of Coke.

It was freezing cold and tasted delicious.

'Do you mind if I make a quick work call?' He had to raise his voice to be heard over the party noise.

'Work? Now?'

He laughed. 'It's the afternoon in LA.'

'Oh, yeah. Er, if you need to work, I can leave?'

'I'll only be five minutes. Why don't you set your reel up? I'm far too old to know how to get YouTube on a television.' He smiled. 'Or stay out here and finish your drink. You've worked hard today. You could probably do with a few minutes' peace.'

He went back into the room, closing the balcony doors behind him. Coco sat on the sofa, took another swig of her Coke, then got out her phone and opened TikTok. She scrolled for a while, glancing up every now and then to see if Fraser was still talking. He caught her looking at him, rolled his eyes and held up a splayed hand, mouthing, 'Sorry, five minutes.'

She looked at the time. She'd already been here ten minutes, and there was no sign of Ingrid. Maybe she should go. But then a message flashed up on her phone. Her heart skipped a beat. It was from Jamie.

Hey last night was fun

'Oh my God, *yes*,' she said under her breath. She didn't answer immediately, not wanting to seem too keen, and thought about how to reply. The line between showing him she liked him and coming across as desperate was very fine.

Yeah had a good time too

He didn't answer for a few minutes, and she worried he was going to leave her on read again. If he did, that was it. She wasn't into games. She sipped her Coke and watched the screen.

Beach tomorrow?

Again she waited. Bide your time, she thought. Not too keen. But then she realised she had some collateral she could use.

Yeah sure by the way im about to drink champagne with ingrid olsson!!

His reply came back immediately, and she grinned.

Wtaf no way??

You know that waitress job? Im in her room!! Hehe

Fuck youll be famous soon

Coco smiled. As she stared at her phone, the words began to swim. She looked up, and her head listed as if she'd spun circles. 'What the hell?' she whispered. She tried to stand, but her knees felt weak.

'You OK?' Fraser asked, appearing at the balcony doors.

'A bit ... faint ... that's all.' Her speech was slurred, as if she'd been drinking.

'You've worked a long day. I bet you haven't eaten.'

She shook her head and felt herself sway.

He pointed at the Coke. 'Finish it. The sugar will help.'

Coco's mouth felt dry and sticky, her brain woolly. She blinked hard, struggling to stabilise her vision, fearful she was about to throw up. She leant forward, head in her hands, breathing slowly and deeply. 'I don't feel so good.'

'You're a very pretty girl, you know.'

She lifted her head. The expression on his face made her blood run cold. Then she turned her faltering vision on the bottle of Coke on the table. Shit. Had he *spiked* her?

'I need to go ... Mum will be here ...'

'Best stay put until you feel less faint. Don't want you falling and cracking your head open.'

She closed her eyes and tried to still her wheeling head. She heard the voice of the girl in Trégastel.

You shouldn't be there!

I know, Coco called back. *I know!*

'Maybe water?' She forced the words out, doing her best to sound sober.

'Sure.' He went back into the suite. Coco fumbled for her phone on the seat beside her. She managed to grasp it, but her fingers wouldn't work, and when she tried to type the unlocking code, she got it wrong twice. Concentrate, she told herself. Third time lucky, and she opened the last text from her mum and punched letters as best she could.

Help mum in ind

Movement caught her attention. Fraser was walking back through the doors. She pressed send and shoved the phone down the side of the sofa cushion.

Her eyelids felt so heavy. What the hell had he given her?

Don't sleep, chérie. *Don't sleep!*

Coco mustered everything she had. She needed to buy some time, wait for the right opportunity then get the hell out. 'Tell me … acting … how … do I get a job?'

He sat down beside her, his body touching hers. She tried to shift away, but he moved with her and kept close to her. 'Well, it certainly isn't all down to talent. You only need to look at who gets the work to know that.' He turned a little, facing her, resting an elbow on the back of the sofa. 'You need to make friends with the right people. I'm sure your mother's told you that, hasn't she?'

Coco blinked hard, desperate to focus. She felt the girl in Trégastel willing her on.

Good, chérie. *Good! You are doing so well!*

Fraser reached for the bottle of Coke. 'Have some more.'

Coco regarded the bottle for a moment or two. She clasped it, the glass cool and hard in her hand, and tipped it to her lips, keeping her mouth shut, swallowing none of it. As she did, she tried to unscramble her thoughts.

Hit him with the bottle, chérie. *Then run!*

Good idea! She raised her arm and drew the bottle backwards. Coke poured down her wrist. With a low grunt, she mustered all her power, ready to smack the bottle against his head.

Fraser caught her wrist, his hand closing like a snare. His smile fell away. Then, quick as a rattlesnake, he thrust his other hand over her mouth.

'Silly girl,' he said through gritted teeth.

The charade was over.

CHAPTER TWENTY-EIGHT

For twenty-five years I'd held Julian Draper responsible for playing a part in my mother's brutal death. Of course I took the blame too. I'd been neglectful of Mikey and my mother from the moment I left home. Though I would never know if I could have altered the tragic course of history, I would always have to live with the notion that if I'd called Mikey back that one time, my mum would still be alive. My reason for not calling back, for not being able to leave my room, was Julian.

But now I'd discovered it wasn't Julian at all.

It was someone else entirely.

And that someone else was with Coco right now.

I kicked Anne-Marie's silver sandals off at the bottom of the staircase and ran upstairs as fast as I could. I caught up with the others at the end of the corridor, just as Ingrid was pressing her card to the key reader.

'On the balcony,' cried Cami as we rushed into the room.

We could see them through the glass, lit by incongruous soft uplighting, Coco on the sofa, Fraser's body engulfing hers, her hands ineffectively paddling against him.

Cami yelled and Debbie cried out. Nick flung the balcony door open and lunged for Fraser, grabbing him by his jacket and yanking him off Coco as if pulling a wolf from a lamb.

Coco gave a small sob of relief and collapsed back on the sofa like a rag doll.

Fraser stumbled backwards, indignant surprise etched into his face. 'What the *fuck*, Nick?'

Debbie ran to Coco and pulled her close, stroking her hair, kissing her forehead.

'Mum?' Coco's voice was a feeble slur. 'He ... he ...'

'Shush, angel. You're OK. You're OK now,' Debbie soothed, doing up the buttons on her daughter's shirt with trembling fingers, her lips pursed, trying not to cry.

'What the hell are you all doing?' Fraser shouted.

'What the hell are *you* doing?' Nick shoved him on the shoulder.

Fraser swiped his hand away. 'Don't touch me.'

Debbie snapped her head around to look up at him, her livid eyes burning. 'You animal,' she spat. 'She's a *child*.'

Fraser's face fell in apparent shock. 'A child? She's twenty-three. She told me.'

'Does she *look* twenty-three?' Debbie cried.

'Well, I mean, yes. Why would I doubt what she told me? Whatever you're insinuating, you're wrong. This is all above board.'

'Above board?' Nick shook his head. 'Jesus, Fraser.'

'Fuck me, Nick, chill out. We were kissing, for Christ's sake! We were about to go down and dance. We were chatting about acting. Had a couple of drinks. She asked if she could kiss me—'

Coco made a noise and shook her head. 'No,' she said weakly. She shook her head again.

'Look at her,' Nick said. 'Even if you thought she was older, she's clearly drunk.'

'She was sober when she—'

'Sober? Look at the state of her! She can barely open her eyes, let alone give consent.'

'Consent? Christ, Nick. She was all over me.'

'Not drunk. I ...' Coco pushed herself off her mother and sat upright, swaying as she pointed at the coffee table. 'The … the Coke.'

My eyes fell to the bottle, and from nowhere came a flash of Fraser at the rag dance, standing on the outside deck of the boat holding two drinks. Pink umbrellas. White plastic cups.

I'd drunk both.

Oh my *God*. I felt sick.

Fraser scoffed. 'This is insane. She finished her shift, asked if I'd watch her showreel, I didn't want to, but I said yes, as a few of you – including you, Nick – told me helping her was the right thing to do.' He glanced at Nick as if challenging him to deny it. 'So we came up. Drank a bit. Then she came on to me. Maybe I should have been stronger.' He shrugged. 'We had a kiss, and the next thing I know, you lot burst in like a raid.'

'You're forty-three,' Nick said. 'I can't believe you'd do something like this.'

'Why are you always so goddam sanctimonious? *Jesus*. It's a wedding. It was a kiss. Don't be such a bore.' Fraser took a breath and shook his head as if growing impatient. 'Do you have any idea how many of these women come to me? Desperate for fame, desperate to get noticed. She knew exactly what she was doing.' He needled his eyes into Debbie. 'You told her this was her chance to get noticed, didn't you? I've met *thousands* of mothers like you. You're playing innocent now, but it was you who told her to do whatever she could to speak to me today.'

Debbie's face fell. Her mouth opened as if to speak, but then Fraser turned on Ingrid. 'And *you* remember how it was, of course. Ingrid Olsson – nonentity to megastar with a couple of below-par blow jobs.' He laughed. 'It's how the business works.' He cast a glance at the rest of us. 'Surely you weren't naïve enough to think the new Mrs Draper got where she has on talent alone?'

Ingrid's expression was diamond-hard. 'Fuck off, arsehole. And by the way, you're fired.'

Fraser shrugged. 'You'll be over in a year or so anyway. People will tire of you. And frankly, you're a pain in the neck to deal with.'

'God, you're an arrogant bastard. You know you're the biggest open secret in the industry, don't you? The whole of LA knows what you're like.'

'Since when was liking women a crime? Or is this just another opportunity to take aim at successful white males? Men like me are the enemy now, aren't we? Scourge of society. It's such bullshit. Women have used men since the dawn of time. They know what they want and they know how to get it. Men have always been the victims of female ambition, and they always will be. And now, because of this, you're up here accusing me of some frankly libellous transgression.'

'*I* didn't want anything.'

The others turned to look at me. My heart was pounding.

'What?'

I repeated myself louder, amazed I was able to form words. 'I didn't want anything from you.'

Fraser's face twisted with scorn.

'The night of the rag dance.' I paused. 'It was you, wasn't it?'

Someone took hold of my hand. I glanced to my side to see who it was.

Cami?

I resisted the instinctive urge to push her away. Her grasp seemed to give me strength.

Fraser laughed dismissively. 'That was centuries ago. Christ, we were kids. We had sex once. Truly awful sex.'

Tears prickled my eyes as my strength leaked from me.

'And you say you didn't want anything? You wanted so much! You'd have done anything to be a part of our group. You were gagging for it from any one of us who'd have you.'

'No!' The shock of his words choked me. 'I didn't want to. I—'

'Trust me. You wanted it.'

'You gave me a drink. Two drinks. Pink umbrellas. I didn't drink anything else that night, but I was all over the place. I couldn't remember a thing. You drugged me.'

He dismissed me with a shake of his head. 'Drug you? As if I'd have to drug anybody. You're delusional. You always were. You constructed some insane love story between you and Nick, which apparently you're still living. You changed how you looked. How you spoke. You pretended you knew how to ski. Told us your father died, when really he was a spineless thief. Oh, and let's not forget you've a murderer in the family. You're a bitter, twisted woman, past your sell-by date and clearly unstable.' He stared at me with hard, unwavering eyes, every word piercing me as if he was throwing daggers. 'I have never drugged anybody—'

'Liar!' Cami's voice was low and flat, her body statue-still. She dropped my hand and moved closer to him.

'Not you too,' Fraser said, sneering at Cami with disdain. 'You're being unbearably tiresome today.'

'Don't speak to—'

'Shut up, Nick. Seriously. How dare you all pile in here like a group of vigilante lunatics?'

'Enough,' Nick said forcibly.

Debbie stood, leaving her daughter slumped on the sofa. She walked over to Fraser, fists clenched at her sides, eyes burning with fury. He loomed over her small frame. She looked up at him. 'You are a predator. All these women? And my precious child. You should be in prison.'

Fraser gave a spiteful laugh, which echoed around the balcony, the remnants of his matinee-idol facade sliding off to reveal his monstrous true self. 'Prison? I know all women are crazy, but this wins the prize. Vix wanted me. Ingrid used me. God knows what Cami's on about. And your *precious child*?' He looked down at Debbie, mouth a twisted snarl. 'That cheap slut came here today with two things on her mind. Fame and fortune. Her pretty little doll-face on billboards all over—'

Debbie slapped him hard across the cheek. His head flipped to the left, then slowly back to look at her, eyes thunderous. He snarled and drew back his hand.

'No!' Nick shouted.

A movement caught my eye, Coco lurching forward, stumbling towards Fraser. As she reached him, he shoved her hard with his raised hand. The force sent her flying backwards. She fell against the coffee table, crying out as she hit her head. Debbie roared. With her teeth bared, she went for him, battering her hands against his chest, clawing at him with the might of an angry lioness. He crossed his arms over his face to protect himself from the barrage and kicked out violently. His foot connected with her knee and she fell to the floor with a yelp.

'Fucking bitch,' he growled, and drew his leg back to kick her again.

Then came a blood-curdling cry.

Cami ran at him, hands stretched out in front of her, face set with ugly rage. There was a thump as she made contact. The power of it sent Fraser reeling backwards, their combined weight ploughing into the balcony railings. There was a creak and a crunch, then a godawful screech of metal. The top railing had wrenched free from its fixtures on the wall.

Fraser's arms flailed as he desperately tried to regain his balance. He grabbed Cami's wrist, and she lurched forward. She tried to pull back, tried to get purchase, but her feet slipped on the decking. I lunged and snatched at her dress, holding on tight as the railing gave way altogether with an almighty pop.

Time was suspended. It was as if somebody had pressed pause on a television remote. Fraser's face contorted, his eyes and mouth growing wide with panic. Nick grabbed Cami too and we held on to her. There was a sharp tug forward as the entire structure of the railings tore away from the brickwork.

Fraser's hand slid down Cami's wrist, his knuckles white as he tried to grip on. His hand slipped into hers, and for a moment it looked as if they were holding hands in a dance. The two of them held each other's gaze. His face full of fear, hers full of hatred.

One by one her fingers uncurled, and as they did, Fraser's grip on her failed.

He fell backwards, his arms and legs wheeling, hands clawing the night sky.

Cami, Nick and I collapsed backwards.

A split second later, there was a sickening thud from the terrace below.

Then nothing.

Nobody moved a muscle or breathed a word. We were frozen on the balcony like subjects in an oil painting.

Then I turned my head to look at Cami, my voice quiet. 'He raped you too.'

Her eyes shone with a film of tears, and she nodded.

CHAPTER TWENTY-NINE

There was a collective exhalation of breath as we all kicked back into motion.

'Holy shit,' Ingrid whispered.

Nick was the first to move. He walked over to the gaping space where the railings used to be and peered over.

'Be careful,' Debbie said.

'Can you see anything?' I asked.

'It's difficult from up here. Too dark.'

Coco moaned softly as Debbie held her.

'Did he hurt you?' I asked her.

She managed to shake her head, curling herself deeper into her mother.

'I'm sorry, baby,' Debbie whispered then. 'I'm so sorry.'

Ingrid put her hand on her forehead. 'What the fuck are we going to say to the press? I'm not losing everything over a prick like him.'

'We need to get down there,' Cami said. Her hand trembled as she reached out for Nick to help her up. 'We should call an ambulance.'

The four of us left Debbie and Coco where they were and ran out of the room.

None of us alerted anybody as we walked quickly along the corridor. It was as if we were stuck in our own surreal nightmare, cut off from the world. As we walked around the outside of the hotel to the back terrace, the marquee a hub of music and dancing, laughing and singing, I wondered if this might be a practical joke. One of Julian's elaborate stunts. That all we'd find on the terrace below the balcony was a note.

Ha! Just joking!

There was no note.

Fraser lay motionless on the paving stones. A pool of blood encircled his head. His eyes stared upwards, the moonlight reflected in them, glinting like flecks of jewel embedded in his retinas.

Cami stepped closer, her arms folded across her body, hugging herself tightly. She stared down at him, then gently touched him with the toe of her shoe. She winced as if trying to dislodge the memories that speared her.

Nick inhaled and moved to go to her. I grabbed his arm and held him back. 'Leave her for a moment,' I whispered.

Cami crouched down and leant over his body. She whispered something, too quiet for us to hear. Then she stood.

I let go of Nick and he went to her, enveloping her in a tight embrace.

Debbie joined us from the shadows, gasping as she took in the gruesome sight. 'Oh my God,' she whispered, and crossed herself.

Cami stepped away from Nick. She was shivering as if she'd been out all night in a storm. 'We need to call the police.'

'Did he really do what Vix said?'

She took a deep breath and nodded. 'That's why I wasn't going to come today. I changed my mind when you said he couldn't make it. I felt sick when I saw him here.' She put her hands up to cover her face.

'When did he do this?'

'The night we split up. The night you …' She glanced at me quickly.

Nick's face twisted and a moan of pain came from deep inside him. He reached for her hand and lifted it to his mouth to kiss it.

'After you left, after we fought, Fraser came over.' Her words were spoken in quiet monotone. 'He knocked on my door and said Tilly had told him what had happened and he wanted to check I was OK. He had a bottle of wine.'

She flinched, and I imagined the painful recollections that were battering her.

'We talked. It was nice to have a friend with me. I drank two glasses, but felt really sick. It came on so suddenly. The last memory I have was telling him I didn't feel very well.' She paused. 'When I woke up a few hours later, he was dressing. He said, "It's best we don't tell anybody about this. Especially Nick." I called you straight away. I wanted to tell you, but I couldn't. I was so ashamed and guilty. I knew how upset you'd be and I couldn't do that to you.'

Nick appeared to be in physical pain. 'That's why you were in such a state.'

'When I saw you, I just wanted us to get back together. I couldn't risk telling you. I didn't want to ruin things. I was scared you wouldn't believe me, because … because he … he was your friend, but also because of the way you'd looked at me when you walked in on us on New Year's Eve—'

Nick interrupted her, his voice cracked with emotion, anger mixing with the pain. 'Of course I'd have believed you.'

'I didn't want to take the chance.' She started to cry then. 'I should have told someone.' She looked at me. 'When I heard you accuse Julian tonight, knowing Julian was with us that night, I realised what Fraser had done.' She wiped her eyes on her sleeve. 'What happened to you was my fault. What happened to Coco and God knows how many others. If I'd told somebody back then, maybe I could have stopped it all.'

'That's not how it works.' It was Ingrid. She was staring down at Fraser, her voice calm and controlled. 'Men like Fraser Jenner are Teflon. You'd have been shouted down. Told you were drunk. Trying to make your ex-boyfriend jealous. Doing it for revenge.

They'd make you feel like you were crazy. You heard him tonight. *I* was asking for it. *You* were asking for it.' She gestured at Debbie. 'Your daughter.' She shook her head. '*Screw* him. The world hasn't lost a hero. Just another entitled fuck.' She stared back down at him and for a moment said nothing. Then she looked up at Debbie. 'Where is she, your daughter?'

'In the car. I took her out the back and used the side path. Nobody saw us. She seems OK. She didn't drink much of the Coke. She's a bit woozy, but I didn't want her to see ...' She pointed at Fraser.

Ingrid nodded. 'Right, everybody has to listen carefully. We're going to call the police and this is what we're going to tell them. Debbie, go and get in your car and drive straight home. From this moment on, you two weren't in that room at the time, OK? You collected Coco after I chatted to her for a few minutes about acting.'

Debbie nodded as if she'd been given military orders by a sergeant major. 'But what about Darren – the manager? He saw us running upstairs. And those security guards?'

'We'll just say we got up to the room and decided to have a private party. Put some music on. Fraser was hammered on all that champagne and cognac. Dancing around the balcony like an idiot. Showing off. We told him to be careful. Then he tripped and fell against the railings. We all saw it happen. A tragic accident that ruined my wedding.'

Cami shook her head. 'No. I ran at—'

'You ran to grab hold of him. You did everything you could to stop him falling.' Ingrid sounded so convincing, I found myself believing her version of events. Fraser was wrong about her having no talent.

I cleared my throat. 'You tried to save him.'

Ingrid nodded. 'I heard you tell him to stay away from the railings when he was leaping about.' She looked at Nick. 'Isn't that right?'

'You can't lie for me,' Cami said. 'We have to tell the truth.'

Nick reached for her hand. 'We will tell the truth. Fraser fell against the railings. You tried to stop him falling. We're lucky you didn't fall with him.'

Ingrid looked at Cami.

Cami hesitated.

I stepped closer to her and turned her to face me. 'Don't let him ruin your life any more than he already has.'

We held each other's gaze for a moment. I smiled, and she took a deep breath in and let it out slowly through pursed lips. Then she nodded.

'Good,' Ingrid said. 'Right then. Ready?'

We exchanged looks, then nodded in unison.

'Debbie, off you go. Get Coco home.'

Debbie didn't hesitate. She turned and trotted off around the back of the hotel, disappearing into the shadows.

Ingrid's face became fear-stricken. She started jumping up and down, agitated, then opened her mouth and screamed. 'Help! Oh my God! *Help!* There's been an accident! We need help! Somebody help us!'

Darren arrived at the French windows. His face was a picture of horror as he took in the scene.

'He's fallen from the balcony,' Nick said urgently. 'He's not breathing. Quickly, please. We've got no phones. You need to call an ambulance.'

CHAPTER THIRTY

Cami

Victoria stayed with us for a few days following the wedding. The unspoken need to huddle together was overwhelming.

She was quiet when I took her up to our spare room. She put her bag on the bed and clasped her hands in front of her. We looked at each other. There were so many words, it was impossible to know which ones to choose.

'Sleep as long as you can,' I said. 'There's a towel in the bathroom. Do you need anything else?'

She shook her head. 'You've both been very kind.'

At least I think that's what she said. The words were almost too quiet to be heard.

When she told us a couple of days later that she wanted to visit her mother's grave, Nick didn't hesitate in offering to go with her. Their relationship had always been a strange one. She was so obviously in love with him from the very beginning, whilst he had this undeniable protective urge. It was as if he'd found a baby bird with a broken wing in that first week of university, and once he'd nursed her back to health, perhaps grown addicted to her obsession, he couldn't bring himself to let her go. At college, I'd struggled with their codependent friendship. I loved him so much and it was tough watching her try to steal him from me. Watching them go back to the house they shared without me. Watching her laugh at his jokes, touch him at every opportunity, shine all her attention on him like a spotlight. I was ashamed of my jealousy. If only I could go back in time and reassure my younger self she didn't need to feel insecure because Nick loved her deeply. I wasted so much of my youth masking my vulnerability with bravado and attitude, clothes and make-up and jewellery, pretending I was confident and strong when underneath I was terrified of rejection.

In the wake of Fraser's death, I saw Victoria in a different light. In some macabre way, what he'd done stitched us together and gave us common ground. Like Nick, I now felt protective of her. Victoria needed kindness.

'I can't ask you to do that,' she told Nick. 'I'll be fine on my own.'

I took her hand. 'We'll both come.' She started to protest, but I interrupted her. 'You can't go alone. Not after everything's that happened.'

In truth, I wanted to go. I needed distraction, needed to keep my mind busy. The empty hours, both day and night, were plagued by violent recollection. I relived the moment I let go of Fraser's hand over and over and over. As time passed, guilt crept in. Whatever he'd done, however rotten he was, I'd caused his death and I would live with this until my final breath. There wasn't only guilt. There was also visceral rage. Rage at what he'd done to Victoria and me. Rage at what he'd intended to do to Coco. Rage at his narcissistic refusal to accept blame and inability to show even a sliver of remorse. Rage that he wasn't the only one, that these men walked amongst us, taking what they could with no thought for the consequential damage.

Later that night, in bed, I rested my head on Nick's chest. 'Can I ask you something?'

'Of course,' he replied, closing his book and laying it on the bedside table.

'What happened in Paris?'

'Paris?'

'With Vix.'

He gave a small sigh. 'Honestly, nothing. I told you that at the time.'

'Yes, but at the wedding she seemed to think differently.'

'It was years ago.'

'I know. I won't be angry. I promise.'

He stiffened, then eased his arm from beneath me and shuffled upright, leaning back against the headboard. 'Most of it you know. She called. She was desperate. Her brother had been released and she'd convinced herself he wanted to hurt her. She talked about killing herself. She begged me to come. Said I was the only one she could turn to.'

I knew all this. I'd been with him when she phoned. Standing next to him when he'd given her myriad excuses.

'You have to go,' I'd said, even though it was the last thing I wanted him to do. 'Imagine how you'd feel if she did something stupid.'

'I haven't seen her in fourteen years. Surely she has other friends?'

'Maybe she doesn't.'

Of course he went. The thought of her alone with her fear and dark thoughts had pulled on his heartstrings.

Now he lay back down and turned on his side. I turned on the pillow to face him. He was lit by the moon through a gap in the curtains, and I thought about how much I still loved him, how much I still wanted to reach out and touch him.

'We met at a café near Charles de Gaulle. Then we walked for a bit. She didn't mention her brother. She seemed happy, actually, as if we were on holiday. I asked her if she was still worried, but she said not now I was with her. She said we should go to the Louvre to see a Delacroix painting. It was *Liberty Leading the People* and she burst into tears when she saw it. She said she'd been dreaming of that moment – seeing this painting in Paris with me – since college.'

'Why?'

He shrugged. 'Apparently we'd talked about it after the pub one night and I'd showed her a picture of it in a book. I couldn't remember that. Then we ate at a brasserie and I walked her back to her hotel. When we got there, she asked me to come up.' He sighed and shook his head, made a face of regret. 'She started crying and said she was scared, that the nights were the worst, that every time she heard a footstep, she thought it was him. So I took her up. Then she asked me to lie next to her until she fell asleep. I know I should have left, but I couldn't face her crying and I kept thinking about what you'd said – that if she did anything silly, I'd never forgive myself. So I lay on her bed, on top of the covers, both of us dressed.' He rested his hand on my cheek. I turned my head enough to kiss his palm. 'I didn't sleep; it all felt so wrong. I got up early to leave and she told me she loved me. She asked me to leave you so we could finally be together.' He sighed. 'I didn't know what to say. I didn't want to hurt her. So I said she was very special, but I couldn't leave the children because they were too young and needed their father.'

'Why didn't you tell her you didn't feel the same way?'

He sighed. 'I'd told her so many times and it never made any difference. And I couldn't stop thinking about what her brother had done. It made me uneasy.'

'Because you thought she might hurt you?'

'Maybe. I don't know. I just wanted to get out of there. But I should have told her the truth and I should have told you exactly what happened. I love you, Cami, and I always have.' He hesitated, then stroked his fingers down my cheek. 'I'm sorry I wasn't there to stop Fraser doing what he did. I'm sorry you went through that and have lived with it for so long.'

'Shush,' I said. 'Don't talk about him. I don't want him anywhere near us.'

Nick pulled me to him, and from the chair in the corner of our room, Fraser's ghost smiled and raised a glass of cognac.

The three of us didn't talk much on the journey to Manchester. The déjà vu was hard to ignore. Twenty-five years earlier, we'd made a similar journey, sitting with Vix, skin pale, stunned by what her brother had done, but also, we now knew, dealing with the aftermath of Fraser's assault.

Nick and I sat on a bench in the graveyard and watched her tend her mother's grave. She cleared it of weeds and placed a bouquet of flowers at the foot of the headstone, then she cried, her head bowed and shoulders juddering.

Victoria stared out of the train window on the way back. Her eyes flickered back and forth over the landscape as it raced by. 'I was a terrible daughter,' she said after a while. 'I should have gone home more.'

'Don't think like that. We were young and living brand-new lives. None of us went home.'

She shook her head. 'I turned my back on her and I'll never forgive myself. If I could live those months again and do everything differently, I'd do it in a heartbeat.'

Nick stood and stretched his back. 'I'm going to the buffet car. Anybody want anything?'

'Coffee would be lovely.'

'I'm fine, thank you,' said Victoria.

We watched him walk through the doors, then she looked at me. It was clear she wanted to say something.

'Go on,' I said.

She stared fixedly at her hands for a moment. 'Thank you for coming with me today.'

'No problem. We—'

'And I want to apologise.'

'Apologise? For what?'

'For how I behaved at college. The things I said.' She paused and took a breath. 'And did.'

I reached out and took her hand. 'Water under the bridge.'

'Thank you,' she said sincerely.

'And I hope we can be friends?'

She smiled. 'I'd like that.' Then she remembered something. 'Oh, by the way, I had an email from Coco.'

'How's she doing?'

'She's fine, she says. She didn't talk about the wedding. She was more interested in telling me that her and Jamie are now *exclusive*.'

'The confusing vocab of Gen Z dating,' I said with a rueful smile.

'She also said she told Debbie she wants to concentrate on her A levels and have a break from acting.'

'Did Debbie take it OK?'

'Coco didn't say. I imagine the poor woman is still pretty shell-shocked and happy to be out of that world for a bit.' Victoria paused. 'And you?' She hesitated. 'How are you?'

How was I after pushing my rapist to his death from a balcony?

I considered the question. 'Up and down. Nick's been amazing. I should have told him sooner. I've been living with what Fraser did for so long. You know, even after twenty-five years I can feel him on me.'

'I sometimes wake in the night unable to breathe because his hand is covering my mouth.'

'I shouldn't say this out loud, but ...' I lowered my voice to a whisper, 'I don't regret what happened to him. It haunts me – his face as he fell and the horrific sound as he hit the terrace – but I'm not sad and I'm not sorry. He deserved it.'

Victoria didn't reply, and I realised how callous I must sound. 'Am I bad for saying that?'

'Bad? No, you're not bad,' she said. 'It was Fraser who was bad.'

The police never questioned the story we told them. The fixings that attached the railings to the wall were rusted and loose. If anybody had leant against them they could have given way. I'd heard a rumour Lowencliffe Hall was being sued by some sort of health and safety body.

The police found a small bottle of flunitrazepam on him, a drug also commonly known as Rohypnol. Julian maintained the pills were for Fraser's insomnia, something he'd apparently suffered with since his late teens.

'I remember him bragging he could get any drug he wanted using the prescription pads he stole from his father's office,' Nick mused. 'Do you remember that?'

'Vaguely. Do you think Julian knew what Fraser had planned for Coco?'

'God, surely not?' Nick shook his head vigorously, as if trying to rid himself of the mere idea of it.

'I mean, he gave him the key to their room. What if he's always known? What if he knew what was going to happen when he left Fraser with Victoria?'

'Why would Julian allow that?'

I shrugged. 'Who knows? There's always a conspiracy of silence around predators. Bystanders willing to turn a blind eye and enable the behaviour. Maybe he always knew what Fraser was really like?'

Nick was quiet for a moment. Then he stepped closer to me and took hold of my shoulders. 'I want you to know that if Fraser was still alive, I'd kill him.' I had never heard such unbridled malice in his voice before. 'I'd fucking kill him.'

Following Fraser's death, numerous women in the film industry, including Ingrid, came out with accusations against him of sexual assault and rape. Some were badly kept secrets, some confirmed industry rumours, others were out of the blue. Many of the accusers were high-profile actresses, and this prompted a backlash of criticism. Social and mainstream media was full of counter-accusations, suggesting these women were washed-up has-beens trying to resurrect their careers, crazy, bitter harpies harbouring vendettas, intent on libelling a man who wasn't alive to defend himself. A variety of vile hashtags trended for months.

With each new voice came another shudder of disgust and regret. I couldn't stop myself feeling responsible for every attack. Nick told me repeatedly that the only person to blame was Fraser. But I kept thinking back to that evening. Fraser standing over me, my body aching, my vision blurred, making out we'd had consensual sex, and instructing me not to tell anybody.

Me doing as he said.

Reason told me Ingrid was correct; nobody would have believed me. His barrister would have told the jury I'd been drinking, that I'd willingly let him into my room, that I was the type who wore tight tops and short skirts and danced suggestively in nightclubs. I would be painted as yet another drunk girl regretting her decisions and attempting to ruin an innocent boy's life with false accusations.

Serial predators always got away with it.

I stared at Fraser's ghost and watched the smile fall from his face.

'Not this time,' I whispered. 'This time you didn't.'

EPILOGUE

Five years later
Victoria

I wait in the hotel's opulent lobby for Cami and Debbie. As Ingrid's guests, we're living the high life. My room overlooks Hyde Park and has a minibar stocked with an array of snacks and drinks. There's a six-foot bed with Egyptian cotton sheets, and a fluffy dressing gown hanging on the back of the bathroom door. It's so sumptuous, I took a video of the room to send to Anne-Marie.

Earlier today, Ingrid sent three stylists to do our hair and make-up. We drank champagne and chatted while we were primped and polished.

'Bloody hell,' Debbie said as a girl massaged patchouli oil into her pedicured feet. 'This is the life.'

Anne-Marie insisted I buy myself a new dress, so I made time to go shopping and found one in a small boutique on Carnaby Street. I have tried to stop costing things in caricatures. Since Ingrid's wedding, I've been inundated with commissions. Apparently all she has to do to help a career take off is share a post to her thirty million Instagram followers. Trudy Greenmore, the potter who made the sea-glass bowl I gave to Ingrid and Julian as a wedding gift, is another beneficiary. Ingrid put up a picture of the bowl and tagged Trudy, who now has her own shop in St Ives, plus two London galleries that sell her ceramics.

Though I am painting full-time, I still do the odd shift for

Fabian. I'd miss him if I didn't and it's a good opportunity to study the faces of his customers. When I returned to Marseille after the wedding, I vowed not to waste any more of my life yearning for a fantasy that could never exist. I'd lived too long under the weight of unrequited love and trauma. It was time to choose happiness.

The first thing I did was dismantle some barriers and open myself up to meeting new people. Anne-Marie has become a true friend. We make each other laugh and I know I can rely on her. A year ago, Laurent came into my life. He is a friend of Fabian, a piano teacher who lost his wife to illness a few years ago and is kind and gentle with a soft sense of humour. We enjoy walking by the sea and shopping in the market. I love listening to him play. When I'm with him, I feel safe. The overwhelming passion I felt for Nick has been replaced by a comforting affection. A few weeks ago, I plucked up the courage to paint a self-portrait. Before I'd been scared of what I might see – perhaps still haunted by the grotesque mouse I'd drawn when I arrived in London – but the painting is the one I'm now most proud of. There is an inner calm shining through, contentment and an air of self-confidence that surprises me. When Laurent first saw it, he was moved to tears.

'*C'est parfait, chérie*. The real you.'

For the first time in as long as I can recall, I am happy.

Cami, Debbie and I have a WhatsApp group. Our experience on the terrace of Lowencliffe Hall glues us together. At the beginning we stayed in contact as a means to help us process what had happened. But we grew to genuinely like each other. The irony isn't lost on me.

Cami emerges from the lift. She is a vision in a long black dress with a halter neck, her hair pinned up in an elegant chignon, her skin flawless. Around her neck she wears the white pebble, clasped in silver, on a silver chain.

'I like your necklace,' I say.

She smiles. 'Nick gave me the stone when we got back together, the day after what happened with Fraser. He told me it would bring me luck and keep me safe. I thought I'd lost it, but it turned up when I went through some boxes last year. Nick asked a jeweller to turn it into a pendant for our anniversary. I love it. It feels like an amulet.'

'It's lovely,' I say. There is no need to say anything more.

After Ingrid's wedding, I went back to my French therapist. There were things I needed to reframe. Nick and I were never star-crossed lovers torn apart by a fairy-tale witch. My infatuation had twisted my perception of reality like a hall of mirrors. Nick and Cami met and fell in love in their first term of university. Cami was never the villain. Nick's friendship for me was that and nothing more. I have clarity now.

Debbie is dressed in an emerald-green dress with tassels on the hem, matching heels and an all-over fake tan. She squeals and runs across the foyer to hug us both. We make our way out to the limousine that is waiting outside the hotel. Inside the car waits more champagne in an ice bucket, a platter of artfully arranged sushi, and a note from Ingrid reading, *Enjoy, lovely ladies!*

Cami opens the bottle and pours three glasses.

'Photo!' Debbie cries. We huddle together, glasses raised, and she snaps a selfie.

As we drive, I watch London passing outside the window. Tall buildings, bright lights, hustle and bustle. I wonder what my life might look like if I'd stayed here rather than catching a train to Paris. Would I still be an artist? Would I be married with two children, a house in Putney and a golden retriever? Maybe I'd be living under the arches with nothing more to my name than a grotty sleeping bag and ragged shoes.

Debbie leans forward and stares up at the buildings. 'Not sure about London. Don't think I trust it.'

We both sit back against the leather seats.

'You must be so proud of her,' Cami says.

Debbie beams, her face almost unable to contain her smile. 'I *knew* she'd be a star.' Pride and love overflow from her. 'I knew it the day I first held her.'

It's not only Debbie who is proud of Coco. I am too. She's the closest thing I've got to a child of my own. Since the wedding, we've remained in contact. Last year she came to stay with me in France. She asked if we could visit a town in northern Brittany called Trégastel.

'Why?' I'd asked.

'I need to thank someone.'

She didn't meet up with anybody in person, but she said it was OK, she'd say her thank you on the cliffs. The spot she took me to reminded me of Stack Point, I place she'd taken me to when I'd visited them in Cornwall previously.

We arrive at the South Bank and are dropped beside the red carpet, near a large sign reading *The London Film Festival*. The assembled press and cameras turn to look at us in case any of us are famous. When they realise none of us are, they turn away.

Ingrid rushes over to us when we walk into the reception area. 'You made it! Well done. Isn't this fabulous? I feel like a proud mother hen.' She laughs and looks at Debbie. 'God knows what you must be feeling.'

'Ready to shit myself, if I'm honest.'

Ingrid makes a face of horror. 'Oh God, please don't. That is not the type of publicity Coco needs tonight.'

Debbie opens her mouth to say something, but Ingrid's attention has turned to a man, who she grabs and pulls our way.

'Digby, darling. Meet my friends.'

Digby de Vesey regards us with a peculiar look on his face, as if trying to work out in what universe the three of us can be friends with Ingrid. Ingrid's third husband – following her divorce from Julian five weeks after their wedding, there was a Las Vegas marriage to a young rock star that lasted three months – is balding, with a stomach that strains against his Savile Row waistband. He wears an old boys' tie and an expression of haughty disdain that perfectly befits a sixty-year-old MP with his sights set on Downing Street.

He leans close to her ear. 'I'm going to need a stiff drink to get through this.'

Cami and I exchange a look as he wanders away without acknowledging us. Ingrid smiles. 'He owns half of Kensington and we've been trending on Twitter almost continuously since we were papped in Quaglino's. A girl's gotta hustle.' Then she winks. 'Right, I must circulate. But see you later. You're coming to Claridge's for the after-party?'

She doesn't wait for our answer and flits away to throw her arms around somebody else.

'She's bonkers,' Cami says with a laugh.

Debbie stares after Ingrid, eyes shining with adoration. 'She's beautiful.'

We take our seats and all three of us crane our necks in search of Coco.

'There she is!' I say, tapping Debbie on the knee and pointing.

Coco is in the second row. She's chatting and laughing with the young man next to her. As I watch, he leans in to kiss her cheek. She smiles.

'Oh Debbie, she looks so happy.'

'I love her new haircut,' Cami says. 'But I can't see her dress. Do you have a picture?'

Debbie gets her phone out and scrolls through her photos. The dress is a simple cream slip, silk, with fine straps. Coco's wearing it with red suede ankle boots and a wide metal choker. Her hair has been newly cut and is silver-blonde with blue tips, short and choppy.

'Stunning,' Cami says. 'Like a young Kristen Stewart.'

Coco finished her A levels, getting good grades in English, psychology and drama, then went to study English literature at Southampton. Whilst there, she joined the film society and began working on her idea. She and Ingrid had connected on Instagram after the wedding, and when Coco posted about wanting to fundraise for a film she was making, Ingrid sent her a private message to tell her she'd recently set up a production company and was looking for young filmmakers and writers for her mentoring initiative. They met for coffee, Ingrid loved the idea, and the rest, as they say, is collaborative history.

In the press interviews Ingrid has given, she speaks highly of Coco.

She's a super-talented writer. Her imagination is incredible. She thinks out of the box and never takes the obvious route, bringing fresh, innovative ideas to the industry with a focus on female-led content. Coco is an exciting young writer with a glittering career ahead of her, and I am thrilled to be supporting someone with such limitless potential.

No wonder Debbie can hardly breathe.

When they get to the nominees for Audience Award for Best Short Film, Cami reaches for my hand and I take Debbie's. She is trembling and mouthing a silent prayer, her eyes closed.

'And the winner of the award for this year's best short film goes to ... *Blind Date.*'

The three of us jump up and clap wildly. I turn and give Debbie a hug. Fat tears of happiness are barrelling down her cheeks.

Coco, the handsome young man and three others, all of them in their early twenties, walk on to the stage. Coco takes the award and grins. She waits for the applause to die down.

'Wow. I mean, seriously. I don't know what to say!' She places the award on the podium and the five of them hold hands, jiggling about with excitement. Then Coco stands tall, her expression becoming serious. She lets go of the boy's hand and addresses the room with poise and composure. If she has any nerves, there's no sign of them. 'I wrote *Blind Date* because I didn't want to stay silent. I wanted to highlight the issue of men in high places using their power to take what they want, remaining unaccountable while the women they abuse are left to carry the scars. Society needs to keep striving to make it easier for women to come forward. And when they do, we need to listen. We shouldn't still be having this conversation. In the wake of Me Too, we all hoped women would feel able to speak out. Maybe, even, that they'd be safer. The landscape felt altered. But the reactionary kick-back, the emergence of that certain brand of toxic masculinity, rode roughshod over advances made, dragging us back to an even darker time. We have to shine a light into the shadows.'

There's a moment of quiet in the auditorium, everybody transfixed by this fierce young woman, fire burning in her belly.

'We are blessed to be here. Blessed to be able to make films we believe in. This shows we *do* have a voice and that voice will be heard.'

More riotous applause.

'Our heartfelt thanks go to Olsson Films for getting behind this project with such enthusiasm. There is nobody in this industry who is as passionate about seeking out and nurturing new talent and providing a spotlight as Ingrid. For your faith and encouragement, we are eternally grateful.'

In the audience, Ingrid kisses both hands and throws them out towards Coco.

'Thank you to the cast. You are all incredible.' She looks at the boy next to her and smiles. He grins back. 'Of course we want to say a huge thank you to everybody who voted for *Blind Date*. We were up against some brilliant films. And then to a group of women I must thank from the bottom of my heart. These are the brave women who so generously and fearlessly told me their stories. Sometimes it was painful. Sometimes it was angry. Sometimes it was cathartic. But for them to trust me the way they did means the world. Without these brave, inspirational and *wonderful* women, there would be no film. This award goes to you with my love.'

While the crowd claps and cheers, Coco scans the audience, hand above her eyes like a ship's captain looking for land. When she finds us, she smiles and holds the award out in our direction. Cami reaches for my hand again and squeezes it. She has tears in her eyes, but they aren't tears of sadness; they're tears of joy and love for the glorious young woman we shared our experiences with.

When the applause settles, Coco smiles. 'And lastly, my mum.'

Debbie squeals and waves frantically. 'I'm right here!'

Coco laughs. 'My final thank you goes to you. Without you, none of this would have been possible. Your love and support from the very beginning has been incredible. Thank you for believing in me. Thank you for being my loudest cheerleader. Thank you for being such an amazing mother. And, well, this will look pretty cool on your mantelpiece, don't you think?'

Debbie clutches her hands beneath her chin and beams.

Coco raises the award, arm straight, fist strong, and punches the air.

Acknowledgements

Some books are harder to write than others. Like squeezing blood from a stone. This one, for reasons unclear, was really fun to write! Perhaps it was the nostalgia of revisiting university years. I loved my time at university and was lucky enough to meet a group of friends, brilliant in all senses of the word, who I'm still close to thirty years later. Sian, who I met in our second term, is an integral part of my book-writing process. I'm in awe of your insight and attention to detail. You're a wonder. Sara, who I met on the second day, is a rock in my life. As a first reader, your kind words are always valued. Holly, the daughter of two more of my closest university friends, who I've had the joy of watching grow into an amazing young woman, now one of my first readers. Thank you for your enthusiasm for my stories. Chris – my husband of twenty-five years – and I met in our first term of university. At the time, he had no idea he was destined to read hundreds of drafts of my books. Thank you for believing in me, for your positivity, your love and support, and for being the man you are. Here's to the next twenty-five years …

Thank you to Kate Mills my editor, Rachael Nazarko, and all those at HQ and beyond who've worked so hard to bring this book to the shelves. I am hugely privileged to be published by such a talented and dedicated team. Broo, my agent of seventeen years (can that be right?!), thank you for never wavering in your support, kindness and encouragement. You're a legend.

To auction winners Cami Cameron, Julie Rainer and Lou Austin (nee Drummond), thank you for lending me your names for three of the characters in this book, and bidding so generously to raise funds for Book Aid for Ukraine and Thames Valley Hospice.

And to my readers, thank you from the bottom of my heart. I love nothing more than writing books for people to enjoy, and send love and gratitude out to each and every one of you.

Thank you, as always, to my parents for their support and love. My three inspirational daughters. The friends who keep me laughing. Cos, Lisa, Tammy, Jenny, a special mention to you. And my sister, Melissa, the best little sister, always there for me in myriad ways. This book is dedicated to you.

Looking for a gripping and atmospheric thriller, packed with tension and stunning twists? Try *The Haven*...

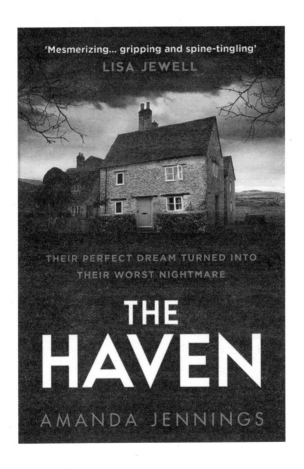

The Haven is available now!

Ready for an emotional family drama,
packed with suspense, obsession, and deceit?
Try *The Cliff House*...

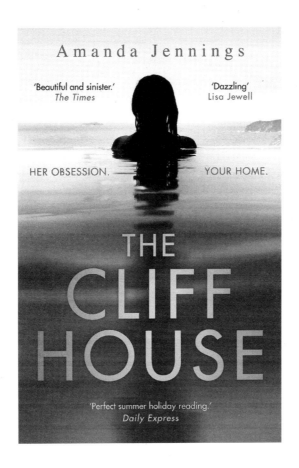

The Cliff House is available now!

Looking for a thrilling psychological suspense novel about lost love and buried secrets? Don't miss *The Storm*...

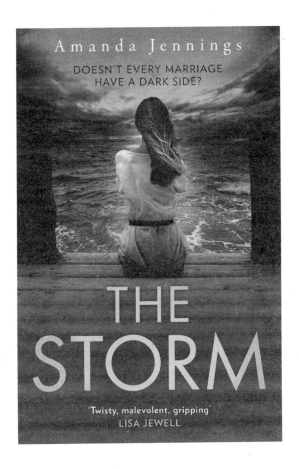

The Storm is available now!

ONE PLACE. MANY STORIES

Bold, innovative and
empowering publishing.

FOLLOW US ON:

@HQStories